DILLON

USA TODAY & WSJ BESTSELLING AUTHOR
SIOBHAN DAVIS

This paperback edition © December 2024
ISBN-13: 978-1-916651-52-4

Edited by Kelly Hartigan (XterraWeb) editing.xterraweb.com
Proofread by Imogen Wells of From the Beginning to the End
Research and critique by The Critical Touch
Cover design by Shannon Passmore of Shanoff Designs
Imagery/graphics used in cover design © bigstockphotos.com and depositphotos.com
Interior graphics © depositphotos.com
Formatted by Zsuzsanna Gerhardt of Midnight Readers PR using Vellum

Book Description

Growing up in Ireland, I always felt like something was missing. I had an idyllic childhood, yet I was never truly happy.

After Mum explained about the adoption, I constantly questioned my existence. Despite being surrounded by love, I struggle to accept it or reciprocate.

When my bio dad shows up, trying to buy my silence, a switch flips inside me, and I let my demons run free. Nothing matters except revenge.

Then *she* lands in my lap –the love of my twin's life—and it feels like fate.

Except nothing goes according to plan. I was supposed to steal her heart—she wasn't supposed to steal mine.

After she runs back to him, I'm left heartbroken and shattered. The hits just keep on coming, and my pain turns to anger. Revenge takes center stage again, and the perfect opportunity presents itself when Simon dies.

Meeting my twin sets a devastating chain reaction in motion, and I'm drowning under the weight of my sins.

Vivien is struggling to cope in the aftermath of her crushing loss. Repairing the damage is my number one goal, because I won't leave her to handle this alone. She can hurl hateful words at me and do her best to push me away.

But I am going nowhere.

Protecting my family is my sole priority. Vivien and Easton need me, and this time, I won't let them down.

A Note from the Author

This book is a companion novel to *Say I'm the One* and *Let Me Love You*. It is not intended to be read as a stand-alone romance.

As with the original duet, this book is recommended to readers aged eighteen and older due to mature content. Some scenes may be triggering. Please refer to the list on my website—www.siobhandavis.com/triggers.

Although this book uses Irish phrasing and speech patterns, it has been written in American English to keep the spelling and grammar consistent with the previous books in the series. In a few places, UK English grammar has been used where it made the most sense for that particular scene.

I have loved being back in this world and being back in Dillon's head. Most all of the content in this book is brand-new scenes. Any existing scenes (told now from Dillon's POV) included are because they were a key scene or my readers asked me to include them and/or they were needed to keep the continuity/flow of this story. I hope you enjoy the book and it gives you additional insight which will add to the overall series.

Happy reading.

Love, Siobhán.

Glossary of Irish Terms & Sayings

Irish people express themselves differently, and I've tried to keep this book as authentic as possible. It might seem like the way some things are phrased is odd, but it's just a cultural difference. The explanation given is in the context of this book. Also includes pronunciations.

4x4 – four-wheel drive/pickup truck.

Aisling – female Irish name. Pronounced Ash-ling.

Aoife – female Irish name. Pronounced Efa.

Bathroom press – bathroom cabinet.

Bin – trashcan.

Bird(s) – woman/women.

Bollocks – balls/testicles.

Boot – trunk.

Canteen – cafeteria.

Catriona – female Irish name. Pronounced Cat-ree-na.

CCA – the secondary school in Kilcoole.

Centra – convenience store.

Ciarán – male Irish name. Pronounced Kir-awn.

Chemist – pharmacy.

Chill – cool.

Clown – idiot.

Cooker – stove.

Copped on to it – realized it/figured it out.

Crisps – chips.

Cutlery – silverware.

Deadly – cool.

Dunnes Store – large retail and grocery chain.

Eamonn – male Irish name. Pronounced Aa-man.

Eejit – idiot.

Eimear – female Irish name. Pronounced Ee-mer.

Full stop – period/end of.

Gaff – house/home.

Gee – slang for vagina.

Gobshite – idiot.

Grand – okay/fine.

Hob – stove top.

Hound – player/manslut/manwhore.

I'm made up for ya – I'm happy for you.

Is not on – not accepted/not cool.

Jocks – boxers/male underwear.

Junior Cert/Certificate – state exams you sit in 3rd year of secondary school, approximately age 15.

Knickers – panties.

Leaving/Leaving Cert/Certificate – state exams you sit in 6th year of secondary school, approximately age 17/18.

Lift – elevator.

Locked – drunk/smashed.

Locker – nightstand/bedside table.

Longitude – open-air music festival held at Marley Park in Dublin.

Loses the plot/ loses the head – gets angry.

Mate – friend/bestie/buddy.

Motorway – highway.

Naggin – a 200 ml bottle of alcohol.

Press – cupboard.

Right gob on her – potty mouth/outspoken/opinionated.

Rowing – arguing.

Rubbish – trash/garbage OR it can mean something that is crap.

Runners – sneakers.

Secondary school – high school.

She's in bits – she's really upset/devastated.

Spar – convenience store

Stretched up – gone through a growth spurt.

Tesco – large grocery store chain

The jacks – toilet/bathroom.

The Liffey – River Liffey in Dublin.

Torches – flashlights.

Tracksuit bottoms – sweats/sweatpants.

Treatment rooms – spa rooms.

Trinners or Trinity – Trinity College Dublin/TCD.

UCD – University College Dublin.

Uni – abbreviated from university.

Wanker – prick/asshole/jerk.

What's the story? – what's up?/what's the plan?

Zip – zipper.

DILLON

Part One
PRE-VIVIEN

Chapter One
Age 6

"Where's Ash?" I ask, poking my head around Mum and looking for my sister.

"She's with Nana, love." Mum messes my hair as she smiles at Nigel and tells him thanks.

I hold the strap of my guitar case as I squeeze past Mum out onto the step. I wave at Daddy, and he waves back. He's leaning against the side of the car waiting for us. It's weird that my sister and little brother aren't in the back seat.

"I'll see you next week, Dillon," my guitar teacher says, leaning down and lifting his hand for a high-five.

I smack Nigel's hand the hardest I can, grinning despite my missing front teeth. Shane keeps calling me goofy. He said Da used to call him that all the time when he was my age. I still don't know what it means. My older brother is super annoying. Mum says it's 'cause he's a teenager now. But Shane's always been annoying. Just 'cause he's older doesn't mean he gets to tell me what to do. He's not my daddy.

"Good job today, Dillon." Nigel's smile gets bigger. "I'll see you next week, and don't forget to practice."

"I won't!" I call out, jumping off the step onto the driveway and running towards Daddy. He laughs when I charge at him, wrapping his arm around me and kissing the top of my head.

"Where is everyone?" I ask, looking up at him as he takes the case off my back. "And why aren't you at work?" In the year since I first started my lessons, Daddy never comes to collect me because he's always busy with the farm. It's always Mum, Ash, and Ro.

"They're over at Nana's. Your mum and I wanted to talk to you alone."

My frown is instant. "About what?"

Daddy scratches the back of his head before opening the boot and carefully putting my guitar inside. "Let's wait until we get back to the house."

My frown deepens.

"If the wind changes, your face will stay all grumpy like that," Mum teases, coming up beside me.

"You always say that, and it never happens," I remind her, climbing into the back seat while my parents get into the front.

"Come sit in between us," Mum says, patting the empty space on the fallen log. There are a few of them on the grass around our playground. My stomach feels funny, and I rub it as I jump down off the swing.

Daddy built the playground last summer close to the house so Mum can see us and so we don't bother Daddy when he's working. He moved some of the cows to a new barn on the other side of the farm, and he gave me and my brothers and sister the old barn to play in. It's still being novated, and we're not allowed inside until it's all clean. But Uncle Eamonn came over and helped Daddy build our playground in the grass at the back of the barn, and it's so cool! We have our own slides, swings, and a climbing frame, and they made a football pitch on the other side with two goals and everything! Shane and Ciarán play football for St. Anthony's, but I don't really care about football.

I only care about my guitar.

And Ash.

My sister is my best friend. Just don't tell Jamie or Cillian.

"Did I do something wrong?" I peek at Mummy and Daddy, wondering if I'm in trouble again.

"No, honey." Mum takes my hand as Daddy puts his arm around both of us.

That lump in his throat moves around before he speaks. "We wanted to talk to you about something important, and then we're going out for pizza and ice cream."

"I want chocolate chip!" I shout, and the pain in my tummy goes away.

Daddy chuckles. "You can have all the chocolate chip ice cream you want."

"But what about Ash and Ro and Ciarán and Shane? They'll be sad if they don't get pizza and ice cream too."

"We're all going, Dillon." Mum kisses my hair. "Your nana is going to drive them to the restaurant in Greystones to meet us."

"Cool." I snuggle into Mum's side. She's always all warm and squishy.

Daddy coughs, and I look up as he and Mum look at one another. The pain in my tummy is back.

Mum kisses the tip of my nose, smiling at me in that funny way she does sometime. "We love you very much, Dillon."

"I know." Mum says it all the time to all of us. She even says it to Daddy when she thinks we aren't listening. I squeeze her tight. "I love you, Mummy." I twist my head around. "You too, Daddy."

"You have brought so much joy into our lives, Dillon. We all love you so much."

This is getting boring. "Okay. Can we go for pizza now?"

Mum smiles, and Daddy squeezes my other hand. "Not yet, love," Mum says. "We wanted to talk to you about adoption. We know you're curious. We didn't talk about it yesterday when you first asked because we wanted to find some quiet time to talk with you alone."

That's what they want to talk about? I wish I hadn't said anything yesterday when I got home from school, but I was afraid I'd get in trouble for punching Ross, and I had to tell my parents he was being nasty to Charlie and saying mean things like nobody wanted him 'cause Charlie is 'dopted. "I asked Charlie McGovern in class today, and he told me everything." I jump up. "So, can we go now? Puh-lease?"

Daddy lifts me back onto the log. "I was adopted," he says, and my eyes pop wide.

"You didn't have a real mummy and daddy?" That's what Charlie said it means. But he's not sad. He's happy. His 'dopted mummy and daddy are really nice to him, and they even gave him a Spider-Man bedroom for his last birthday and everything.

"Everyone has a mummy and daddy," Mum says, tucking some of my hair behind my ear. "It's how babies are made, but sometimes, for various reasons, that mummy and daddy aren't able to look after the baby."

"That's sad." I have a pain in my heart now.

"Sometimes it is," my daddy says. "But sometimes it's not so sad because other mummies and daddies adopt the baby and love and care for him in a way the other mummy and daddy couldn't."

I scrunch my nose, not really sure what they mean.

"Sometimes it's the best thing for the baby," Mum says. "Lots of married couples can't have babies, and they have so much love to give."

"Like my parents." Daddy pats my shoulder. "They tried to have children of their own for a long time, and they couldn't."

"Why not?"

"It's complicated," Mummy says. "But it's not important now.

Dillon

What is important is that your granny Mary and grandad Jack adopted your dad, and he had the best life with them. They loved him and cared for him, and he was very happy."

"I love my granny and grandad. Why do they have to live in Kerry? It's so far away." We only get to see them a few times a year, unlike my other nana and grandpa who live in Greystones. We see them all the time.

Daddy rubs his beard. "I'll call your granny and see if maybe we can visit them over Easter for a few days."

"Yay!" I hop up again. "Can we get pizza now?"

"You need to sit down and let us finish telling you." Mum pulls me down onto her lap. Daddy moves in right beside us as Mum's arms go around me.

"Being adopted was the best thing that happened to me," Daddy says. "My life could have been very different if your granny and grandad hadn't opened their home and their hearts to me. Your uncle Eamonn is adopted too."

"The things Ross said yesterday were cruel and untrue." Mum rubs my back while biting on the side of her lip. "Charlie is loved, and it makes no difference whether he was adopted or not. Jenny and Ian are his real parents in all the ways that count."

"Just like your granny and grandad are my real parents too."

I lean back against Mum, wishing we could just get to the pizza and ice cream part.

"We need to tell you something, Dillon. We weren't planning to tell you quite yet, but this seems like the right time to mention it." Mum brushes her fingers across my cheek. I look at her and then my daddy. That weird feeling is back in my stomach.

"We adopted you when you were a baby, Dillon," Mum says.

I just stare at her.

She holds me tighter, staring into my eyes. "Your biological parents—the mummy and daddy who made you—weren't able to care for you, and they asked us if we wanted to love you and cherish you and have you be a part of our family, and we said yes, yes, yes because you're a very special little boy, Dillon."

"It's something I've always wanted to do." Daddy takes my hands in his much bigger ones. "I wanted to give that special experience to another child so they could enjoy all the wonderful things I did growing up."

"Your daddy and I have lots and lots of love to give." Mum's voice sounds strange, and there's water in her eyes. "Your Auntie Eileen told us about you, and the minute we met you, we knew you were ours."

The pain in my tummy is in my chest now. It's like someone is hammering on me from the inside.

"We loved you instantly, Dillon, and we were happy we could give you a home." Now Daddy has water in his eyes.

There's a strange taste in my mouth, and I snuggle in closer to my mummy, feeling cold all over.

"You are our son in the same way Shane, Ciarán, and Ronan are. We love you boys and Aisling equally." Mum puts her finger under my chin. "Do you understand what we are saying, love?"

I nod, holding on to her shirt even though I don't really understand.

"It's a lot to take in." Daddy kisses my forehead. "I was a bit older than you when I found out, and it was confusing at first. But you don't need to worry about it for now, and it doesn't change anything."

"We're your parents. Your family." Mum squeezes me so hard it feels like my bones might break. "And we love you to the moon and back." She puts kisses all over my face. "Don't ever doubt how much you are loved, Dillon."

"Okay."

"Do you have any questions? Is there anything you want to say or know?" Her forehead is all scrunched up as she stares at me.

I shake my head, and she hugs me closer.

Daddy wraps his arms around both of us. "We just needed you to know. If you don't have any questions right now, that's fine."

Dillon

"In time, you will." Mum holds my face in her hands. "Don't bottle it up, Dillon. Come and talk to us about your feelings. You can tell us anything, and we'll understand."

"When you have questions, come to me or your mum, and we'll do our best to answer them. I promise."

"Okay," I say, and they both have funny expressions on their faces. "Can we get pizza now?"

Chapter Two
Age 12

"**D**illon Thomas O'Donoghue! You are so dead!" My sister screams at me, pushing her long, wet strawberry-blonde hair off her face and trying to look mad. But her lips are twitching, and I know she's trying not to laugh.

I walk into the cold Irish Sea in my T-shirt and shorts, heading towards her. "Look! I'm in my clothes too. You can't get mad at me for throwing you in now."

"You're a dickhead." Ash fake glares at me.

"Tell me something new," I tease.

"Joke's on you, sucker!" Ash yells, snorting laughter as she grabs my arm and pulls me down fully under the water.

We stay in the sea, swimming, splashing one another, and messing about as the few other people on Kilcoole Beach pack up their things and leave. "Come on. We better get home before Ma starts looking for us." I hold out my hand, and my sister links her fingers in mine as we stumble out of the sea, shivering, with our clothes stuck to our skin. Grabbing the pink towel, I wrap it around Ash, rubbing my hands up and down her arms and across her back like Ma does.

"Fuck off fussing and dry yourself. I can hear your bones rattling." Ash flings the blue and green towel at me.

"Ma will kick your arse if you keep cursing," I remind her as I drag the towel through my messy brown hair before wrapping it around my shoulders.

"You curse as much as I do." Ash pulls off her swim shoes and shoves her feet into her runners.

"I'm a boy."

She digs her elbows into my ribs. "That's sexist. What the fuck has that got to do with anything?"

"You heard Ma. It's not ladylike. She can hardly say that to me now, can she?" Bending down, I grab my backpack and pull out my runners, switching my swim shoes for them before dumping both our swim shoes in the bag and grabbing my mobile phone. I got one for my tenth birthday. Now all of us have phones except for Ronan. He has another year and a bit to wait before it's his turn. Ma only let us have phones for safety, and as I stare at all the missed calls and texts, I kinda wish I didn't have one. "Fuck." I sling the bag over my shoulder and sigh.

"What's wrong?" Ash grabs the phone from my hand, reading the most recent text. "Shit. She's going to kill us. I bet she'll ground us."

"We can sneak out if she does." Snatching my phone back, I send Ma a quick text saying we're on our way home. Not that it'll cool her down. Da is the quiet one in our house, and Ma is the one who always loses the plot.

Ash slaps her hand to her forehead. "I totally forgot we were supposed to clean the chicken coop this afternoon."

I'm not admitting I remembered and it's why I suggested we sneak off to the beach after lunch. Putting my phone in my bag, I take my sister's hand and start walking. "It's summer holidays. We shouldn't have so many stupid chores," I grumble, kicking a stone as we leave the sandy part of the beach and walk across the stony stretch before we hit the side of the train tracks. "Jamie doesn't have to do any chores." I look left and right, checking to ensure no train is coming before I walk my sister across the wooden slats.

"Maybe he should. Their house is always dirty and smelly." Ash's nose wrinkles in disgust as we walk through the turnstile and out onto the road.

Even though it's almost dinnertime, it's still bright out as I push Ash in front of me, walking on the opposite side of the road. Ciarán said at least that way you can see the cars coming.

"It's not that bad," I lie, feeling the need to defend my friend.

"It so is." Ash glances back at me. "His da gives me the creeps."

"His da is a wanker." Jamie had a black eye the last week of school 'cause he put himself between his parents when they were fighting. He lied to everyone and said he tripped over his school bag and fell face-first into the door handle, but he told me the truth. I said when we're older and bigger we can give his dickhead da a few black eyes to get him back.

"We're lucky," Ash says quietly. "I know Ma loses the head sometimes, but it's only 'cause we're always getting into trouble, and we drive her mad. But she cares about us, and she loves Da. I'm glad they don't fight like Jamie's parents do."

"Yeah." I grip the strap of my bag. "Me too." My best mate has it rough.

"Don't blame Ash." I fold my arms and stare at Ma as she flaps her arms around and shrieks at us. "It was all my idea. I made her do it. Don't ground Ash. It's not fair."

"Shut up, clown." My sister glares at me. "I can fight my own battles." Her lips purse as she stares at Ma. "I was a willing partner in crime. I'll take the same punishment as Dil."

I roll my eyes. She always does this even though she promised me outside she'd let me take the fall. No sense in both of us being officially grounded.

Ro sits at the kitchen table, pretending to read one of his comics while watching out of the corner of his eye and listening to every word. Behind Ma, Shane smirks and flips me the bird. I can't resist doing it back to him.

"Dillon!" Ma shouts. Her eyes look like they are bugging out of her head. "No cursing or obscene gestures will be tolerated in this house. You're grounded for two weeks now."

What the hell? Come on! She's making a big deal out of nothing. It's not like anything happened to us, and so what if my brothers had to do our chores? We'll do theirs tomorrow, and then it's all even. No need for any fucking grounding.

"No, I'm not!" I shout back. "I start secondary school in two weeks. I'm not being grounded for the last two weeks of my holidays!" I glare at her. She can't do this! "So what if we missed cleaning the stupid chicken coop! Shane and Ciarán already did it! You're just being mean for the sake of being mean."

"Dillon." Ma lowers her voice on purpose, and I can tell it's an effort to do it. "This is more than you missing chores. I have told you both, countless times before, how unsafe it is walking back from the beach on your own, yet you keep sneaking down there when my back is turned. I don't know how else to drive the point home. It's not safe. Every time you sneak off there, you put your safety and your sister's safety at risk."

"I'm twelve, and Ash is thirteen. We're old enough to walk to the fucking beach by ourselves." I'm sick of being treated like a baby!

Dillon

"Dillon! Language!" Ma snaps, rubbing the side of her forehead.

"Jamie's ma lets him walk everywhere by himself!"

"I am not discussing what any other parent does. That's up to them to decide. I am talking about you and your sister's safety, and that's nonnegotiable to me. You are still children, Dillon. Children under our protection and care."

"I would never let anything happen to Ash." My hands ball into fists. Ma knows I would die before I'd let anything happen to my sister. "I'd throw myself in front of a car if she was in danger. You don't have to worry."

The angry look on Ma's face fades away. "You're such a good brother, Dillon, but I don't just worry about Ash. I worry about you too, and I don't want anyone throwing themselves in front of cars, which is why you're not allowed to walk to the beach without Shane, Ciarán, or me or your dad. Those are the rules, and you have broken them too many times this summer. I was too lenient before. But not this time."

"I'm not being grounded the last two weeks of my summer holidays. I'll stay home tomorrow. That's enough grounding."

Shane shakes his head, and I'm gonna knock that stupid grin off his face as soon as Ma is done with this stupid crap.

"It's not up to you, Dillon. I'm the parent, and this is my decision. I'll talk to your father on the phone tonight, and he'll agree. You need to learn this lesson before it's learned the hard way."

Da is in Kerry with Uncle Eamonn fishing this week. We stayed with our grandparents last week but came back with Ma on the bus on Sunday.

"This is stupid." I kick my backpack across the kitchen floor in a temper. "You're not the boss of me. I'm not staying grounded for two weeks."

"Dil," Ash whispers. "Just agree, and we'll work on her later or get Da to change her mind when he gets home." Ash has Da wrapped around her little finger. He's a big softie when it comes to his only daughter, so it's possible she'll work her magic on him. But he's not

15

due home for another three days, and I'll go crazy if I have to stay at the farm all that time.

"No." I shake my head. "I'm not doing it."

Ma mutters something under her breath. "I'm your mother, and you will not give me cheek, boy." She waves her finger in my face, and she looks angry again. "Keep this up, and I'll ground you for a month!"

I don't know why I say it, but she just makes me so mad sometimes. "No, you're not!" I shout. "You're not my real mother, and you don't get to tell me what to do!"

Tears instantly fill her eyes, and I want to take the words back, but I can't.

"Apologize, you little prick." Shane storms up to me, grabbing my shoulders.

"Shane, don't." Ma pulls him away. "Go to your room, Dillon. You too, Ash."

I stomp up the stairs to the bedroom I share with my little brother and slam the door closed. Throwing myself on my bed, I bury my face in my pillow and try to ignore the pain in my chest and the sobs building behind my eyes. I know I shouldn't have said that. I hurt Ma, and I hate myself. I don't know why I have these thoughts or why I keep saying horrible things. I hate feeling like this, being like this, but I can't make it stop.

Chapter Three

Age 12

The door opens, and I lift my head as Ash slips into my room. She climbs onto the bed and hugs me, but I push her arms away, sniffling as I sit up against my headboard. "Don't hug me. Hug Ma. She deserves your hugs, not me."

"You deserve all the hugs in the world, Dil." Ignoring me, she moves up the bed and wraps her arms around me as best she can. She rests her head on my chest, and I put my hand on her back. "What you said to Ma was cruel, but I know you didn't mean it. She knows that too."

"I can't stop the crap that comes out of my mouth sometimes. I bet they regret adopting me." It's not the first time I've thought that.

"Dillon, no." Ash sits upright, holding my face in her hands. Her eyes are glassy as she stares at me. "Of course, they don't. They love you. We all do."

I hold my sister a little tighter. "I don't know why. I'm always getting in trouble at school. I play my guitar way too late at night, keeping everyone up, even though Ma has told me to stop it so many times. I moan about doing chores all the time, and I'm always sneaking out and usually bringing you with me."

"You're a free spirit, Dil, and societal norms are trying to quash your spontaneity and crush your creativity."

My sister is only a year older than me, and she's way smarter, but there's no way she said this. I don't even know what it fucking means. I arch a brow as I stare at her. "What?"

She giggles. "I heard Shane saying it to Ma and Da last week. He was defending you. I liked the sound of it, so I memorized it."

"You're going to rule the world someday, Ash." I truly mean that.

"As long as I get to do it with you by my side."

I squeeze her closer, already feeling better. "Try stopping me."

"Hey."

We both look up, finding Shane in the doorway. "Can I talk to Dil alone for a bit?"

Ash looks to me. I know if I say no she'll refuse to leave me, but this isn't her fight. "It's okay."

Ash looks unsure as she looks from me to our oldest brother.

"He's safe, Ash." Shane smirks as he moves into the room. "I'm not going to beat the crap out of him though he deserves it."

I nod because it's the truth. I have more than deserved it, plenty of times, but Shane has never beat me up. He prefers to annoy the shit out of me using his words.

"I just want to have a chat with him. Man to man."

"Go. I'll be grand."

She hugs me one final time before jumping off the bed. "Go easy on him," she warns Shane as she passes. The door shuts behind her as Shane sits on the edge of my bed.

"Ash would walk over hot coals for you."

"I know. I'd do the same for her." Lots of my mates have sisters, and all they do is bitch about them. I'm lucky because my sister is chill, and she's everything to me.

"I love the bond ye have, but you really should stop getting her into trouble."

I lift a brow in his direction. "You ever tried talking Ash out of anything after she's made up her mind?"

Shane chuckles. "We all share the same stubborn streak except for Ro maybe."

I put new meaning to the word. Sometimes, I wonder whether I got my legendary stubbornness from my bio mother or father. I know I'm frowning as I force thoughts of those wankers from my mind.

The humor dies on my brother's face. "You know what you have to do, Dil." He gives me that look. The one that says he means business.

"I didn't mean it." I hug my knees to my chest.

"We all know that." Shane leans in closer. "I don't know what kind of shite is going through your head, Dillon, but I know it's crap." He grabs the back of my head. "You're our brother. You're their son. End of, Dil. Whatever bullshit is going on inside here." He presses his finger to my brow. "It's not the truth. I wish they'd never told you."

"Why did they?" I have often wondered that myself.

I was only six and all it did was confuse me. Ma has tried to talk to me a few times, but I don't want to speak about it. I want to forget I'm adopted. I want to feel normal, like the rest of my brothers and my sister. Talking about it will only keep reminding me I'm different. I get enough of that when I look in the mirror. My brothers all look alike, and though I have brown hair and blue eyes, same as Shane and Ro, I still look totally different to them, and I hate it.

"That little shit Ross Kenmare is to blame. Ma and Da had planned on telling you when you were ten, but after Ross started bullying Charlie at school, they were afraid to keep it from you. Everyone knows everyone's business in Kilcoole. It's no secret you were adopted. They were afraid you'd find out from Ross or someone else."

"I wish I'd never known."

"Then put it out of your mind." Shane shrugs. "Force yourself to forget it."

If only it were that easy.

"It doesn't matter a bit to any of us, so if it's bugging you that much, just forget about it. You're one of us. It doesn't matter whose gee you came out of."

"Fucking gross."

Shane grins. "You won't be saying that for much longer."

Shane still babies me too. "Talk to me about Rihanna's gee, and I'm there, mate. Just leave Ma out of it."

Shane chuckles before his "serious" face reappears. "Listen to me." Shane grips my arms. "I'm not going to be around as much once I start back at UCD, and you and Ciarán need to step up and help Ma when I'm too busy with classes and studying. I know you can't help it, but try to dial down your troublemaker setting, yeah?"

"I thought you didn't want to crush my creativity or some shit."

"That sneaky little bitch." Shane shakes his head, but he's smiling. "No one wants to crush your spirit, Dil." His gaze lands on my guitar where it's propped against the wall. "I've said it before, and I'll say it again. You're a future superstar in the making." He puts his hand over his heart. "I know it as much as I know I'll be taking charge of the farm as soon as I graduate and diversifying before it's too late."

I've heard him arguing with Da over the dinner table about diversification, but I usually tune out farm talk as it bores me to tears.

"But you can't say that crap to Ma, Dillon," he adds. "You've really hurt her this time."

I slide my legs off the bed. "I'll say sorry."

Shane stands the same time I do. "I think Ma is right and it'd do you good to talk to someone."

"I don't need a psychologist," I scoff. "I'm not talking to some shrink." Some stranger isn't going to help me make sense of the shit in my head when he doesn't even know me.

"It might help, Dillon."

"I'm going to talk to Ma," I say, brushing past him.

"Dil," he calls after me, and I stop in the doorway and look over my shoulder.

"I know we haven't always gotten on, but you're my brother, and

I'm here for you. You can talk to me about anything. I'll always make time for you, okay?"

I jerk my head in acknowledgment before walking off downstairs.

Ma is standing at the cooker in the kitchen when I walk in. She looks back and stops stirring whatever's in the saucepan as I walk over to her. I can barely get the words out over the lump in my throat. "I'm sorry, Ma. I didn't mean it."

"I know you didn't."

I wrap my arms around her. "It's not what I think," I whisper. "I don't know why I said it. I'm really sorry."

She runs her hand back and forth across the back of my head. "I wish you'd talk to me, Dillon, or talk to someone, anyone. It's not healthy to bury your feelings inside. They need to come out."

"I don't want to talk about it, Ma," I whisper.

"And that's exactly why you should." Her soft tone normally comforts me, but I hate disappointing her, and I know I'm still doing it.

I ease out of her embrace. "You can ground me all year. I'll take whatever punishment I deserve."

"One week, and you'll do extra chores around the house and the farm."

"Okay." I shuffle on my feet. "I really am sorry."

"I know, honey." She presses a kiss to my cheek. "I love you, son."

I want to return the sentiment, but the words just won't come. They haven't for a few years now.

She puts her hand on my arm. "It's okay, Dillon. Don't beat yourself up about it. I just want you to be happy. We both do, and we love you so, so much. I wish there was a way to cut open my heart and show you so you'd believe it."

"I believe it," I say even though I'm not fully sure that's the truth. Some days, I don't know what I believe.

"You're so precious to me, Dillon, and I worry about you." She pats my cheek. "I won't force you to speak to a professional, but at least speak to your sister or to Shane or even Cillian or Jamie. Don't let those feelings fester inside you because one day they will explode, and it won't be pretty."

Chapter Four
Age 14

I hear the shouting from outside as I walk up Jamie's driveway, and I inwardly cringe. Fuck. I don't know how my best mate lives with all the constant arguments. His parents are a bleeding nightmare. A loud noise claims my attention just as I reach the Flemings' front door, and I whip my head to the side. My eyes pop wide as the sitting room window shatters into pieces and a guitar, *a fucking guitar*, comes sailing through the broken glass, landing unceremoniously on the overgrown grass of their small front garden. "What in the actual fuck?" I mutter to myself, lifting my hand to knock on the door when it's suddenly torn open from inside.

Jamie has a face like thunder as he storms outside, slamming the door shut behind him. "I need to get fucked up."

"Okay." I look at the smashed guitar as we walk past with pain in my heart. "What the fuck did the guitar do to anyone? That's messed up."

"My entire life is messed up." Jay pulls out a box of smokes, offering me one.

We light up in silence as we walk on autopilot towards the main street to meet up with our other friends. "Wanna talk about it?" I run a hand along the back of my neck as I glance at my mate.

He shrugs, pulling a long drag before blowing smoke clouds into the chilly air. "Not much more to say. Same ole shite, different day." Tension brackets his mouth. "Ma seems especially mad this time, but neither of them will tell me what he did now."

I zip up my jacket as we turn left onto the path which leads to the main part of town. We puff away as we walk, keeping stride with one another. We've both stretched up a lot the past year, and we're the tallest of our friends.

"Does Shauna know?" I ask. Jamie's older sister is his only sibling. She's four years older, and she recently moved to Belfast to study social work at uni, leaving him alone in the hellhole he calls home.

"Doubt it. She took off the second she finished her Leaving, and you know she hasn't been back to the gaff since. She calls me every couple of weeks, but she never wants to speak to Ma or Da. Not that I blame her. I'd get out now too if I could."

"You could move in with us." I don't know if Ma would want to get in the middle of the rowing Flemings, but she's fond of Jamie, and he often stays over. I think she'd be open to considering it.

"I can't leave Ma on her own with him. They'd kill one another." His shoulders hunch as we approach Byrne's car park at the top of the road, where the rest of the boys are already huddled together. "Don't say anything to Cill," Jay says in a low tone.

"You don't need to say it. I never tell him the things you tell me." Jamie is embarrassed, and I'm not one to blab. Cillian doesn't need me to say it anyway. He's got eyes and ears. Most everyone in town knows Jamie's parents have a shit marriage and they should have broken up years ago.

Shane said the rumor around town is Jay's da cheats on his ma when he travels around the country playing with his band. During the week, his da works for the council, but at least two weekends a month, he books gigs with his piece-of-shit band. I've heard them play, and they're fucking awful. But somehow, they have gathered a

24

bit of a cult following over the years. You'd swear Conal Fleming was fucking Bono the way he goes on sometimes. He's the biggest loser. My da may not have much to say, but at least he doesn't go around bragging or cheating or embarrassing any of his kids.

"Boys," I say in greeting when we reach our gang, tossing my empty butt on the ground and smashing it under my boot. "What's the story?"

"Jono's bro thinks he can get us into the McGettigan party." Cillian rubs his hands and grins.

I narrow my eyes on the noticeable mark on his neck and react on instinct. Grabbing him by his jacket, I shove him up against the wall. "My sister better not have given you that," I snap.

"What?" Jamie frowns, looking between me and our other best friend.

I haven't told Jay I suspect Ash and Cillian are messing around. He sulked big-time a few years ago when I told him Cill gave Ash her first kiss. That didn't go down well, and the guys butt heads a lot these days. The three of us have been best friends since we were little, and I don't want my sister getting in the middle of whatever is going on with us. It's not just Jamie. There is distance between Cill and me too that wasn't there previously. I'm finding we have less in common, and I suspect the reason we don't see as much of him now is because he's sneaking around with my sister.

I see how both my mates stare at Ash. I don't like it, but I get it. She's beautiful, smart as fuck, and she has a fiery personality with a right gob on her that seems to send all the guys at school wild. I got the new scar over my right eyebrow two weeks ago after a fight with this prick at school who was talking crap about her. Got suspended for three days for fighting, and my parents were not happy. But they weren't too heavy-handed with the punishment when they discovered I was defending my sister, though Ma would prefer I used my words not my fists.

"Is this a trick question?" Cill tosses his dirty-blond hair out of his eyes with a jerk of his head.

"Just yes or no, Cill." I release my hold on him but keep my glare firmly in place.

"If I say yes, you'll go nuts. If I say no, meaning it's some other bird, you'll go nuts. I can't fucking win with you, Dil."

"Fucking hell." Jamie glares at Cillian before removing a naggin of vodka from the inside pocket of his jacket and taking a vicious swig.

I yank Cillian around the corner, away from prying ears. "Do not mess my sister around, Cill. Make it official or end it."

Ash tells me most everything, but she's been quiet about Cillian. Which is how I know something is going on. That and the puppy-dog eyes they give one another when they think I'm not looking. I'd have to be blind to not realize they're mad about one another. I know Ash isn't saying anything so if it ends badly it won't impact my friendship with Cill, but deep down, she knows it won't matter. My loyalty will always belong to my sister. If Cillian doesn't treat her right, he'll be dead to me, and I won't lose any sleep over it.

"You won't go nuts?" He crosses his arms and leans back against the pub wall, arching a brow in my direction. "You've always told us Ash is off-limits."

"That didn't fucking stop you, did it?"

"I can't help how I feel." He pushes off the wall and straightens up. "I love her. She's it for me, Dil. I don't see anyone but her. Tell me you're grand with it so I can do this right."

"I'm not exactly excited about it, but it's not my call. It's not yours either."

"She loves me too. She's been afraid to tell you."

Bullshit. Nothing scares Aisling O'Donoghue. She's trying to protect me and denying herself in the process. "If it's what Ash wants, I won't stand in your way. I just want her to be happy."

The goofiest smile ghosts over his mouth.

Fucking hell. He's a total goner.

"Thanks, mate. I promise I'll treat her like a queen."

"You fucking better." I thump his upper arm, but it's only half in jest. "I'll beat the ever-living daylights out of you if you hurt her."

"I won't. I swear."

I nod and grab him into a headlock. He punches me in the gut, and I let him go.

"Jamie won't like it," I say.

"That's not my problem."

"It will be if it gets messy."

"Jamie's just pissed she picked me, but he'll get over it."

I run my hands through my hair, wondering when both my friends turned into pussies. I seriously need to get drunk. "Sort that shit out with him, and maybe I won't rearrange your face."

"What's going on with Cill and Ash?" Jay asks as we walk towards the McGettigan farm. It's only a quarter mile from my house, which will be handy for getting my drunken arse home later.

I swipe the naggin from his fingers and decide to just put it out there. "He says they love each other. I told him to make it official or fuck off." I take a swig before passing the bottle back. "You have any issue if they start going out?"

"Me?" He fakes surprise, but he's fooling no one. "Why the fuck would I give a shit?" He drains the rest of the vodka and tosses the empty bottle over a bush as we walk down Lott Lane.

I could call him out on his bullshit, but I'd rather not. If he likes my sister, her new relationship will soon cure him of those feelings. It's not like Ash has even noticed. All she sees is Cillian.

"Good." Removing two cans of cider from my backpack, I pop the tab on one and hand it to Jay. Thank fuck for Jono's older brother, Graham. He turned eighteen a few months ago, and he has no issue buying booze for us. Unlike my stick-up-the-arse brother. Ciarán is also eighteen, but he refuses to help a brother out.

"Time to get fucked up." He brings the can to his mouth.

27

"Yup." I open my drink and knock back a mouthful of warm cider. "Just remember girls are distractions we don't need," I say, eyeballing him. Jamie and I have been discussing starting a band, and between the band and school, we'll be busy. We don't need girls getting in the way of our plans.

We both grew up with a guitar in our hands and bonded early over our love of music. I have a notebook full of songs I've written over the past few years, and I'm itching to let the words roam free. Ma won't let me consider it until after the Junior Cert, but as soon as next summer hits, I'm putting our plans into action.

If Jay likes my sis, he'll soon get over it when we start the band and have birds throwing their knickers at us nonstop.

"True, but I wouldn't mind getting my dick sucked on the regular. Wanking just isn't doing it for me anymore."

We share a grin thinking back to last month where we both had our first blowjobs in the toilets of the community center—the highlight of the lame teen disco I'd only attended 'cause Ash wanted to go.

We're both locked by the time we get to the party taking place in an outbuilding on the McGettigan farm. It's mostly older kids from fifth and sixth year in attendance. Jono's brother is here, and he's vouched for us, though he told us we're on our own if we get into any trouble. Cillian, that sly fucker, disappeared somewhere en route to the party. Took a detour into my house is my guess. Cill likes to talk a big game, act like he's the big lad, down with drinking and partying, but the truth is, his parents are proper religious, and it's messed with his head. So, yeah, Cill doing a disappearing act is nothing new.

We knock back the rest of the cider, smoke some weed, and head to the dance floor, buzzing and dancing like dopes, until I spot Eimear Tallon and Nina Campbell looking right at us. They're off to the side, holding bottles of that fruity alcohol shit all the girls seem to drink. Eimear licks her lips and tilts her head in a "come here" gesture, and I don't need to be told twice.

I've had a hard-on for Eimear since first year, but she usually doesn't give me the time of day. She's sixteen, and even though I'm only a few months away from fifteen, she's always rejected my flirting, telling me I'm too young for her. I'm hoping that might have changed since I took a big growth spurt over the summer. I'm almost as tall as Shane now, and my shoulders and arms are ripped from farm work and my weekly sessions at Bray Boxing Club. From the look in Eimear's eye, she's appreciating my efforts.

It's a miracle I don't come on the spot with the way she's eye fucking me.

I grab Jay's arm. "Come on, lad." I'm already rock hard behind my jeans as I haul him off the dance floor with me. "I think it's our lucky night."

"Let's go!" he says, grinning when he sees the girls waiting for us.

"Be chill," I warn him. He's more fucked up than me, and I'm not blowing the only chance I might get with Eimear.

"Eimear. Nina. Looking beautiful, as always," I say when we reach them.

"You don't look so bad yourself, Dillon." Eimear's gaze moves up and down my body.

"You still meeting Lawlor?" I ask as Jamie pulls Nina off to the side and starts talking to her.

"Nah. I broke it off with him." She leans in closer, putting her hand on my chest before she looks up at me. "He was too serious, and I'm only looking for fun."

"Fun's practically my middle name."

She giggles. "Cheesy, but I bet it's true."

I slide my arm around her waist, pulling her in flush to my body, letting her feel what she does to me. "You want a good time, babe, I'm your man." I can't stop the cheese flowing from my mouth, but Eimear doesn't seem to mind.

"Shut your mouth, O'Donoghue, before I change my mind." She wraps her arms around my neck, pressing her gorgeous body against me. "Or maybe I'll shut it for you." She grabs my face and pulls it down to hers.

I'm grinning like an eejit as my lips descend, claiming her mouth in a hard kiss. I'm fairly sure some cum is leaking in my boxers when she shoves her tongue in my mouth and grabs my arse through my jeans, and I really hope I don't embarrass myself.

"Let's go outside," she purrs into my ear, taking my hand and guiding it through the gaps in our bodies and up under her skirt. "I need a different kind of kiss," she adds, licking my ear and dragging my fingers along her knickers.

Jamie and I trade matching smug grins as both older girls lead us outside the barn, and we're still wearing them an hour later when we stumble back to my gaff after epic blowjobs that culminated in us coming all over the girls' tits.

Chapter Five
Age 15

I slice my hand through the air in a cutting motion when my sister sticks her fingers in her ears, instantly silencing the room. I don't blame Ash. We're fucking terrible. Toxic Gods, my arse. We're more like Toxic Gobshites right now. My sigh is heavy as I turn and look around at Conor, Jamie, and Aaron. We need to get our act together before Simone Sullivan's birthday party in eight days, or we'll never hear the end of it.

Initially, Ma had said we could have the play barn for band practice, but after a week, Da and Shane cleared out a smaller concrete shed that was full of old rubbish a bit farther away from the house for us. We all pitched in to buy a secondhand sofa and a table and chairs as well as some other bits of equipment we needed. We want this to be a creative hub where we write and perform music.

I threw Toxic Gods into the mix as a suggested name for the band, and it was the only name we all agreed on—Ash's very vocal protests didn't count. A few days later, Shane showed up with a large board bearing the name, tacking it to the wall, and now it's official. My brother also got us a coffee machine. We've had our ups and downs, my brother and I, but he's been really supportive of the band, and I'm finding he's less annoying as I get older.

Shane graduated from UCD in May though the grad ceremony isn't until September. He did really well, 'cause he's a big fucking nerd. I'm hoping I did enough to pass my Junior Cert, though I'm not holding my breath. The exam reports aren't released until October, so I'm making the most of my summer in case I get grounded for the rest of my life when the results come out.

"You're all out of sync," Ash says, leaning against the far wall. She's our biggest supporter, and she hangs out with us every session. She is really excited about the band and happy for me. She wants us to succeed, and she has cool ideas, which is why we all listen to her. "Like, individually, you all play great, and you know the material, but you haven't gelled. You haven't found your flow."

"What do you suggest?" Jay asks, reaching a hand up to check his hair is still intact. I swear he's worse than a girl since he got a faux hawk and dyed the tips of his hair white blond.

"I suggest you stop drooling over my sister's tits." I say it low so Ash doesn't hear.

"Can't help it. They're much bigger, and have you seen what she's wearing?" He doesn't disguise his approval as his gaze rakes over her crop top and small denim shorts.

"Unfortunately, yes." Since Cillian and Ash started going out—and they're clearly banging—she's been dressing sexier. Ma and Da have no clue because she exits the house wearing jeans and a top and changes in the barn before leaving to meet her boyfriend. Her current wardrobe seems to consist mostly of crop tops, skimpy skirts, tight dresses, and high heels. My sister is beautiful, and she looks all grown up now. Unfortunately, Cill isn't the only mate who's noticed.

"Cill will kick your arse if he catches you." Things are already strained between the three of us, and the dynamic has changed a lot. Cillian isn't into music, so he's not part of the band, and he has shown little interest in getting involved in any way. It's only helping to highlight the divide in our friendship and the fact we don't have that much in common with him anymore.

Jamie is pissed Cill is with Ash, though he's claiming it's 'cause Cillian isn't good enough for her. With the rate the two of us are kissing girls, he's not exactly brokenhearted, so maybe it's the truth. I'm not completely happy Cill is fucking my sister, especially when they seem to argue and break up all the damn time, but it's not my call to make. She says she loves him, and I've been warned not to interfere, so I'm trying to stay out of it.

If this is how relationships are, I want no part of it. I'm happy messing around with random girls, and my dick isn't complaining. I haven't fucked any girl yet, but I'm planning to rectify that this summer.

"The words are coming from my mouth, Jamie, not my fucking tits."

Ash's snarky tone yanks me out of my head. I thump my mate in the arm, sending him a warning look. "Ignore this clown," I say, "and repeat your suggestions. I was zoned out."

She rolls her eyes and mutters under her breath before pushing off the wall and walking closer to us. "I've been googling it, and these are the kind of issues most new bands experience. Aaron," she calls out, peeking past us to fix her stare on our drummer. "Typically, the drummer keeps time and the other band members align to your beat. You need a click track. I've emailed you a link to some software you can use to create it. That'll help you all to keep to the same beat so you're in sync. You're in charge of that, Aaron. You keep the rhythm, and the others will follow your cue."

Aaron nods his head enthusiastically, rolling his drumsticks between his fingers like the show-off he is. "Cool."

"But the rest of you need to tighten up as well." She puts her hands on her hips, letting her gaze skim over me, Conor, and Jay. "So, you need to pick one song to master, to find your rhythm as a band, and once you've got that one song nailed down, then you should be good to move on to others. So, what's the song?"

"Easy," I say.

"'Breakeven,'" Jamie and I say together. We lift our hands for a knuckle touch. "It's the perfect song." Contemporary alternative rock or pop rock isn't really my thing, but I make an exception for The Script and Coldplay. Mostly I'm into U2, The Foo Fighters, Nirvana, Imagine Dragons, Jane's Addiction, The Cure, Green Day, No Doubt, Fleetwood Mac, Bon Jovi, and I could go on.

Recently, Jay and I have snuck out a few times to watch local indie rock bands play in pubs and venues across the city center. We're both over six feet now, and we look older, plus we've got deadly fake IDs, so getting in hasn't been an issue.

"Okay. So, here's how it's going down," Ash says as Cillian enters the shed. She hasn't noticed him yet; she's too focused on us. "You'll all practice your individual parts of 'Breakeven' religiously, every night alone, and record it. Listen back, correct anything that needs correcting, but listen to the beat, inhale the pulse, live and breathe it. Then at band practice, you try it a few different ways. One at a time, with drums, without drums, with the click, without it."

"Babe." Cillian slides his arms around her from behind and nuzzles her long, wavy hair with his nose. The pussy is obsessed with her hair, always running his fingers through it or sniffing it, and I saw him fucking brushing it one time. Weirdo. "Leave the band stuff to the band. What do you know about it?"

"A lot more than you," she snaps, pushing his arms away and turning around to face him. "Dil's been playing guitar since he was five and explaining things to me for as long. I've spent hours listening to Jamie and Dillon play. Plus, I'm good at research. I don't have to be a musical genius to discover how other bands have overcome the teething problems they faced at the start."

"Doesn't mean you're qualified to tell them what to do. It's not like you're their manager." He chuckles at whatever expression is on her face.

"She is," I blurt because I don't like the way Cillian is treating my sister, and honestly, with how invested she is, it only makes sense.

Dillon

Jamie's mouth curves into a smile as he nods. Aaron eyes me in a way that says he's cool with it, and Conor...well, Conor exists in his own little world. He's currently sitting on the floor smoking a joint with his guitar beside him. I'll explain it to him later, and he'll be grand.

Conor only moved to Kilcoole when he was nine. He lives with his grandparents, and he keeps to himself. The lad is chasing some demons, not that I'm one to throw shade. No one was more surprised when he turned up to audition than me. I had no clue he was into music or that he could play bass guitar like a fucking legend. Jamie was a little concerned letting him into the band, but I like he's quiet and a deep thinker, and who cares if he's perpetually stoned? As long as he plays like that, I couldn't give a flying fuck what he smokes. Conor said he's written some stuff too, so we're gonna join forces and see what magic we can create with our words.

Jamie and I have known Aaron since we were little kids. We all go to the same school. Although none of us are friends per se, we know his crew, and he's sound and a kick-ass drummer, so it was a no-brainer to let him join.

Seems like setting up the band was easy in theory, not so much in reality. But I'm confident with Ash's help we'll get over this initial bump. Which is why Cillian Doyle doesn't get to spout stupid shit at my sister and get away with it. "Keep your nose out of shit you know nothing about, Cill, and if I hear you disrespecting my sister like that again, I'll knock you the fuck out."

"You're such a stuck-up-cunt at times," Jamie says. "You need to chill."

"Shut the fuck up." Cillian glares at Jamie. "Jealous prick," he adds under his breath.

"Okay, enough." Ash threads her fingers through Cillian's, pulling him back. "Let's go. The session is finished anyway."

"Sure, babe." His arms go around her again, and I puke a little in my mouth when he slams his lips down on hers and kisses her in a way that leaves no one in any doubt he's staking his claim. For Jamie's benefit, I'm sure.

"I'll catch you later," Ash says, surfacing for air a minute later. "Remember what I said, and practice, practice, practice," she calls out before Cillian steers her out the door.

"I don't like that guy," Conor says.

"I'm beginning to agree with you, mate," Jamie adds.

Simone Sullivan's eighteenth birthday party is equally the worst night of my life and the absolute best. Worst because our first public performance as a band is a complete fucking disaster. We're still all over the place, and it shows. While the girls dancing in front of the stage were full of admiration, the guys shouting insults and throwing bottles at us from the corner weren't holding back.

And best because it's the night I lose my virginity.

I'm drowning my sorrows with a bottle of beer, propped against the bar in the large marquee erected on the grounds of the Sullivan mansion in Enniskerry, when the birthday girl comes up to me.

Simone is beautiful with gorgeous reddish-brown hair and the most stunning hazel eyes. She's way out of my league, but that doesn't mean I won't try to get in her knickers. Her body is like my every wet dream come to life, and I'm having a hard time keeping my eyes on her face and not looking down the front of her strapless black minidress. Her tits are huge, and they're right there in front of my face. I spring an instant boner. "Having a good time?" I ask, adjusting the erection digging into the zip of my ripped jeans as I flash her a flirty grin.

"Nope." Grabbing my bottle, she empties the rest of my beer down her throat. I use the opportunity to sneak a look down her dress, and I almost die on the spot. Fuck me. I need to get my hands and my lips on those titties. Saliva pools in my mouth, and my cock aches with need.

She slams the bottle down on the counter and drills me with a poisonous look. "Your band is shite. I just broke up with my cheating arsehole of a boyfriend, and I punched my best friend and told her to go fuck herself after I caught her banging my fella in the downstairs loo. My cake was *red fucking velvet*. Like what the fuck is that? What the hell is wrong with good ole chocolate fudge cake? Which is what I asked for, but Mum ignores anything I say."

She grabs a half-empty bottle of beer from the counter and takes a quick swig before putting it down and grabbing me by the shirt. "I hate most everyone here, and I don't know why I even bothered having a party because I'm having a shit time, and to top it off, I'm not even drunk!" Her eyes flare with frustration before darkening when they lower to my mouth.

"Sounds like you need to destress." I run the tip of my finger up her bare arm as she relaxes her iron fist in my shirt. "It's not too late to turn your birthday into a fun night." I trace my finger across her collarbone. I'm so fucking tempted to bury my hand in the gap between her tits, but I think that might be pushing it.

Ma always says all good things come to those who wait, so I'll hold off on groping her tits in public.

She laughs. "I suppose you're offering?"

"Hell yeah." I cock my head to one side and flash her another flirty grin.

"I'll admit you have a lot of stage presence. You look like you belong up there." She moves in closer, placing her hands on my hips. "You look the part too." She drags her eyes up and down my body, lingering on the noticeable bulge at my crotch. "Your band needs to get their act together, but *you* have something special." Her lips land on my jaw the same time her hands land on my arse. "And a great arse."

I move my lips to her ear. "Want to take this somewhere private?" My arms go around her back, and I press her in against me, ensuring she feels how hard I am for her.

Her pupils are blown when she lifts her head and stares into my eyes. "You do owe me after that rubbish performance." Her eyes glint with desire, and my palms are itching to explore every delicious inch of her.

"I do," I readily agree, fully prepared to lie if she asks me how old I am.

But she doesn't.

"I get horny when I'm pissed off." She links her fingers in mine and leads me out of the marquee. When she looks up at me, a naughty grin is dancing over her lips. "And I'm really fucking pissed off tonight."

Pushing her up against the wall, I cage her in between my arms. "Challenge accepted," I purr before crashing my mouth to hers.

Chapter Six
Age 16

"**D**illon, can I come in?" Ma asks, knocking on the door but waiting to open it.

"Yeah." I sigh, closing my notepad and preparing for the speech I know is coming. I've been expecting it since I was almost expelled from school on Monday.

Ma quietly opens the door and slips into my bedroom carrying a white envelope in her hand. Now that Shane is living in a house with his girlfriend, Fiona, and Ciarán is in college in Galway, Ro and I finally have our own bedrooms. I never minded rooming with my chill little bro, but it's sick having my own space.

I scoot up the bed, resting my back against the headboard as Ma sits on the edge of my mattress. Her hand lifts to the purple-black mess that is my current face. With gentle fingers, she tips my chin up, examining my swollen nose. It's broken in three places, but thankfully, there isn't serious damage, and it'll heal in a few weeks. I've been icing it and taking paracetamol for the pain. At least I don't have a broken jaw like Ross Kenmare. He needs surgery, and he's been told it could take up to six months for his jaw to fully heal. Fucker won't be able to speak for a few weeks, and I'm betting the whole of CCA is secretly patting me on the back for putting that dickhead in his place.

How was I to know Megan was lying when she said her and Ross were on another break? Those two are as on-again, off-again as Cillian and Ash. I never would've fucked Megan if I'd known she was still with Ross. I'm an asshole, in many ways, but I don't tolerate cheating, and I'm pissed Megan lied.

"Is it still hurting?" Ma asks, yanking me out of my head.

"Nah," I lie. "It's not too bad." It's worse at night when I lie down, so I haven't been doing much sleeping. It's just as well I'm suspended from school for two weeks.

"Your father and Shane met with Ross's parents, and they've agreed to drop all this nonsense talk of suing you."

"I wasn't worried." I run my hands through my messy hair. "He hit me first. It was self-defense."

"I know you didn't have a choice, but you broke his jaw, Dillon, and he's facing months of recovery time."

"Maybe next time, he'll shut his stupid gob." My fingers fist the duvet as I recall our argument. I said some horrible things about Megan that weren't nice, but the dickhead was making out like I took advantage of his girl when the truth is she was the one who initiated sex. He hit me when I said it wasn't my fault his bird was a cheating slut, and I laughed until he started spewing personal shit about me.

Everyone knows you fuck around 'cause you've got mommy issues.

Poor little Dillon, his real mommy and daddy didn't want him, and now he's looking for someone to love him, but no one gives a shit.

Everyone knows the O'Donoghues only took you in out of pity.

Girls only want you for one thing.

No one wants to keep you because you're damaged goods, O'Donoghue.

You're a pathetic loser.

We were punching one another in between his insults, but things took a serious turn when he slammed my face into the wall and busted up my face and broke my nose. Rage, unlike anything I've felt

40

before, consumed me, and I grabbed his head and bounced it off the wall like a fucking ball. It's a miracle I didn't kill the fucker.

"Love." Ma's hands are warm against my cheeks. "Talk to me, please."

"That prick deserved it, and I'm not sorry."

"Violence is not the answer, Dillon. Ash told me the things he said, and it's unforgivable, but you should have walked away. Ignoring bullies is the best way to handle them."

"I'm sixteen, not six, Ma. The only way to handle bullies is to beat the shit out of them." Pain flares in her eyes, and I hate I'm so often the cause of it. "You should've given me back when you had the chance."

"Don't talk rubbish, Dillon. You were not a choice. You were fate. The moment I held you in my arms, you were *mine*, and that hasn't changed." She moves in closer. "You were always meant to be with us, and as long as there is air in my lungs, I'll never stop trying to prove that to you." She places her hand over my chest. "You're as much mine as Ro, Shane, Ciarán, and Ash are, Dillon. There is no difference in my heart. What can I do to make you believe that?"

Tears well in her eyes. "You're my son, and I love you so damn much. It breaks my heart to see you hurting yourself with false truths. You are loved. Wholly and completely. There might have been moments where I've wanted to give all of you back at some point, but I wouldn't trade you or your siblings or our family for anything."

I wipe a tear from her eye. "Don't cry, Ma. You know how much I hate it."

"I wish you could see yourself the way I see you. The way we all see you."

"I cause you nothing but trouble and pain."

A sob rips from her mouth. "That is not true. You've always had so much spirit, Dillon. You're so full of life, but you feel things so deeply. Deeper than any of my other kids." She pats my chest. "You take things to heart so intensely. It can be a good thing and a bad thing. You're too stubborn for your own good, but you have the biggest heart. The way you care for your brothers and sister is beautiful. You moan about doing chores, yet you're the first one to lend a hand when your da or me needs it. I don't like you fighting, but you're always fighting for the underdog or defending yourself or your siblings. You don't look for trouble, son, it just seems to find you."

"I'm sorry for always causing problems for you." I avert my eyes, staring at the duvet as that empty void inside me grows wider. I hate disappointing my parents, and I'm always doing it. I wish I was more like Shane or Ciarán or Ronan. Ro is a little mischief-maker, but everyone loves him, and he never resorts to using his fists if he gets in a fight. Ash and me are the temperamental ones. Even if she's gotten into a few scraps herself, she's got better self-control than me. I'm the only one they're constantly called into the school office over. I know what Ma believes, but the truth is, their lives would be much easier and less stressful without me. They did this good deed, taking me in when my bio parents didn't want me, and all I do is repay them in stress.

Some days, I really fucking hate myself. I wish I wasn't like this, but there's some self-destruct button inside me I can't help pressing. The only time I truly feel at peace is when I'm with the band, songwriting, or playing my guitar. Music soothes my soul when little else does.

"Look at me, son." She takes my hand and forces my gaze to hers. "I wouldn't change a single thing about you, Dillon. You coming into our lives was a blessing. There is so much good in you and so much talent. I am proud of the man you are becoming."

"You cannot mean that." I point at my face. "Look what I did! I nearly got kicked out of school. I let my temper and anger take control instead of walking away and ignoring the prick."

"I'm not happy about the fighting, you know that, Dillon, but it only defines you if you let it. I know you don't want to talk about this, but we're going to. You are internalizing all your feelings, and it's not good for you, son. You've got to let it out. I know your music is an outlet, and it's wonderful you have that, but you need to voice your feelings to deal with them. Shoving them into the furthermost corner of your mind is not healthy."

She hands me the envelope. "Your Auntie Eileen left that for you." Tears fill her eyes again, and I pull her into an awkward hug.

"I still can't believe she's gone," I say. Ma's only sister died last year from cancer. She worked for an adoption agency in London, and I'm here because of her. Auntie Eileen never married, and she came to us for Christmas every year, but I can't say we were especially close. That said, Ma has been really upset since she passed, and we've all been trying our best to comfort her.

"Nor me." She smiles through her tears as we break our embrace. "I never thought my younger sister would go before me. She still had so much living to do."

I hand her a tissue from the box on my bedside locker.

"Thanks, love." She dabs at her eyes and blows her nose before tossing the tissue in the bin. "Your aunt left instructions on how to find your bio parents, should you want to," she tacks on the end when I open my mouth to protest. "You need to be eighteen to get your original birth certificate, but her friend at the agency will personally handle your case. You can reach out to her next year, and she'll explain more."

"They didn't want me," I hiss. "Why the fuck would I want to find them?"

"Dillon." Ma holds my hand tight. "Your mother died giving birth to you, love."

"What?" My entire body goes into shock.

"Your parents were American, and they were married. Your mother died, and I suppose your father didn't feel like he could care for you on his own."

I just stare at her, and the words float around my head, not fully landing.

"That's as much as I know," she says, answering the question before I've asked it. "They don't give you specifics on purpose."

"I'm American?" I blurt.

"You'll always be Irish to me, but technically, yes. I'm guessing you'll be able to get an American passport after you turn eighteen should you want to."

"I don't have any plans to do that or to look *him* up." In some weird way, it actually helps knowing my bio mother didn't give me up. It hits differently when it's your mother.

"Grief is a powerful emotion," Ma says. "I've often wondered if he regretted the decision he made."

A harsh laugh erupts from my chest. "It can't have been much of a marriage if he gave up the last remaining piece of his wife on this earth."

"I've thought that too, but we don't know the circumstances. Perhaps he couldn't afford to raise a child on his own. Maybe he knew the best option for you to grow up with love was to give you away. There could be any number of reasons."

"Well, I guess we'll never know because I have zero interest in looking for a man who didn't want me."

She runs her fingers through my hair. "That's your choice, Dillon. I just want you to know should you change your mind, at any time in the future, we'll support you. Don't hold back out of fear of hurting us."

I'm not lying when I say I don't want to find my bio dad. He's a dick, and I want nothing to do with him. But I would be lying if I said I hadn't thought of it from time to time. The other reason I won't ever look for him is Ma and Da. I couldn't hurt them like that. I have messed up so much with my parents, but I never want them to feel like they're not enough for me when they're everything.

I would have nothing if they hadn't stepped up, and I owe them so much.

More than this sorry pathetic excuse of a son they've ended up with.

The least I can do is honor them by not seeking out the man who threw me away like I was nothing.

She places a soft kiss on my cheek. "We're secure in our love for you and your love for us, and whatever you need, you've got it. All I ask is that you tell us before you begin the process." She places the envelope into the drawer of my locker. "Keep that safe. In case you change your mind."

"I won't."

She smiles, squeezing my hand again. "You're young, Dillon. There is plenty of time to think about it." Leaning in, she kisses my brow. "You should rest before dinner. I know you're having trouble sleeping."

"I'll try." I crawl under the covers, and she tucks me in like she used to when I was little. Her adoring gaze warms all the frozen parts of me as she sweeps my hair back off my forehead.

I love you.

My heart is bursting with everything I feel for my ma, and I want to tell her. I know how much it would mean to her to hear me say these words after so long, but they just won't come out. Whatever is broken inside me shows no signs of healing. Pain comingles with regret, frustration, and disappointment. I want to be so much better for my mum, but I don't know how to fix this.

"Okay, love. Rest. I'll send Ro to get you when dinner is ready." Releasing my hand, she stands and walks towards the door. Ma stops and turns around, smiling softly at me. "I understand why you don't want to meet your biological father, but I have always been so grateful to him." Her eyes turn glassy. "You wouldn't be my son if he hadn't made that decision. My life would be infinitely less bright if he'd made a different decision. I don't know if that helps or hurts, but I just wanted you to know."

Chapter Seven
Age 16

I don't sleep, but I stay under the covers, contemplating everything Ma just said. I know I got lucky. As much as my parents piss me off at times, they are seriously good people, and for the most part, I've been happy. It's not their fault there's something lacking inside me. I don't know how to explain it without making them feel guilty or like they're responsible because they're not. I'm just dysfunctional. A patchwork of jagged pieces with a hole where the core should be. It's part of the reason why I don't speak about this shit. There's always this hollow ache inside me, like I'm missing a vital part of me. Even at times when I'm super happy, it's still there—a constant gnawing ache inside. I don't know what it means or if it's fixable, but as long as it exists, I don't feel whole.

The door creaks open, and I twist around, widening my eyes when I see Kelly Rogers creeping into my room. I sit up and stare at her as she grins and skips across the carpeted floor towards me. "What the fuck, Kelly?"

"Hey, Dillon. I just wanted to see how you're doing. Everyone's so worried at school." She plonks her skinny arse on my bed like it's commonplace to just steal into someone's house without invitation.

I have no idea why she is here unless she's trying to use me to get to my sister or Cillian. Ash hates her guts because she's always following Cill around like a puppy dog, and she's been a bitch to my sister. She has a rep for going after other girls' guys and for stirring up shit any chance she gets.

"How did you get up here?" There's no way Ma would've let her upstairs. Girls are not allowed in my room, and I have no problem complying with that rule. I take them to the play barn or the band outbuilding to fuck them instead.

"The front door was unlocked, and your ma was busy in the kitchen, so I just snuck up here." She giggles, and the sound is like rusted nails scraping over my skin.

"You need to leave, Kelly."

"Not before I've given you your present."

In a lightning-fast move, she peels back my duvet, grabs the waistband of my tracksuit bottoms, and tugs them down to my thighs.

News flash—I'm not wearing boxers.

"Kelly, no." I swat her hand away as she moves to grab my dick.

"Let me blow you, Dil. You must be bored out of your mind, and it'll distract you from the pain."

"I wouldn't let you touch me if you were the last girl on the planet," I snap, pulling my bottoms back up and covering my very flaccid dick. Nothing about this girl turns me on, and trust me when I say that means a lot because it doesn't take much to get me hard. "In case my words or my soft cock is too subtle for you, both of us have zero interest in getting with you. I'd rather ask Jamie to blow me than let your vile lips anywhere near my dick, so fuck off and don't ever fucking come back."

"There's no need to be so mean." Her hands ball into fists as she stands. "You're an ungrateful dickhead, and I was only being charitable because you're injured. Under normal circumstances, I wouldn't touch your disease-ridden cock," she lies.

"Yeah, whatever. Get the fuck out."

Dillon

She shoves her middle finger up at me before stomping out of my room, slamming my door after her.

Good fucking riddance.

The next day, Ro tells me she burst into his room, dropped to her knees, and gave him his first blowjob before leaving. Manipulative little bitch. I laughed my arse off when Ro told me how he panicked when he started coming in her mouth, so he pulled out mid-flow showering her face with cum and getting some in her eye. She left his room bitching him out and cursing all O'Donoghue men.

It was karma at its finest, and it couldn't have happened to a more deserving girl. Ro wasn't aware of the bad blood between Ash and Kelly, and now he feels bad. I told him to forget about it and steer clear of her if she tries anything again.

Ro and I agreed Ash doesn't need to know and we'll keep it a secret to the grave.

"I'm freezing my bollox off, mate," I tell Conor, rubbing my hands together to keep warm and wishing I'd brought extra blankets. Deciding to head to Killiney Hill for a songwriting session in the middle of November was a ridiculous decision. It was my idea because I like coming up here to think, and I thought it might get our creative juices flowing. We came up late in the day, after the families and kids were gone, and our only forethought was to bring a couple of torches, beer, and weed. Next time, I'm bringing sleeping bags, food, and a tent. "Do you think your grandpa could come get us earlier?"

He shakes his head. "He doesn't get off work until nine." Wind-tossed strands of his long, straggly dark hair curtain his face. "Have another toke." He passes the joint back to me.

I swear that's Conor's answer to everything.

I've got the worst case of blue balls. *Have a toke.*

I can't write this fucking essay. *Have a toke.*

Cill and Ash's relationship drama is doing my head in. *Have a toke.*

But maybe he's on to something. He's constantly spaced out, but he's a fucking dynamite bass guitarist and a decent songwriter. We work well together as songwriting partners, and we've already written enough for one album. Together, we come up with the harmony, and I'm usually the one to add the lyrics, though Conor jumps in when I'm stuck, and his input is always spot-on.

"God knows what kind of shite we're writing," I say as I accept the weed and take a long puff.

"Bob Dylan wrote songs while stoned," Conor replies, sitting cross-legged. "Tons of artists write their best hits when high. Drugs and music go together like peanut butter and jam."

"If you say so." I smirk as we pass the joint back and forth in between working our way through the beer. The one good thing about freezing our asses off at the top of Killiney Hill on a winter's night is the beer is nicely chilled.

We play our guitars as we work on the melody for a new track. Then Conor gets a text from his grandpa saying he's on his way, so we pack up and start the trek down to the car park.

"What's a song you like you'd never admit to in public?" Conor asks as we try not to trip over the uneven path in the dark.

I don't even have to think about it. "'I Knew I Loved You' by Savage Garden."

"Why?"

"It's the lyrics and the sentiment behind them. It resonates with me personally."

"How?" He brushes stray branches out of the way, and I duck my head to avoid a piece of bark in face.

Maybe it's the beer or my semi-stoned state or the fact I know with complete confidence that Conor will never tell a soul what I confide in him, but I find myself opening up without hesitation. "My entire life I've felt like there's this void inside me. I'm constantly searching for a sense of completion—the missing pieces I need to feel whole. Those lyrics could've been written especially for me, but it's more than that. It's the notion that fate is out there waiting to be claimed. It gives me hope that whatever I'm seeking is out there. That there could be a time when I don't feel so empty. Where I'm *enough*." I shrug as we exit the narrow path and hit the back of the car park. "It just speaks to me."

"You want to dream someone into life," he says, nodding as we walk across the large empty space in the direction of the headlights streaming towards us.

"You know the song?" Savage Garden are not a current or cool choice among my peers, but Conor has always danced to his own beat.

"Music is my only companion. There isn't much I don't know."

"You know about the emptiness, don't you?"

He stops and turns to me with a rare lucid look. "Darkness is who I am. That is a given."

"What happened?" I ask as curiosity gets the better of me. I'm not normally one to pry.

"Maybe someday I'll tell you." He starts walking towards his grandpa's car, and I keep pace with him.

He stalls with his hand on the door handle, glancing sideways at me. "Hang your hopes on the stars, O'Donoghue. It might be too late for me, but you can still pack your bag for outer space."

I'm cleaning out the cow barn when Da's rusted brown 4x4 comes to a noisy stop outside.

"Dillon," he calls out, and I stop what I'm doing and jog to the entryway. Da leans out the driver's side window. "Get in. I need your help with the fencing on the top field."

"I thought Shane was helping with that?" Although my brother manages the business side of running the farm, he's very hands-on too, and I know he was working with Da to replace some of the rotten wooden fencing around the larger field.

"Fiona was feeling under the weather today, so he stayed home to look after her." Shane only told us last week he's knocked his long-term girlfriend up. Baby's due next year. It wouldn't be for me, but Shane's happy as a pig in shite. Ma is super excited at becoming a granny, and it's helping to distract her from her grief.

I climb up beside my ole man and we take off. Country music plays in the background as we amble over the bumpy path towards the rear of our extensive farm. Da doesn't speak, but it's just his way.

He puts me to work immediately, hammering the posts into the ground while he secures the panels. It's repetitive work, but it's soothing on the brain. The only sounds out here are the rustling of the wind through the trees, the intermittent chirping of birds, the pounding of two hammers, and the screaming of my own thoughts.

Since Ma and me had our little talk last month, I've thought a lot about my bio parents and what she said. There's an overwhelming sense of sadness I never had a chance to know my mother. I've wondered what part of America I was born in and what my life might have been like if I'd grown up there. Would I still have found music? Was one of my bio parents a musician? Is that where I get this calling from? Would I still have felt this ache inside? Is that missing piece the mother I never knew? Guilt crawls up my throat at that thought, like always, and I swing the sledgehammer harder as if it can pound the horrible thought from my brain.

I don't want to believe this hole inside me is from missing the woman who gave me life when I have the best fucking mother in the world. It feels like such a disrespect to Ma to even think such a thing. That cannot be the reason for the emptiness I feel. But I sure as fuck am not aching for that prick that gave me up with little consideration.

I'll be seventeen in two months, and I can start a conversation with my aunt's friend in the agency that will lead to finding where I came from. I haven't changed my mind, per se, but a part of me wants to confront that man and ask him *why*? Why did he discard me so easily? Why didn't he want to cling to me as something precious created with his wife before she died? Perhaps their marriage was like Jay's parents' marriage—a totally shitty one—and he saw a two-for-one opportunity to terminate it permanently.

I don't know.

And that's the problem.

What if this ache is because I'm missing the truth? Will it always exist unless I have all the answers? Should I take a risk and find out in the hope it will help me to find the closure I so desperately need?

I don't know.

I hammer in another post, lost in thought as I move my way around the field, working in companionable silence with my dad.

I don't know what I'm going to do, but at least I'm kind of working through it in my own head.

"Let's call it a night." Da clamps his hand on my shoulder. "Nice job," he says, admiring my handiwork.

I'm good with manual labor. Good with my hands. I like to keep them occupied. Music, English, history, and woodwork are the only subjects I like at school and the only ones I put any effort into.

The current argument with Ma is over Irish. I want to stop going to Irish class as I don't plan to sit the Irish exam for my Leaving. It's technically a requirement by law, and if you want to go to certain colleges in Ireland, you need it. But uni isn't in the cards for me even if I did briefly consider studying history at Trinity. I'm dedicated to the band and music, and that's not going to change. I'm in fifth year now, and I'll be sitting my final exams in a little over a year and a half. I don't see the point in going to Irish class when I'm not going to do the exam. But Ma and the school board are digging their heels in and making me go, which is fucking stupid and a complete waste of my time.

I help Da load our surplus supplies in the back of the vehicle, and we head off back to the house for dinner.

"Did it help?" Da asks as we enter the house and walk upstairs to get cleaned up.

My brow puckers. "What?"

"I do my best thinking out in the fresh air, keeping my hands busy." He squeezes my shoulder. "There's a lot more fencing to be done, son, if you need it."

Chapter Eight

Age 17

"I warned you, Doyle. I told you what'd happen if you hurt my sister." I land a vicious kick to Cillian's side as he lies on the ground in our play barn. Jamie and I dragged him here the instant he left my house after breaking my sister's heart for the second time today.

Ash's devastated face resurrects in my mind. As long as I live, I'll never forget her anguished cries in the school hallway this morning after that little bitch Kelly told her she was pregnant with Ash's boyfriend's baby. It's the worst betrayal, and the fact my mate—now ex-mate—didn't even have the balls to tell my sister himself is the final nail in the coffin. "How fucking dare you let her find out from that slut!"

"I love Ash, and I didn't know how to tell her!" Cill looks up at me through pleading eyes, his face already bruising.

I level another savage kick to his ribs, hoping I broke them. "You don't fucking know the meaning of the word!" I roar.

Cill curls into a fetal position on the ground between me and Jamie, moaning and constantly repeating he's sorry.

"Sorry means jack shit, dickhead." Jamie delivers a swift kick to his balls, and Cillian howls in pain before breaking into sobs.

He's such a pathetic prick.

Crouching down, I get all up in his battered face. "Ash was always way too good for the likes of you." I punch his nose, and blood gushes out of his swollen nostrils. Let him get married looking like the ugly piece of shit he is. Gripping his chin, I force his gaze to mine. "Kelly doesn't even compare. That slut snuck into my bedroom and tried to suck my dick. When I told her to fuck off, she went and sucked Ro's dick. That's the kind of girl you cheated on my sister with."

"I know she isn't in Ash's league! I messed up."

Understatement of the century. "I hope you're miserable as fuck with that cunt because you deserve it."

"It was a mistake," he snivels, wrapping his arm around his middle. "I was locked, and she pounced. I felt sick the next day when I realized what I'd done. When Kelly told me she was pregnant, I panicked. I was trying to convince her to get an abortion. I'd no idea she was going to blurt it to Ash, I swear."

He really is a piece of work. He would've said nothing to Ash if Kelly had aborted the baby. He makes me sick. How was I ever friends with this wanker?

"It doesn't fucking matter now." Jamie bitch slaps him in the face, and Cillian yelps. "You've agreed to marry that skank. That says it all about the kind of pathetic prick you are." Jay presses his boot in hard between Cill's legs, and he cries out in pain.

"Ash doesn't see it now, but you've done her a favor. Now she can find a decent bloke, someone worthy of her," I say, spitting in his face. "You're scum, Doyle. We should probably thank you for being a cheating dickhead, but I'm not thanking you for shit."

I jerk my head at Jay in silent communication. As much as I want to continue beating the shit out of that asshole, I'm not doing time for Cillian Fucking Doyle. My sister needs me, and she's my priority.

We lift the sniveling bastard by the arms. "You stay away from

Ash, Cillian," I warn as we drag him towards the door. "If you love her like you say you do, you will leave her alone. You've hurt her enough. End all contact. It's the only way she'll heal."

"Don't give us any reason to come for you again," Jay says as we toss him on the dirt outside the barn. "Next time, we won't go so easy on you."

After we dump Cillian outside his house, we hop back into Shane's Beamer and get the fuck out of there before Cill's prissy mother comes out and goes mad at us. Shane doesn't let me borrow his pride and joy that often, but he didn't want Ma seeing the state of Cillian. He wasn't about to let Cill soil his precious car, and I had no issue shoving that prick into the boot. It's good enough for the shithead.

I'm saving up for a Kawasaki, and now I have a learner's permit and can legally drive, I can't wait until I have my own set of wheels.

I drop Jamie at his house first, killing the engine out front because I need to set some ground rules. "I need to say something." I eyeball my mate.

"If this is about Ash, it doesn't need to be said."

"It does." I drill him with a warning look. "My sister is completely off-limits, Jay. I know you liked her before, and I want to make sure you know this isn't an opportunity to get with her."

He pins me with an angry look. "Give me some fucking credit, Dil." He tugs on his new eyebrow piercing while glaring at me. "The girl is fucking heartbroken, and I'm not a selfish prick."

I know he's not. He's also not good enough for Ash. He's too much of a hound like me. "I'm not just talking about now. I'm talking about forever, Jamie." Grabbing the back of his neck, I press my forehead to his. "You're my brother, Jay. There isn't much I wouldn't do for you, but Ash is the exception. She's not the one for you, mate." I ease back. "You hear me?"

He looks pissed. After a couple tense beats, his shoulders relax, and he sighs. "I hear ya, Dil, and it won't be an issue. All right?"

I nod, relieved. "Thanks for backing me up and for taking our side."

"Don't thank me for that. I'm always Team O'Donoghue." He flashes me a devilish smile as his fingers curl around the door handle. "Besides, I've been dying to knock the shit out of that prick for years. He had it coming." He gets out and leans down. "If I can do anything else to help, let me know."

Dillon

"You're killing me, Ash," I say when I enter her bedroom to find her curled on top of her bed, hugging the giant teddy Cillian won for her last month at Funderland and sobbing like it's the end of the world. She doesn't move, acknowledge me, or stop crying. A heavy sigh cleaves my lips as I kick off my runners and lie down on the bed beside her. Curling my arms around her from behind, I tuck her in close. "He's not worthy of your tears. He's a piece-of-shit human who never deserved you."

Ash cries harder, and I decide to shut up and just hold her. A few minutes later, she turns around, buries her face in my chest, and continues sobbing. I kiss the top of her head, feeling helpless. Her pain is my pain. My chest feels tight, and my hands itch with a renewed need to beat the crap out of her ex. I hope he's in physical pain. He deserves to hurt for the agony he's inflicted on my sister. This is the last thing she needs in the run-up to her Leaving Cert in June. Unlike me, Ash wants to go to college, and she's set her heart on going to Trinity. If Cillian ruins that for her, I will fucking bury that dick six feet under.

Ash clings to my shirt, soaking it, as she cries. I didn't know a person could cry that much. I feel fucking useless as I dot kisses in her hair and rub a hand up and down her back. I don't really know what else to do.

"Dil," she croaks in a raspy voice sometime later, lifting her chin and staring at me through red swollen eyes. "Make it stop," she begs over a sob. "Make it go away." She slaps a hand over her chest. "It hurts so much."

"If I could take all the hurt and pain for you, I'd do it in a heartbeat, Ash."

Her soul-crushing cries bounce off the walls of her bedroom. "How could he do this to me?"

"He's a selfish coward and a disloyal prick. I will never forgive him for this."

"I want to die," she wails, and her entire body is shaking as she clings to me.

"No, Ash. Don't ever fucking say that."

"This is killing me, Dil," she says in a shrill tone. "In my dreams, it was always me carrying his baby and *me* walking up the aisle to him. Not that fucking scheming, manipulative, slutty bitch!" She dissolves into another round of tears, and only for the fact Ash needs me I would be paying another visit to Cillian Doyle and making good on my promise to bury him alive. Right now, I honestly think I'd be capable of murder. I want to rip him apart for doing this to my sister.

"They deserve each other. Let them rot in hell together." I brush hair back from her face and kiss her forehead. "I know this feels like the worst thing in the world, Ash, but you will get over it. Get over him. There is someone better out there for you. Someone amazing who will treat you like the fucking queen you are. This happened so you'd find the right person one day."

"I already had him," she sobs, fisting her tiny hand in my wet shirt. "He was mine. He was my forever."

I don't agree. Those two were only ever heading for Splitsville, but I don't voice that opinion. She won't hear me now. She won't hear any of it. So, I shut my mouth and let her purge her thoughts, holding her and comforting her the only way I know how.

The next couple of months are rough. On the one hand, things with the band are going well, and we've got a regular Friday night spot at a pub in Bray Harbor. Our set is mostly covers, but we throw in three of our own tracks, and they have gone down well. But it's hard to enjoy the fact we're now getting paid to play music when my heartbroken sister is falling apart before my eyes.

That bitch Kelly is prancing around school, wearing tight, non-uniform clothes to draw attention to her growing belly, with Cillian on her arm, pawing at him any chance she gets, purely to gloat and piss my sister off. I came this close to hitting a pregnant girl last week when Kelly started loudly discussing her wedding plans at the top of her voice in the school canteen, on purpose, knowing Ash was in listening distance.

Ash has refused to return to school since then, and Ma and Da are really worried about her. She has barely opened a book since the end of January when all this shit went down, and she's been in constant trouble at school for not showing up and not turning in her homework.

Ash only leaves her bedroom to do chores around the house and to eat, though she mostly picks at her food, and she's definitely looking way too skinny. I've been making her some of my chocolate protein shakes and forcing her to drink them, so at least she's getting some nourishment into her. She refuses to talk to or see her friends, and she has lost all interest in Toxic Gods. Instead, she hides in her room, listening to sad songs, watching even sadder movies, and crying over photos of her and Cillian in between bouts of stalking him with his skanky fiancée on social media.

Cillian hasn't attempted to talk to her since that last day, and I'm glad he's at least doing this one thing for her. It would be so much worse if he was still sniffing around her.

I'm the only one she'll allow in. Ash is pushing everyone else away. I want to be there for her, but, I swear to god, if I have to sit through *The Notebook* one more time, I'm gonna throw the TV out the fucking window. And I think I've developed a permanent aversion to mint chocolate chip ice cream. For weeks, it was the only thing Ash ate, so I bought cartons of the stuff because, as bad as it is for her, it's better than an empty stomach.

"Get up," I say on Saturday morning, pulling the covers back. I've decided some tough love is in order. I'm not standing by and watching my sister piss her life away over the shithead any longer.

"Go away, Dil." She yanks the covers back over her pajama-clad body. Her voice is devoid of all emotion, and it hurts me so much to see her like this.

"I know you know what day it is." I move to her wardrobe and grab some clothes.

"Which is why I'm not leaving this room today."

"Get the fuck up." I throw jeans and a black hoodie down on the bed before walking to her dressing unit to grab underwear and socks. "Aisling O'Donoghue always has the last word, and there is no way in hell my sister is letting that cheating prick and his skanky slut get away with what they did." Tossing her things on the bed, I hover over her, putting my face all up in hers. "I know you're heartbroken, but this isn't you. Fuck them, Ash. They don't get to suck all the light from your eyes. They have taken enough from you, and it's time for some payback."

A tiny spark flares in her eyes, and inside, I'm fist pumping the air. "Did you have something in mind?"

"Get up and find out."

Come on, Ash. I'm silently praying, begging my sister to find her fighting spirit. If she can't do this, I won't push any harder than I already have. Jamie, Jono, and I are prepared to do this alone, if necessary, but one thing is certain—Cillian Cheating Doyle and Kelly Slut-face Rogers are not getting married today without feeling the wrath of the O'Donoghues. They can fucking bank on it.

Chapter Nine
Age 17

"What are you doing?" Ash whispers as I round the back of the wedding car on a solo mission, leaving Jamie and Ash to continue egging the silver Rolls Royce the soon-to-be newlyweds have hired for the day.

"Adding one final touch." I smirk as I shove a couple of potatoes into the exhaust, using a stick to push them up the pipe out of sight.

"Jono just messaged," Jamie says, pelting the last egg on top of the roof. "We need to drive the car back."

The wedding driver is a local guy, well-known for being a big gambler. His usual MO is to leave the car outside the church while the ceremony is taking place and head to the bookies. Thank fuck for his predictability today. Jono was already in the bookies waiting, and he snuck the keys out of his pocket when he wasn't looking and ran up here with them. Then he ran back to keep an eye on him.

Thankfully, there wasn't anyone around when we drove the car from the church up the road and into the rear of the car park adjacent to a small apartment building. It's always empty during the day, and we've been able to work without interruption or an audience. There's no fun in getting caught sabotaging their wedding day although they'll definitely know we did this. Can't do jack shit without proof though. As an added precaution we're all wearing black hoodies and bandanas covering most of our faces.

"You two head home," I say. "I'll drive it back and take the heat if anyone sees me."

"Like fuck you will!" Ash shakes her stubborn head. "If we get caught, we *all* own this shit." There's my ballbuster little sis. It's good to know she's still in there underneath all the heartache and pain.

Jamie grins and hugs her. "That's my girl."

My scowl is instantaneous. Jamie flips me the bird as he lets Ash go and gets into the passenger seat. I climb behind the wheel while Ash gets into the back. "They'll have one more surprise," Jamie says, glancing back at Ash with a wide grin.

I start the engine and reverse around the corner.

"My cousin Elaine made their wedding cake," he explains, "and I paid her a visit while she was baking it and added laxative to the mix when she was out of the room."

I burst out laughing as I drive through the gate of the apartments. "Nice one, mate."

Through the mirror, I catch Ash's smile. "That'll give them the shits for hours. Thanks, Jay. You're my hero."

I groan as the compliment soaks into his skin and he beams like he's just won a Grammy. I might have to have words with my best mate again.

"Thought that was me," I joke as we head towards the church.

"You're my savior, Dillon," she quietly says. "You're the only reason I can even get out of bed each day."

The atmosphere sobers, and pain lances me straight through the heart. I hate this for my sister, and I wish I could make it all go away.

I love you. I think it, but, of course, I can't say it. "You're my everything, Ash. I would do anything for you."

She offers me a watery smile through the mirror. "Same."

Jamie's Adam's apple bobs in his throat as he looks between the two of us. In that moment, he knows it's been really, really bad. I've told Jamie Ash is struggling, but he doesn't know the details. She wouldn't want anyone knowing how bad it is.

"What're you doing?" Jay asks, frowning as Ash sits on the floor in the back, spreading a cloth across the seat in between chugging red wine from a bottle.

"Rubbing red wine into the leather. I can't have it too visible, or she won't sit down, but I reckon a fine layer of red wine will still work wonders on her white dress."

"That's diabolical." Jamie chuckles. "I approve. But remind me to never get on your bad side."

"Or mine." I side-eye him with intent.

He just rolls his eyes and watches Ash at work.

"They might not leave for the hotel in this car when they see the state of it," I say.

"Oh, they will." Ash smears the back seat with the rest of the red wine while I swing the car around in a U-turn. "Mrs. Doyle might be proper religious, but she's a snob at heart. She won't have them showing up to a five-star hotel in their old Toyota. She'll go mad when she sees the car, but she'll swing into action. She'll get water from the garage and make the driver clean the egg off."

"But she won't know about the red wine or the surprise in the exhaust pipe until it's too late." Jay waggles his brows.

"I hate both of them, I truly do, but that won't kill them or hurt their..." She sucks in a sharp breath, and her lower lip wobbles. "They won't get poisoned by fumes, Dil, right?" Her worried gaze meets mine in the mirror as I near the church.

I hadn't actually considered that, and the truth is, I don't know. It's a common prank around these parts, and I've never heard of anyone getting toxic poisoning. But that slut is pregnant, and the baby is innocent. "The hotel is close by, and the car should break down on the way, so I don't think it's a big concern. But I'll send an anonymous message to the driver telling him there are potatoes in the exhaust pipe to be on the safe side." I don't want anyone's death or illness on my conscience.

"Come on," Jay says when I kill the engine. "Let's get the fuck out of Dodge."

A few cars driving past the church slow down as we get out of the car, but they don't stop, and they don't know who we are as we all have our hoods up, our bandanas covering most of our faces, and our heads down as we run off through the housing estate across the road, taking the shortcut at the end of the estate, which leads onto Lott Lane.

I tell the others to go on while I stop to message the driver via the contact form on his wedding car hire website, hoping it sends the message straight to his mobile phone. Then I run to catch up with my sister and best mate, and we cut through some fields, staying well away from the road and entering our farm through a loose fence at the rear of our property. Ash and I used to use it a lot when we were younger to sneak off the farm unnoticed.

We fist pump the air, laughing and hollering as we make our way to the Toxic Gods outbuilding where we burn our bandanas and change our clothes on the off chance any of the wedding party show up here with scowls and accusations.

"I would fucking love to be there when they come out of the church and see their car." Jamie slaps his knee and grins.

"Or when she gets out of the car at the posh hotel with red wine stains all over the back of her dress." I chuckle. "I wonder how long it'll take someone to point it out?"

"Maybe we should sneak into the hotel later and watch the shit go down after the cake is cut." Jamie howls with laughter at his pun, and it feels good to have done something. Maybe we're petty assholes for trying to ruin their big day, but the cunts brought it on themselves. They're the reason I'm trying to hold my heartbroken sister together.

A strangled sob rips through the air, instantly slicing through our amusement.

Jamie and I whip our heads around to the sofa where Ash is sitting. Tears are streaming down her face, and she's doubled over, hugging herself and shaking.

Dillon

"Shit, Ash." I grab my sister onto my lap and fold her into my arms as she breaks down. "It's okay."

"It's really not." She hiccups over more sobs. "I could forget while we were trashing the car, but he's still up there in that church saying his vows to *her*."

"It's gonna be okay, sis." I smooth a hand down her hair. "It won't always feel like this."

I hope.

I mean, what the fuck do I know about how she's feeling? The only feelings I've ever had for a bird are the ones in my dick, and they are fleeting and completely hormone driven. I have no clue what it's like to be in love or to think you're in love because, honestly, how much can you be in love at our age?

I carry Ash to the house, tucking her in bed, before I head back to the outbuilding to get ready for band practice.

"I didn't realize she was still so upset," Jamie quietly says as we tune up our guitars.

"She's in bits, mate." As I tighten my guitar strings it feels like I'm tightening the invisible strings around my heart. When Ash hurts, I hurt. It's that simple.

"We should have beat him bloody," he says in a clipped tone.

"I might yet," I honestly reply.

"Dillon! I need you to get to the house quickly!" Ma's panicked tone over the phone sends blood rushing to my head. In the background, there is lots of noise and multiple raised voices.

"What's happened?" I ask, instantly removing my guitar and setting it down. I make a slicing motion across my throat so Jay, Conor, and Aaron know practice is finished for today. We've been at it for hours, and it's late now anyway.

"It's your sister." Ma's voice cracks.

My anxiety spikes instantly. Ash has been super quiet in the three weeks since the wedding, like she's breaking all over again. "Is she okay?" My heart thuds painfully against my rib cage as I sprint out the door and race down the road towards the farmhouse.

"She won't stop screaming and throwing things. She won't listen to any of us," Ma cries.

"I'm on my way. Tell her I'll be there in a minute." I hang up, shove my phone in my pocket, and run harder than I've ever run before.

I'm panting by the time I stumble into Ash's bedroom. She's stopped throwing things, but her room is destroyed. Books, smashed picture frames, broken jewelry, and spilled perfume bottles litter the floor as I pick my way through the mess to get to my sister. The teddy bear Cillian won for Ash is ripped apart, and fluffy particles are floating in the air. Posters have been torn off the walls, lying in shreds across her bed. Her laptop dangles precariously off one side of her desk, the screen displaying a multitude of spider cracks. Her desk chair is broken, and wooden spindles lie haphazardly under the open window. The net curtain blows softly, offering a glimpse of the moon resting high in the pitch-black sky.

Ash is sitting quietly on her knees in the middle of the devastation, wearing pajamas, just staring straight ahead. Her face is pale, and she looks exhausted. Dropping down beside her, I pull her into my arms. She doesn't move; she just sits there in a daze with Ma, Da, and Ro standing helplessly in the doorway with concern written all over their faces. "I've got her," I tell them, subtly nodding in Ro's direction. He's only fourteen, and he doesn't need to see this.

Da pulls Ro away, steering him back to bed while Ma hovers reluctantly. "It's okay, Ma. I'll take care of her." I tighten my arms around my sister, pressing a kiss to the top of her hair. Strawberry-blonde strands stick to her cheeks and her brow, but I gently remove them, tucking them behind her ears as Ma softly closes the door, leaving me with my sister.

"What happened?" I ask, sweeping my fingers across her cheek.

She gulps but says nothing.

"Please, Ash. Talk to me."

Slowly, she turns her head and looks at my face. Her throat is hoarse when she speaks, the words uttered in a monotone voice. "Cillian showed up." She looks at me as if she's looking through me. "He said he was sorry, he still loves me, and he only married her because of the baby. He said we can still be together."

I grind my teeth to the molars and work hard to strangle the potent rage flowing through my veins.

"He said nothing had to change. It didn't mean we have to be over." A bitter laugh escapes her mouth, and her eyes blaze angrily. "He said we could still fuck one another behind Kelly's back, that she didn't have to know."

My entire body vibrates with bone-deep fury.

"Then he kissed me."

I take deep breaths trying to calm down.

Her lips curl into a snarl. "I bit his lip and drew blood. Then I scratched his face and started screaming. I totally lost it. Threw the chair at him as he was escaping through the window."

As soon as she mentioned his name, I knew the coward had snuck in through her bedroom window. He'd been doing that for years when they were a couple.

She shucks off my embrace and stands on wobbly legs. "I'm tired. I want to go back to bed."

"Ash." I climb to my feet and reach for her.

"It's okay, Dil." She smiles weakly. "This actually helped. All I was good for was sex. That's clearly all I meant to him. I never meant to him what he meant to me. I see that now."

I don't think that was true, and I'm not sure I believe this has genuinely helped, but now isn't the time to get into all that. Together, we clean up her room in silence, salvaging what we can and dumping the rest in black sacks. Then I make her tea with honey and lemon, and after she drinks it, I turn off the overhead light and lie on top of the bed with my arm over her while she's under the covers. I have every intention of sneaking off to find Cillian and reacquaint him with my fists, but I fall asleep beside my sister, and the next thing I know, Ma is shaking us to get ready for school.

Ash refuses to go to school, and Ma doesn't have the heart to make her after last night. It's not like she's been present at school much lately anyway. I'm not so lucky. I offer to stay home with Ash knowing it's Ma's day to volunteer at the local nursing home, Da is already at work on the farm, and Ro will be at school. Ma refuses to let me stay home, but I can make that work to my advantage. After getting dressed in my school uniform in record time, I skip breakfast and leave the house early, running across the road from my farm, straight towards Cillian's house.

Kelly was bragging at school last week that Cillian's parents renovated the playroom downstairs, turning it into a master bedroom with en suite bathroom for the newlyweds. It's no wonder her big mouth gets her into so much trouble.

She made this too easy. The window is open, and I climb inside with zero hesitation. The shower is on, and Cillian is the only one in the bed, still fast asleep and oblivious.

But not for long.

Dragging that sad sack of shit out from under the covers, I beat him to a pulp with zero remorse. Red-hot rage is the blood flowing through my veins as I pummel his face and his bare torso, not giving him a chance to retaliate. "You don't get to disrespect my sister like that after everything you've done," I roar, landing a particularly vicious punch to his gut. At some point, his wife must have emerged from the shower, but I was too busy fucking up her husband to notice. Kelly is screaming and cowering in the corner, wearing only a towel, cradling her stomach like her baby needs protecting from me. As much as I hate her, I would never lay a finger on her or her unborn child.

Mr. and Mrs. Doyle rush into the room a few minutes later. I punch Cillian's da in the face when he tries to pull me off his son.

"Tell them what you did!" I roar, shoving Cillian up against the wall. His face is awash with blood, but it's telling he's not even

70

attempting to fight back. He knows he deserves this. "Tell your pregnant wife how you crept into my sister's bedroom last night and told her you still loved her."

Kelly's screeching reaches new heights as Mrs. Doyle helps her husband to his feet, but I tune her out. Bitch is giving me a headache. "Man the fuck up, Cillian. Tell them how you kissed Ash without her permission and told her you wanted to keep fucking her because you only married Kelly to do right by the baby." I land another savage punch, and he spits blood out of his mouth. It's possible he might have broken a tooth or two.

"That's enough." Mr. Doyle grabs my arms and yanks me away from his son. Cillian slithers to the floor like the slimy snake he is. "Elizabeth, call the police."

His wife moves towards the door. "While you're at it," I calmly say, "don't forget to tell them about your son's breaking and entering and forcing himself on a woman who isn't his wife. Be sure to mention that. I can just see the headline now in *The Wicklow People*." Appearances are the only thing besides God and her precious family that matters to Elizabeth Doyle.

She falters in the doorway, casting a worried glance at her husband.

Mr. Doyle lets me go with a shove. "Leave, Dillon, and don't come back."

I turn around and smirk. "Tell your son to stay away from my sister and my house. I won't come back here as long as he keeps the fuck away from Ash."

Mrs. Doyle cringes as if cursing in her presence paints a dark stain on her soul.

"He won't be going anywhere near your slut of a sister," Kelly hisses, having stopped her screaming and shrieking. I guess she's Cillian's mouthpiece now. I doubt her mother-in-law is impressed with her language either.

"Brave words for a skank who got herself knocked up before she's even finished school," I sneer. "Or are they stupid words from a bitch

71

so desperate to hold on to a man she had to steal she'd overlook his blatant cheating while she's carrying his child? I'd put a tracking device on that one, Kelly." I jab my finger in Cillian's direction. He's sitting on the ground with his knees bent and his head cradled in his hands. "You're going to need it."

I purposely shove Mr. Doyle's shoulder as I walk towards the door. Elizabeth plasters her back to the wall like I'm the devil and she doesn't want to even breathe the same air as me. I can't help leaning into her face and fixing her with my most menacing stare. "Fuck, fuck, fuck, fuck, fuck." She slides sideways, ducking away from me, and runs to the safety of her husband's arms. I laugh as I shove my torn, bloody knuckles in the pockets of my school trousers and saunter off shouting "fuck" repeatedly at the top of my lungs.

Chapter Ten
Age 17

Opening the school app on my way home, I submit a fake absence report so they don't issue an automatic text to Ma. There's no way in hell I'm going to school today and leaving my sister alone. I'll forge Ma's signature on a note in my journal tomorrow, and I'll make myself scarce if she returns to the house at lunchtime to check on Ash as I suspect. By the time she gets home this evening, she'll be none the wiser.

The house is quiet when I return, and I'm guessing Ash is still sleeping. I take a long hot shower and change into a tracksuit before tending to my shredded knuckles. I'm not going to bother hiding them from Ma because it'd be impossible. When she asks, I'll tell her I beat the crap out of that prick Cillian. She won't be happy—she hates me fighting—but I doubt she'll do anything about it when I tell her what he did.

Barging into Ash's room, I brace myself for a day eating mint chocolate chip ice cream and watching *The Notebook* on repeat, grinding to an immediate halt in complete and utter shock when I find my sister passed out in her pajamas on top of her bed surrounded by a few empty tablet boxes and a half-empty bottle of vodka loosely clutched in her hand. My heart slams into my rib cage, and blood rushes to my head. The ringing in my ears is so loud it's deafening. Pain races across my chest and I can barely breathe. I'm rooted to the spot initially, frozen with shock, until reality slaps me in the face and I move.

"No, Ash!!" I cry, rushing towards her as anxiety surges through my veins. "No, no, no." Lifting her limp wrist, I press a trembling finger to her pulse point, but I can't feel anything. "Fuck no. No, no, no!" Sweat beads on my brow as I shake her shoulders. "Wake up, Ash! Wake the fuck up now!" Moving my fingers to her neck, I'm relieved to feel her pulse against my clammy skin. It's weak as fuck, but she's still alive.

I feel like collapsing on the floor, but I can't fall apart.

My sister needs me.

My hands are shaking as I remove my phone from my pocket and call 999. As I wait for the call to connect, I examine the tablet boxes, finding both empty. A few stray tablets are hidden in the creases of her duvet, but it looks like she's swallowed most of them. "What the fuck were you thinking, Ash? How could you do this?" I sit on Ash's bed, resting my back against the headrest as I wait for the call to connect.

"You're through to Rita. Who am I speaking with?" the responder says.

"Dillon O'Donoghue."

"What's your emergency, Dillon, and which service do you require?"

"Ambulance. Please hurry. It's my sister. She's swallowed all of my mother's sleeping pills and drank vodka." Gently, I lift Ash, placing her head in my lap, praying like I have never prayed before in my life. I'm shaking all over as terror takes hold of every part of me. She can't die. I won't let her.

"What's your location, sir?"

I rattle off our address as I place my fingers back on her neck. "Hurry, please hurry. Her pulse is really weak."

"We'll get an ambulance to you as soon as we can, Dillon. I'll stay on the line until they arrive."

"I can't. I need to call my parents."

She calls out my number to verify it's correct, tells me to hang up and call my parents, confirming she will ring me back in five minutes.

I cradle Ash in my arms as I call Da. He's the closest, and I need him. The instant he picks up, I burst into tears.

"Dillon, what's wrong? Are you hurt or in trouble?"

"Da," I sob, almost choking on my tears as I rock my unconscious sister in my arms. "It's Ash. She tried to kill herself."

"Dear God, no." His pain is palpable.

"She's still breathing, but her pulse is weak as shit. The ambulance is on its way," I croak. "Call Ma and get home now."

"I'll be there as quick as I can." He hangs up instantly, and I silently plead with him to hurry up. I'm terrified something is going to happen to my sister while I'm all alone, and I don't know what to do! Why the fuck didn't I check in on her when I first got back? And why the hell did I take such a long shower?! I should have checked on my sister first. If she doesn't... Oh god, I can't think that... Ash has got to be okay. I won't ever forgive myself for failing her. I should have fought Ma and stayed home from school with Ash instead of focusing on beating that shithead. If I'd been here, this wouldn't have happened.

This is all that prick's fault.

He did this, and I'm going to fucking end him for it.

I don't care. I'll go to jail.

At least if he's dead, he can't hurt her anymore.

Cillian's betrayal and cruel selfishness caused this.

As long as I live, I will never forgive that cheating bastard.

But I can't think about him now. I rest my head on my sister's head as tears roll down my face. Just then, I remember the lady from 999. She hasn't called yet. She said five minutes, and it must be five minutes now, right? Why isn't she ringing me back?

I check Ash's pulse again, and it's still faint, but her heart is beating, and that's all that matters right now. What if it stops beating? The horrible thought lands in my head and I immediately panic. Anguished sounds slip from my lips as I hold her closer, and my frantic brain tries to remember the things I learned when I did a first aid course in transition year, but I'm drawing a blank. "Hang on, Ash," I cry, hugging her and sobbing. "Help is coming. Just hang on until we get you to hospital. Do it for me. You can't leave me. Please, Ash. Please hold on." I can scarcely see through my blurry eyes. "I love you," I whisper. "I love you so much. Please don't die."

"Your daughter is stable," the doctor tells my parents as Shane, Ro, and I huddle around them in the small waiting room at St. Vincent's Hospital. Ash was taken to ICU after she was admitted to A&E, and we've spent a few agonizing hours waiting for news.

"Oh, thank God," Ma says before dissolving into tears.

Da bundles her in his arms. "Can we see her?"

"She is getting settled in a room. One of the nurses will come to get you shortly." He glances at me and my brothers. Ciarán is driving here from Galway, and he should be arriving any minute now. "Only two at a time. She's still unconscious, and she'll be drowsy for a little while."

"Is she going to be all right?" I ask.

"These are Aisling's brothers," Ma volunteers, sniffling. "Our other son is en route. He goes to college in Galway."

"Aisling is very lucky. Who found her?"

"Dillon did." Ma touches my arm.

"You got to her in time." The older man eyeballs me. "A few minutes later, and it might have been too late."

"Guess it's lucky I ditched school then." I shudder to think what would've happened if I hadn't made that decision.

"For once, you won't hear any arguments from me, son." Ma shucks out of Da's embrace and hugs me. "Ash might not be here if you didn't go back to the house," she says over a sob. "You saved her life, Dillon. I love you so much." She quietly cries as I hold her against me, barely able to swallow over the lump wedged in my throat. We came so close to losing Ash. Too close.

"When can she go home?" Shane asks.

"Either later tonight or early tomorrow morning. She'll be released provided her vitals look good and after our psychiatrist has spoken with her and verified she's not a threat to herself. Lucy is the psychiatrist on shift today. She'll talk to you after she speaks with Aisling and recommend appropriate supports and treatments for aftercare."

"Thank you, Doctor," Da says, and the man leaves.

We sit in strained silence, drinking shit coffee from the machine, until a nurse appears fifteen minutes later and Ma and Da leave with her to see Ash.

"Why did you skip school?" Shane asks while Ro buries his head in his phone.

I fill Shane in on what happened last night and this morning.

"You should have killed the little shit," Shane seethes, balling his hands into fists.

"I might just after this."

"No, you leave that cunt to me."

"What're you going to do?"

"That prick needs to fuck off out of Kilcoole, and I have a few ideas on how I can make that happen." Shane clamps his hand on my shoulder. "That can't have been easy. Are you okay?"

"I'll be okay once I see Ash." I shrug like I didn't just age a hundred years in the past few hours. To say I was terrified is an understatement.

Shane surveys my red-rimmed eyes but says nothing, just squeezes my shoulder one final time and drops it.

Ma and Da come back the same time Ciarán arrives, the latter looking pale and stressed. I can't imagine that three-hour drive was much fun. We all hug him, and then Shane and I leave to visit Ash.

Siobhan Davis

She looks so tiny in the bed, and my heart aches anew.

"What the hell happened to her hair?" Shane whispers as we claim seats on either side of her bed, both of us taking her hands.

My eyes widen when I see the hacked jagged strands of hair resting high on the nape of her neck. "I don't know," I choke out. "I didn't even notice."

"All her pretty hair gone." Sadness shrouds his face. "That fucker has so much to answer for."

"I hate him," I say through gritted teeth. "I want to kill him with my bare hands for doing this to her."

"He doesn't get to ruin your life like he's tried to ruin hers." Shane leans in and presses a soft kiss to her cheek. "You leave this to me, Dillon." He drills me with a sharp look. "I mean it. No one has done more for Ash than you. Now it's my turn. I'm her big brother, and I need a chance to protect her. Let me handle it now. You take care of her."

"You've got Fiona and the baby to think about."

"I'm doing this for Ash. End of."

Well, okay, then. "Fine." I nod my agreement. I'll focus on my sister and leave Cillian Fucking Doyle to Shane.

78

Chapter Eleven
Age 17

Silence descends except for the steady beeping of the machine Ash is hooked up to. We both stare at her in numbed shock. All of this is still so surreal. I regret the day I befriended Cillian Doyle, wishing I had never brought him into our lives. Lifting Ash's hand to my lips, I kiss her warm skin, so grateful the ambulance came fast and we got here in time. I can't even imagine what it'd be like if we'd been too late. I honestly think I would've died too. I wouldn't have survived if I'd lost her. My sister means the world to me.

Sometimes, I feel guilty that I love her with so much intensity. I mean, I love my brothers too and my parents, but it's always been different with Ash. Us two have been joined at the hip from the time we were little. I feel sorry for Ro. Shane and Ciarán are close, and I have Ash. As the youngest, Ro tends to be on his own, and I often wonder if he feels left out.

I make a vow, then and there, to include him more. He's been pestering me a lot lately to jam with us. He started drum lessons eighteen months ago, and while he uses the Toxic Gods outbuilding to practice every day when we're not there, I haven't let him play with us as I don't want to piss Aaron off. It took us a while to gel as a band, and we get along for the most part. I don't want Aaron to feel threatened if Ro starts jamming with us.

But maybe Jay and I can practice with him one day a week, and perhaps I can convince Shane to come see us play in Bray one Friday night so Ro can come too. Ma won't let him go to the pub on his own, and Ash has been MIA for months now.

Ash doesn't wake properly until the middle of the night, and I'm the only one in the room with her. Shane took Ma, Da, and Ro home earlier. Ciarán is asleep in one of the chairs in the waiting room. The psychiatrist didn't get to see Ash today because of some emergency that held her up. She's coming to see her first thing in the morning, and provided she's happy, Ash can go home then.

They tried to kick all of us out at nine when visiting hours are officially over, but I refused to leave. We were lucky one of the nurses on night duty is the older sister of Ciarán's new girlfriend, Susie. She fixed it so two of us could stay. Ma wanted to stay, but Da made her leave. She was exhausted and nodding off in the chair.

When Ash slowly blinks her eyes open, I stand and lean over her, careful not to crowd her even though every instinct demands I pull her into a tight hug and never let her go. "Hey you." I clear my throat, overcome with emotion when her blue eyes meet mine. In brief panicked moments, I worried I'd never get to see them again.

"Dillon." Her voice sounds scratched raw as she looks around the room with a small frown.

"You're in St. Vincent's ICU," I explain, pulling the chair right up beside her and sitting back down. "How do you feel?"

"Like shit. My head hurts, and my throat and my stomach are sore."

I take her hand in mine. "You're going to be okay."

"I'm sorry," she whispers, her eyes filling with tears.

80

"I know." I pat her hand. "But if you ever do anything like that again, I'll fucking follow you, Ash. I swear." As much as I was worried, I'm mad at her too.

"I just wanted it to stop, Dil. I'm in so much pain, and I just wanted to silence all the screaming in my head. I didn't stop to properly think about it. What it'd do to you, Ma, Da, and the others. I just needed the hurt to end."

"Promise me you won't do this again, Ash."

"I promise." Her solemn eyes meet mine. "I mean it."

"You scared me," I quietly say.

"I'm so sorry." Silent tears stream down her face, and I lean in and hug her.

"Shush, it's okay." My fingers reach for hair that isn't there. "Why did you do this?" I ask, feeling the ragged edges of her new pixie haircut.

"He was always playing with my hair, said he loved it. Every time I looked in the mirror, I would see him there, running his fingers through it." She reaches up, touching the ends of her much shorter hair. "I'm not sorry I did it, though I probably should've waited to go to the hairdressers."

I wasn't sure what kind of mood Ash would be in when she woke, but I'm glad she seems more like herself. The sadness is still there. The hurt too, but there's a resignation, an acceptance of sorts, that was missing before. Perhaps doing what she did was the wake-up call she needed though I would never have wanted it to come about like this.

I ease back and stare her straight in the eyes. "You can get it fixed, and you can fix your heart too, Ash."

"I need time to mourn him and mourn all those stupid dreams I had."

"They weren't stupid. Only that prick was."

She averts her eyes, looking to one side.

I gently cup her cheek. "You will get through this, Ash, and I'll be with you every step of the way."

She sniffles, nodding. "I'm thirsty."

I pour her some water from the jug on her locker, elevate the bed, and help her to sit up a little. I hold the plastic cup while she takes a few sips, and that's how the nurse finds us. She talks quietly to Ash, asking her a few things, before checking the machine and her vitals, and then she leaves again.

"Where's everyone?"

I fill my sister in on all that she missed, and gradually, her eyelids droop shut. "Sleep," I say, helping her to lie down flat and pulling the covers up over her. "I'll be right here when you wake up."

The next couple months are difficult for my sister, but she is finally starting to turn a corner. She decided to defer sitting her exams because she has missed too much time, and she'll re-sit sixth year. It means we will be together for our final year, and we'll both be doing the Leaving at the same time next year. I like that, and I like that this takes the pressure off Ash so she can concentrate on getting better.

I drive her to therapy every week, and when I'm not at school, working, or with the band, I spend every spare moment with my sister. Gradually, she is healing and the old Ash is starting to resurface. We are all so relieved.

I don't know what Shane did or said, but the week after Ash returned home from the hospital, Cillian and Kelly packed up and moved to Cork to stay with his grandparents. I assume they transferred to a school there, but I really couldn't give a flying fuck as long as they stay away from my sister. I'd be happy if they never came back to Kilcoole.

During the summer holidays, Toxic Gods books a second regular gig at a pub-slash-nightclub in Wicklow on Saturday nights. Ciarán has graduated UCG, started a job with Microsoft, and he's living in a flat in Greystones with Susie now. They have come to see us play in

Dillon

Bray and Wicklow a couple of times, letting Ro tag along as Ash still hasn't ventured back onto the social scene.

Ro is champing at the bit to play with us and pestering me nonstop to get rid of Aaron and bring him on board instead. He's such a clown. My little bro is nowhere near ready to fill Aaron's shoes, and even if he was, I wouldn't boot the guy out just to accommodate Ro. That would be a seriously shitty thing to do. Ma would also string me up. Unlike me, Ro does well in school, and she doesn't want the band distracting him from his studies.

Shane and Fiona had a little girl, Chloe, and she has us all wrapped around her tiny finger.

A few nights a week I work behind the bar at a local pub for extra cash. I'm saving every spare penny I earn towards my motorbike and leaving home. The band has already decided we'll be moving into the city center after we finish school next year. We're going to try to get a few gigs around town and start making a name for ourselves on the indie rock scene in Dublin.

It's late one Thursday night in early July when my world turns upside down.

I'm the last patron to leave Bray Boxing Club, and I wave at Pete as he locks up and heads towards his car while I stop to have a smoke. The bus isn't for another twenty minutes, and I have plenty of time to walk to the bus stop.

I'm leaning back against the wall at the side of the club when a new model BMW 8 Series pulls up to the curb. I puff away, feigning disinterest, as an older man, wearing a sharp fitted black suit gets out of the back seat. His blue eyes narrow on me as he approaches, and all the fine hairs on the back of my neck stand to attention. Not a single dark hair is out of place on the man's head, and his clean-shaven jaw and smooth tanned skin make it hard to put an exact age on him. He projects arrogant confidence as he heads straight towards me.

I straighten up, throwing my ciggie on the ground and stamping it out under my boot, instantly on high alert. Clutching the straps of my bag tighter, I study him as he comes near. I don't know the man. I'm one hundred percent certain I've never set eyes on him before, yet somehow, he's familiar. His silver watch glints under the streetlamp, and it looks like an expensive one. In fact, his whole demeanor screams wealth.

I level a glare at the rich prick when he stops directly in front of me. If he wants trouble, he's come to the right place. I won't hesitate to take this dick down if necessary. "What do you want?" I say in a cold unwelcoming voice. I'm a few inches taller than him and broader in the shoulders, and I enjoy looking down at him.

His eyes roam over me with a calculated stare. "You're Dillon O'Donoghue." His American accent is unmistakable, and my breath falters as the realization instantly hits like someone just plunged a dagger straight through my heart.

No.

I clutch the wall behind me for support when my legs feel like they might go out from under me.

This cannot be happening.

But it can't be a coincidence. Why else would a stranger come looking for me at ten o'clock at night when he's clearly far from home?

After a lot of soul searching, I reached out to Auntie Eileen's friend at the adoption agency a few weeks ago. I told her I'd like to receive a copy of my original birth cert. She said she'd fill in the paperwork and get things moving, but it wouldn't be released to me until I was eighteen. I wasn't sure what, if anything, I was going to do with it, but now it looks like that decision has been taken out of my hands.

I push off the wall a little and straighten up. It's a miracle my voice rings out loud and clear when I'm shaking on the inside. "Who are you?" I ask though I suspect I already know.

"My name is Simon Lancaster. I'm your father."

Chapter Twelve
Age 17

R age is instantaneous, and I don't hold back. I blurt my emotions without hesitation. "You're not my father. My father is Eugene O'Donoghue, and he's ten times the man you are. You're just a DNA contributor."

"If this attitude is any indication, I'd say the way he raised you is definitely lacking, and your statement is questionable in the extreme."

I grab his shirt and get all up in his face. "You don't get to show up out of the blue after giving me up and disrespect my parents. If I have an attitude, it's because *your* DNA flows in my veins."

He grips my wrist. "Take your hand off me. Now."

I'm tempted to smash his face into the wall, but I let him go because it's obvious he has money, and he's already proven he doesn't give a shit about me, so it wouldn't take much for him to come after me if I hurt him. I try to calm down. "Why are you here?"

"We need to have a conversation. We'll talk in my car."

"We'll talk right fucking here." I fold my arms and glare at him. There's no way I'm going anywhere with this man.

He looks all around and up at the sky. "I'm not speaking out in the open," he says, lowering his gaze and refocusing on me. "Get in the car."

"Fuck you."

"You're just proving I was right to give you up." His cold tone matches the icy sheen in his eyes.

"Again. Fuck you." I shove past him. "I don't care what you have to say. Just fuck off and leave me alone. I want nothing to do with you." I'm grinding my teeth as I walk off.

"Half a million dollars says you want to hear me out," he calls after me.

Now *that* gets my attention. I slow to a stop a few feet away from his BMW.

He catches up, stopping in front of me again. "I have a valid reason for being here. I just need five minutes of your time. I know you've reached out to the adoption agency in London and you're curious. Listen to what I have to say, sign on the dotted line, and I'll deposit the money in your bank account. Then we can both go back to our lives and pretend like this never happened. We don't ever have to see one another again."

Wow, he's a real piece of work. He's only shown up because he wants something from me, and as soon as he gets it, he'll disappear for good. Why the fuck would I give him anything? He abandoned me, and he has no interest in having any kind of relationship with me. Hurt replaces the blood flowing through my veins, and I swallow thickly, averting my eyes before he sees any of that emotion on my face. Who cares if this asshole doesn't want me? I don't need him. I've gotten along fine without him up to this point.

I'm tempted to tell him to fuck off again, but I want to know why he's here and what he's proposing. Plus, half a million dollars is a lot of money. I'd be an idiot to turn it down without at least hearing what he has to say. Purposely shoving my hurt to one side, I school my features into a neutral line and meet his eyes. "Why look me up now?"

"You'll have access to your birth certificate when you turn eighteen. It wouldn't be difficult for you to find me or..." His gaze roams my face slowly. "It's remarkable really."

I frown. "What is?"

He stares at me for a few tense beats. Ignoring my question, he says, "I'm the CEO and part owner of a big movie production company. I thought I'd preempt things and save us both the awkwardness. I don't want you, and it seems you don't need me. No point in wasting either of our time."

How can I have come from this wanker? Is he even human? Inside, I'm a whirlwind of explosive emotions. This has all come at me out of nowhere, and my emotions are ping-ponging all over the place. I refuse to let this jerk hurt me any more than he already has, so I cling to indifference and try to squash my anger and my pain. "Why should I trust you? How do I know you are even who you say you are?"

He removes a driving license from his wallet and shows it to me. The address says he lives in L.A. "This could be fake." I have no clue what American licenses look like. I hand it back to him as he passes a folded piece of paper to me.

"That's your birth certificate."

I unfold the paper and examine the details. "This says the baby's name is Rhett Lancaster." I look up at him. "This isn't me."

"Your mother named you after Rhett Butler from *Gone with the Wind*. It was one of her favorite movies."

"So, why isn't it my name?" I mean, I'm not unhappy it isn't. I definitely dodged a bullet there. I can only imagine the slagging I'd have gotten in school if I was Rhett O'Donoghue. But I know my parents, and they wouldn't have changed my name.

"You didn't deserve to keep it," he snaps. "She died and the name died along with it."

"Felicia Maria Lancaster," I whisper, speaking my bio mother's name for the first time. If this prick is telling the truth, that is. All of this could be a lie, though I'm struggling to understand why any Yank would show up out of the blue and spout lies when there is nothing to gain from it. I'm too old to be kidnapped and trafficked. I don't have anything of value to be stolen, and this guy isn't short of money. Unless he's a complete psycho, I doubt he's crossed the ocean to murder me. He has some of the details of my adoption, and the resemblance between us is too strong to ignore.

No, unfortunately, this is legit. He is the man who helped to give me life, and he's a complete dick.

"My wife." I hear the pain in his tone and lift my head, watching his Adam's apple bob in his throat. "Your mother." His eyes narrow into pointed daggers. "You murdered her when you were born."

I stumble back, and the piece of paper escapes my fingers. "What?" Ma told me my mother died in childbirth, but to say I *murdered* her? It's not like I haven't thought of how she'd be alive if I hadn't been born, but I've never thought of it like that. Murder suggests intent and how could a baby intentionally kill anyone? "I couldn't. I wouldn't... You can't say that to me." Hurt mixes with anger as he bends down and retrieves the errant certificate.

"Didn't anyone ever tell you the truth hurts, boy?" He shoves the paper at my chest, and I immediately push him away and step back. "Phrase it however you want, but it doesn't alter the facts. The love of my life died giving birth to you. She only lived long enough to give you a name. You took Felicia from me, and I'll never forgive you. You're lucky I gave you up for adoption because I'd most likely have killed you had I taken you home. I couldn't bear to look at you then. Like I can't bear to look at you now."

He glares at me with so much hatred burning in his eyes it's not hard to see how much he truly loathes me. Pain spreads across my chest making breathing difficult.

"You ruined my life, and I won't let you ruin Reeve's."

"Reeve?" My brows knit together.

"Your brother." My eyes pop wide as I stare at him. "Reeve is your twin brother. Felicia was a big *Superman* fan, and she named Reeve after the actor Christopher Reeve. Looking at you is like looking at him." He thrusts his phone in front of my face, showing me a picture of himself with a guy who looks scarily like me. They are both wearing suits and fake smiles. Reeve's hair is a bit lighter in parts, and he's got a mole over his lip, and his nose doesn't look like it was ever broken fighting, but other than that he looks identical to me. A shiver works its way through me, and I'm drowning in a pool of confusing feelings. "Get in the car, Dillon, and I'll explain."

My legs are like jelly as I walk in a daze to the car. A guy jumps out from behind the wheel and opens the back door for Simon.

Simon slides in, looking up at me with a scowl. "Get in the other side."

I move as if on autopilot, almost taking a tumble when I step off the curb. I have a brother? I'm a twin? I open the door and flop onto the back seat, beside the wanker, in total shock.

"Reeve is an actor, and he's going to be a big star. He doesn't need any skeletons in the closet causing issues for him. The last thing he needs is his long-lost twin resurfacing."

"He lives with you?"

He nods.

"Does he know about me?" I ask. My voice doesn't even sound like my own.

"I told him when he was twelve." Simon flicks a piece of lint off his trousers. "I offered to reunite him with you, but he said no. He didn't want you either." His cruel eyes bore into mine. "We are just fine without you."

"So why are you there then?" I bark, fighting the urge to curl into a ball and rock. Even my twin didn't want me? How am I so bad? Unless they've been watching me and all the fighting and trouble I get into seemingly validates their opinion.

"To make sure you don't mess things up for my son."

I'm not quick enough to hide the hurt from my face even though it's all kinds of fucked up because I'm not his son in any of the ways that count. But I'm barely holding it together, and I can't shield everything from him. Knowing he kept my twin but rejected me hurts. "Reeve asked me to come talk to you. You can't come forward, Dillon.

No one can know you exist. You are never to contact Reeve. You need to slink into the shadows and stay there. Pretend like you're invisible, if you will."

"I hate you," I say through gritted teeth. "I hate both of you."

He shrugs, like it's no big deal, pulling a stapled document out of a large envelope. "This is an NDA. Nondisclosure agreement," he adds. "Sign this, agreeing to never approach Reeve and never to talk about him or me to anyone, ever, and I'll give you half a million dollars."

"Hush money." I clench my hands into fists.

"Protection for my son." He shrugs again, and I'm so tempted to smash my fist in his face and fuck up the illusion he presents to the world. He might look rich and polished, successful and confident, but behind that veneer, he's the devil.

"I'm guessing Reeve was born first." It's the only explanation that makes sense.

"Felicia held him in her arms. She was so happy until the midwife said there was another baby, and then everything turned to shit."

"Only a sick fuck would blame innocent babies for something uncontrollable."

"I don't blame Reeve. I blame you."

Wow, this dick doesn't hold back. I stare straight ahead, unable to process all this. I'm only now realizing the driver didn't get in the car. He's outside on purpose, I'm betting, so he's not privy to this disgusting conversation.

"No." I swivel to face him, the leather squelching underneath me with the motion. "You can take your money and shove it up your ass. I'm signing nothing."

"That would be a big mistake, Dillon." He flips the document to the last page and removes a shiny silver pen from the outside pocket of his jacket, handing it to me. "Sign it, and let's be done with this."

"Fuck you." I swat his hand away, and the pen drops to the floor.

"You don't want to make an enemy of me, boy. I'm very powerful, and I can make your life hell."

"Do your worst. I don't care."

"Sign the NDA, Dillon."

"No, screw you." I open the door and get out. If I stay in that car for much longer, I'll choke the life from his pathetic body. I lean back in and fix him with my most hateful expression. "I'm signing nothing. Fuck off back to America, you evil piece of shit." I'm not giving him what he wants, tempting and all as the money is. I want nothing from this wanker or my self-centered twin. The two of them can rot in hell for all I care.

"One million." He stares me straight in the eye, looking unruffled. "I'll double it to one million."

I'm sensing people rarely refuse him, and he's used to writing a check to get what he wants.

Not this time, dickhead. "I'm not for sale."

Slamming the door shut, I storm off in the direction of the bus stop. With every step, the horror of what just transpired sinks deeper into my skin, pushing through sinew and muscle, brushing past bone, and attaching itself to my very soul. I'm shaking and shivering by the time I reach the bus shelter, and the icy chill clings to my body even after I've gotten home, crept up the stairs, and taken a long hot shower.

Chapter Thirteen
Age 17

R ed-hot anger is my constant companion in the days that follow. Along with a bottle of JD. I don't even attempt to hide my drinking from my parents. Bitterness and resentment replace the blood flowing through my veins as I attempt to drown my spiraling emotions at the bottom of a whiskey bottle.

I completely lose the plot when an envelope arrives with an updated NDA and my birth cert, throwing shit around my room as my pain runs free. I'm panting and sweating by the time I've finished rearranging my room. I'm surprised Ma didn't barge in when she heard all the noise.

Everyone is asking me what's wrong, but I can't tell them. Vocalizing it will only confirm how worthless and rejected I feel. If I say it out loud, who's to say my family won't draw the same conclusion? I have brought nothing but trouble into their lives. If they aren't already regretting taking me in, they would after I tell them. The two people who should love me most hate my guts, and they want me to disappear and pretend like I don't exist. Knowing I'm that inconsequential is a hard pill to swallow. It hurts real fucking bad. I've tried telling myself what they think doesn't fucking matter, but it's not helping. Inside, I'm consumed with pain and anger, and it's eating me up. It's bad enough I'm having to deal with all of this. No sense in letting everyone else suffer along with me.

I'm seconds away from shredding the NDA when I think better of it. This is evidence of who Simon and Reeve Lancaster are to me. It's leverage. Perhaps it'll come in handy at some point. If Reeve is going to be as big of a star as the dickhead thinks, maybe I'll go to the press. If my darling twin brother becomes Hollywood's next golden boy, my revelation could be worth a lot. It might be a way to pocket some easy money and stick the knife into the Lancasters' backs at the same time. Of course, I'd also be outing myself, and I'm not sure I want to do that either. But at least it gives me options. Ha! Bet that asshole didn't consider this before he posted the paperwork to me.

Sliding the papers back in the envelope, I tuck it into the shoebox I keep at the top of my wardrobe, hidden behind a bunch of old *Rolling Stone* magazines.

I receive the first text message that same day. It's sent from a different phone number to the one listed with the paperwork, but I know it's from *him*.

> Sign the NDA.

> Keep your mouth shut.

> If you speak out, the O'Donoghues will pay the price for your selfishness.

He doesn't need to elaborate for me to imagine what he might do. He's rich and powerful, and my parents are no match for the likes of him. Knowing he's tied my hands is so frustrating. I wonder why he's offering me money at all. Surely, he knows all he has to do is threaten my family and I won't breathe a word. I would never risk it. I'm beyond frustrated he has the upper hand, but I will find a way to get him back even if it takes me years.

Receiving the paperwork and the text only adds to my torment, and I spiral deeper. Dark emotions stab me from the inside until I'm nothing but a shredded, bloody mess of organs, tissues, and cells. The hollow ache that has always lived inside me expands, threatening to smother me completely. The pain is like a thousand tiny daggers constantly stabbing me all over. My head and my heart are so fucked up, and I'm falling apart at the seams.

I lash out at everyone, just wanting the world to fuck off and leave me alone.

Jamie is worried when I'm a no-show for our Friday and Saturday night gigs. Aaron is pissed, and Conor is zoned out as usual. I finally drag my arse out of bed on Monday to practice with the band, and it's the only bit of peace I've found since the dickhead flipped my world upside down. I vent my emotions through music, passing out on the sofa in the outbuilding a couple of nights.

The next Friday, I'm completely fucking locked when I take to the stage for our regular gig in Bray Harbor. Ironically, it's my best performance to date, and the crowd are going wild by the time we finish our set. Girls crawl all over me as I make my way to the bar to grab another beer. I'm starting to sober up and fuck that shit. I don't want reality to come crawling back in, kicking and screaming. So, I down a beer, gratefully accept the tequila shots Phoebe and her friend Sammie buy me, and then I take them both around the back of the building and take turns fucking them.

That becomes a regular pattern as July turns into August. When I'm not asleep, I'm either drunk or stoned. Conor and I spend a couple nights up at Killiney Hill, completely off our faces, and if I could get away with smoking weed every day, I'd happily stay stoned forever. But Catherine O'Donoghue would never let me get away with it.

"Get up," Ma shouts in an angry voice as she whips the covers off me. "This ends now, Dillon. I am not going to stand by and watch you throw your life away."

"Fuck off." Lifting my head, I glare at her before tugging the covers back over me. "It's summer holidays. I'll get up when I fucking want to."

"You'll get up now, young man." She moves for the duvet again, but I curl it around my body and hold on to it with a tight grip. "You have chores to do."

I haven't lifted a finger to help out since that fateful night. "Fuck chores. Fuck life." I have a vise grip on the duvet, and we tussle as she tries to pull it off me, and I cling more possessively to it.

"Dillon, please." She gives up a few seconds later. "If you won't tell me what's wrong, at least talk to your sister."

"There's nothing to talk about," I repeat for the umpteenth time. "You're like a broken record, and you're giving me a fucking headache. Just go away and let me sleep."

"I want to know what happened. You were perfectly fine leaving for boxing that Thursday, and all of this started the next day." The bed dips as she sits down. "Did someone hurt you? Please tell me."

"For the last fucking time, Ma, no one hurt me," I lie. "And nothing happened. This is the new me. Get used to it." Anger burns like acid in my gut, and I squash the need to scream from the top of my lungs. Inside, I'm screaming all the time, and it's exhausting.

She vigorously shakes her head. "This isn't you. This angry person saying all these cruel things is not my son."

"I'm not yours!" I shout, pushing up on my elbows. "I'm just some stray you took in, and I bet you regret it. Well don't worry, *Mother*, I'll be eighteen in five months, and I'll get out of your hair then."

Tears roll down her cheeks, and a sharp pain stabs me in the chest. "That isn't true, and you're not leaving."

"You can't stop me." I sit up against the headrest and reach for my cigarette box, plucking a joint I premade and lighting it up.

Dillon

"There is no smoking in the house, Dillon." She tries to grab the joint, but I stretch my arm up out of reach.

"This is my room, and I'll do what the fuck I like in it."

She closes her eyes for a few seconds. When she reopens them, they are flooded with concern that only pisses me off. She should hate me. Why doesn't she? "Is this about Ash? Because what happened to her was not your fault. Just like you're not responsible for what happened between her and Cillian. No one has done more for your sister than you."

"Get out of my room, Ma," I say before taking a toke of my joint. "I have nothing to say to you."

The rational part of my brain knows I'm taking my anger out on the wrong people, but the fucked-up part of my brain can't stop the fury coating my skin like a blanket. No one gets it. There is nothing anyone can say that will make this better. I'm just angry twenty-four-seven. Every word, every look, and every action aggravates me. My only respite is anesthetizing myself with booze, weed, and women or losing myself in music.

Music lets me channel my pain into art. Music isn't looking to dig into my head and understand the workings of my brain. It's not trying to coax me into speaking when I have nothing to say. It doesn't try to force my emotions to the surface to purge them.

Music just lets me be.

"Why are you still here?" I snap when I realize Ma is still in the room. I blow smoke circles in her face, knowing how much she hates when I do that.

"I'm beginning to think you're possessed by some demon or evil spirit," she says, standing. "Maybe I need to call Father Mannion."

"Try it and see what happens." I puff on my joint and blow more smoke in her direction. "I'll strangle the fucker with his rosary beads before he can spout any religious crap about God and how everything happens for a reason. Fuck God. And fuck Father Mannion." What the fuck has God ever done for me? He killed my mother to give me life and saddled me with an evil prick for a sperm donor and a selfish bastard for a brother. My own flesh and blood didn't want me, and despite what my parents have said, I know they only took me in out of pity. Girls are happy to spread their legs for me, but none of them want me for *me*.

No one wants the real me.

I'm forever destined to be the reject, second best, a charity case.

"You can't say those things about Father Mannion, Dillon. Take them back. It'll be a black stain on your soul."

"My soul is already pitch-black, Mother." I crack up laughing. She's just too funny.

"What's so funny?" Ash asks, materializing in my doorway.

"There is nothing funny about blasphemy." Ma plants her hands on her hips. "And your soul is not pitch-black, Dillon. It's just troubled."

I laugh harder as Ash steps into my room.

"Blasphemy?" Her forehead wrinkles as she looks to me to reply.

My laughter fades out, and I continue puffing my joint, refusing to look at my sister.

"I thought maybe Father Mannion could have a word with Dillon, but—"

"Jesus, Ma. Get real. You have more chance of Dillon talking to Father Fucking Christmas than Father Mannion."

"Language, Aisling O'Donoghue."

Ash rolls her eyes before her gaze latches on to the joint between my fingers, and she frowns. "You seriously need to lay off that shit, Dil. It's scrambling your brain."

"That's the plan."

"Please tell me what's wrong." My sister crawls up onto the bed beside me as I spy Ma creeping out of the room. "I just want to help you the same way you helped me."

"I don't need any help."

She places her head on my shoulder. "I know how you must've felt now," she quietly says. "Please let me in."

I swing my legs out of the bed and stand, hearing the soft thunk as her head drops onto my vacant pillow. "I just want to be left alone. Why the fuck doesn't anyone get that?" I roar, grabbing my clothes off the floor where I left them last night and hurriedly getting dressed.

Ash stands in front of me, watching me shove my feet into my boots. "You're breaking my heart, Dil."

I grab my keys, wallet, phone, laptop, hoodie, smokes, and a half-empty bottle of JD and stash them in my backpack before zipping it up. Swinging the bag over one shoulder, I jerk my head up and eyeball my sister. "That wasn't me. That was Cillian."

She sucks in a shocked gasp, and I feel instant regret when her soft sobs follow me out of the room, but it's not enough to go back there and apologize. My heart is heavier than usual as I leave the house, slamming the door shut behind me.

I head to the Toxic Gods outbuilding, and the first thing I do is secure the lock I bought yesterday to the door. That'll keep people out unless I want them here. My sleeping bag and a spare pillow are already strewn across the sofa, and I plan to sleep here the next few nights. At least that way the endless questions and the pointless nagging will stop. Plonking my sorry arse on a chair, I grab my guitar case and prepare to indulge in some musical therapy. I tune up my guitar and play, losing myself in the music in between knocking back swigs of JD. I'm not sure how long I've been playing when I'm interrupted by a knock on the door.

"Wanker!" Jamie yells, pounding his fists on the door. "Open the fuck up!"

I set my guitar down, unlock the door, and open it a smidgeon. "You're not coming in if you're here to lecture me."

"What? Fuck no." He dangles a plastic Centra bag in my face. "I brought rolls and crisps and beer to wash it down."

My stomach rumbles, reminding me I haven't eaten anything since lunch yesterday. Opening the door wider, I step back to let him in. He arches a brow as I flip the lock behind him. "Where'd that come from?"

"Woodies." I snatch the bag from his hand and rummage inside.

Jay doesn't say anything else about it, and we devour our food in silence.

"By the way, practice is off," he says around the last mouthful of his roll. "Aaron and Conor have the shits."

"Nasty."

Jay nods, swallowing the last of his food.

"Wanna jam for a bit and then get fucked up?" I ask, rolling up the tinfoil and tossing it in the bin.

"Sounds like a plan." He clamps a hand on my shoulder and moves over to his guitar.

This is the reason Jamie is my best friend. He doesn't push. He understands what it's like to have shit to handle. To not want to talk about it. Like I understand if I ever want to speak about it, he will listen. If I'm gonna share what's happened with anyone, it'd be Jay. But he's got his own problems. He doesn't need mine too. And in the same way, I don't want to burden Ash with it when she's still healing, and I can't tell my parents because it would fucking gut them.

I know I'm being a prick, but I'm just trying to protect them.

There's no point in all of us being mad.

I've got enough anger to fill the world's oceans and then some.

Chapter Fourteen
Age 17

"I told the boys we'd meet them in Molly's in a while," Jay says, shoving his phone in his jeans pocket.

"I'm ready now." I place my guitar in its case and lock it.

"You smell and your hair looks like dead raccoons are nesting there."

"Fuck off." I thrust my middle finger up at him. "Bet I could still get laid more times than you."

"Not a fucking chance in hell, lad." He grabs me in a headlock. "Go shower, and I'll do the same."

"Nah," I say, shoving him away and unlocking the door. "I'm not going back to the house. All they ever do is nag the fucking shit out of me."

"Shower at mine." He shrugs. "It's on the way anyway."

We head to Jay's house and take turns showering. I'm brushing my teeth at the steam-clouded mirror in the bathroom when Jamie comes in. "Here." He hands me a clean shirt, jocks, and socks. "Hurry up. The asshole just got home, and they'll kick off any second now."

By the time we make it downstairs five minutes later, his parents are letting rip at one another. There's a loud crash from the kitchen as we creep down the hall towards the door. His mother's high-pitched shriek hammers at my eardrums as we pull the front door closed behind us.

"Sorry about that." He kicks dirt across the driveway as we walk, and a muscle pops in his stubbly jawline.

"It's cool. Not like it's your fault."

"It's fucking embarrassing is what it is."

I sling my arm around his shoulder. "It's really not." I want to add I know all about embarrassing, but it's not like we're in a competition for having the shittiest bio dad. If we were, I'd say it's a close call between Conal Fleming and Simon Lancaster.

"I'm immune to it these days, but anyone else seeing that shit reminds me it's not normal. I don't know why they didn't split up years ago. Honestly, I'd be happy if I never saw either of them again."

"You can move into the outbuilding with me," I suggest, letting my arm slide off his shoulders.

Jay glances sideways at me as he lights up a spliff. "You're living there now?"

I shrug, flicking strands of semi-dry hair out of my eyes. "For the next few nights anyway. No one bothers me there."

"It's that bad?" he asks, passing the spliff to me.

I inhale deeply, drawing the hypnotic scent of weed and tobacco deep into my lungs. "They won't leave me alone, and I'm sick of sounding like a broken record. I just want some peace and quiet." I hand the spliff over.

"I hear ya." He takes a smoke and passes it back. "My parents tossed Shauna's mattress in the shed. I'll grab that on my way back."

"So what? She's planning on never coming back?" I'm kinda pissed at his older sister. She always looked out for him growing up, but now she's in college up The North it's like she has forgotten he exists, and that's not cool. Maybe she thinks 'cause he's seventeen that he doesn't need her anymore, but she's his only real family besides us.

His jaw tightens. "Looks that way." I suspect he wants to say more but doesn't too. And I understand that sentiment fully.

"We'll be out of here by this time next year."

"I'm so ready to be done with school. I can't wait to move into town and focus on the band."

"Same, just keep saving."

Jay has been laboring all summer in between our gigs while I've been taking as many shifts as I can at Lee's, Aaron is working in a restaurant in Greystones, and Conor has been helping his uncle at his carpentry practice. Anything we're not drinking or smoking is going towards equipment and the apartment we intend to share with the band. We'll need at least a few months' rent in advance to cover us until we get some gigs in town. But I'm confident it won't take long. We're getting really good, and we have a loyal local following. All we need is one venue in town to take a chance on us, and we'll prove ourselves.

I'm also stashing money away for my Kawasaki, and I should have enough to buy a secondhand one just after we finish the Leaving. That's if I finish it. I haven't ruled out bailing after my birthday in January. What the fuck do I need the exams for anyway?

All the lads are there when we arrive at Molly's, and the place is buzzing for a Thursday night. Turns out Shelby Sullivan is having her eighteenth birthday here. Reminds me of her older sister's eighteenth and losing my virginity. In between knocking back beers and laughing with my mates, I check the room to see if Simone is here, but she's not. Shelby isn't quite in the same league as her sister, but she's got great tits, and the more beers I drink, the more attractive she gets. I also remember someone telling me she liked me, and apparently, she was upset her sister fucked me. That could be advantageous now.

Kylie Walsh is currently sitting in my lap, and I've been kissing her a bit, but I'm not interested in anything more. I never go back for seconds. She was a shitty lay anyway, and she's got clinger written all over her face. Nah, fuck that shit. Kylie's gotta go. I turn my head when she moves to kiss me again. "Run along now, babe."

She squirms on my lap, licking her lips and tugging her top down lower, shoving her tits all up in my face. "I want you to fuck me again. It's all I've been thinking about since we banged."

I lift her off my lap, placing her feet on the ground. "It's not happening, Kylie. You know the score. I told you it was a onetime thing, and I meant it."

"But you've been kissing me all night!" She pouts, planting her hands on her hips.

"*You've* been kissing *me*, and I'm over it. Plenty more fish in the sea, babe." I lean in and press my mouth to her ear. "Jamie likes you," I lie, in the mood to shit stir. "And his lap is looking lonely." Only cause Melissa just left it to go to the bathroom three seconds ago.

"Really?" She looks dubious as she glances back at my mate.

"He's too shy to approach you." I don't know how I get those words out without laughing. Jamie Fleming doesn't have a shy fucking bone in his body.

"You wouldn't mind?"

"Not a bit. Go for it." I give her a little push in Jay's direction and walk off, heading towards the birthday girl.

Shelby is talking with some nerd from school, but I shove him out of the way and flash her my most flirtatious smile. I've got a nice buzz going from the alcohol and the spliff I smoked earlier, and now I'm horny and I want to fuck. "Happy birthday, Shelby."

"Thank you." Her voice is barely a whisper as she stares up at me with these big doe eyes.

Up close, she's much prettier. Or maybe it's the beer talking. Her cheeks stain pink, the color darkening when I twirl my finger around a lock of her wavy, brown hair. "You look gorgeous tonight."

Her face is so red I almost expect to see flames scorching a path along her skin.

"I have a gift for you," I say, waggling my brows and licking my lips.

"You do?" Surprise registers on her pretty face.

"Yeah." I lean in, and she steps back until her spine meets the wall. Caging her in with my arms, I cock my head to one side. "You ready for it?"

Her eyes grow impossibly wide as she gulps and nods. Then I lean in and kiss her, hard and possessively. Pretty sure she's never been kissed like this before if her tentative explorations are any indication. Her pupils are dilated and her chest is heaving when I pull back, breaking our lip-lock. "Want another gift?" I brush my lips over hers as I nudge her with the semi in my jeans.

She nods quickly, and I silently fist pump the air.

"Come home with me, and I'll make it a birthday to remember."

Her eyes light up. "Okay."

Twenty minutes later, I've convinced her to ditch the party, and we leave with Jamie and Melissa to head to my place. Jamie is laying into me for the stunt I pulled with Kylie as the two girls talk among themselves.

We stop to retrieve the mattress from Jamie's shed on the way, and when we reach the farm, I tell Jay to use the play barn while I take Shelby to the band building. I've no issue in fucking her with Jay and Melissa in the room, but I'm pretty sure Shelby wouldn't like that if the nervous glances she's been giving me on the way here are any indication.

When we get inside the outbuilding, I lock the door and push her up against it, dragging the back of my knuckles up and down her face. "I want to fuck you. Can I?"

Her head bobs, and a blush steals across her cheeks.

"Are you sure? I need you to say the words."

"Yes, I'm sure," she replies in a timid voice, and something occurs to me.

"You have done this before, yeah?"

She nods. "Yeah."

"This will be the only time. There will be no repeat performance.

I don't have time for a girlfriend. I'm focused on my band. If you're expecting more from this, you should leave now."

"I'm fine with it, Dillon. I know this is your usual MO."

Not sure if I'm happy girls around the town are talking about me or not. "Okay." I lean in and kiss her neck. "If you want me to stop, just say so, and I will."

I feel her up at the door, kissing and groping her until she relaxes. Then I bend her over the sofa, roll a condom on, pull her dress up, and fuck her hard while fondling her tits. When I'm done, I dispose of the condom and grab two waters from the small fridge while she fixes herself. "Thanks for the fuck, babe."

Her neck and face are flushed as she wraps her arms around herself and stares at me with expectant little puppy-dog eyes.

For fuck's sake. I fucking told her the score. Why the fuck is she looking at me like that? Girls are crazy, and they wreck your head. I'm never having a girlfriend or getting married. How da fuck does any man put up with that shit? Any momentary release I just felt is now gone as irritation surges through my veins. "You need to leave." I hand her a water and steer her to the door, patting her arse as I push her outside. "See ya around."

After she's gone, I message Jamie to let him know the coast is clear. He messages back to say he's going to sleep in the play barn with Melissa. I warn him to get her out of there early before Da starts work and finds them.

I try to sleep, but I'm too wired. I toy with the idea that's been on my mind consistently the past five weeks since the asshole appeared in my life. I can't avoid it forever, and I might as well get it over and done with.

Sitting upright on the sofa, I grab my bottle of JD and open my phone. I log into Instagram and type Reeve Lancaster into the search bar. There are tons of results, and my stomach coils into knots as I tap into his official page. He's got thousands of followers, and all his posts have decent likes and comments. I scroll through a few posts as I drink JD. All the blood leaches from my skin when I zoom in on a photo of him. The resemblance is uncanny. If we were standing beside one another, there is no doubt we are brothers.

Staring at my mirror image makes it all the more real. Pain slashes through my chest, cutting deep. I can't help imagining what it would've been like if I hadn't been adopted. If we'd grown up together. Would he still hate me? Or would he fill the hollow ache inside me like the missing piece? Guilt joins hurt in slapping me upside the head. Thinking these thoughts feels so disloyal to my family. As if I'm wishing they were never part of my life.

It's all so fucking confusing.

I drop my cell on the sofa and take a huge mouthful of whiskey, relishing the burn as it glides down my throat. Leaning my head back, I close my eyes and fight the turmoil swirling in my chest.

I *hate* that I look so much like the brother who doesn't want me.

I want to share *nothing* with that prick.

If there was a way to replace the DNA flowing through my veins, I'd do it in a heartbeat. Hell, I'd scrub my brain with bleach if it'd remove all knowledge of both Lancasters from my mind.

I want to erase Reeve's existence from my life in the same way he's erased mine from his.

As I think about it, I realize there's something I can do that'll help.

Before I pass out, I mentally form the plan in my head, determined to act on it ASAP.

Chapter Fifteen
Age 17

"**D**illon O'Donoghue!" The pounding on the door is in sync with the pounding in my head as I slowly come to. I've a crick in my neck from falling asleep at an awkward angle, and it tastes like mothballs have taken up residence in my mouth.

"Open this door, dickhead, or I swear I'll fucking tear it down," the somewhat familiar female says.

Shoving the sleeping bag off my lap, I drag my hands through my messy hair as I stifle a yawn and head towards the door.

"Come out here and show yourself, you fucking coward!" the woman adds in a shrill tone.

I rub my sore head. I do not need whatever drama this is, but the bitch sounds unhinged and ignoring her doesn't seem like a smart plan. "Keep your hair on," I say as I unlock the door. "I'm—Simone?" My recollections have not done her justice. Simone Sullivan is a total knockout. Way sexier than her younger sister. "Hey, babe." I waggle my brows and flash her a flirty smile. "If I'd known you were stopping by, I'd have cleaned up." I open the door wide, smiling as I gesture for her to come in. "I don't usually go back for seconds, but I'll make an exception in your case."

"Un-fucking-believable." She glares at me like I'm the devil incarnate, and I frown before it registers in my hungover brain.

"Shit."

"Yeah, shit." Grabbing my wrinkled shirt, she yanks me outside. "How dare you treat my sister like that!" She shoves my chest, and steam is practically billowing from her ears. "Especially after I made sure you had a good time losing your virginity. You could at least have shown my sister the same respect instead of treating her like a whore and shoving her out the door the instant you'd come!"

"Hang on here a sec." I massage my throbbing temples. "Are you saying Shelby was a virgin?"

"Of course, she was a virgin! You fucking wanker!" She pushes my chest again, and I stumble back a little.

Out of the corner of my eye, I spy Shane loitering in the near distance, no doubt listening to every word. I shake my head, sending him a warning glare to butt the fuck out. "I didn't know. I asked her, and she lied." Folding my arms across my chest, I drill her with a dark look. "I don't know what your fucking problem is, but I suggest you take it up with your sister. I didn't mislead her. I told her out straight what the story was. Not my issue if she's got a problem with it now."

"You're such a prick," she says as tears fill her eyes. "She's liked you for years. Only God knows why."

"Sounds like you're in no position to throw shade. You knew that, and yet you let me bang your brains out. Sounds fucking hypocritical to me."

"I didn't know! If I'd known how she felt, I would never have fucked you that night. I shouldn't have fucked you anyway, but you caught me at a vulnerable moment."

"Rewrite history if you want, but I know what happened."

"That doesn't fucking matter!" she screams, pacing in front of me. "How could you hurt Shelby like this, Dillon? She has liked you for so long. She saved her virginity for you, and then you just cruelly took it without any regard for her feelings."

"She liked it." I really don't know why this bitch is making a big deal out of nothing. "If she didn't, she would've told me to stop, and she didn't."

"She didn't even come! And you fucked her so hard she's sore and in pain today." She shakes her head. "I didn't think you were like this. I have never regretted fucking anyone as much as I regret fucking you."

Join The Regrets Club, sweetheart, along with everyone else I seem to have let down.

I shrug before shoving my hands in the pockets of my jeans. Don't know why she bothered coming here to stir shit up. It's not like I can turn back time and reinstate her sister's hymen. "You done now? 'Cause I've got shit to do."

"My god, you're not even a tiny bit sorry, are you?"

"What the fuck have I got to be sorry for?" I yell, stalking forward and pushing my angry face all up in hers. "Shelby is the one who lied. I didn't do anything wrong, so fuck off home and tear strips off her because I'm fucking done with this shitty conversation."

"You're a complete prick, Dillon O'Donoghue." She stabs my chest with her finger. "You stay the hell away from my sister. Shelby's a good girl, and she's going places. She doesn't need the likes of you bringing her down."

"Your sister already spread her legs for me. I have no reason to go near her again."

She lunges at me and manages to scrape her nails down my cheek and knee me in the balls before Shane hauls her off me.

"Fuckkkkk!" I hiss, gently cupping my junk and trying not to pass out from the pain.

"You need to leave, Simone," my brother says, keeping his arm around her as he walks her to her car. "I'm really sorry about all this. Dillon's going through some stuff right now, and he doesn't mean it."

"Yes, I do!" I shout, still hunched over and cursing the bitch every which way to Sunday. "Fuck off apologizing for me."

My brother glares at me over his shoulder before helping Simone into her car. I straighten up and adjust myself behind my jeans. Fuck, that hurt. They have a hushed conversation for a few minutes while I stand there stewing. I'm tempted to throw rocks at her car as she drives off, but I manage to restrain myself. I don't trust her not to come back and try to castrate me. Bitch has serious issues.

"What the actual fuck was that all about?" Shane shouts, putting his face all up in mine. "How could you do that to that poor girl?"

"Fuck off, Shane." I push him away. "I didn't do anything to that *poor girl* that she didn't want. Everyone needs to get off my fucking case. You're all acting like I fucking raped her!"

"Well, you said it." Shane pins narrowed eyes on me.

"What'd you say?" My dark tone slithers in the gap between us, flexing with warning.

"You heard me." The stubborn cut of his jaw confirms he won't back down.

"It was consensual. You take that back, Shane."

"You've been acting like the devil's spawn for weeks. It's only a matter of time before you do something that'll land you in jail, and I'm done with the way you're treating Ma and Da. This bullshit ends now, Dillon."

"Fuck you." I push my chest into his. "You take it back, Shane. You fucking take it back!" I jab my finger repeatedly in his chest.

"I'll take it back when you apologize to everyone for acting like the antichrist."

"You're not my fucking father, and I don't answer to you!"

"If you were my son, I'd have you tossed in a cell until you came to your senses. No O'Donoghue goes around treating girls like shit. That's not who we are, but maybe the DNA flowing through your veins is proof you're not really one of us. You can't be if this is how you treat people."

All semblance of humanity leaves me as his words strike deep and true. Letting out a giant roar, I ram my fist in his face. And then it's on. We throw punches at one another, landing blows on each other's faces and upper torsos. When he gets me in a headlock, I bite his hand and punch him in the nuts. As he's hunched over, I slam my fist into his side, and he loses it, pushing me back before headbutting me. I stumble on my feet, almost tripping, but I recover fast. My vision is still blurry as we charge at one another, hitting, punching, and shouting, until we're forcibly pulled apart.

"That's enough," Da says, restraining my arms behind my back. Ro is tugging Shane back. Blood leaks out of Shane's swollen nose, and one eye is already closing as he hugs his side and glares at me. "What on earth is going on?" Da asks.

"He called me a rapist!" I snap, spitting blood on the ground. My lip stings, and my cheek is sore as well as my stomach. Shane managed to land a few savage punches to my gut, and I bet they'll bruise.

"What? Why?" Da asks, looking between me and Shane with a puckered brow.

Shane quickly explains what happened while I quietly seethe. Now my entire family will know. Great, that's just great.

"Dillon has a lot he needs to apologize for, but you were out of line, Shane," Da says.

"Someone had to try to punch sense into him." Shane shucks out of Ro's embrace.

"You said that on purpose?" Ro arches a brow, and Shane's head bobs.

"I don't think you're a rapist, Dil," Shane says, slowly approaching. "I shouldn't have said that, but if you don't stop all this bullshit, that could become a reality. You're so out of it most days I don't know how you can even walk straight."

"You're an asshole," I hiss at him as Da tightens his hold on my arms.

"So are you."

"I know, and I don't care."

Sadness ghosts over Shane's face. "I'm sorry for starting a fight, and I'm sorry for saying you weren't an O'Donoghue."

A muscle pops in my jaw as I stare at my brother. We've always had a tumultuous relationship, but the past few years, we have mostly gotten on. Shane calling me out on my shit is expected. The only surprise is he didn't do it sooner.

"I didn't mean that, Dillon. You're one of us through and through. It's why when you hurt we all hurt." Ro nods in agreement as Shane continues. "When you do something wrong, we all accept that responsibility. You didn't technically do wrong by Shelby Sullivan, but you didn't treat her right either. That's not you. I don't give a flying fuck what you say, but that is not who my brother is. Wherever he's gone, bring him the fuck back before it's too late. If you won't talk to us or your friends, go and talk to a professional, but this has got to stop, Dillon, before someone ends up really hurt." His chest heaves, and his eyes radiate pain when he adds, "That someone could be you."

He walks away with his arm around Ro's shoulders, talking to him as they head towards the house. Da only releases me when they've gone inside. I move to walk into the outbuilding, but Da stops me with a hand on my chest. "Hold up there, young man. You're weeks behind on your chores, and you're working on the farm with me today. If you can't vent your emotions through words, do it with your hands in a meaningful way."

Chapter Sixteen
Age 17 to 18

"Oh my god." Ma slaps a hand over her chest, pinning me with a horrified stare as I take a seat around the dinner table. "What have you done?"

I don't bother answering. Nothing I say will be right. I knew Ma wouldn't be happy, but I didn't do this for her.

"I like it. It's very edgy," Ash says, smiling as her gaze roams over my newly dyed white-blond hair before clocking the eyebrow, nose, and lip piercing. "Very rock 'n' roll."

"Why did you have to pierce your lovely skin?" Ma maintains the look of horror on her face as she examines my piercings. "You look like a member of a gang."

Ash's lips twitch. "Ma, lighten up. Loads of guys have piercings these days. Tattoos too. I was thinking of getting a stud in my nose."

"You should do it," I say, placing three thick-cut slices of beef on my plate. "It'd look cool with your hair." Ash has embraced her pixie cut, and she's determined to keep it that way. She said she's never wearing her hair long again. Personally, I think she should wear it long to spite Cillian Doyle. He's no longer around anyway. I wouldn't let that prick take anything else from me, if I was her, but it's her call.

Either way, my sister looks beautiful. Her shorter hair showcases her pretty face. I'm guessing when we return to school she'll have no shortage of offers, though I doubt Ash'll be interested. She says she is turned off guys for life. It won't last forever, but I think she's right to avoid distractions and concentrate on school. She's determined to go to Trinity next year.

"You'll have even more birds fighting all over you." Ro smirks. "Maybe I'll transform myself too."

"Over my dead body, Ronan O'Donoghue." Ma waves her finger in his direction as she puts a large bowl of veggies on the table. "You are perfect the way you are. You don't need to change a thing. The same goes for you, Dillon. I don't understand why you had to do this." She leans in with concern etched all over her face. "Are those green contacts?"

"Yeah," I say, spooning a dollop of mashed potatoes on my plate. "What of it?" I challenge her with a look.

"You have such beautiful blue eyes. Why would you want to hide them?"

"Because I hate them!" I bark, slamming a spoonful of veggies onto my plate. "It's my face, my body. I'll do what the fuck I like, and you'd better get used to it as I plan to get lots of ink." I've already booked an appointment with a guy in Bray who came recommended by Jono's brother. He did his ink, and it looks sick.

"Dillon. You will watch your tone with your mother." Da fixes me with a stern look that is rare. "We talked about this last week. You will not disrespect your mother or raise your voice at this table."

"Fine." My chair scrapes off the tiled floor as I push it back and stand. "I'll leave." I storm off with a chorus of voices calling after me.

Dillon

I'm strumming on my guitar, trying to fit a melody to some new lyrics I've written, when Ash shows up.

"Open up, dumbass. I have food."

I let her in and snatch the covered plate from her hands, ripping the tinfoil off and diving into the roast beef dinner I so stubbornly left behind. I was just about to order pizza when she showed up. She watches me quietly as I devour my dinner and lick the plate clean.

"How long are you going to stay out here?" she asks.

I shrug. "I dunno. If it had central heating and a shower and a microwave, I'd probably never go back inside the house."

"I miss you." She eyeballs me with solemn eyes. "If I promise to not ask you what's wrong again. If I drop it, can we go back to being friends?" She audibly gulps. "We're back to school in three days, and I feel sick at the thought of it. I can't do it without you."

Instinctively, I reach out and take her hand. "You're still my best friend. You and Jay. And we won't leave you to handle CCA alone. We've got your back. Always."

The next few months roll by at a snail's pace. It's always the way when you're itching for something to happen. I can't wait to finish sixth year, do my Leaving, and then move into town. Simon sends me regular texts warning me to keep my mouth shut, which I ignore. I block his number every time, but he seems to have an endless supply of mobile phones and an annoying ability to send me into a red-hot rage.

I'm still consumed with anger and still struggling to handle all my emotions. The first few months of school are tough. It's hard to care about something that means fuck all to me. So, I put zero effort in. I show up—because Ash needs me there—but I don't do my homework, I refuse to do after-school study, and I'm rude to my teachers with zero fucks to give. I'm constantly in detention, and after getting into a fight with Kelly's brother—when he spoke crap to Ash—I almost get expelled, but Shane manages to talk the school board around. Ash pleads with me not to do anything else, so I suck it up and stop with all the bullshit. She helps me with my homework, and we study together, and I try to keep my nose out of trouble.

I'm still wallowing in pain and self-loathing and still burying it with booze, weed, and birds at the weekends, but I find a way of living with it, and I stop taking my hurt out on my loved ones. Consequently, they stop nagging me to talk, and things settle down at home.

Ma is upset as I gradually ink my body, starting with my arms, and then I get a large tattoo of a scorpion tattooed on my back. It put a considerable dent in my savings, but it was worth it. I researched options for months until I settled on it. The symbolism—determination, rebirth, resilience—resonated most with me. When I look in the mirror, it's a permanent reminder I can be whoever I want to be as long as I fight those who seek to tear me down. I'm not just the sum of the DNA that flows through my veins. I am my own person, and Simon Lancaster can do nothing about it. He doesn't control me. I own every part of myself, even the cruel twisted parts, and I alone decide my actions and my fate. Every time I look at the scorpion, it reinforces my determination to fight back. It's a reminder that one day vengeance *will* be mine.

Someday, somehow, I will pay Simon and Reeve back for the pain they continue to cause me. Someday, they will know what it feels like. I will find a way to make them suffer, and only then will I fully be reborn.

What's most important now is when I look in the mirror, I see *me*.

I don't see him.

It feels like the first victory of many.

Christmas comes and goes, and then it's my eighteenth birthday. I celebrate with the band after our gig in Wicklow on Saturday, and Jamie and I go back to this older bird's gaff where we take turns fucking her and her friend. Fun times. I stagger home in the early hours, high as a kite and drunk off my face, sporting a happy smile and a smug dick.

Dillon

I told Ma I didn't want a party, but of course, she didn't listen to me. She throws a surprise party on Sunday night with all the family and extended family. Both sets of grandparents are here. Da's parents traveled up from Kerry for the occasion. They shower me with presents, most of which are cards with cash, which is much appreciated. As everyone sings happy birthday to me and I blow out the candles on the large cake Ma and Ash made, I feel incredibly unworthy and full of shame for how I treated my family last year.

They didn't deserve that. I wish I had a time machine so I could go back and erase all the cruel things I said and hurtful things I did.

I'm helping Ma clean up the dishes after the party when I finally pluck up the nerve to apologize. "Ma." I dry my hands on the tea towel after putting the last plate away in the press.

"Yes, love."

"Thank you for the party and the presents and the cake."

She beams up at me, her face shining with love. "You're only eighteen once, and it needed to be celebrated properly."

I'm not sure I agree. Every birthday feels tainted to me now knowing my twin is in L.A. celebrating his birthday as if I don't exist. I wonder what he got for his eighteenth. Probably a luxury car or an apartment or something ridiculously expensive.

Whenever my mind wanders to Reeve, I think about all the ways in which our lives are different. I haven't wanted for anything in my life, and I know I have a lot to be grateful for, but it's not the same as growing up uber rich and having everything your heart desires at the click of your fingers. Resentment bubbles up my throat, like always, when I think about him. My twin has it so easy. He hasn't had to battle with feelings of inadequacy and rejection for most of his life. He hasn't had to hear our father say he wishes he'd never been born. He doesn't live with the guilt that he murdered our mother.

"Love." Ma cups my cheek. "Where'd you go?"

"I'm here." I smile, batting my nerves away as I tentatively hug her. "I'm sorry, Ma," I whisper as her arms automatically go around me and she squeezes me tight. "I'm sorry for everything."

She chokes on a sob, and I hold her closer. "I know you are."

"I didn't mean any of those shitty things I said. I hate myself for being so cruel to you and everyone."

Tears cling to her lashes as she clutches my face in her hands. "All that matters is you're back to yourself. We were so worried, Dillon. I woke every morning not knowing if I'd find you the way you found Ash." Her voice cracks, and tears spill down her cheeks. "Knowing your kids are hurting and you can't do anything to help is one of the most soul-crushing things to endure. I feel like I failed both of you, and—"

"No, Ma." I shake my head. "You didn't fail me or Ash. I was the one who failed you. It won't happen again, I swear, and I never once thought about ending things, so put that worry from your mind."

It's the truth. I won't give Simon and Reeve Lancaster the satisfaction of wiping myself from this planet. That'd make it too easy for those pricks. Besides, after everything that happened with Ash, I could never put my parents and my siblings through it again. I'm embarrassed I caused them more pain when they were still dealing with the aftermath of Ash's pain. My sister is doing much better now, though she's not fully back to herself, but she's turned a corner, and we're all relieved.

"I just want you to be happy. Health and happiness is all I want for my kids." She brushes her fingers through my lighter-colored hair. She's gotten used to my look, though she's still not a fan of the ink or piercings, but she's stopped giving me grief about it. "Are you happy yet, Dillon?"

"I'm getting there. I still have some other shit to sort out in my head, but I'm not unhappy."

"I'm glad you have your music, and you know we'll support you with your move to the city, but you've got to promise to ring me regularly, and I'll expect you at Sunday dinner at least once a month."

"I can do that."

Dillon

Before I know it, our exams are finished and I walk out of CCA for the last time feeling like a convict walking out of jail. We stick around Kilcoole during the summer while we apartment hunt in town. I want to ensure Ash gets her place in Trinity before we leave home. The Leaving Cert results come out, and miracle of miracles, I actually pass. I give my sister all the credit. Ash is the one who forced me to do homework and study with her. My sister gets five hundred and twenty points, and I'm so fucking proud of her. She's in the top twenty percent for the entire country, and it's a massive achievement. She's gone through a lot in the past eighteen months, and she deserves all the good things coming her way.

Her offer comes in from Trinity, and we're all happy for Ash, though it doesn't extend to Ma and Da letting her apply for one of the dorms. They are still worried about her mental state, so they make a deal with her. She will live in Kilcoole and commute to and from college each day for first year, and then they'll contribute to her getting her own place next year. It's a fair compromise, and she agrees. I'm not the only one trying to make things up to our folks.

Jamie surprises everyone by getting offered a place in Trinity too. I knew he'd applied for the CAO, but I didn't think he was serious about college. The course he's doing is only twenty hours a week, so he'll still have time to study and participate fully in the band. And, of course, any gigs we manage to land in town will be at night, so it's doable.

We find a three-bed place in Temple Bar, put down the deposit, and prepare to move in two weeks' time. I buy a secondhand black and silver Kawasaki EN500. It's an older model German import, but it has low mileage, I got it for a steal, and it's a pillion bike. I wanted to ensure I had a seat so Ash can stay over sometimes and I can drive her back home the next day. Ma hasn't stopped crossing herself any time I get on the bike. She hates it, but I'm an adult now, and she can't stop me.

Texts from Simon are still frequent, but I just treat them like I do any other spam text. They go unread, deleted, and blocked.

Stalking the Lancasters online has become my new obsession. I
need ammunition for revenge, and I need to keep tabs on both men if
I'm to devise a viable plan. Many nights are spent trawling the
internet for information on the dickhead and my loathsome twin.

Simon Lancaster attends a lot of movie premieres, always with a
different woman on his arm. The devil in my ear whispers I seem to
be a lot like him, but I punt that meddling voice away. I am *nothing*
like my prick of a sperm donor. I refuse to accept any similarities
except for the physical ones I can't deny. Apart from pics at
premieres, there is the odd interview or quote he gives about an up-
and-coming production and a few pics of him playing golf with the
director Jonathon Mills, but that's it.

There is a lot more content available on my twin, though there
are no personal pics on his socials. All his posts are movie related.
Many of them show that slut Saffron Roberts draped all over him.
She looks like trouble in a pint-sized package. I can see why some
guys might be into her, but she does nothing for me. Everything about
her turns me off. She's fake with a capital F and trying way too hard.
From the way she's clinging to Reeve and looking at him in the pics, it
seems like she's set her sights on him.

Wonder what his girlfriend thinks about that?

There is very little about Vivien Mills online, apart from some
photos of her with Reeve when they were kids attending movie
premieres with their famous parents. I found her Insta account, but
there are no pics of Reeve, which seems weird when they grew up
together and, apparently, they're a couple. Their parents are best
friends, and they live beside one another in a wealthy part of L.A. So
why is there no evidence of them on either of their socials? It makes
no sense. I found some threads for the movie where fans were specu-
lating on the nature of their relationship. A few girls who profess to
be Vivien and Reeve's classmates say they've been a couple for years
and they are very much still together.

Vivien Mills is absolutely stunning. Drop-dead gorgeous. The
most beautiful girl I've ever laid eyes on, and now I hate my brother

122

even more. If he deserves any bird, it's that Roberts slut. She seems like karma. Reeve Lancaster does not deserve a girl like Vivien. She's far too good for him.

My finger traces over the image of Vivien's gorgeous face on her most recent post. She's laughing alongside a pretty girl with long red hair and vibrant green eyes. Vivien doesn't appear to be wearing much makeup, and she's dressed in skinny ripped jeans and an off-the-shoulder shirt. Glossy dark hair tumbles over her shoulders and down her back. She seems rather unassuming for a Hollywood princess. Her eyes are magnetic. Big and wide, they are framed by thick black lashes with golden flecks shimmering amidst warm honey-colored irises. They draw me in and steal all the breath from my lungs. I stare at her picture for way too long, noting every detail of her perfection and hating my twin with every molecule of my being.

Outwardly, Vivien looks happy, but behind her smile and laughing eyes I detect a hint of pain. Perhaps it's because I can relate to it so well, but all is not as perfect as it first seems. It intrigues me—*she* intrigues me—and I spend hours searching through her posts and everything I can find about her online.

When I fall asleep that night, I'm not dreaming about the voluptuous blonde I banged earlier, I'm dreaming about the fresh-faced L.A. beauty who seems to have captured my twin's heart.

Chapter Seventeen
Age 19 to 20

"That's the last box," I say, dumping it on the counter in Ash's compact studio flat. The gaff is freshly painted and clean, but the furniture is dated, and the olive-green bathroom and blue kitchen cupboards look like a throwback to the eighties. My sister is on a tight budget, and she's lucky she found this place. It's cheap and only a few minutes' walk from our place, so that's all that matters.

"Thanks for helping me move in." She wraps her arms around me, and I lean into her embrace. Her head doesn't even reach my chest these days, and it only makes me more protective of her.

"Are you sure you want to do this, Aisling?" Ma asks from her perch on the sofa. Her hands are curled around a mug, and there's a plate of biscuits on the coffee table in front of her.

Da borrowed a van from his brother to transport Ash's stuff from home. Ma traveled with Da while Ash came with me on the bike.

"For the umpteenth time, yes. Stop worrying, Ma." Ash releases me and moves over to sit beside our mother.

"That's an impossibility. I'll never stop worrying even when you're married with your own kids or when you're old and gray. You'll always be my babies." She hugs Ash while smiling at me.

She often says that, and I know she means it. Ma loves something fierce. The usual knot tightens in my gut as my chest swarms with love. I wish I could tell her how much she means to me, but I'm still all twisted up on the inside and still battling the same demons I've been fighting for most of my life.

"We should make tracks, Cath," Da says over his shoulder as he washes his hands in the kitchen sink. "I'd like to make it back before we hit rush-hour traffic."

"I'm not sure I can leave you." Ma's eyes fill with tears as she clings to Ash. "I only have one baby at home now, and he can't wait to leave either."

"Don't take it too personally. It's just hard for Ro to still be in school and not living with the rest of the band," I say.

Aaron moved abroad with his family a few months ago. His sister is very ill, and she's getting treatment overseas. He didn't want to leave the band, especially now we are establishing a name for ourselves on the Dublin indie scene, but given the circumstances, he didn't want to be thousands of miles away should anything happen. It was understandable, and we didn't mind too much because Ro has been bending my ear for years about joining Toxic Gods and we knew we had a fully trained replacement already waiting in the wings.

To be honest, the vibe is better with Ro as our drummer. It feels like this is always how Toxic Gods was meant to be. It also means Jay and I now have our own bedrooms. I love Jamie like a brother, but he's a messy fucker, and while we often tag team girls, banging birds together all the time was getting old. Having a private space to fuck girls makes life easier even if I still kick most of them out after we're done. I don't like waking up with random girls in my bed.

We bought a sofa bed for the sitting room, and Ro sleeps there at weekends after we play our regular gigs at Whelans and Bruxelles. Both pubs are big venues on the indie rock scene in Dublin, and we have amassed a hardcore following who show up for us week in and week out.

After Ro sits his Leaving Cert next summer, we plan to look for a four-bed townhouse in Inchicore or Drumcondra. It won't be as central as our current place, but any four-bed gaffs in the city are way out of our price range. If we live a little farther out, we can get around . on our bikes or use public transport.

Uncle Eamonn gave us his van when he bought a new one. He could have traded it in, but he knew we needed a van to transport our equipment to and from gigs, and he kindly offered it to us. My uncle is a legend, and we owe him one. Usually, we pay a guy to drive the van back home after every gig so we can stay and party.

"Be happy our children want to be independent," Da says, yanking me out of the inner monologue in my head. He dries his hands down the front of his black cargo pants because Ash hasn't unpacked any towels yet.

"Plus, we don't live a million miles away," Ash reminds her, shucking out of Ma's hold.

"And we come to Sunday dinner at least once a month," I add. I made Ma a promise a year ago when we moved out, and I've kept it.

"I know I'm being silly," she says, standing. "I can't help worrying, and I miss you." She sniffles, and Da pulls her into his arms. "I don't know what I'll do with myself when Ronan leaves and we have an empty nest."

"You have Chloe to keep you busy," I say. "And I'm sure Fi and Shane will give you lots more babies once they get married." My oldest brother is now engaged to his longtime girlfriend, and they're planning their wedding for next summer.

"Ciarán will probably propose to Susie soon and I bet they'll give you more grandkids too," Ash supplies. "Just don't go counting on me. I'm still sworn off relationships."

"Or me," I say. "I have zero plans to ever get married or have kids."

"You might want to change your promiscuous lifestyle then." Ash arches a brow, and I flash her a warning look to quit it. The less Ma knows about the stuff I get up to, the better.

"On that note, we'll go home." Ma hugs us one at a time. "Don't be strangers. Love you." She kisses my cheek. "Watch over your sister, Dillon. Make sure she's safe."

"Always, Ma." She doesn't see Ash rolling her eyes behind her back.

"Don't forget we're only a phone call away if either of you need anything," Da says, slapping me on the back.

"Let me know if you need any more money," he tells Ash as he hugs her.

"I'll be grand, Da. You and Dil have done enough for me already."

I gave Ash half the money for her deposit, and my parents gave her the rest. She worked part-time in Centra Kilcoole while in first year, and she worked full-time this summer to save money for moving to the city. Our parents are paying her college fees, but she buys all her own books and materials. She managed to get a part-time job in Centra on Dame Street, which is only a few minutes' walk from Trinners and not too far from her flat either. I told her I'll help out where I can, though I don't have a lot of spare cash. Any extra money we make is going into a savings account for paying for a recording studio.

"Do you need help unpacking?" I ask after our parents have left.

"Nah. I'll manage. I know your shift starts in a few hours. Go home and rest." Her face sours.

"What's that look for?"

"Nothing." She starts unloading the box on the kitchen counter.

"Ash."

She sighs. "Is Aoife living at your place now?" She nibbles on her lip as she removes items from the box, looking everywhere but at me.

"No. Why'd you ask?"

We met Aoife at Whelans a couple months ago. She's one of a number of girls who follow us around, eager to fuck us. Unlike the other girls, she's chill, and we decided we'd appoint her as our regular band bird. Feels a little crass thinking that, but she's fucked me, Jay, and Conor, on several occasions, so if the cap fits... There is no shortage of pussy if we want it, but having regular pussy on tap has its advantages, so we're trying this out.

Ash shrugs, but her shoulders are corded into muscles, and she's not fooling me. "She just seems to always be there lately."

I think I know what this is about. She's jealous Aoife is sleeping with Jamie. I have a suspicion that something happened this summer between my sister and my best mate. I have no proof. It's just a gut feeling. When I asked Jay, I'm pretty sure he lied to my face. I used it as an opportunity to warn him to keep his fucking hands off my sister.

After Cillian, I'm extra protective of my only sister. She's fucked a few blokes at college, but I always make sure they know I'll rearrange their insides and their faces if they hurt her. Ash doesn't seem interested in getting serious with anyone. She appears happy to just have casual sex, and I'm okay with it. Less chance of her being betrayed that way. Ash needs to find a nice, decent guy when she's ready to commit to a relationship again. The last thing she needs is a hound like Jamie Fleming. And I'm not being hypocritical. I'm as much of a slut as he is. I just don't want that kind of guy for my sister even if he is one of the best guys I know.

Anyway, if something was going on between them, it's definitely not now. Jay has been with several girls these past couple weeks, including Aoife. Ash is back to constantly bitching about him, and my mate goes out of his way to avoid her. It's for the best. Jamie is not the man for my sister. End of.

"She's not moving in, but she's convenient pussy," I explain. "She doesn't mind us sharing her, and she's not looking for anything but sex."

"If you truly believe that, you're an idiot. That slut has gold digger written all over her."

"Hey now. You were the one who gave me a big fucking lecture about not referring to women who sleep around as sluts."

"That's different." She empties the box and begins flattening it. "I was talking about equality. Girls like Aoife have an agenda. They use sex for manipulation and self-gain. Those girls are sluts in my opinion. Girls who have regular consensual sex, with one or more guys, for pleasure's sake, are not sluts. They're embracing their sexuality and exploring it in a safe way with no ill intent. They're no different to you or Jamie or Conor." Her face pales. "Or Ro, I guess. Ugh." She rubs at her chest. "I still can't believe our little brother is having sex. I used to watch him getting his nappy changed and feed him his bottles. It feels so wrong."

A chuckle rumbles from my chest. "If it's any consolation, the groupie scene is not really his scene." I've never had a girlfriend, but my little brother has been in regular relationships since he was fourteen. He's a right little Casanova. He's had a few one-night stands too, but I'm not telling Ash he's reaping the benefits of being in the band. She's already traumatized enough.

"Fact. He's a total charmer, and the girls only love him for it." She folds her arms and leans back against the fridge. "Keep Aoife away from him, Dil. I don't trust her, and Ronan is still only seventeen."

He's almost eighteen and way more mature than I was at that age, but I know Ash's concern comes from a good place. "I don't think he's interested anyway, but I'll make sure she stays away from him."

"Happy birthday, birthday boy!" My bed bounces as Ash jumps on it waking me from a deep sleep.

I don't know what time it is, but I bet it's way too early. It was after five before I crashed, and I had plans to sleep most of the day away. "Go away." I pull the covers over my head, but my sister is not to be deterred.

She yanks the covers back down. "No. We're going out to celebrate your birthday whether you like it or not."

"Hard pass." I scrub at my eyes and turn flat on my back. "You know I don't give a crap about my birthday, and it's not like this is a special one."

"You're twenty, Dil. You're no longer a teenager. That makes it special. Besides, you wouldn't let me do anything last year, so you owe me."

"It's my birthday, but somehow, I owe you? Fuck my life." I scrub my hands down my face.

"Open your present." She places a gift-wrapped parcel on my chest.

"Ash. I said no presents." I know she doesn't have much spare cash, and I'm not lying when I say I don't want to acknowledge my birthday. It's not anything to celebrate. All it does is make me think of that self-serving, smug prick of a twin. He's Hollywood's current golden boy, and I can't open up the internet, turn on the TV, or walk past a newsstand without seeing his annoying face.

Simon still texts me threats, but they are less frequent. His precious son is a big star now, and his rejected one hasn't outed the secret, so he's probably not too concerned anymore. Which is just the way I want it to be. Lull him into a false sense of security, and when he least expects it, I'll drop the bomb and ruin them both. I still haven't worked out the how, but they say patience is rewarded, so I'll bide my time.

"It's your birthday, Dil. Everyone deserves presents on their birthday." I don't tell her the threesome I had with two busty redheads last night is all the present I need because I can imagine how that news would go down.

Ash is proper into Toxic Gods again, and she comes to all our shows, which means she has a front row seat to Groupieville and Depravity Land. To say she's unhappy is an understatement. She's been nagging me to find a girl outside the scene to settle down with, but it'll never happen. I'm happy with the way things are and see no reason to change it.

Sitting up against the headboard, I tear the paper open, grinning as I examine the small bag of branded guitar picks. "These are cool." I tip the custom picks into my hand and examine them in more detail. They're red and black, and the skull design has a serpent crawling through the eyes and the words TOXIC GODS scrawled over the emblem. "Thanks, sis. I love the design."

"It's still not right, but I saw a shop on Etsy that did custom picks, and I couldn't resist ordering you some." She pulls her legs up onto the bed. "I got more picks for the others. I knew the assholes would only steal yours if I didn't."

"That was thoughtful. They'll love them."

"I still think you should've changed your name. You guys are really fucking good, and I have a real good feeling about the band."

She's starting to sound like Ro, and I wonder if he's asked her to put some pressure on me. He's so hyper and already planning world domination. I'd be happy if we could produce our own albums and sell them within Ireland and maybe play gigs up and down the country. We'd make a comfortable living, and it's achievable with a little effort. "I don't think Toxic Gods does you justice," she adds.

"You sound like a nagging wife," I joke as I slip my finger under the sealing on the envelope which was the other item in the gift. "And our fans love the name." I eyeball her. "It's staying."

Ash watches me remove the item from the envelope with barely contained excitement. "No way, Ash." My eyes are out on stalks as I look at the Longitude ticket. It's a massive event staged every summer in Marley Park, featuring a ton of bands and some big names. "This is too much. How'd you even afford it?"

"You know I worked a few extra shifts over Christmas and New Year's, so I had extra money."

"You should be keeping that for yourself." I lean in and hug her. "Thanks, Ash."

"Ugh. Get off." She pushes me away. "You smell like beer, tacky perfume, and regret."

I chuckle as I set my gifts on the bedside locker. "Trust me, I have no regrets." I flash her a wide-lipped grin. "Tania and Rosanna were the perfect way to say goodbye to my teens."

"Gross. It's like you're incapable of sleeping with just one woman."

That's not true at all, but I don't feel like correcting her.

Ash hops up off the bed, scowling at it like it just bit her in the ass. "I probably caught something sitting there."

Laugher rumbles my chest. "I keep my room clean, and I regularly wash my sheets. You didn't catch anything."

"Hope you wash your dick too."

"I'm always double bagged, sis."

She covers her face with her hands, mumbling, "TMI, Dillon."

"You started it." I smirk.

"And I'm ending it." She plants her hands on her hips and fixes me with her no-bullshit look. "Get showered and changed. We're all going for wings. Your lunch is my treat. By the way, the guys have tickets for Longitude, and I have one as well. We're all going together."

"Can't wait." It's months away yet but definitely something to look forward to. It's a nonstop three-day-long session, and I'm already on a countdown.

"Oh, and Dil," she says, lingering in my doorway as I fling the covers off my body. I look up. "Aoife is not invited."

"Fine by me." Despite what Ash thinks, we are not glued at the hip to Aoife. She's around a lot at the weekends when we play gigs and have parties, but I don't tend to see much of her during the week. I have been working some temporary shifts behind the bar at Whelans at night, to earn extra cash, and during the day when I'm home practicing and writing lyrics, she's at work in Dunnes. Jamie meets up with her a few lunchtimes, and he fucks her the most.

To be honest, she's becoming a little too clingy for my liking, and I don't like the superior attitude she throws around sometimes with other girls. I've told the lads if she keeps it up, she's out. I think Ash may have hit the nail on the head last September and she has an agenda. "Will I get to meet the Yank?" I yawn as I stand, stretching my arms up over my head.

"I asked Grace, but she's not feeling great today, so she passed. I think she's a little shy, but I'm sure you'll get to meet her soon."

Part Two
IN MY VIVIEN ERA

Chapter Eighteen

Age 20

"She's fucking gorgeous," Jamie says to Ronan as I return to our usual table in Whelans with fresh beers. Aoife scowls and scoots in closer to Jay's side.

"Who is?" I ask, setting the tray with the drinks down on the table before sinking into a chair.

"The Yank," Jay replies.

"Is she here?" I ask, sitting up straighter and looking around the crowded bar for any sign of my pint-sized feisty sister and her new sidekick. I'll admit I'm curious. Ash hasn't shut up about Grace since they met at Trinners.

"Not yet," Ro says, staring at his phone. "They are on their way."

"I bumped into them in The Buttery during the week," Jay supplies. I'm surprised this is the first time he's mentioned it.

"She's not that gorgeous," Aoife pipes up, sulking and scowling because the risk of competition threatens her perceived position within the band.

She hasn't gotten the memo yet that her place is temporary. It's not like any of us would settle down with a girl who openly shares herself among us. I'm not judging her. I think it's cool she owns her sexuality, and I love she's down for anything, but she's not exactly girlfriend material.

Not that I ever want one of those.

Love is for pussies and fools.

"Do I detect a hint of the green-eyed monster?" Ro asks, grinning before he knocks back his beer.

Jay slides his arm around Aoife's shoulders. "I didn't say I was going to bang her. Just acknowledging she's a real looker."

"Depends on your taste," Aoife replies through tight lips and gritted teeth.

Her attitude is starting to grate on my nerves. I was fine to keep her around when she seemed satisfied with casual sex, but she's getting needy, and I'm thinking the time to cut her loose may be approaching.

I can't stand clingy women. Especially when we have always been up front with her. We told her it would never be more than sex, and she agreed.

I stand, deciding to check things with Ron before our set, to ensure everything is in hand, rather than sit here with the pouting possessive groupie now climbing into Jay's lap.

"Hey, Dillon." A vaguely familiar brunette sidles up to me, brushing her hand against my chest. "It's been a while."

Aoife shoots daggers at the woman as she pushes her tits into my chest, and I'm not having this.

"It has," I lie because I have no fucking clue who this girl is, but I'll go along with it. I think it's time Aoife learned a valuable lesson. "What's up?"

"Hopefully you." A seductive smile graces her full lips as she discreetly slips her hand in the gap between our bodies and palms my cock through my jeans.

"Is that an offer?" I flash her a smile all the ladies love, inwardly chuckling as her eyes pop wide, her cheeks flush, and her lips part with longing.

She snaps out of it fast. "Absolutely." Her smile expands as she gently squeezes my hardening dick.

"It'll have to be quick. We're on soon," I say, grabbing her hand and pulling her with me as I force my way through the crowd, heading for the staff door at the rear of the main room.

———

"Thanks for the blowjob," I say fifteen minutes later as I lead the girl out from the back into the main area of the pub. Still don't know her name, and I have no interest in learning it. It was a pretty shit effort, but at least I got to blow off some steam before we go on stage. I kiss her quickly. "See you around," I say, pretending I don't notice how her pretty face twists into a frown as I walk away.

I'm an asshole. I readily admit it, but it's not like these women don't know what they're getting into. Everyone on the indie scene in Dublin knows I'm not into commitment.

I am making my way towards our table when the strangest sensation washes over me. All the hairs on the back of my neck stand to attention, and an electrical charge coasts along my skin. My heart picks up pace, thumping quicker, as butterflies swoop into my stomach.

What the fuck?

Then I see her. Standing beside Ash. The girls have their backs to me as they face a clearly excited Ronan. He's still seated, staring up at the Yank as if the sun shines out of her arse. I roll my eyes. My little brother is so obvious. He knows it and refuses to change. He wears his heart on his sleeve and carries lust in his eyes without shielding it from the object of his affection. He rotates through girls almost as fast as me. Unlike me, he likes having a girlfriend, and he usually has a different one every month. He falls in and out of love as fast and as often as Taylor Swift.

I hang back on purpose, drinking Ash's new friend in, wondering if she's the source of my weird reaction. Her dark hair hangs in waves down her back, looking shiny and thick and perfect to wrap around my fist if we were fucking. She's tall, even accounting for the added height from her black and gold stilettos, making Ash appear even smaller than her five feet three inches. I can't see much of her body as she's got a coat on, but the ripped black jeans she's wearing are molded to slender legs I already know would look good wrapped around my head. My dick perks to life as I walk towards them, wanting an introduction.

Ash already warned us off her new best friend, and while I probably should keep it in my pants, I suspect that's going to be problematic. "If it isn't my favorite sister," I say from behind Ash, cutting across the conversation she's having with Grace, Cat, and Ro. "About time you showed up."

Ash whirls around and smacks me in the upper arm while her friend remains oddly rooted in place. "I'm your only sister, clown, and that joke's getting real old."

"Is this the Yank?" I ask, wanting to get a look at her face. If Jay says she's gorgeous, she must be. He's a fussy fucker, and he only likes 'em pretty.

Ash thumps me again. "Be nice, Dillon," she warns as Grace slowly turns around.

Shock renders me mute when our eyes lock and I get a look at her face.

No. Fucking. Way.

She's gorgeous all right. Even more so in the flesh. With her flawless skin, expressive big hazel eyes framed by long thick black lashes, perfect nose, high cheekbones, and fuckable lips, she is smoking hot. My fantasy woman in more ways than one. The pictures I have seen of her online have not done her justice at all.

She is definitely the most beautiful woman I have ever laid eyes on.

That weird electric current I felt a few minutes ago pulses and strains in the small gap between our bodies as we stare at one another.

I'm guessing shock is registering on my face when I spot the panic in her eyes.

Interesting. Does she suspect I know who she is? Or is there a more sinister reason for her reaction. My eyes narrow, and admiration gives way to anger as I think about why she is here and whether her meeting my sister is a coincidence.

That fucking asshole Lancaster.

I grind my teeth to the molars and clench my fists at my sides as I consider the very real possibility this is a setup.

Every few months, that asshole who spawned me reaches out, reminding me of the offer he made. It's not like I've forgotten. That meeting with him when I was seventeen is imprinted in my brain, no matter how badly I wish I could scrub it away. The contract resides in a secure hiding place at the back of my wardrobe. Not sure why I don't just rip that shit into pieces, but my gut tells me to hold on to it. It's a decent amount of money, but I refuse to give the sperm donor or my brother what they want.

Fuck them both.

Let them stress over it.

I have zero desire right now to let anyone know Hollywood's new golden boy is my twin. I don't want that kind of attention. But they don't know that, and I'll use it to my advantage. There may come a time when I need that ammunition, and I'm keeping my options open.

Besides, I don't want that prick's money. He can shove it up his pompous arse and choke on it.

A muscle clenches in my jaw, and Vivien Mills, my twin's precious girlfriend, takes a step back, fear and confusion clouding those stunning greenish-brown eyes. The table rattles, and some of the drinks spill.

"Watch it," Jamie snarls, drilling her with a look. "Or the next round's on you."

"Stop complaining," Ash says to Jay while yanking on my arm. "A little drink got spilled. Big deal."

Why is she here? And why is she masquerading as someone else? Did Simon put her up to this? Is that why she looks so terrified? Is she afraid I have already figured out who she is? If she thinks she's going to influence me into signing that contract, she can think again. And if she thinks she's going to use my sister to get to me, I will fucking ruin her. Fuck the freaky connection simmering between us, and I don't care how gorgeous she is. No one gets to hurt my sister. That shit will never happen again on my watch.

The skin on my knuckles blanches white I'm clenching my hands so tight. I glare at her, pouring all my venom into the look so she gets the message loud and clear. If Vivien is here to cause trouble, I'll be the one bringing it to her. The Lancasters will rue the day they tried to manipulate me. If she's a part of whatever game they are now playing, I won't hesitate to take her down too.

What if she is here to spy on me? To report back to Simon on whether I'm being a good boy and keeping the news of my bio family to myself?

Ro gets up and shoves me a little, leveling me with a warning look. "You're being rude."

Ash snorts. "Are you even surprised?"

"I'm Ronan," my brother says, smiling at the spy with stars in his eyes. "Ash and Dillon's brother, but please don't hold that against me."

"Grace." She smiles back at him, and a snarl builds at the back of my throat. "Nice to meet you."

I'm not buying this sugary-sweet act. Not for a single second do I think she is being genuine. Reeve Lancaster's bitch doesn't randomly show up in Dublin. That girl's got an agenda, and I need to figure out what it is ASAP. I sharpen my eyes and drill her with a lethal look that usually has grown men shitting their pants. "Why are you here, *Grace*?" I hiss, trying and failing to rein my hostility in. I'm sure it's projecting from me in waves, but I don't care. Let her see I'm onto her.

She thrusts her shoulders out, brazenly staring me in the eyes, and I'll give her some credit for that. "Ash invited me." Her husky voice is confident and alluring, and it's doing strange things to my insides.

It only makes me hate her more.

"In Ireland," I add in a clipped tone. Bitch knows what I mean, and if she wants to play this game, I'm more than up for the challenge.

Her brow puckers. "What does it matter why I'm here?"

"Just answer the question," I snap, my eyes briefly flickering around the space, wondering if her jerk of a boyfriend is here too. Then I remember he's promoting his new movie in the US, and it's most likely she is here alone.

She squares up to me, narrowing her eyes. "I don't owe you any explanation, and is this how you always treat new people you meet?"

"I'm suspicious of anyone who comes into my sister's life." I lean down, putting my face all up in hers, trying to ignore how utterly exquisite she is up close. "Especially nosy Americans." If that doesn't make it clear, I don't know what will.

"Wow. Generalize much?" She crosses her arms over her gorgeous rack and glowers at me like I'm the devil.

Close, sweetheart. Real close.

"You're pissing me off now, Dil." Ash's nails bite into my arm as she yanks me away from her friend.

"Fact." Ro nods.

"What's going on?" Aoife asks.

I wondered how long it would take her to interject herself into the conversation. I knew her anger at me for disappearing with a girl who wasn't her wouldn't last long. "Nothing." My jaw is tense as I circle my arm around Aoife's shoulders before dropping into the empty seat bedside Jamie and situating her on my lap.

Aoife babbles shit in my ear as she feels me up, but I'm not paying her any attention. My gaze is laser-focused on the American spy. I tune my surroundings out as I try to figure out why she is here. Ash evidently doesn't know her true identity. Rage spikes in my blood.

143

How fucking dare she try to pull the wool over my sister's eyes? What the fuck has Ash ever done to her?

I snap out of my angry haze as Vivien removes her coat and scarf, exposing a revealing outfit. My dick hardens as my gaze roams over the figure-hugging jeans that showcase her slim legs and shapely arse to perfection. She's wearing a sheer black lace top that exposes her bra and a sliver of tantalizing tanned skin.

Straightening up, she turns around and fixes me with a heated stare. My eyes drink her in as if she isn't the enemy.

Fucking hell.

She is sex on legs.

Her bra is fully on display underneath the risqué lacy top, leaving little to the imagination. Her chest heaves under the underwired cups as we stare at one another. My gaze dips lower, over her flat stomach, toned waist, and the soft curves of her hips. I hate my bio brother, for many reasons, but I've got to begrudgingly admire his taste in women because Vivien Mills is a bona fide knockout.

Every guy within our vicinity is looking at her with lust in their eyes, and my little brother is about to bust a nut in his pants.

Aoife's arms tighten around my neck, like a choke hold, and I feel the hatred oozing from her pores. Aoife isn't the smartest chick on the block, but she's not dumb either. She knows competition when she sees it, and she won't like this girl one little bit.

I may be able to use that to my advantage.

"Wow. You're beautiful," Ro says because he has no chill. His words break whatever shit was going down between Vivien and me, and she ends our stare, looking away and smiling at my brother.

I tune them out, focusing my attention on Jay and Conor. The latter looks as disinterested as ever, and I wonder how long it will take him to nuke all his brain cells with weed. I don't know if the guy is ever sober. Not that I care. As long as he gets up on that stage and performs, I couldn't give two shits if he's stoned or drunk.

"Told you," Jamie says, waggling his brows and grinning. "Sexy, feisty, and her tits are the real deal."

Dillon

Aoife is peppering kisses along my neck as she grinds against the semi in my jeans, thinking it's all for her. I actually wish it was. I don't want to get hard for the Yank. She is the enemy, and I need to find a way of conveying that to my sister without admitting the truth. No one knows who my bio dad and brother are, and it's going to stay that way.

Whatever the reason behind Vivien Mills' relocation to Ireland, she is not going to succeed.

Hell will freeze over before I let Simon and Reeve Lancaster trample all over me.

If they are using her to achieve their goal, they are going to regret it.

I'll send their precious princess back to L.A. a broken shell of a woman, and they'll wish they never crossed me.

Chapter Nineteen

Age 20

"**S**top." Aoife's blonde head pauses mid-suck when I speak, and she stares up at me with bits of drool clinging to the corners of her mouth. "I'm not in the mood tonight."

She releases my dick with a loud pop, and I tuck my flaccid length back in my boxers and zip up my jeans. "What's wrong? You love my blowjobs."

She's acting like she's the fucking blowjob queen when she's average at best. Aoife still doesn't get her best talent is her convenience and availability. She's nothing special in the sack. "I'm not feeling it tonight," I lie. Truth is, I'm fixated on a different woman, and Aoife's touch feels all wrong.

She purses her lips before whipping her top off and sliding her bra straps down her arms, exposing her boobs and hard nipples. "Play with my tits while I grind on top of you. Bet that'll do the trick." She climbs eagerly into my lap and smushes her tits in my face.

It irritates the fuck out of me. I have zero interest in touching her right now. Or maybe ever. Everything about her is all wrong. "I said I'm not in the mood," I snap. "Go fuck Jamie or Conor." Lifting her off my lap, I set her feet on the ground and look away as she fixes herself.

"Did I do something wrong, Dillon?"

Her eyes glisten with unshed tears when I lift my gaze to meet hers. Fuck, I hate when girls cry. I purposely dial down my irritation. "No, babe. I've just got a lot on my mind."

"You haven't fucked me in weeks."

"And?" I narrow my eyes and silently count to ten.

"I miss you. You fuck me real good, Dillon, and I need your cock inside me."

Irritation flares again, and it's an effort not to lash out. I just want her to go. How difficult is that to understand? I shouldn't have to repeat myself. "Not tonight, Aoife. I've got shit to do."

Snagging my laptop from the top of my dresser, I sit down against the headboard, stretch my legs out on top of my duvet, and pop the lid up. Top of my priority list is researching the current status quo between Vivien *Grace* Mills and Reeve Lancaster. I haven't looked online the past few weeks as it's been crazy busy between Christmas and New Year's, and I stayed in Kilcoole until a couple days ago to help Dad and Shane finish building the new greenhouses for the flower farm.

From the instant I met Vivien in the flesh earlier tonight, she is all I can think about. I need to know what agenda she has. To find out if Reeve or Simon sent her here to spy on me. Her annoyingly stunning face resurrects in my mind, and my cock jerks a little in my boxers, proving it's still in working order. Guess Aoife just isn't doing it for me anymore.

"She won't be interested in you, Dil. Don't bother wasting your time." Aoife's sharp tone claims my attention and yanks me back to the moment. I lift my head. Her hands are planted on her hips, and the vulnerable teary look from a minute ago has been replaced by a superior, challenging expression.

"I don't know what the fuck you're talking about."

"The Yank." She spits out the words like they're poison. "She's so far up her own arse she can't see anything else. I know her type. She only dates rich pricks who can buy her expensive things," she scoffs. "You can't afford her, Dil. Besides, she wouldn't slum it with you, no matter how gorgeous you are, so you should get that idea out of your head, she's—"

"Jealousy is not a good look on you, Aoife," I say in a cold tone, cutting across her. "Neither is sounding like a pissed-off girlfriend. You're a convenient hole to fuck when no other pussy takes my fancy. That's it." Who the fuck does she think she is spouting that shit at me? I have been nothing but completely honest with her from the very start, and this bullshit is the very reason I'm anti-girlfriend. "If this arrangement no longer works for you, I'll talk to the lads, and we can part ways."

"Don't do that," she blurts, widening her eyes. Panic is clear in her tone. "I'm happy with how things are. I just don't want to see you get hurt. Girls like her—"

"Get the fuck out of my room, Aoife." I glare at her. "Now," I add when she still hasn't moved.

"I'm sorry, Dil." Tears well in her eyes, and I'm so done with her theatrics. "I'm just looking out for you."

"Get out!" I roar. "Get the fuck out and stay out."

She scurries out of the room, slamming the door behind her, and I can finally breathe. I tap out a message to Jay telling him to keep her away from me, and then I go down the Viv-Reeve rabbit hole.

A couple of hours later, I'm thoroughly confused. I have missed a lot of drama in my twin's life recently, most notably how he very publicly cheated on his long-term girlfriend with Saffron Roberts. Ha! I could've called that years ago. Told you she was karma. The news broke on Christmas Day when E-News ran a video showing Reeve in a very passionate lip-lock with his slutty costar at a Boston club. They had their hands all over one another, and he was devouring her mouth like a starving man. It isn't a good look for a guy who's supposedly in love with his childhood sweetheart.

Reddit was a great source of intel, and it seems a few months previously a video taken at a college frat party was shared online, showing Vivien Mills dancing provocatively with men who were not my twin. Gotta say, that shocked me. Didn't think she had it in her.

While the video has officially been removed from everywhere, I messaged one of the Reddit users who had a copy, and she sent it to me. Vivien's drunken, teary-eyed confession to whomever took the video was cringeworthy in the extreme. She isn't shown in the best light, but I'm guessing it's been doctored to make it so. I actually felt a little sorry for her while watching it, and I wonder if that video is the reason she was attacked in December.

Pictures of my twin wheeling her out of hospital firmly reminded me she's the enemy. What I don't get is why she's in Ireland. Is she that pathetic she'd forgive Reeve so easily for humiliating her in front of the entire world? Did she cheat first that night at the frat party and Reeve was given a free pass? Or has she done something worse and this is her way of making it up to him? Or maybe it's none of the above and she is here because she wanted to get away from him and the circus that seems to follow him everywhere he goes?

I don't know, and I can't tell if she's here to spy on me or if it's a complete coincidence. But how likely is that? It doesn't seem plausible, which brings me back to my spying theory. Well, two can play that game, and it's time she had a taste of her own medicine.

Dillon

In the few weeks that follow, I put my sleuthing hat on and shadow Vivien any chance I get. It's not difficult because she leads a pretty boring life, only venturing out to attend classes at Trinners, go shopping, or go for a walk. The rest of her time is spent at her swanky apartment overlooking The Liffey. Sometimes, I see her through the window of the downstairs gym, pounding away on the treadmill, looking a million miles away with the saddest expression on her face.

I'm a few paces behind her as she walks down Grafton Street, using the throng of Saturday morning shoppers to hide me. She emerged from M&S a short while ago with a bag of food in one hand and a bunch of flowers in the other, heading in the direction of her apartment. I know Ro and Ash are going to her gaff for lunch today, so she's obviously getting supplies in.

Her feet falter as she passes a newsstand. She moves in closer, reading something, and I hang back, leaning against a wall beside a shop front, straining my head to see what's captured her attention. I risk moving a little closer, pulling my hoodie up over my head to hide my distinctive hair.

I'm close enough to hear the painful sob she emits before she takes off, rejoining the flow of foot traffic. I quickly read the magazine headline as I walk past: REEVE AND SAFFRON ARE DATING!

I'm lost in thought as I rush to catch up with her. If she's upset because of that headline, does it mean they have broken up and she came here to escape him and all the drama? Or has she figured out I've been following her and it's a deliberate ruse to lead me off the scent? Except, if she was sent here to spy on me, wouldn't she be the one following *me* around? Wouldn't she actually be working out ways to spend time with me instead of avoiding me? Ash says she has refused to return to Whelans and the only time she socializes with them is Thursday nights when I'm not around.

I'm still confused and getting more irritated by the minute. I can't believe her showing up in Dublin and befriending my sister wasn't part of some elaborate plan. It's way too much of a coincidence to be true.

Up ahead, Viv darts into a side street at the bottom of Grafton Street, and I shove people out of my way so I don't lose her. When I round the corner, I almost have a heart attack on the spot as I narrowly avoid colliding with her. She's stopped in front of a shop on the quieter street, with her bags and the bunch of flowers at her feet, and her face is buried in her hands while she quietly cries. Every sob feels like a dagger sliding between my ribs. Briefly, I consider stopping, but I force my feet to keep moving because she can't discover I've been trailing her around town all morning. It takes effort to walk away when every instinct urges me to bundle her in my arms and comfort her.

It's a troubling thought, one that keeps my feet moving forwards. Screw following her the rest of the way home. She's not likely to detour, and I've got band practice in ninety minutes. I risk a quick glance over my shoulder when I hit the end of the street, needing to check she's okay before I leave. A tightness spreads over my chest as I watch her frantically swiping the tears rolling down her face while she tries to reassure the older couple standing in front of her that she's all right.

My mind is heavy on the walk back to Temple Bar. I don't know what to think about Vivien Mills. I don't think she was acting back there. I don't think she has worked out I've been following her. So, does it mean she's no longer with him and her showing up here *is* pure coincidence? I still struggle to accept that. The only thing I know with certainty is she's occupying far too much space in my head, and maybe I need to just take a step back and let her make the next move.

"Hey, Dil," Aoife says when I enter our apartment, sashaying towards me wearing Jamie's shirt. It falls mid-thigh, covering the fact she's most likely bare underneath. It's too big on her, and it falls off one shoulder, revealing the swell of a tit. It does nothing for me. None of the girls hanging around us the past few weeks have done anything for me. Took a girl home the past two Friday nights and sent them packing shortly after. Couldn't get it up for either of them. It's embarrassing, and I didn't feel like repeating the experience last night, so I drove the van home after our set and went to bed sober for a change.

The only time I get hard these days is imagining Vivien Grace Mills on her knees sucking my cock. Or bending her over my bed and fucking her until she's screaming my name and creaming all over my dick. Or dragging her into the bathroom at Whelans and banging her senseless. It seems there's no limit to my fantasies when it comes to my twin's girl, and at this point, I've fucked her countless times, in multiple positions, and they all end with her squeezing the cum from my body until every last drop is gone.

I've got issues. I know.

"Dillon." Aoife's aggravation is transparent in her tone. Girl does not like being ignored.

Shaking all thoughts of Vivien from my mind, I offer her a tight smile. "Hey." Pushing past her, I open the fridge and remove the things I need to make a sandwich.

Sliding her arm along my back, she peers around the fridge door and eyeballs the four-pack of Heineken lying on the middle shelf. "The beer is a gift from me."

"Why are you buying me beer?" I ask, shucking out of her hold as I grab the lettuce and close the door with my butt. Aoife usually shows up empty-handed and spends the weekend drinking our beer and eating our food, so this is not the norm.

"It's a peace offering." She hops up on the counter beside where I lay my ingredients.

"I don't want anything from you." Not if it comes with conditions, which I suspect this does.

"See, that's the problem." She runs her bare foot up the side of my leg as I butter two slices of bread.

"Knock that shit off." There was a time I enjoyed her touch. But not now.

"Please, Dil." She slides off the counter, plastering her body to my side and pleading with her eyes. "Tell me what I can do to fix things."

"You're making a big deal out of nothing and crowding me while I'm trying to make a fucking sandwich doesn't help your case."

"Babe, come here." Jay saunters into the kitchen wearing track-suit bottoms and nothing else. "Let Dillon be." He whispers in her ear and swats her arse. Aoife turns to look at me before she disappears in the direction of the bedrooms.

"I'm getting a bit sick of her always being around," I admit as I slice tomatoes.

"What's up with that?" He leans against the counter and drills me with a look.

"I'm thinking she might have reached her best-before date."

Jay chuckles. "Harsh, mate."

I shrug. "She's getting too clingy for my liking."

"It's only 'cause you're not paying her any attention. Just bang her brains out, and she'll ease off."

"I have zero interest in fucking her." I add cheese and ham to my sandwich and cut it in half.

"Seems like you have zero interest in fucking anyone these days. What's the story?"

"Just haven't been feeling it." I fill the kettle with water to make tea.

"Does this have anything to do with the Yank?"

I swing my gaze to his as I switch the kettle on. "Why would you ask that?"

"I saw the way you were with her that night in Whelans. You couldn't keep your eyes off her. Even when you had your tongue down Aoife's throat, your eyes were following Grace."

Wow, Jay is far more observant than I've ever given him credit for. "I'm wary of her and watching out for my sister."

"If you say so."

He tosses me a smirk as I snag a mug from the overhead press. Ignoring him, I add a tea bag to the mug and pour in boiling water.

"That was the last time you fucked anyone, right? Aoife said you couldn't get it up that night. Then the next week, when we were doing her together, you walked off with a limp dick before we even got started. If you've got a thing for Grace, it's cool, mate. No need to hide it."

"The fuck?" I pin a savage glare on my best mate even though he's not the one I'm angry at. "Aoife needs to learn there's a time to open her mouth and a time to fucking shut it," I snap.

"She shouldn't have said anything, but she feels threatened by Grace."

"She's got to go," I hiss, dunking my spoon in the mug. "Either claim her as yours or tell her to fuck off. Conor hasn't screwed her in weeks, and I'm not fucking her again."

"I'm still having fun with her, but if she bothers you that much, I'll tell her to take a hike."

"Just keep her out of my way, Jay," I say, plating my sandwich. "Make sure she knows the score."

Chapter Twenty

Age 20

"Isn't it amazing?" Ash squeals as she bounces on her large new bed. "I'm still pinching myself I get to live somewhere like this for free!"

"Is it really free though?" I rake my gaze over the luxurious king bedroom with en suite bath as I try to ignore the pounding in my skull. We went at it hardcore last night, and we're all suffering today.

"Grace says I only have to pay for my food. Everything else is already paid for."

"Nothing in life is truly free. Bet she asks something of you."

Ash wallops me in the arm. "When did you get so cynical and so suspicious?" She folds her arms and glares at me. "Grace is my friend, and there is no big agenda. You need to quit giving me shit about her and quit treating her like a pariah. She's nice, Dillon. If you'd just stop acting like an overbearing oaf, you'd see that."

"You hardly know her, Ash."

"I know enough to know she's a good person, Dil. This arrangement works for her too. She's lonely living by herself. We're both getting something out of this."

"We'll see," I murmur. The jury is still very much out on the Yank.

"That's the last of them," Ro says, depositing a box heaving with books on the floor in front of the fitted white wardrobes. Conor trails in after him, placing his box on the desk. He drops onto the chair, straddling it backwards and staring off into space.

"Tell this one to stop raining on my parade, will ya?" Ash looks at Ro while jabbing her finger in my face. "He's putting me in a bad mood."

"He just needs to get laid." Ro smirks. "It's been a while."

"Shut up." Ash whacks Ro. "Dillon's gotten laid enough to last him a lifetime. A bit of abstinence never hurt anyone."

"Can everyone shut the fuck up about my sex life." I glare at my siblings.

"What sex life?" Jay quips, poking his head into the room. "Nuns have more sex than Dillon O'Donoghue these days." I flip him the bird, and he chuckles. "This place is sick, Ash," he adds, looking around.

My sister's expression is guarded as she glances at Jamie. Things don't appear to be as strained between them, but they are still acting a bit off around one another. "Yeah, I lucked out."

"So, when's the housewarming party?" Ro rubs his hands together and waggles his brows.

All the fine hairs lift on the back of my neck, and fiery tingles skate over my skin. That's how I know she's close. My body is reacting instinctively just like the first time I met her. What the hell is up with that? A foreign feeling spreads across my chest as my heart beats faster, slamming against my rib cage when I turn around and my gaze snares hers where she's leaning against the doorway.

Immediately, the room fades away, and it's like we're the only two people here. I'm acutely aware of every little puff that escapes her lush lips, every flutter of her eyelashes, and every subtle lift of her chest. Electricity charges the air between us and every nerve ending on my body is hyper alert as we stare at one another.

Dillon

Fuck me. She's so beautiful.

Air punches from my lungs as my breathing stutters, and I struggle to understand my visceral reaction to her. I've never felt like this with any girl before. *Ever.* The thumping behind my chest wall ramps up until my heart is thrashing about like it's as unhinged as I appear to be.

Vivien breaks eye contact first, and my surroundings come back with a resounding slap. A low grumble builds in my chest as she smiles at my brother. Ro hasn't shut up talking about her. That he likes her isn't in doubt, but I won't let him act on it. Whatever is going on with Vivien Mills, she will not be tangling my little brother up in it.

"I guess we can come up with something," she says, shrugging.

Her dark hair is pulled up in a high ponytail, and a few wispy strands have escaped, framing her stunning face. Her face is devoid of makeup, and she's only wearing leggings, an oversized T-shirt, and runners, yet she still steals all the air from my lungs. How is it possible for any woman to be so completely and utterly gorgeous? I cannot think of a single celebrity who outshines her.

Hanging back, I purposely keep quiet and subtly study her. There is no evidence of her meltdown from yesterday on her face. Her skin is flawless, her eyes bright and clear, her lips full and tempting. Amber flecks radiate from her eyes, which are more green than brown today. It's hidden well, but her heartache is still there, and it's like a punch in the gut.

It makes me uneasy.

Why do I care if she's hurting?

She should've known better than to get involved with someone like Reeve Lancaster.

That selfish asshole was always destined to hurt her.

He's incapable of thinking about anyone but himself.

Concern turns to disgust as I contemplate how weak she must be to have fallen for his shit for years. If she's hurting, it's her own fault for being too gullible.

Jay slings his arm around her shoulders and leers at her. "Make sure your favorite band is on the guest list, babe."

My glare is instantaneous, my growl trapped between my teeth as I fixate on how her tight body is pressed all up against my best mate's. My fingers twitch at my sides. He'd better remove his arm or...

Or what, fuckface?

Dragging my hands down my cheeks, I'm confused by my reaction to her. It's been over three weeks since I shared the same room as her, and I'm annoyed my body is already highly attuned to her presence. I don't want to be attracted to her, and I'm sick of thinking about her. Maybe Jay is right, and I just need to fuck this stupid fixation away.

The only good thing is my muse is back after a worrying hiatus, and I'm writing tons of new songs. Conor and I are going up Killiney Hill tomorrow night for a songwriting session.

"My favorite band is Coldplay, and I'm doubting they'd accept the invite." Vivien's breathy tone coils around my body like smoke and fire, heating my blood and sending delicious shivers cascading up and down my spine.

"We have a few Coldplay tracks on our set list," Ro confirms, edging closer to her. He shoots Jay some serious side-eye. "Dillon's voice gives me chills when we play 'God Put a Smile on Your Face.' Invite us, and maybe we'll play it for you." He flashes her a flirtatious grin, and I visualize tossing my brother out the window.

"I doubt the management company would be happy with a live band blaring rock music around the building," Ash says, grabbing my arm and trying to convey something with her eyes.

"Yeah, I don't want to risk getting kicked out." Vivien chews on the corner of her delectable mouth. "My mom went to a lot of trouble to get this place for me."

Spoken like a true Hollywood brat. A pampered princess who doesn't want for a single thing. This place must cost a fortune, and she's hasn't lifted a finger for it. Same as my twin. They get handed everything on a plate, and it makes me sick.

Dillon

"I'm out," I tell Ash through gritted teeth. "Call me if you need anything." Leaning down, I kiss her cheek and pull her into a quick hug.

"Be nice, Dil," she whispers. I draw an invisible halo over my head with my hand and purposely leave the apartment without acknowledging or speaking to Vivien Mills.

"Just let Aoife come," I say, shrugging as I finish my beer and slam the bottle down on our regular table at Whelans. We finished our set two hours ago, and now we're getting ready to leave for Ash and *Grace's* housewarming party. I'm already pretty locked, and I have to remind myself Vivien is using her middle name here so I don't slip up and give the game away.

"No." Ronan shakes his head. "Ash was insistent she wasn't invited. We can't offend Grace by disrespecting her wishes."

"It's fine, Dil." Aoife sidles up to me, preening and smiling because she thinks I'm going to bat for her. I only said it because it's obvious Vivien—*Grace*—really doesn't want her there, and I'm down to stir up some shit tonight. "I don't want to go to that prissy bitch's party anyway."

"You've changed your tune," Jay says quietly in my ear. "Thought you were done with Aoife?"

"I'm thinking she might still come in handy."

Jay chuckles. "You're an evil prick, O'Donoghue."

"Takes one to know one." I waggle my brows as someone wraps their arms around me from behind. Aoife instantly scowls, but that's no surprise. She hasn't been quick enough lately to hide her territorial ways.

"I'll come with you, Dillon." I have no clue who she is, though the whiny voice is vaguely familiar. From the way she's pawing at me, it's a safe bet she's someone I previously fucked, so maybe she'll do. Her

161

hands are all over me before she ducks under my arm, pushes her body flush against my front, and smiles up at me.

Ah, fuck. Now I know why I semi-recognized her voice. Breda gives off Grade-A clinger vibes, and I already fucked her a couple of months back, and the sex was shit. I don't go back for seconds, and I've been avoiding her for weeks, but she's a catty bitch, and I think she'll play her part perfectly, so I'll bend my own rules this one time. "Okay, let's go."

Aoife opens her mouth to object, but Jay shuts her up with a hard kiss. "We'll see ya tomorrow, babe." He grabs her arse in both hands and devours her mouth for a few beats before pulling back. "Make sure you get a taxi home. I'll talk to Mick outside and tell him to hold one for you."

Aoife isn't happy as we walk off, but she's not following, so she got the message.

I'm fighting Breda and her grabby hands off the entire taxi ride to Ash's new gaff, second-guessing my decision to invite her. Briefly, I consider ditching her when we get to the apartment building, but I'm not showing up without a bird on my arm, so I let her stay, hoping I don't end up regretting it.

The crowd cheers when we enter the packed living room, and we lap up the adoration like the smug assholes we are.

"Yay! You made it!" Ash squeals, rushing towards us.

My eyes dart around the room, looking for my sister's new roomie. Vivien is standing a few feet away, with her back to us, talking to some nerd wearing a jumper over a polo shirt and too-tight jeans. I bet his balls are constricted and sweating. Like, who the fuck wears that shit to a college party?

Slowly, Vivien turns around, and it's a miracle I don't fall flat on my arse. She looks incredible in a strapless lacy black and red top with ripped skinny black jeans and high heels. Fuck, her body is a work of art, and my hands are dying to explore every sinful curve. I suspect I'm being far too obvious. I've probably had one too many beers, and the joint we shared outside isn't helping either. But fuck it.

162

Dillon

I don't care if she notices I'm staring at her. She is so incredibly gorgeous, and I can't drag my eyes from her. My lips twitch as I tilt my head to one side and blatantly stare at her. Let's see how she reacts to my obvious attention.

Waves of lustrous dark hair tumble around her glistening bare shoulders. The golds and browns painted on her eyelids make her eyes seem bigger and wider. Her glossy red lips would look great wrapped around my dick. The instant that thought lands in my brain, all the blood in my body rushes south and my cock starts hardening. Breda has impeccable timing because she chooses that exact moment to shove her hands into my pockets from behind, her fingers brushing against my erection through my jeans.

Great. Now she'll think I sprung a boner for her. I brought her here tonight for one purpose only—to piss Vivien off—and it seems to be working if the displeasure and disgust on *Grace's* face is any clue. The challenge will be fending Breda off because I have no intention of fucking her tonight or any other night. One round of bad sex with her was enough for me. But, for now, she's serving her purpose, and I'll figure the rest out later.

Chapter Twenty-One
Age 20

T he party is still going strong, and I'm completely locked. My eyes haven't strayed from Vivien's for long tonight, much to Breda's annoyance. She's driving me insane—groping me, trying to grab my dick, and attempting to kiss me. "Come on, Dillon," Breda pleads in a whiny voice. "I'm dying to fuck you again."

I almost roll my eyes. These bitches are so unoriginal. Doesn't she realize desperation is a major fucking turn-off? She's been nagging me all night, and I seriously regret inviting her. I tune her out as my gaze lands on Vivien again. She's still in the middle of a group of classmates, deep in conversation with Cat and two other girls. It's safe to say she'll be preoccupied for a while. Time to do some snooping. "Come with me." Grabbing Breda's hand, I shove my way through the crowd dancing on the living room floor and out to the hallway where the bedrooms are.

A couple are dry humping at the end of the hallway, thoroughly engrossed in one another. Three girls are chatting and laughing as they line up outside the main bathroom. No one is paying us any attention as I remove a small flathead screwdriver from my back pocket and pick the lock. "What're you doing?" Breda asks as I open the door to Vivien's room and switch on the light.

"Stay out here and keep watch." I kiss her hard and fast, purely to obtain her obedience. It's a miracle I don't puke in her mouth because I have never felt less into a kiss than this one. "Rap three times on the door if you see the princess returning."

"Princess?" She scoffs, looking offended. "Don't you mean skank?"

Pretty sure the one thing Vivien Mills isn't is a skank. "Sure, babe." I squeeze her arse and force a sexy smile. "Be a good girl, and you might get rewarded," I lie.

I slip into the room and shut the door behind me before Breda can start mouthing off. My eyes flit around the room, taking note of everything. It's neat and tidy. She gets bonus points for that. All the accessories are girly in the extreme, but there aren't many personal touches.

After opening her wardrobe, I trail my fingers along all the designer clothing hanging inside. Pulling some drawers open, I discover neatly folded shirts and jumpers and another drawer with exercise gear. Then I hit the jackpot. I'm grinning like a bona fide perv as I rifle through her underwear drawer, my fingers toying with lacy knickers and bras and other sexy lingerie. My cock is at full mast, straining against my zip as I lift a pair of virginal white silk and lace panties to my nose and inhale. I'm leaking precum imagining Vivien's hot, tight body wearing these and only these. Before I can talk myself out of it, I stuff the knickers in my back pocket and shut the drawer.

Wandering over to her bed, I study the two framed photos on top of her locker. It's telling there are no pictures of her and Reeve. It's a solid piece of evidence that he no longer has a place in her life. Lifting the photo of her with her famous parents, I trail the tip of my finger over her gorgeous face, pretending the longing surging through my veins and the blood pumping into my hard dick doesn't exist because I can't lust after this girl.

Dillon

"Dillon!" The door creaks open, and I curse under my breath. I whip around, discreetly setting the photo down before Breda notices.

"Get out," I snap as she enters the room, shuts the door, and walks towards me. I don't like her invading Vivien's private space. She was a complete bitch to her earlier, not that I did anything about it. It was fun watching the Yank get her knickers in a twist.

Hypocrite, the devil in my ear whispers. *I know. You can add stalker and pervert to that list too,* I silently snark.

"Let me take care of that." Breda grabs my junk through my jeans.

I'm about to open my mouth to tell her to fuck off when I see them. A massive bunch of pale purple roses sitting pretty in a large glass vase on her desk. The florist card is propped against the vase, in plain sight, the writing easy to read.

Happy Valentine's Day, baby.
I miss you. I love you.
Yours always, Reeve.

Rage is instantaneous, so I don't protest when Breda tugs my zip down and pushes me back onto the bed. I fist my hands in Vivien's spotless white duvet as I quietly seethe. Why the fuck is she going around acting all mopey and sad if she's still with him? What kind of sick fucking game is this?

I'm vaguely aware of Breda shoving my boxers and jeans to my ankles and spreading my thighs wide. My eyes land on Vivien's face in the photo of her with her red-haired friend, and as Breda lowers her lips over my erection, I imagine it's Vivien's mouth going down over me. I glance down at Breda's bobbing head, but her hair is too black to be Vivien's rich chocolate brown, and it shatters the illusion. So, I close my eyes, arch my head back, and visualize Vivien in my mind as Breda slurps on my cock like it's a lollipop.

Air whistles over my dick when Breda suddenly drops me from her mouth. "What the fuck do you think you're doing?" she snarls, and my eyes pop open.

Turning my head, I find Vivien standing at the end of the bed, her wide eyes pinned to my dick. She's staring at my cock piercing like she's an innocent virgin seeing a dick for the first time. I had it done last year, and though I had to abstain from sex for six weeks while it healed, it was the best decision I ever made. Birds go crazy for it, and I'm not surprised Vivien is staring.

My erection swells, hardening to the point of pain the longer she looks. I need to come so fucking badly, and I want to yank Vivien Mills to her knees, tug down her top, and blow my load all over those gorgeous tits.

Of course, whiny fucking Breda has to ruin things, like usual.

"Get the fuck out!" she screeches, and Vivien blinks rapidly, finally tearing her eyes from my aching cock.

Spreading my thighs wider, I fix her with a smug grin as I say, "You're welcome to join us, princess. The more, the merrier." I keep my eyes trained on her face as I stroke my hard-on and lick my lips, loving the flush crawling up her neck and onto her cheeks. Her chest is heaving, and I bet if I thrust my fingers inside her knickers the evidence of her arousal would be coating my skin.

"Get lost, bitch," Breda says because the cunt is determined to ruin all the best parts of tonight.

My mouth hangs open a little as Vivien rushes out of the room. What the hell? I crack up laughing. This is comedy gold. This is Vivien's room. Vivien's apartment. And she's going to let some little tart speak to her like that? Where's the feisty attitude she's shown me gone?

Seconds after the thought lands in my brain, Vivien rushes back into the room and grabs Breda by the hair, tugging her away from me. "This is my room and my apartment, and you've outstayed your welcome. Get the fuck out!"

That's my girl.

Not your girl. She's Reeve's, the devil in my ear reminds me.

Not if I have anything to do with it.

"Let go of me, you stupid bitch!" Breda looks at me with pleading eyes.

Yeah, I'm not interfering in this. I'm happy to let it play out and see how far Vivien takes it. Girl fights are spank-bank ammunition gold.

"Jesus," Ro says, bursting into the room quickly followed by Ash.

My sister shrieks. "For fuck's sake, Dil, put your cock away unless you want to scar me for life."

I'm smirking as I lean back on the bed, not in any hurry to re-dress as long as Vivien keeps sneaking looks at me. This night is turning out to be immensely entertaining. "Liking what you see, princess?" I ask, flicking my tongue out so she gets a look at that piercing too. I want her imagining what it'd feel like if I fucked her with my tongue and my cock.

She fakes disgust as she eyeballs me, but her body language doesn't lie. She wants me. She wishes she was riding my dick and reaping the benefits of my piercings. "You're every bit as disgusting as your friend. And stop calling me that."

"Are you decent yet?" Ash asks, still hiding her eyes.

"Nope." I waggle my brows and throw a flirty grin in Vivien's direction. "I might just stay like this. There's nothing more freeing than being at one with nature."

The look on the princess's face is priceless. "I think your brother is an exhibitionist, or he likes trying to shock people. Pity it won't work on me."

She's such a little liar. I'm loving this, and I could do it all day with her.

"Get fucking dressed, Dil," Ash barks, losing all semblance of patience. "Or I'm telling Ma you flashed my new best friend."

Ash would do it too. "You sure about that, *Princess Grace.*" I wind Vivien up on purpose as I slowly tuck my cock away and fix my clothes into place.

"Think what you like about me. I don't care." She shrugs, but her shoulders are tense.

That got to her. Interesting. Deciding to push her buttons a little more, I put my face all up in hers. Fuck, she is exquisite. I know I sound like a broken record, but I can't help it. Her beauty blows me away every time I'm near her. I spot a smattering of freckles across her nose, barely visible under her makeup, I haven't noticed before. Her pretty eyes flare with anger, and this is my kryptonite. "I think you do care. You want everyone to love you because Mommy and Daddy always told you what a precious princess you were. It bugs you that I can't stand you. That everything you represent annoys the fuck out of me." There's some truth mixed in with the lies.

"Everything I represent?" she shouts, forcibly pushing me back.

That definitely hit a nerve. My gaze snags on the roses again, twisting my emotions and cranking my rage higher. I unleash it all on her without hesitation. "Pretty little princess with her pathetic purple roses in her palace rented with Mommy and Daddy's money," I hiss. Who the fuck is she to act so indignant?

Ash hits me and yells some, but it's like background noise as I face off with Vivien in a silent battle.

"Wow. That's some fucked-up generalization right there. You know nothing about me. Nothing about my life. And you don't get to come into my apartment and spout this shit at me."

Oh, she's really pissed now. Good. I like seeing her all riled up when she drops the crowd-pleasing façade and her claws come out. *Show me the real Vivien Grace Mills, princess.* Show me you're not a pathetic rich bitch who lets her cheating boyfriend stomp all over her heart. I can't help pushing her further. "You think you're so superior, like all arrogant rich wankers."

"How did you get in here?" she snaps, folding her arms. The motion pushes her magnificent tits up higher on her chest, offering a tantalizing glimpse of tanned, soft mounds that has my cock swelling to life again.

She's glaring at me, and it only makes me smile wider. "I picked the lock."

Shock splays across her face while Ash loses the plot, screeching and screaming at me.

Vivien shakes her head. "Wow. You're really something else."

"I am."

"That wasn't a compliment." She turns to Ash as Ronan reenters the room. I didn't even realize he had left, but I'm guessing he took the trash out, which I'm grateful for. "I'm sorry, Ash," she continues. "I know he's your brother, but he's a giant bag of dicks, and I don't want him here. I'm not going to be insulted in my own fucking home just because he's got some massive stick shoved up his ass."

I have to smother my snort of laughter. *Giant bag of dicks.* She's so American. It's fucking adorable and downright intriguing. She has hypnotized me like no other woman ever has before. "Careful, princess. You've just used up your cursing quota for the year."

"Fucking hell, bro. Stop annoying the girl," my brother says. "You need to lay off the weed and the booze, man."

"Either that or get a personality transplant," Vivien deadpans, and inside, I'm grinning large. This is the real Vivien. I want to see more of this girl, not the pale imitation my twin forced her to be.

"I'll talk to him," Ash says, beseeching me with her eyes to cut the crap. "We were coming to get you because we kicked everyone out except our friends. We're up on the roof, and the guys are going to play their guitars. Let me knock some sense into this dumbass, and we'll follow you up."

"If he says one more nasty thing to me or he calls me fucking princess again, I'll throw him off the roof and make no apology for it," Vivien says.

"Come on, Grace. Let's get fucked up," Ro says.

I bet he's loving being her knight to my devil. Enjoy it, brother, because it won't be lasting long. Even in my inebriated state, the seeds of an idea are forming.

"Sounds like a plan." Vivien links her arm through my brother's and pointedly ignores me as they exit her bedroom.

Chapter Twenty-Two
Age 20

I'm nursing the mother of all hangovers the following morning as I lie in my bed, absently watching the TV in the background, as I consider everything I learned last night. The more I think about my new plan, the more I'm convinced it's the best course of action. Now that I'm sober, I see the situation for what it is. Vivien and Reeve are broken up, but he's fighting to get her back. That puts a completely different spin on things. She hasn't been sent here to spy on me. I'm guessing she probably knows nothing about me. Simon said it himself. Neither of them want the world knowing I exist, so I doubt Reeve even told the girl he grew up with. It wouldn't exactly paint him in the best light.

No, the more I think about it, the more I realize I've gotten it all wrong. Vivien doesn't know Reeve has a secret twin brother. She has come to Ireland to get away from him and all that Hollywood bullshit. That's why Ash told me to go easy on her last night, admitting she is brokenhearted and my shitty treatment of her is only making things worse. It still blows my mind she ended up befriending my sister, but maybe karma is on my side this time. Because the perfect opportunity for revenge has landed in my lap.

My plan is genius. I'll make Vivien fall in love with me and send her back to him even more heartbroken than she is now. Reeve wants her back, but he can't have her. I'm going to make her *mine*. She'll be so in love with me she'll never want him back. Let him feel the eviscerating pain of rejection and abandonment. I am at least owed this much. Reeve Lancaster has taken everything else belonging to me, so it's only fair I take something that belongs to him. Something so precious he won't ever recover from it.

Guilt battles with smug satisfaction inside my head and my heart. Now I know Vivien doesn't have an agenda, I can't help feeling empathy for her. Reeve has already done a number on her heart, and it's not fair to plan to do the same, but life isn't fair. I've learned that lesson, and it's time she did too. I don't want to hurt her, but this is war, and there are always casualties during war. Always innocent victims.

Vivien is collateral damage, pure and simple.

She will pay the price for my revenge, and I hate this will hurt her, but I don't have a choice. Only a fool would let this opportunity pass them by.

"You missed a great session last night, mate," Jamie says when he returns home a few hours later. I'm sitting in one of the armchairs in the living room, jotting some lyrics down.

"I already told him." Ro pokes his head out from the duvet he's hiding under on the sofa.

We're both hungover as fuck today, and I'm guessing Jay is the same. Conor still hasn't emerged from his room, so I'm betting he's royally fucked too.

"Vivien has the voice of an angel." Ro's dreamy face whenever he speaks of her is really starting to get on my nerves.

"So you've said," I drawl, narrowing my eyes on him. "At least ten times."

"It's true," Jay says over a yawn, kicking his boots off and dropping into the other chair. "I got the biggest hard-on when she started singing."

I have a sudden urge to wrap my hands around his throat and squeeze. He deserves it for his obnoxious flirting with Vivien last night. Except I know he did it on purpose to wind me up. Despite my protests, he knows I have a thing for her.

"We should totally get her to sing with the band. She could be our secret weapon," Ro adds.

"Nah, she'll never go for it," Jay says. "She was serious when she said she'd hate the attention."

"You her best buddy now or something?" I snark, doodling on my notepad. Maybe I shouldn't have been such an ass to the princess last night. I hate that I missed out on what appears to have been a bonding session.

"I got to know her more last night," Jamie adds. "She's cool, and I don't think she's playing Ash. I don't think that girl has a bad bone in her body."

"Grace is amazing, and she's so fine," Ronan says, his tone matching his dreamy expression.

I chuck my notepad at his face.

"Ow," he moans, swatting it away after it hits him in the nose. "What's that for?"

"You sound like some teenage girl mooning over 1D."

"I like her. How is that a crime?"

"She's too old for you."

"I'm almost eighteen, and she's only nineteen. How the fuck is that too old?" Ro glares at me.

"She's almost twenty, and you're still only seventeen." I'm splitting hairs, but so what? I need Ro to drop all fantasies of him with Vivien even more now I've decided on my plan. "Plus, she's still upset after her recent breakup."

Until I swoop in and glue back the fragments of her broken heart. *Only to rip it apart again*, the devil snarls in my ear.

"She told you that?" Ro arches a brow, sitting up under the duvet and running a hand through his messy dark hair.

"Ash mentioned it last night." In between reaming me out of it for my shitty attitude. My sister told me Grace's ex really did a number on her and she's hurting bad. Guilt sits on my chest, but I force it to subside. I've made up my mind. I'll just have to find a way to deal with it.

"I'll help her to forget him," Ro says.

"It's not happening," I bark, rubbing my throbbing temples. "Find your next girlfriend somewhere else."

"Shut the fuck up, Dil. You don't get to dictate every aspect of my life."

"Hey now," Jay cuts in. "We don't come to blows over a woman. Ever."

"He doesn't get to tell me who I can and can't like. It's bad enough I have to deal with his bullshit about the band."

"Bullshit?" I sit up straighter and outright glower at my little bro.

"We have a real chance, Dil. Everyone says it, and the feedback from the EP is phenomenal," Ro says.

We released a six-track EP three months ago which was very well received. Momentum and sales are building all the time, so my brother isn't wrong.

Ro's eyes widen, like always when he's talking about the band potential. "We could make it big, bro, but you need to adjust your mindset. We need to strike now! We need to hire a manager and try to get a recording deal. We're never going to get anywhere if we just focus on Ireland. Think outside the box, Dil. We need to expand our horizons and start thinking bigger."

"He makes a lot of sense," Jay supplies.

"I'm not disputing that." We've had this conversation several times lately. "Or the fact we could make it big. All I'm saying is, do we really want that?"

Ro snorts out a laugh. "What the fuck kind of question is that? Who the fuck doesn't want to be rich and famous with girls hanging off their every word? Who doesn't want to make their passion a reality and travel around the world living the dream? Come the fuck on, bro. Stop talking shite."

"You're looking at it with rose-tinted glasses, Ro. Being rich and famous has a dark side," I say. "Celebrities have no fucking privacy, and trust goes out the window. There's a reason so many famous people are addicts. They turn to drink, drugs, and sex to block out all the dark shit. Can you honestly say you want all that? You want to leave Ireland and barely see our families? Live overseas, hidden behind gates and walls because you can't leave your house without being besieged?" I drag my hands through my hair. "Doesn't sound like a dream to me."

Maybe I'm hesitant because I've seen how Reeve's and Vivien's lives have played out over social media the past few years. Hell, you only need to look at Vivien to see the burden it's put on her. The girl flew halfway around the world to avoid the spotlight, and Ronan wants to shove us into it at warp speed?

I'm not convinced, and the thought of moving to America and potentially running into Simon and Reeve is something I have to consider too. It could work to my advantage. I could twist the knife and make Simon nervous every time I gave an interview. But I have a feeling if we got a recording deal without me having signed the NDA it'd somehow disappear or end up a disaster. I don't think Simon Lancaster will let me build a music career in the US without signing my freedom of speech away. He's powerful enough to make things difficult if I don't play things his way.

It's a tangled mess, and it's not like I can explain it to the band.

"Not every celebrity becomes an addict, and we never do hard drugs," Ro replies.

It's the one rule I laid down when we moved into the city two years ago. Weed and booze are one thing, hard drugs quite another. It's a slippery slope, and we've collectively agreed as a band to never go there.

"I'm just saying you need to think about it more, and we should learn to walk before we try to run. We're getting more radio play and starting to earn decent money from the EP. Let's start releasing more of our material and let it build organically from there. If something comes of that, then grand, let's roll with it, but I don't think now is the time to get too ahead of ourselves."

"That makes sense too." Jay plops his sock-covered feet on the coffee table.

"You're sucking all the joy out of my life," Ro huffs, yanking the covers back up over him and lying down.

"Dramatic much?" I tease.

"Fuck off, Dil." He shoves his middle finger up at me, but there's no heat behind the words.

Ro doesn't hold a grudge for long. Unlike Shane and me when we get into disagreements. We're both as stubborn as one another and can last days cold-shouldering each other. Ro gets over his anger as quickly as it comes on, and it's hard to ever stay mad at him. He doesn't understand I'm trying to protect him, as much as myself, because he's high on life with the band and enthusiastic and excited for the future. I am too, but with caveats.

"I know what you mean about the fame, Dil," Jay says a few minutes later, looking deep in thought. "And I think being aware of that at the outset is half the battle, you know?"

I nod because I don't disagree.

"I have a gut feeling we're going to make it big," Jamie adds. "Maybe I'm wrong. Maybe it's wishful thinking, but I think we should all be open to at least considering it."

"I'm not closed off to it, Jay. Just cautious. I don't want to lose myself to the machine. I love playing music. I love it up on that stage. I just refuse to sacrifice who I am in the process. Fame and money will mean fuck all if we're miserable."

Dillon

It's been two weeks since I last saw Vivien, and I'm on edge as I scan the room, looking for her. I've been dying for an opportunity to apologize and start putting things in motion. Ash managed to convince her to come out tonight, and I'm determined to make things right with her. She should be here by now. Ash said they were coming to Whelans early, and I was expecting them to have arrived while we were upstairs. Ro and I were just interviewed by *Hot Press* magazine, and I'm buzzing. It went well, and it'll give us a good bit of exposure when the article is published.

Tingles of awareness tiptoe up my spine, and relief pours through me when I find her across the crowded room, sitting in a chair on the outside of a table in our regular area. I could pick her out in a crowded room if I was blindfolded based on instinct alone, which is kind of nuts but doesn't make it untrue.

I take my time savoring her like a good wine, dragging my gaze up and down her luscious form, admiring every delicious inch of her. Vivien's hair is wavy tonight, and she's gone for an edgier look that still manages to be soft. My dick is throwing a party behind my jeans as my hungry gaze devours her. She looks incredible in a pink one-shouldered top, tight-fitting black leather trousers, and black knee-high fuck-me boots. *Yes, please,* I think as I lick my lips and toy with my eyebrow piercing.

I stifle a moan when I spot Breda hovering around the band at the second table. I knew bringing her to the housewarming party was a mistake. Her stalking has massively ramped up since then, and I'm close to losing my sanity. I've been about as subtle as a wrecking ball telling her I have no interest in her and we're done. The girl either has skin as thick as a rhinoceros or she's thick-skulled and brain dead. My money is on the latter. I don't know what else I can do to drill the message home. I just want her to fuck off and leave me alone.

My gaze skims over the rest of our crew. Aoife is draped all over Jay, and Conor has an unfamiliar blonde perched on his lap. I sigh as I spy my little brother heading towards Vivien with that lovesick look on his face again. Fuck. I scrub my hands down my face as I watch Ro drool all over her. I don't want to hurt my brother, but he's got to back off. Truth is, I don't think Vivien sees him as anything more than a friend, and I'm hoping I'm right. I don't want to force Ro's hand. I'm hoping Vivien will handle it instead.

I hang back, frowning as I watch Ro and Vivien's interaction. It appears to get a little heated, and I wonder what that's about. My eyes follow her as she stands and walks to the bar, not missing the interested looks she picks up from several guys along the way.

Back off, fuckers.

She's *mine*.

As I head towards her, determined to grovel at her feet, if necessary, I try not to focus on the fact I don't have a fucking clue how to romance a woman and get her to agree to be mine and mine alone.

Can't be that hard though. Right?

Chapter Twenty-Three
Age 20

D amn, her arse looks good enough to eat in those leather trousers. I'm frothing at the mouth as I take a few moments to appreciate the rear view when Vivien speaks in a clipped tone. "What do you want, Dillon?"

I bend down, planting my lips against her ear as she faces the bar, refusing to look at me. "You to look at me, for starters."

She shivers, and I silently fist pump the air. Round one to O'Donoghue. Twisting around, she looks up at me, and my breath falters in my lungs.

Fucking hell.

How is it she gets even more beautiful every time I see her?

Electricity crackles around us as we stare at one another. Her tongue darts out, licking her lips, and I'm transfixed by her mouth. The craving to taste her is riding me hard, and my body is reacting in all kinds of interesting ways being this close to such perfection.

"What?" she says, averting her eyes.

Nuh-uh. I know I'm not the only one feeling this. She doesn't get to ignore the chemistry we share. "Look at me," I command, tilting her chin up with a finger. Fiery tremors skate up my arm from the touch, and it's like being zapped by lightning. This has never happened with any girl before.

"Why?" she snaps.

"Because apologies should always be made face to face. Only cowards apologize when someone is looking at their feet."

"Okay. I'll bite." She cocks her head to the side, eyeing me curiously.

I lift a brow, fighting a lip twitch. "Didn't peg you for a biter."

"I've been known to bite," she says, deliberately tugging her lower lip between her teeth.

Oh, princess, you are so out of your league with me.

"My sister and Jamie tell me I'm wrong about you." I purposely move in closer until there's barely any space between us. "Maybe they are right." I touch a few wispy strands of hair framing her face, tucking them gently behind her ear. The same magnetic zap coasts over my hand and up my arm when I touch her, proving it wasn't an isolated incident.

Another little shiver goes through her, and I know she's feeling it too.

We stare at one another, and I get lost in her pretty eyes. She's so close I feel her warm breath fanning across my face. Delicate floral scents tickle my nostrils, and I inhale a fruity smell from her hair. The atmosphere sizzles with tension, and I'm real close to saying fuck it and throwing caution to the wind. I need to kiss her so badly it feels like I might die if I don't get to taste her lips.

"Dil." A familiar voice ruins the moment, and we jerk back from one another in sync.

What the fuck is with other girls trying to spoil things with Vivien? "Not now, Aoife," I say in a tightly controlled voice, keeping my gaze trained on Viv.

"But—"

I grind my teeth to the molars as I whip my head around. "I'm trying to have a private conversation here. I'll talk to you later."

I refocus on Vivien, not caring to watch Aoife walk away. Just as

I'm about to speak, the bartender snags her attention, and she leans in to place her order. Her arse is all up in my space, and I'm practically melting into a puddle as I stare at it. My fingers twitch with the need to dig into those sculpted cheeks and knead them hard. My dick is straining against my zip, jerking with the need to thrust and conquer and claim.

Fuck me. I sound like one of those trashy romance books Ash reads.

Viv crosses her arms and narrows her eyes at me. I don't care I've been caught drooling over her. "What?" I shrug. "If you don't want guys staring at your arse, you shouldn't wear tight leather trousers."

"Was there a reason you accosted me?"

Oh, princess. You are priceless. "Accosted? That makes me sound like some pervert." I can't help laughing because she has hit the nail on the head. I've lost count of how many nights I've pulled her stolen knickers out from their hiding place and jerked off with them covering my nose or wrapped around my dick.

Vivien full-on glares at me. "Aren't you?"

I seem to have a special knack for annoying her. Don't think that will help with the obvious wooing I need to do, so I lose the grin and plant a serious look on my face. "I'm sorry for acting like a giant bag of dicks." My lips twitch, my mouth transforming into a smile when I see her fighting amusement too.

"Why did you?" she asks.

"I have my reasons."

"And you're not going to share those with me?"

"If it was something I felt you needed to know, I'd tell you." I drag my gaze from her to pay the bartender before she can.

"You didn't have to do that."

"Call it a peace offering." I flash her one of my signature flirty smiles, trying not to preen when a dazed looks appears on her face.

"I think I preferred it when you were mean to me," she whispers before covering her mouth.

"Be careful what you wish for." I wink to lighten the mood because she doesn't understand how prophetic her statement is.

"Stop being so weird," Ash whispers as we work side by side in the kitchen of the apartment she shares with the princess on Wednesday night.

"How am I being weird?" I lift a brow as I chop onions for the chicken curry. We're using Ma's recipe. The one handed down from her grandmother. It was an O'Donoghue family staple growing up, and we all know how to make it from scratch.

"You have barely spoken to Grace since you arrived." She pours a tablespoon of oil into a saucepan on a low heat.

"Did you or did you not tell me a few weeks ago to be on my best behavior?" I drop the onions into the saucepan and stir them with a wooden spoon as Ash chops up chicken.

"Yes, but that doesn't mean ignoring her either."

I look over my shoulder, frowning as I watch Vivien laughing at something Ronan has said as they set the table for dinner. "Doesn't look like she's missing me any."

Ash sets the knife down on the chopping board and stares me straight in the eye. "I see the way you look at her, Dil. It's the same way she looks at you." She casts a glance behind her. "She doesn't look at Ro that way." She resumes cutting the meat, and I mull over her words while adding the finely chopped apple to the onion mix in the pan.

Truth is, I'm not quite sure how to play this with Vivien. I've never had to romance a girl before, and I don't know where to start. I wish I had someone to ask. Conor and Jamie are as clueless as me. Ro has relationship experience, but I don't want to ask his advice for obvious reasons. I could call Shane, but he'll only give me shit and annoy me. Ciarán could help, but we don't have the kind of relationship where I can just pick up the phone and ask him.

So, I'm stuck.

Ash and I finish dinner and call the others to the table. I sit beside my sister, across from Vivien. Ro is sitting beside her because he's tenacious and he's not giving up. I wonder if he feels the electricity charging the air between Viv and me or if it's all in my head.

It's kind of freaking me out. I don't think this is normal. It's like my entire body is plugged into a live socket and every nerve ending is sparking with awareness. I'm quiet as I listen to the others talking, studying Viv when no one is looking. How she can make leggings and an oversized jumper attractive is beyond me. I think the girl could wear a black sack and I'd still be attracted to her.

If I don't get to touch her soon, I might self-combust.

I remind myself, not for the first time, that I can't get attached. I'm not overly worried. I don't catch feelings. I just need to fuck this freaky chemistry out of my system while sticking to the program.

"Are you in, Dil?" Ash asks, and I come back to the moment.

"What?"

She rolls her eyes. "I knew you weren't listening. Grace got us all tickets to see The Frames at Kilmainham on Saturday." She pops a forkful of curry into her mouth.

"Why would you do that?" I eyeball Vivien across the table.

She sets her cutlery down. "I've heard The Royal Hospital Kilmainham is an iconic venue, and The Frames are an under-hyped band. I want to see them, and I thought it'd be fun to go as a group. Consider it my way of saying thanks for welcoming me so warmly."

Ro snorts out a laugh. "If that's the criteria, Dillon doesn't deserve a ticket."

Fact.

"Don't be mean. He has apologized, and they're starting over." Ash is quick to defend me, as always. "Plus, it's meant to be. You guys normally play Bruxelles on Saturdays, but they're closed for renovations, so you don't really have any reason to turn it down."

"I was suggesting we make a day of it." Ro slides his arm along the back of Vivien's chair. "We could meet for brunch, do the GPO and a few other touristy things before heading to the venue."

"We should book the Skyline and Kilmainham Gaol," I say, because the view of Dublin city from the Skyline Tour is spectacular and every visitor should see it. Kilmainham Gaol is steeped in history and not far from the venue, so it makes sense to include it in the itinerary.

"Does that mean you'll come?" Ash asks.

My gaze meets Vivien's, and her brownish-green eyes instantly suck me in. "Yeah. I'm in."

A faint blush steals over her cheeks before she tears her eyes from mine and smiles at Ash. "I'm super excited to do all the things. I can't wait."

Chapter Twenty-Four
Age 20

"What happened with you and the princess at the Skyline?" Jamie asks as we stand off to the side on our own at the venue where The Frames are playing. Ash, Cat, Vivien, and Ro are a few feet behind us. This is an all-standing event, and it's a full-capacity crowd, but we're in the gold circle meaning we're not too squashed and we're close to the stage with a great view. I'm not surprised. Only the best for the Hollywood princess after all.

"She pissed me off," I truthfully reply, tagging a swig from the naggin of whiskey Ash snuck into the venue in her knickers.

Things had been going great today until the subject of Reeve Fucking Lancaster came up. I told Vivien I know who she is. It was going to come out at some point. I thought I'd get it out of the way at the outset so it's one less obstacle between us. But then it turned into a row when I brought up those fucking roses and her so-called ex. She got snippy. I got pissy, and here we are.

Jamie chuckles before grimacing as he takes a mouthful of cheap beer. "Pissing her off all the time won't help you get into her knickers."

"Who said I want to get into her knickers?"

He tosses me a lopsided grin. "You can't still be in denial. This is me, fucker." He jabs me in the ribs. "I'm your best mate. I know when you want someone, and you want her."

I decide to come somewhat clean. "I don't just want in her knickers."

"I know that too."

I arch a brow in silent question.

He smirks. "You two have been eye fucking one another from the start. It's clear neither of you are looking for a one-night stand. It's as obvious as the nose on both your faces."

"I don't think my little brother got the memo."

Jay sighs. "The poor fucker. I hope she lets him down gently."

"He'll be over her by the next day. You know how Ro is."

"I don't know." He runs his fingers through the bristle on his chin. "I think Grace Mills has done a number on both O'Donoghue men."

I fucking hope not, for both our sakes. Things are already complicated enough.

Sometimes, I really wish I'd told Jamie what happened with Simon Lancaster when I was seventeen. I hate lying to him by default, but I can't bring it up now. Jamie is still all cut up about Shauna. His oldest sister—and only sibling—died of a brain aneurysm last year.

It was completely unexpected and came out of the blue. Jamie was in a bad way for months. Almost got kicked out of Trinners for not going to class. Passed his summer exams by the skin of his teeth. He threw himself into the music and the band lifestyle in much the same way I did at seventeen, albeit much less self-destructive.

Now, his parents' marriage is hanging by a thread. Although no one would be surprised if they finally went their separate ways, I know it'd hurt Jay. As crappy as his parents are, they're the only blood family he has left. Them splitting up now, after all the pain they put their kids through, would be like a kick in the teeth.

Dillon

So, yeah, I can't tell Jay even if lying to him doesn't sit right with me.

Same goes for my family for different reasons. If I told the truth now, Ma and Da would beg me to attend therapy and find a way to let it all go. Ro would want me to take the money so we could use it for the band. Ash would beat my ass for involving her new best friend in my revenge plans. Not sure where my older brothers would land. But it doesn't matter because I can't tell them, and at this point, I most likely never will. It's not like anything good would come from spilling the beans after all this time.

"Earth to fuckface." Jamie clicks his fingers in my face. "You totally spaced out, mate."

"I've a lot on my mind," I admit as the first opening act runs onto the stage, encouraged by a loud roar from the crowd.

"I'm here for ya." Jamie clamps his hand on my shoulder and squeezes.

The next three hours fly by. The gig is incredible. All the bands were great, but The Frames killed it. Jay and I kept to ourselves, and the others only sought us out at the end so Vivien could surprise us with backstage passes.

Ro is about to come in his boxers. He's bouncing all over the place like a kid on a sugar high. I'm clenching my hands and growling every time he picks Vivien up and swings her around.

"You look like you're seconds away from beating the shit out of your little bro." Jamie elbows me in the ribs. "Relax, mate. She's not into him."

Then why is she letting him touch her all the time?

"Why do you look so fucking grumpy?" Ash asks, looping her arm through mine as we make our way to the backstage entrance. "Aren't you excited?"

"You'd swear we were meeting the fucking queen."

Ash rolls her eyes, dragging me along. "I know you hate all the celebrity bullshit, but you respect and admire The Frames. Bond with them over music, Dil. This is an opportunity to make some important contacts. Try to pull that stick out of your arse long enough not to blow things, yeah?"

Forcing thoughts of Vivien from my mind, I do as my sister suggests. I owe it to Toxic Gods to make the most of this chance. The guys are down to earth and not your stereotypical band. It's not hard to gel with them. Over the course of a couple hours, we talk music and the industry over a few beers.

I turn a blind eye when Ash slips out of the green room holding hands with one of the crew, like how I ignore the clearly pissed-off look on Jamie's face when she disappears out of sight. Cat and Vivien stick close together, and I never lose sight of the princess even when we're deep in conversation with The Frames. A few crew members approach her, not shy in expressing interest. I'm hugely relieved when she dismisses all of them with a gracious smile.

On the way home in the taxi, I shoot Glen Hansard from The Frames an email with a copy of our EP. He said he wants to listen to it, and it didn't seem like he was just being polite. Still, I'm a little shocked when he reaches out first thing the next morning to say he has already listened to it, and he's impressed. He has a few contacts in Ireland and L.A., and he's going to reach out to some people and then pass on their details. It's extremely generous of him, and I only respect him more for it.

"Let me look at you." Ma grips my forearms, inspecting me from head to toe in the kitchen of our farmhouse.

"Looks like the same troublemaker to me," Shane quips, flipping me the bird behind Ma's back.

"You look thinner. Are you eating enough?"

"Ma, you say this every time I come for Sunday dinner. I eat plenty. Stop worrying." I kiss the top of her head as Shane's fiancée, Fiona, appears in the kitchen holding their three-year-old daughter in her arms.

Dillon

"Uncle Dil-Dil," Chloe screeches, wriggling out of her mum's arms. Her brown curls bounce up and down as she races towards me.

I crouch down and open my arms.

She flings herself at me, and I bundle her up, inhaling the strawberry scent from her hair and the warmth from her little body. "Me missed you," she says, peppering my face with wet kisses as I stand with her in my arms.

"Missed you too, little munchkin." I tweak her nose, and she giggles. "Tell me all your news, cutie."

"I got my last toof. Look!" She parts her lips with her fingers, pointing at a row of cute little baby teeth.

"Well done, princess."

She squirms in my arms. "I gotta show Uncle Ran." It's what she calls Ciarán. I'm chuckling as I set her down on her feet and she instantly crawls into my brother's lap, showing him her teeth.

"Where are the others?" Shane asks, pouring water into his glass from the jug. I stand behind where he's seated at the large table, pressing my body against the wall. Ma has joined Fiona in the kitchen, and they're tending to dinner. Da has his nose stuck in the *Irish Farmers Journal*, but he did acknowledge me when I first arrived. Ciarán and his long-term girlfriend Susie are engaging my little niece.

"They should be here in a sec," I say, just as Jabba and Chewie start barking like crazy out the front, heralding their arrival.

"Uncle Ro and Auntie Ash are here!" Chloe squeals, rushing past me on chubby little legs out into the hall. As much as I adore my little niece, my sore head does not appreciate her exuberance today. I might have had a few too many beers with The Frames last night, and I'm paying for it today.

Ma walks after her granddaughter, untying her apron as she goes.

"You didn't travel together?" Shane asks, but I purposely ignore him, walking over to sit in Susie's seat when she gets up to go to the toilet.

"Hey, bro."

"Dil." Ciarán eyeballs me curiously as he swipes a piece of brown bread from the basket and puts it on his side plate. "Everything okay?"

"Yeah. I was, ugh..." I rub the back of my neck, wondering why this is so hard to get out. I clear my throat and try again. "I was hoping to talk to you after dinner about something. If you have time."

"Color me intrigued." He grins as he butters his bread. "Course, I have time. We're heading over to Susie's parents' gaff later, but we can talk before I leave."

"Cool. Thanks." The chair scrapes across the tile floor as I get up.

Ro walks in with Chloe in his arms a few minutes later as I round the table and reclaim my spot against the wall. He lets her down, and she runs to help her mum in the kitchen. "Sup, bro." Ro grabs me into a hug. "Glad you made it here alive. You're a stupid fucker for getting on that bike so hungover."

"What the fuck, Dil?" Shane sends daggers at me as he rakes an angry gaze over me from head to toe.

My oldest brother hates that I have a bike. He lost a good friend to a motorbike accident when he was twenty-three, so I get it. Shane was very vocal in his protests at the time I was buying my Kawasaki. I know it comes from a good place, but I'm not in the mood for his shite today. "Don't start, Shane. I've already got a headache."

Tingles tiptoe up my spine, and there she is. The Hollywood princess. Looking like a vision in a pretty dress with minimal makeup and the cutest nervous smile. Vivien continues to nuke all the brain cells in my head, and she currently commands all the blood flowing to my dick. It's some kind of voodoo magic because one look is all it takes sometimes to make me so hard I see fucking stars.

It seems I can't stay mad at Vivien for long. This morning, despite my cautious excitement and tinge of trepidation, all I'm feeling is immense gratitude to her for organizing everything yesterday. I know she must have gone to a lot of trouble to set it all up, and she did it out of the goodness of her heart. I was a moody asshole for arguing with her and then giving her the silent treatment. And Jamie is right. I'll never win her heart if I'm short-tempered and ignoring her all the time.

"You're a dickhead," Shane says, but I tune his rant out as I stare at Vivien while Ma makes the introductions.

Shane spouts more bullshit about my bike and how I'm too reckless blah, blah, blah. Then we're all sitting down, tucking into our roast dinner. The conversation is lively, as usual, while we eat, and the topics are ever changing. We talk about the farm, Fiona and Shane's impending summer wedding, and Ciarán's job at Microsoft, and that leads into a conversation about L.A. Vivien visibly tenses, and it's clear why. Ro misses all the obvious clues as he continues to bombard her with questions about her hometown, and she's growing more uncomfortable by the second.

"I'm sure Grace is sick of everyone asking her about L.A.," I interject when Ma is speaking. Vivien is literally sweating bullets by now as the talk turns to celebrities.

"The only celebrity your mother has ever gushed about is Lauren Mills," Da says, suddenly deciding now is a great time to enter the conversation. And what the fuck? How did I not know Ma is a fan of Vivien's mother?

Poor Vivien is noticeably paler as she squirms in her seat. I suspect the cat's about to be let out of the bag. There's no way Vivien will not mention who she is now. Ash offers her friend a sympathetic look before she asks our parents, "Why have I never heard about this?"

"I used to go see all her movies before I was married and had you lot. Then the farm and family responsibilities took over," Ma explains as she starts clearing the table.

I stand. "Sit down, Ma. I've got it." Taking the stack of plates from her arms, I walk over to the sink and set them down.

"You're all too young to remember this," Da says. "But one of her movies premiered at the Savoy in Dublin, back in the day, and rumors were rife that Lauren was going to be there. We got your nana over to mind you lot, and we headed into town early so we could see her."

"Unfortunately, Lauren had to pull out," Ma continues as I walk between the table and the sink, clearing away the dirty plates and cutlery. "Her daughter fell out of a tree and broke her arm. She didn't want to leave her. As a mother, I respected her even more for that."

Vivien looks a bit spaced out, and I'm guessing she's probably reliving the moment.

"She's a fine mother and a fine actress," Da adds. He's been a lot more talkative today than usual. He's generally happy to absorb the atmosphere and listen to all of us talking and arguing on Sundays. You can always tell he's quietly proud and just soaking it all up.

"Grace's surname is Mills," Ro says. "What a funny coincidence."

Vivien looks petrified as she reaches for Ash and clears her throat. "Actually, it's not really a coincidence."

Ro frowns, and a quiet hush settles over the table. Expectant faces stare at our guest.

"You might as well tell them," I say, running my fingers through my hair as I reclaim my position against the wall. I maintain eye focus and nod at her in what I hope are supportive gestures.

"Wait? You know?" Ash's eyes widen as she stares between her friend and me.

"He saw the photo by my bed," Vivien explains.

"So, you two are an item?" Shane asks, pointing between us, and I have a sudden urge to ram my fist in his annoying interfering face.

"No!" I say the same time as Ro and Vivien. I glare at Ro, and he glares right back.

"But you said—"

"Shut up, Shane," Ro and I snap, and this is getting ridiculous.

"My mom is Lauren Mills," Vivien blurts, her voice betraying her anxiety. "I'm her only daughter, Vivien Grace."

Chapter Twenty-Five
Age 20

Vivien tells the story of her childhood accident and explains a little more, looking embarrassed and contrite as she speaks.

"Oh, honey. No." Ma gets up and hugs her. "There's no need to apologize. I just wish I'd known Lauren Mills's daughter was coming for dinner. I'd have taken out the fancy china."

We all crack up laughing because it's such a Ma thing to say, but it helps to break the tension and put a smile back on Vivien's face.

Ash takes Vivien outside to the orchard, and Ma goes with Fiona and Susie to bring Chloe out to the swings while the men finish clearing up the kitchen. After we're done, the others disperse while Ciarán and I head over to the play barn to talk in private.

"God, I have fond memories of this place," my brother says, grinning mischievously when we enter the barn. It still looks the same even though no one really uses the space anymore. A cover protects the snooker table in one corner while over the other side are the sofas, chairs, beanbags, and music system we scored from secondhand stores when we were teenagers. The long table propped under the wall, where we used to store booze and cups for sneaky parties, is chipped and in desperate need of a fresh coat of paint, but it still looks sturdy.

"Fun times for sure." I smirk as I walk towards the snooker table.

"How we managed to get away with so much shite under Ma and Da's noses I'll never know," my brother says, handing me a snooker cue.

"I think they knew, but they preferred we were safe on their property. They turned a blind eye on purpose."

Ciarán shrugs. "I can't see Ma condoning underage drinking."

We lift the cover off the table together, and I fold it up and set it down against the wall. "She's a stickler for rules but also pragmatic. Better we got locked here than at the GAA pitch or wandering around town with cans in our hands."

"True." My brother fixes me with a strange expression while he chalks his stick.

"What?"

"You're growing up."

"That's generally what happens when you get older," I deadpan as I position the balls correctly in the frame and line it up on the table.

"Still a fucking smart-arse." Ciarán leans back against the wall, watching as I lift the frame carefully and set it aside. "You break."

I line up the cue ball and take my shot, breaking the triangle formation and pocketing two red balls in different corners. "Shit talk me all you like, bro. I'm still gonna win."

Ciarán crosses one ankle, and we continue playing as we talk. "I guess it was too much to hope your arrogance might have dialed down a notch."

"You do know I'm in a band, right?" I lean down and line up a new shot. "Ego and musician tend to go hand in hand." Oh, the irony of missing my shot after that statement.

"Except you were always humble about your talent."

I shrug, watching him pocket a red in the top corner as I pluck up the nerve to ask him what I came here to ask him. "So, ah, I wanted to ask your advice." I rub the back of my neck.

My brother looks over at me. "Would this have anything to do with Ash's pretty American friend?"

"You caught that, huh?"

"Your eyes were like heat-seeking missiles following her every move, Dil. You're as subtle as a brick."

"Well, shit."

"Ro likes her too."

"Yeah. I hope it doesn't get messy." I pot another few balls.

"See that it doesn't." He sends me a warning look as I miss my next shot. "Family first, Dil. Make things right with Ronan before you do anything with Vivien."

He sinks the last of the reds, lining up to tap the yellow in the bottom corner.

"Make things right with Ro but not Ash?" I fight a smirk as he misses.

"Don't look so smug, dickhead. You haven't won yet." He stands back while I effortlessly pocket the yellow and set my sights on the green. "And we both know you don't have to square anything with Ash. She's always Team Dillon. I bet she's hoping for this."

"I have fuck all experience dating." I sink the green. "I don't even know where to start with Vivien. Women usually pursue me; it's never the other way around."

"Yep, there's that ego."

"I might be cocky, but it's the truth. I haven't a clue what I'm supposed to be doing."

"It's not rocket science, Dil. Just be yourself. Don't overthink it. Trust your gut and go with the flow."

"I'm not exactly the easiest person to get along with." I pocket the brown, and Ciarán rests his cue against the wall. "I figure I need to tone things down, but I'm not sure I can pull that off."

"I concede," he says, lifting a shoulder. "C'mon. Let's sit and talk."

I rest my cue on the table and follow him to the sofa area, flopping down beside him.

"Don't change your personality, Dil. If she doesn't want you, flaws and all, she's not the one for you."

"I don't think Vivien would expect that, but the shit that comes out of my mouth sometimes is all wrong, and I have a habit of making her mad."

My brother grins. "Passion is not necessarily a bad thing. Just try to use it for good things instead of pissing her off."

I shift around, raising one knee up onto the sofa. "Like what?"

"Be passionate about the things she likes. Listen to her when she needs to talk. Support her when she needs a helping hand or a soundboard."

"But how do I even get to that place? Right now, we have a tentative truce, but she's still wary of me. How do I get her to like me so when I ask her out she won't just laugh in my face."

"Treat her with respect, Dil, and be committed. If you say you're going to call her, call her. If you arrange a time to meet, show up on time. A romantic relationship is essentially a best friend with intimacy. You're incredibly loyal and supportive to your friends, Dil. Start there. Be her friend. Be there for her when she needs it and build on it."

My brother is not bad at this shit. "I can do that," I say, bobbing my head, already feeling more confident.

"Go slow, Dillon, and let Vivien set the pace. Most girls don't put out the instant you meet them. You can't go into this expecting her to be the same as your little groupies." His mouth contorts into a grimace for a couple seconds. "Watch Vivien for cues. Make sure she's comfortable and she knows it's all about her and your needs take second place."

"I'm not an idiot, bro. Vivien is special. I know she's not like the typical girls we hang around with. It's one of the things I like about her." Not being disrespectful to the girls we fuck around with. Just stating the facts. I can't compare the casual sex I'm used to with the potential relationship I'll have with Vivien because they are completely different.

"Just be considerate of her needs. Find ways to show her you care that are genuine. Take the time to get to know her, and then ask her out. If she says no, wait and then ask again. Show her you mean what you say and you're going to fight for her. If you really like this girl, don't give up. Relationships are hard, and they take work, but the rewards are worth it."

"You really love Susie, huh?"

"With my whole heart. She is it for me. I've known it from the minute I met her. I was inexplicably drawn to her in a way I'd never been drawn to anyone else, and when I touch her, it's the most amazing feeling. But it's more than that. She's my best friend, and I know she's got my back like I've always got hers. Making her happy is my number one priority, and my happiness is that for her. We're a team, and we don't plan anything without considering the other person. She's my world. I love her more than I can say."

Right now, I am so in awe of my brother and the confidence that radiates from him in spades. It can be easy to overlook Ciarán because he doesn't have a big mouth like Shane and me, and he's not excitable yet chill like Ro. He's comfortable in his own skin, and he doesn't need to be the center of attention to be happy. He's quietly content and proud. A lot of guys wouldn't dare make themselves vulnerable in front of others, but Ciarán has no hesitation.

"That's pretty profound."

"Yup. That's me. Profound," he jokes.

In an uncharacteristic move, I yank him into a hug. "You *are* profound, and Susie is lucky to have you."

"I'm the lucky one." He hugs me tight before we break our embrace.

"Should we be expecting another engagement soon?"

"Susie knows I want to marry her, but I want to get a promotion first. I'm hoping this trip to L.A. will push me up the career ladder. We want to buy a house, and right now, that's more of a priority than a wedding, but it'll happen. We're both on the same page."

"I'm happy for you." I squeeze his shoulder.

"Thanks, Dillon." His lips twitch. "And who knows? Maybe the next wedding will be yours."

Chapter Twenty-Six
Age 20

On that note, I flee the barn with my brother's laughter following me. Fucker knows I'm never getting married. He gave me solid advice though, and I'm glad I talked to him. I'll feel more comfortable going to him in the future too.

Approaching the orchard from the other side, I spot Vivien and Ash in the distance. They are leaning against an apple tree, and my sister is smoking. We've both gone through phases where we've tried to quit. Unsuccessfully, obviously. Their voices tickle my eardrums as I draw closer from the rear. I tread softly as I make my approach, deliberately eavesdropping on their conversation, wondering if they're talking about me.

"Ro needs to toughen up. He's too sensitive sometimes," Ash says.

"I like that about him. Too often men are told they must be strong. What's wrong with showing vulnerability?" the princess replies, and my scowl is automatic.

"You need to speak to him." Ash says, looking sideways at her friend as she blows smoke circles into the air.

Yeah, fuck this shit. I'm not going to listen to them talking about

Ro. "Speak to who?" I ask in a gruff tone, making my presence known.

"This is a private conversation, Dil. Butt out." Ash shoots me a warning glare as I round the tree and stop in front of them.

"Chloe wants you to push her on the swing," I lie, needing to get my sister out of the way so I can start bonding with her friend. Opportunities to spend time alone with Vivien are limited, and I'm not wasting this one.

"C'mon." Ash stubs her cigarette out on the tree, gesturing for Vivien to go with her.

"Don't let Shane see you doing that. He'll probably have a heart attack," I say, half wishing he was looking out the kitchen window and throwing an epic hissy fit right now.

"What he doesn't know won't hurt him." Ash grins.

"I want to speak to the princess alone," I admit, and a growly noise bubbles up Vivien's throat.

"Dillon. Please. Would it kill you to be nice?" Ash asks.

"I'm trying to play nice, and you're getting in my way." I gently push her back, hoping she gets the hint. "Shoo. I'll escort her highness to you when we're done."

"You're insufferable." Vivien wraps her arms around her body as a gust of wind sweeps through the orchard, swirling strands of her hair.

"You want me to kick him in the nuts?" Ash asks.

"It's okay. I can handle Dillon," she says while attempting to tame her errant hair.

Not likely, sweetheart, but good luck with that plan.

Ash waves before heading off in the direction of the small playground. Shane upgraded our old one for his daughter last year.

"Is that right?" I slouch against the tree, grinning as I cross my feet at the ankles.

"What do you want?" A look of mild irritation flashes in her eyes.

"That's a loaded question." I flash her one of my signature flirty grins as I light up a joint.

"C'mon, Dillon. I'm freezing my ass off here."

Shit. I didn't notice she's missing a jacket, and it is cold. I move closer to her and thrust the joint out. "Hold this." She frowns. "It's not going to bite," I add, trying to smother my amusement.

She's so innocent. I wonder if she's ever smoked weed or done anything naughty in her life. I can't see my annoying prick of a twin ever breaking the rules or encouraging her to let her hair down. Not when appearances are all that matter to the Lancasters.

Vivien shocks the shit out of me by bringing the joint to her lips and taking a long drag on it. I shuck out of my jacket and reach for her hand, stifling a pleasurable groan when her skin comes into contact with mine. Delicious tremors are shooting up my arm from her touch, and I wonder what it'll feel like when we're touching all over. I nearly come on the spot just thinking about it. I shimmy the jacket up her arm, and it's hanging off her shoulder when she starts spluttering.

I chuckle, smoothing a hand up and down her back until she's stopped coughing. "I keep forgetting how precious you are." I know saying that will piss her off, but I'm gonna be unapologetically myself, just like my brother said.

Pushing my shoulders, she glares as she gives the joint back to me. "I'm not some prissy, precious princess," she snaps, angrily shoving her other arm into my jacket. "And I've told you to stop calling me that."

Warmth spreads across my chest as she huddles in my jacket. It's way too big, but I love seeing her wearing it. "Why does it bug you so much?" I ask before taking a quick drag of the joint. "Your boyfriend calls you that or something?" Why do I keep thinking about that prick? A muscle pops in my jaw as I lower to the ground, pressing my back up against the tree.

She joins me, tucking her knees into her chest. "I told you he isn't my boyfriend anymore, and no. If you must know, my dad is the only one who calls me princess, and he says it in a much nicer way than you do."

Ah, fuck. Now I feel like a right piece of shit. I just always assumed she was reacting because Reeve called her that. I didn't even consider it might have special meaning with anyone else. "I'm sorry. I know I'm being a dick. It's my default setting."

"I'm beginning to realize that." She thrusts her hand out. "Hit me."

When I turn to face her, my nose brushes her cheek, and my skin is instantly on fire. My eyes latch on to hers, and I stop breathing for a second. Up close like this, and without any makeup on her face this time, I clearly see the light dusting of freckles across her nose and part of her cheeks. They're adorable. But her eyes. Fuck me. Her eyes are completely stunning. Those little amber flecks I've noticed before are joined by tiny green flecks only adding to their beauty. My chest heaves the longer I stare into her spellbinding gaze, and the need to pull her into my arms and kiss the shit out of her is riding me hard.

"You have the most stunning eyes," I truthfully admit. "You have these little gold and green flecks I've never seen before. They're enchanting." I can't stop myself from leaning in closer. It's like there's this pull between us, sucking me in, consequences be damned. Our noses touch, and I'm toasty warm everywhere even though I'm sitting outside on the ground in the chilly March air in only a light shirt. I rake my gaze all over her gorgeous face with a longing I've never ever experienced.

I want her. I want her so badly.

"Thank you," she says, and her breathy, sexy tone sends heat surging to my cock. Wind swirls around us, lifting more strands of her hair as we stare at one another with minimal space between us. She seems as captivated as me. The scent from her hair and her skin is the most alluring thing I've ever smelled—a delicate, fresh, floral, fruity smell that wraps around every part of me.

It feels like I'm coming out of my skin, and the need to touch her is almost insurmountable.

Go slow. That's what my brother said. I'm only beginning to realize how difficult that's going to be.

"Let me try something." Leaning my head back against the bark, I take a long pull of the joint and close my lips after trapping the smoke inside. I reach for her, sweeping my fingers across her cheek before I pull her face closer. My heart is going crazy behind my chest wall, and butterflies turn cartwheels in my stomach.

I don't know what I'm doing, just that it feels right.

With my heart pounding, I drag my thumb along her lips before pushing it in her mouth. Heat coils inside me when she sucks deeply, curling her tongue around my thumb, and all I can think is how incredible that lush mouth will feel when she's sucking my dick. Precum leaks from my cock, and the need ratcheting inside me feels like a bomb swelling, readying itself to explode.

My eyes lower to her lips when I line my mouth up with hers. I notice her squeezing her thighs together, and what I wouldn't give to ease the ache she must be feeling. She's not in it alone. More precum leaks into my boxers as I fight powerful need. Removing my thumb, I lightly press my lips against hers and release all the trapped smoke into her mouth. I hold her lips together, keeping the heady scent enclosed.

She inhales deeply, briefly closing her eyes, and I'm about ready to detonate. I want to touch her everywhere. Worship her gorgeous mouth with my lips and my tongue. Grab her onto my lap and grind my throbbing cock against her.

"More," she whispers, opening her eyes and meeting mine.

I'll give you everything, baby, if you'll just let me. The thought lands out of nowhere, but I don't dwell on it as we sit side by side sharing breaths and weed and not talking. It's the most content I've been in ages. I'm so comfortable just sitting here, existing with her.

"How'd this happen?" she asks, gently touching the little ridge on my nose.

I lean into her touch, begging her to give me more. "Got into a fight at school. Asshole shoved my face into a wall. Broke my nose in three places."

"Ouch."

"I broke his jaw in two places, so I'd call it even." I shrug before taking another toke of the joint. We're down to the dregs now, and I wish I had more. I don't want her to go. My skin feels like it's lifting off, such is the need to touch her, taste her, claim her, own every inch of her. My inhibitions are lowered, and I've always been a risk-taker, so I just act on instinct. Looking deep into her eyes, I hold her hip and pull her in close until our bodies are touching.

My lips caress hers in the softest touch. I feel it in every part of my body. Tingles are going off like rockets, and I can't deny this any longer. I have never wanted to touch a girl as badly as I want to touch Vivien Grace Mills in this moment. Taking the last drag on the joint, I tilt her chin up and blow directly into her mouth. She inhales deeply, drawing it into her lungs. Her skin is flushed, her eyes alive, and I've never seen anything more beautiful. "You have the most flawless skin," I whisper, brushing my lips across her cheeks in light kisses while my thumb rubs circles against her hip through her dress, and I wish I was touching her bare flesh.

"What are you doing?" she croaks, but she doesn't pull back, and her eyes dip to my mouth, conveying she wants this too.

"I don't know," I whisper, pressing a kiss to the corner of her tempting mouth. Tossing the butt of the joint aside, I cup her face in both palms. "I just know I want more of it." Without stopping to second-guess myself, I smash my lips to hers and kiss her.

"Vivien Grace!" Ash shouts. "Get your tongue out of my brother's mouth and your arse over here now!"

You have got to be bleeding kidding me! Is every woman on this planet determined to come between me and this girl?

I'm beyond aggravated when Vivien tears her mouth from mine after one brief kiss and climbs to her feet.

Lifting a knee, I tip my head to the side and stare at her. "Running scared, Hollywood?"

"That never happened," she says, attempting to sound nonchalant, but she can't hide the little tremor in her voice or the blush spreading across her chest and up her neck. She was as into it as me. "We were stoned, and it was barely a kiss anyway."

I run a hand along my stubbly jawline, smirking at her. "If you say so."

"Ahh. I'm going." She's a cross between pissed off and turned on when she stomps off towards my sister. I'll take that.

I chuckle to myself. She can deny it all she wants, but this changes things, and we both know it. *Game on, Hollywood.* I'm coming for ya, and I'm not taking no for an answer.

Chapter Twenty-Seven
Age 20

In the days that follow, I hide away in my bedroom and write like a madman. My muse is on fire. Jay, Conor, and I jam in the sitting room, working out melodies to my new lyrics on our guitars, and when Ro arrives on Friday, we head to our small rented practice room and start pulling a couple of new songs together.

I haven't seen Vivien since last weekend, but she's all I've been thinking about. It's pathetic to admit, but I've replayed that kiss over and over in my head until it feels like I'm going crazy. I'm jerking off nonstop, and if I don't get to touch her again soon, I might need to be committed. Ash told me her best friend Audrey arrived from L.A. She's spending a few days in Dublin around Paddy's Day, so I guess I'll get to see Vivien soon.

I haven't heard anything from Glen Hansard yet, but it's still early days, and these things take time. Something my impatient little brother does not understand. Ro is driving me nuts going on about it. He's extra pissed off because he heard about my kiss with Vivien in the orchard, though he hasn't admitted he knows, and I haven't said anything to him either. Vivien better be planning to set him straight soon, or I'm going to have to ask her outright. I don't want Ronan hurt. He needs to be left out of this.

I'm in the middle of the best fucking dream, moaning as Vivien strokes my dick and plants kisses along my neck, when reality comes crashing down, instantly rousing me from slumber. My eyes pop open. My bedroom is still pitch-black because it's nighttime and I was sleeping.

Horror engulfs me as I look down at the hand pumping my cock, knowing it's not the hand I want it to be. Gripping her wrist, I pull her hand from my dick and push it away. Flipping onto my back, I glare at Aoife. "What the fuck do you think you're doing?"

"What?" She feigns innocence as she leans down to kiss me.

I shove her back, disgusted when my palm meets bare skin. She crawled into my bed fucking naked in the middle of the night to... what? Seduce me under the pretense of being anyone else? This bullshit ends now. "Jamie," I yell at the top of my lungs, loud enough to wake up the whole county.

"You want to fuck my cunt while he takes my ass?" she asks, climbing onto my lap.

I can't work out if she's dumb or calculated. I push her away—hard—uncaring when she falls off the bed just as Jay rushes into the room. "What's wrong?" he asks in a sleep-drenched tone.

"What's wrong," I say in a cold voice, tugging the duvet up to my waist to cover myself as I sit up against the headboard. "Is that cunt climbed into my bed uninvited and started jerking me off while I was asleep."

His eyes dart wide as his gaze swings to Aoife. Predictably, she's turned on the waterworks, sniveling as she pushes to her feet completely starkers. I look away, not wanting to see any naked part of her.

"What the fuck, Aoife?" Jay says, clearly angered. "That's not cool."

"I miss him," she sobs, "and I just needed to remind him of how good it is between us."

"Listen here, cunt," I snap, jabbing my finger in her direction. "I told you I'm done with you. I don't miss you. I don't want to touch you, kiss you, fuck you. The only reason you're still here is because of my best mate, and he and I will be having words about that." I pin her with the full extent of my glare. "After you get your things and get the fuck out of my gaff."

"Jay." Her lower lip wobbles as she throws herself at Jamie. He keeps her at arm's length as we have a silent conversation with our eyes.

"You need to get dressed and leave, Aoife." Jay's icy tone matches mine. "I'll call you a taxi."

"No!" She flips her gaze on me. "I'm sorry, Dillon. It was a stupid thing to do. I swear it won't happen again."

"You touched me without my permission, Aoife," I say through gritted teeth. "If any man did what you just did, they'd be arrested. Give me one good reason why I shouldn't call the cops?"

She dissolves into tears, wrapping her arms around herself, repeating "I'm sorry" over and over.

"Get her out of my fucking sight, Jay."

After he gets rid of her, he returns to my room. "She was way out of line, Dil, and she knows it too."

"I don't want her around here anymore. If you still want to fuck her, go to her place, and do it there."

He nods. "Fair enough."

"You should cut her loose. She's trouble."

"I don't see much of her anymore, and this is the first night she's stayed over in weeks."

"True, but she still hangs around us at gigs, and she's only going to dig her claws into you more."

"I'll let her down gradually. If I go cold turkey, she's liable to stir up all kinds of shit. Don't worry about me. I know how to handle Aoife."

I hope he's right because I've had enough of her shit.

"What was that all about?" I ask Ro when he materializes beside Jay as we're lining up to go onstage upstairs at Whelans. It's Paddy's Day, and the place is packed to the rafters, so it promises to be a good gig.

"As if you don't know," Ro snaps in a clipped tone.

Vivien had pulled him aside downstairs just before we left. I'd hoped it was to let Ro down gently. I'm relieved she's set him straight, but I get no pleasure in seeing him upset. "I didn't tell her to say anything to you if that's what you're implying," I calmly reply.

The last thing we need is to be at odds right before we're due to play our set. I'm already a little pissed after my run-in downstairs with Breda. Bitch isn't listening, and I'm all out of patience. If there'd been time, I would have asked the bouncers to toss her out on her clingy arse. I plan to speak to the manager this week to get her barred. I've given her more than enough chances. Her harassment ends now.

"Well, the coast is all clear now, bro. I've been friendzoned." Anger underscores Ro's words. "You can go fuck her and toss her aside like you planned all along."

I'm on him in a flash, shoving him up against the wall. "Watch your fucking mouth. Don't speak about Vivien like that."

"It's the truth, and I wish I'd had the balls to tell it to her face, but she'll learn her lesson the hard way."

Jay's sharp gaze bounces between us. He won't intervene. Not unless there's a need. This is between my brother and me. "Vivien is different." I release him with a sigh. "It's not going to be like that. I like her, and I want more than a quick fuck."

"For how long, Dil?" He shoves my shoulder as he brushes past me. "Until you've fucked whatever you think you're feeling out of your system I'm guessing."

"Don't do this, Ro," Jay says. "I know you're pissed, but don't take it out on your brother just because they like one another. Neither of them did it on purpose to hurt you."

"I don't care. You're the one making a big deal out of this, not me." He eyeballs Jay for a sec before shrugging as he glances at me, visibly shaking his anger off. "She's only a girl. Have at it, bro. Plenty more fish in the sea. Am I right?" He's not convincing any of us, but I'll roll with it if it keeps the peace. "I'll have some pretty young thing under me in a few hours. I was never that interested in her anyway."

It's lies, and I want to call him out on his disrespect towards Vivien, but this isn't the place. It's in all our interests for me to just let it go, so I do.

"Family first, bro." I lift my hand for a knuckle touch, relieved when he meets me halfway.

"Always."

"We good?"

"Yeah, bro."

Jay and I breathe a sigh of relief. Crisis averted. At least for now.

I tie an Irish flag around my waist and wrap a green bandana across my forehead as we get ready to go on. Gotta enter into the spirit of things for our national day. The Vanquished come offstage, and we greet one another briefly as the MC announces us, and then it's game on.

The assembled audience roars its approval as we start off with a crowd-pleaser from U2. A sea of green, white, and orange greets us, and it truly is a sight to behold. Hordes of revelers dance and jump around as I hug the mic and lean down into the row of screaming girls up front. Most all the faces are ones I recognize, but I scan the crowd looking for the only face that matters. I purposely skim over Aoife and Breda without acknowledging them. Both girls are right up front, dancing side by side, looking more like friends than rivals, but I don't give a fuck about either of them.

My heart pounds harder when I find Vivien dancing near the front, on the other side, with Ash and her American friend Audrey. Audrey is the redhead from the framed photo by Vivien's bed. I was introduced to her downstairs, and she seems cool. Apparently, Vivien told her Toxic Gods are good, and I'm determined to prove it. So, I put in extra effort to deliver a killer performance, ensuring we don't disappoint.

We move fluidly through songs that are a mix of classic covers and our own music. Hearing your own words being sung back at you from an enthusiastic crowd is overwhelming in the best possible way. Being up here is the most incredible feeling in the world. Getting to perform onstage is my life's dream, and I don't care if I'm performing to one hundred fans or one hundred thousand fans. Experiencing this in any capacity is magical. My soul is only truly happy when I'm singing my heart out, playing my heart out, and entertaining a crowd.

My fingers skillfully pluck the strings of my guitar in a familiar rhythm as we play a popular Foo Fighters number, and I belt the lyrics into the mic, buzzing off the excitement and vibes emanating from the crowd.

My eyes never stray far from Vivien. She looks so fucking sexy in skinny jeans and a tight green shirt. In honor of St. Paddy's Day, she's pinned a sprig of shamrock above her chest and painted little Irish flags on both cheeks. Somehow, she manages to be adorable and sexy at the same time. Her hair is pulled into a messy bun on top of her head, showcasing her stunning face, and it's hard not to just stare at her all the time. I want to get down on my knees and serenade her for the entire show, but I doubt it'd go down well with the masses. I've spotted a few girls in the front row noticing where my attention is straying, and I don't like the looks being tossed her way.

Vivien looks happy, bobbing around and singing her little heart out. Warmth spreads across my chest. I love seeing her like this, and I love that she appears comfortable in my world.

A bra flies over the crowd, landing at my feet. It's a common occurrence. Conor has a whole box load of sexy undies that have been thrown at us on stage. I'm not gonna think about what he does with them, though I'm hardly in any position to criticize. Vivien's virginal white panties are my most treasured possession, and they have a starring role in my best fantasies.

I kick the bra in Jamie's direction, and the crowd goes wild when he picks it up and puts it on his head. Clown.

We finish our set to cries of "more," but it's a multi-band event today and the schedule is tight, so that's it folks. Besides, I have singular focus and the worst twitchy hands. After offloading my guitar to Conor, I jump down off the stage, into the crowd, and make my way towards Vivien. Hands reach out, grabbing me, but I ignore them, making a beeline for the woman who has enchanted me.

Being onstage makes me come alive in every sense of the word. There's a reason rock stars fuck groupies. I'm always on a complete high when I come offstage and usually fucking horny. I might have told Ciarán that ego and rock stars go together, but so does rock stars and sex.

Need swirls in my veins as I push closer to Vivien. I need to put my hands on her before I explode. Longing burns in my eyes as I draw nearer. Ash and Audrey are laughing, and I hear Viv saying, "I'm not sleeping with your brother!" just as I reach them.

I press my mouth to her ear as I come up behind her. "Is that a challenge?" My hands land on her hips as I push all up against her, nibbling her earlobe and struggling to hold on to my self-control. Her floral, fruity scent invades my senses, and I grind my hard-on against her arse while moving a hand up under her shirt.

Her skin is warm to the touch, and my dick is jerking like crazy as she pushes back against me with zero hesitation. I'm so turned on being close to her like this. "Well?" I ask.

"Well, what?" she rasps, moving against me as we dance to the music pulsing around the room.

A chuckle tumbles from my chest. She's too cute for words. "Is that a challenge? Because you know how I feel about those." I trail my hand across her flat stomach as we grind and dance against one another, and it feels like the most natural thing in the world.

Ash stares at me in silent question, and I nod confirming I will take care of her friend. Seemingly satisfied, Ash leaves, taking Audrey with her.

"It's...not," Viv says, stumbling over the words.

Brushing my lips against the elegant column of her neck, I

commit the taste, feel, and smell of her skin to my memory bank. "You don't sound sure," I whisper, holding her tighter when she sways in my arms.

"I'm not one of your groupies," she says, looking back at me with a little frown.

I'm instantly serious. "I know you're not. But you can't deny we have chemistry." My fingers caress the soft skin of her cheek.

"I won't lie about that."

Yes! Finally.

She stares deep into my eyes. "But I'm still not sleeping with you."

Still somewhat delusional, I see. I lean into her face until there's only a small gap between us. "Yet," I say, flicking my tongue lightly against the seam of her lips.

Her hand lifts to my face, and I'm in heaven as she sweeps her fingers across the stubble on my jawline. "Hmm." I lean into her touch, briefly closing my eyes, just wanting to savor the moment and everything I'm feeling. But the crowd won't let me have it, jostling and pushing into us, so I move back a little, keeping her pulled in flush against me, finding a space that isn't as congested. Vivien's back is pressed against my chest, and I hold her tight, unwilling to let her go, as we dirty dance in sync with the music. Our bodies fit against one another perfectly, and we find a natural rhythm as we dance and touch each other.

I never want this moment to end.

My hands explore the exquisite curves of her body while I nuzzle her neck, licking, nipping, and kissing her skin. I wish we were naked, in a bed, so I could do all the things I want to do to her. Her hands glide up and down the sides of my legs and the backs of my thighs as she presses back against me, and every part of my body is straining with need. This is everything but not enough at the same time.

I need more.

I think with her I always will.

Resting her head back on my shoulder, she closes her eyes and moans as we rock and sway to the beat, clinging to one another with greedy hands. I'm totally fixated on her, beyond bewitched, which is why I don't spot the attack in time to stop it.

Vivien screams, and I jerk my head up, glaring at the black-haired bitch staring smugly back at me.

Chapter Twenty-Eight
Age 20

"**W**hat the fuck, Breda?" I bark, noticing the empty pint glass in her hand. What a cunt. I turn Vivien around to inspect the damage. She's fucking soaked. Wispy strands of her dark hair are plastered to her wet brow, and her makeup is sliding off her face. Green face paint is streaking down her cheeks, and her T-shirt is molded to her body like a second skin. I curse, tossing a venomous look in Breda's direction before focusing my attention on Vivien. "Are you okay?"

"I need to go." She tries to free herself from our embrace, but I'm not having it.

"You're not going anywhere."

"I'm a fucking mess, Dillon," she says, and I hate the way her voice trembles.

I should have asked someone to get the bouncer for me and had that bitch tossed outside earlier. Then this wouldn't have happened. Knowing Vivien's recent history, I can guess where her head has gone. I hate that I'm the reason she got a drink thrown over her tonight. Vivien isn't the reason I kicked Breda to the curb. Bitch did that all by herself, and I'm fucked if she's going to take it out on an innocent woman.

Vivien will not be belittled, harassed, or abused on my watch.

"I have a spare shirt in my bag, and I'll take you to the staff toilets to clean up. She's not ruining your night." Taking Vivien's hand, I link our fingers together.

"C'mon, Dillon. It was only a joke," Breda says.

"You're a clingy, jealous cunt, and I'm sick of your shit." I slant her a dark look. "You're not welcome around us anymore, so fuck off."

She goes on a bit of a rant, but I'm done with her. Vivien is my sole priority. I take her to the staff entrance, and we head inside, away from the heat, the noise, and crazy-ass Breda. "I'm really sorry about that," I say as I lead her along the hallway, loving the feel of her warm, soft hand in mine.

"It's not your fault your psycho radar is out of whack," she drawls.

"I'm pretty sure it is my fault," I say as I lead her into the cloakroom. "I only brought her to your party to wind you up, and now she's like a dose of bad breath I can't shake." I grab my bag and drop it on the ground.

"Nice analogy."

I open my bag and search through it for the things I need. "Here." I hand her one of my black T-shirts. "These might help too," I add, offering her a pack of skin wipes. She arches an elegant brow, and I grin. "Don't judge. It gets hot as fuck under stage lights." I stand and point behind her. "Toilet is right across the hall. Take as long as you need. I'll be right here."

I watch her walk off, staring at the door long after she's disappeared inside. Rezipping my bag, I stuff it back in the cubbyhole and head out into the hallway to wait for her.

Things were going so well tonight until Breda had to go and ruin it. I'm betting Vivien is in there telling herself this scene is not unlike the one she just escaped from in L.A. Any progress I've made is most likely undone now, and I'll have to work harder to convince her it's not the same.

Dillon

For one, I'm not my twin. He didn't protect Vivien, and I'm not going to make the same mistake. What happened tonight will never happen again. None of the girls I fucked in the past will be getting near Vivien again. She doesn't deserve to pay the price for their jealousy. I'm just not sure how I can convince her things will be different this time.

The bathroom door opens, and she reappears in front of me, fresh-faced and looking sexy as sin in my shirt. She has it twisted into a knot under her tits, exposing a large section of toned skin I had my hands all over a little while ago. Lust slams into me. "Fuck me." I drag a hand through my hair. "You look too fucking good in my shirt."

I move on autopilot, pinning her to the wall with my body and caging her in between my arms. I breathe in the scent that is uniquely Vivien Mills, and I'm consumed with desire. I need to taste her, or I'll go insane. I'm seconds from crashing my mouth to hers when my brother's words return to me. I need to go slow. Let her set the pace. It hurts me not to take control and give us both what we want, but I need to learn patience from somewhere. Right now, I see the conflict raging across her face, and I know she's talking herself out of it before she confirms it with her words.

"I need to go." She pushes on my chest, and I take a step back. Her eyes lower to the floor.

"Don't do that." I hold her chin and tip it up so those pretty eyes are looking at me. "Don't shut me out. I know you were into it downstairs." I touch her cheek. "I promise I'll tone down my default setting if you don't push me away."

Her gaze dips to my mouth, and I lick my lips as lust wars with logic inside me. My movements are slow as I press my body against hers, giving her time and space to stop me. Sweeping my fingers along her neck, I rub my nose against hers, wanting to be much closer but knowing I can't force this even if she wants this deep down inside.

She drops her wet shirt to the floor and grabs my waist. I take that as my cue to keep going. My lips replace my fingers at her neck, and the little breathy moan she emits when my mouth glides against her soft flesh is music to my ears.

She needs me as much as I need her.

I kiss up and down her neck, wanting to move to her mouth and worship her lips but she's got to give me permission. Her hips buck against mine, and there's no way she doesn't feel my erection. "I know you want this as much as me," I whisper, moving my lips to her jaw and edging closer to her mouth. "Stop fighting it. Give your body what it needs." Taking a chance, I run one finger along the waistband of her jeans, and that's all it takes to break the spell.

"No." Vivien pushes firmly on my shoulders. "I can't do this."

I immediately release her and step back, knowing I've lost her. Disappointment swirls in my veins, but this isn't about me. She's stopping this for a reason, and I need her to say it. "What are you so afraid of? I won't hurt you. I promise." Pain spreads across my chest when her eyes automatically fill with tears.

"You shouldn't make promises you don't know you can keep."

Instinctively, I reach for her, needing to hold her and comfort her, but she evades my touch, running along the hallway and exiting through the door.

I don't immediately follow because Vivien is right. I'm lying to myself as much as I'm lying to her. I can't promise Vivien I won't hurt her. Not when my entire plan hinges on her falling so desperately in love with me she'll be a broken shell when she returns to him.

I don't know how long I stay in the hallway, torturing myself with so many conflicting emotions and thoughts, but my heart is still heavy when I finally make my way outside.

Vivien, Audrey, and Ash are long gone by the time I make it back downstairs to our regular table in the pub. I order a beer and take a seat beside Conor, still all up in my feelings. Ro is making out with some bird in the corner—that didn't take long—and Aoife is perched on Jay's lap. Breda isn't around. Lucky for her as I'm liable to do anything to that bitch if she dares show her face here again tonight.

I'll definitely be calling the manager tomorrow and getting her barred.

"Dillon."

Hell no. I do not have the patience for this. "Fuck off, Aoife," I say without even looking up at her.

"I need to say something, and I swear I'll never come near you again."

I snort out a harsh laugh. "You sound like a broken record, and your words are empty." A lot like the ache in my chest, which is back full force. I swallow a mouthful of beer, wishing I could rewind time and get a do-over.

The seat dips beside me, and I growl in annoyance, planning to ignore her until she gets the fucking message and pisses off.

"I'm so sorry about last night, Dillon. It was unforgivable, and you're right; if any man did that, there'd be hell to pay."

Against my better judgment, I turn my head and look at her.

She stares at me with big, sad eyes, clutching her hands nervously in her lap. "I'm disgusted with myself and so incredibly sorry for treating you like that. I know I don't deserve it, but I'm hoping some day you can find it in your heart to forgive me. It was a mistake. You've been telling me, and I haven't been listening. That's all on me."

Her eyes drop to her lap. "I know we are over, and I respect your decision. I won't touch you again or even speak to you unless you want me to. I promise I will respect the boundaries you've set. I understand I'm not welcome to stay over at your place, and that's totally fine. I get it." She raises her gaze to mine. "Just please don't take all this from me." Her eyes dart around the crowded pub. "I don't have much in my life. I hate my job. My family suck. I don't have many friends. I live for this scene. Music soothes my soul, and getting to be around the band, to feel like a part of something, it matters more than I can say."

Her voice is meek, and she seems sincere, but it's so hard to trust any of the girls that frequent the indie scene.

"I won't cause any more trouble. I promise. Just please don't cut me off from the band." Her eyes well up as she pleads with me. "I'm begging, Dil."

I hope I don't end up regretting this. "As long as you stay away from me and respect my boundaries, I can give you one final chance, but this is it, Aoife. One more strike, and you're permanently out."

"Thank you, Dillon." She moves to hug me but stops herself in time when she sees the expression on my face.

"This extends to Ash and Vivien too," I add. "You will show them respect."

She readily nods. "I swear I won't cause any problems."

"Make sure of it," I warn before returning to my beer and my sulking and dismissing her.

Chapter Twenty-Nine
Age 20

"We should find a manager now," Ro argues as we get ready to leave our place for our regular Whelans set.

I work hard not to lose my temper. "We have a manager," I snap through gritted teeth.

"Ash has no experience and no industry contacts," Ro continues. "This could be our only shot, Dil. We can't fuck it up."

"The guy has only just reached out to me. It might go nowhere." Trying to regulate my brother's expectations is starting to feel like a full-time job.

"We need to be prepared for all possible outcomes, and Ro has a point about Ash," Jamie interjects.

I glare at my buddy. "You're happy to push her out after all her support?"

"Of course not." Jay glares back at me. "I want Ash involved. We all do, but she'd be the first one to agree we need to find an experienced manager to help us navigate any opportunities that might come our way now. She can still be involved in some capacity and in time take on more of an active management role."

"This is a moot point, and I'm done discussing it without Ash." I snap my guitar case closed and sling it over my shoulder.

"Fine. Let's talk to her after our set." Ro folds his arms and levels me with a challenging stare.

He's like a dog with a bone since I got the text this morning from a scout for a major US label. The guy asked me to send him the EP and any other demo tapes we have, which I've already done. Nothing may come of it, and if something does come of it, I fully trust my sister to negotiate on our behalf. So what if she doesn't have any record management experience? Aisling O'Donoghue is a rottweiler, and she won't let anyone pull the wool over our eyes. But it's not just up to me. We're not a dictatorship, and it's looking like I'm in the minority. "Okay." I jerk my head in acknowledgment. "Let's go. We don't want to be late."

"Where's Vivien?" I ask as my gaze roams the packed pub looking for Ash's new best friend.

"She's not here."

My scowl is instant along with a sinking feeling in the pit of my stomach. "How come?"

"She's a bit depressed since Audrey left. She said she wasn't in the mood to come out, and I didn't push it." Ash is momentarily jostled to the side by a rowdy group entering the bar. "Hey, watch it, dickheads!" she shouts after them.

Subtly, I slip my foot out, catching the last prick in the leg, smirking when he stumbles forwards, taking a few of his mates down to the floor with him. Fuckers. Ignoring the dicks, I peer deep into my sister's eyes. "Is she still pissed over what happened on Paddy's Day?" Viv filled Ash in before I got the chance to tell her.

"She hasn't said anything since, but I know she's worried about being a target for the groupies."

"I would never let anyone hurt her."

"I know that, but words aren't going to prove it to her." Sympathy splays across her face as she runs her fingers through her short hair. "Viv has dealt with a lot, and it's only natural she's cautious."

"It's understandable, but I just want a chance to prove it'd be different with me."

"You really like her, huh?" Ash can't contain the massive grin spreading across her mouth.

"We've got a connection, and I want to see where it goes."

"Oh my god." Ash's eyes light up, and she jumps up and down on the spot, clapping her hands and squealing. "Imagine you get married! She'll be my sister for real!"

"Steady on, Ash. I haven't even asked her out yet."

She grips my arm, beaming up at me. "But you're going to, right?"

"She'd have to show up for me to ask."

"I'll get her here next week. Promise."

"Don't get your hopes up, Ash. I like her, but I'm still not relationship material, and marriage and kids are not on the cards for me." I have considered how Ash will react to everything, and this right here is what I'm afraid of. Ash is already daydreaming about me and Viv together forever, and it only adds to my guilt.

Just not enough to stop my revenge plans.

She'll get over it in time, and she'll forgive me. My sister always does.

Ditching my friends after our set—much to their protests—I take the van and head back to our apartment. The idea came to me while I was onstage, and I'm not second-guessing myself. Ciarán said to be myself, and this feels like the right thing, so I'm doing it. Making a pit stop at the local Spar, I grab some Cadbury's chocolate and a box of Lyon's teabags for Viv. Briefly, I consider buying her flowers, but it might be overkill, and I don't want her to feel pressured. I just want to do something that will hopefully make her feel better.

At home, I wash her shirt from the other night and read her article in the Trinity student newspaper as her top dries in the dryer. Vivien is a good writer, and her piece about being an American student in Ireland is eloquent and professional while being personable too.

There's no denying she's got a big set of lady balls. It can't have been easy uprooting her whole life to come here, especially when the person she has grown up with betrayed her so publicly. Her heartbreak has been obvious to see. It only makes me hate my twin even more. How could he have a girl as special as Vivien and throw it all away for someone like Saffron Roberts? Vivien is levels above that man-stealing ho.

Saffron reminds me of Kelly. Last I heard, Cillian is back in Kilcoole with his slut of a wife and their little daughter. He's studying business at UCD and working nights and weekends for an insurance company doing online customer service. Apparently, they were living in a rented apartment in Stillorgan, but he's moved back home so they can save for a house. Kelly is working one of the tills in Tesco Greystones, and Mrs. Doyle minds their kid when both parents are working. Doesn't sound like a lot of fun to me, but Cill got what he deserves. Thankfully, Ash is fully over him now, and anytime she sees either of them around the town, she holds her head up high and ignores them.

I get up early on Saturday morning and deliver my package to Ciara, the manager on duty, in Viv and Ash's apartment building.

She promises to take it straight up to Vivien. I had considered hand-delivering it, but I didn't want to make it awkward.

I'm walking back to our place when my phone pings with a text from her.

> Thanks for the care package. It was a really thoughtful gesture. The chocolate is yummy.

It's accompanied by a picture of her holding a mug of tea with an open bar of chocolate on the table. I send her back a short reply.

> You're welcome.

Warmth spreads across my chest as I tuck my phone back in my jeans pocket, and I'm still smiling when I get home.

Ash calls over the following afternoon when we're all lounging around the sitting room recovering from a late session in Bruxelles. She jumps onto the sofa beside me and leans into my ear. "She loved it. It was the perfect thing to do."

"I'm glad."

"Who knew you could be so romantic?" Ash smiles wider.

"It was only some tea bags and chocolate. Let's not get carried away."

"It's the thought that counts, and you went to the trouble of washing her shirt too." Ash has a swoony look on her face I haven't seen in years.

All because I washed a shirt? Women are strange creatures.

"I've also convinced her to come out on Friday so you can ask her." She waggles her brows.

"Ask who what?" Ro inquires as he carries a tray laden with biscuits and mugs of tea.

"Dil's going to ask Viv out."

I glare at my sister as Jamie snorts with laughter, and Ro's frown deepens. I don't know why my little bro is looking so pissed off when he's shacked up with Zara now.

"What?" Ash shrugs, feigning innocence. "You didn't say it was a big secret."

"That was implied," I deadpan, reaching for a mug.

"I never thought I'd see the day." Jay's smug grin expands when I flip him the bird.

"It's not a big deal, and it's not what we need to discuss." I purposely change the subject. We didn't get to talk about the manager issue on Friday because I left straight after our set.

"Ro and I spoke about it," Ash says, dunking her digestive biscuit in her tea. "And I agree you should look for an experienced manager."

"Ro should not have spoken to you without the rest of us," I say through gritted teeth, shooting daggers at my meddlesome little brother.

"It makes sense, Dil." Ash clings to my arm and snuggles into my side. "I love how loyal you are to me, but it's my loyalty to all of you that means I'm A-okay with this. I want Toxic Gods to succeed, and if you get professional representation, they can steer you in a way I can't."

"You know us, and you're smart," I protest. "You'll learn the ropes fast. I don't think we should underplay the importance of having someone we trust acting on our behalf."

"That's a valid point, but how do we marry the two?" Conor says, surprising us all with his contribution. I learnt long ago that Con soaks everything up like a sponge. He rarely misses anything even if it seems like he's living in his own little world. But it's not often he speaks up.

"I was thinking maybe I could be mentored by the person," Ash says, straightening up. "We could make it a condition of whatever management contract you sign so they have to show me the ropes. After I finish my degree, I'm considering doing an MBA, and then I could take over managing you in the future, when the timing is right." Her gaze bounces between all four of us. "Unless things take off quickly, and then I can revise that plan."

"I like it," Jay says, and Conor and Ro bob their heads in agreement.

"I still think Ash is good enough, but I know when I'm outnumbered."

"This is the right call, Dil." Ash squeezes my arm. "Let me do some research. Find a few people I think will be a good fit, and then we can discuss whether to approach them now or wait until we have a concrete offer from a label."

Chapter Thirty
Age 20

I'm sweating buckets by the time we finish our set, and I just need to get this over with now before I throw up. I was tempted to message Ciarán to ask if it's normal to be this nervous asking someone out, but I'd get shit for it for eternity, so I nixed that idea. During our set, I worked hard not to constantly stare at Vivien, so as not to draw attention to her like I did on Paddy's Day, but it's hard because I just want to look at her all the time.

My hands are shaking, and sheer terror has an iron grip on my heart by the time I make my way downstairs. I seriously hope I don't mess this up. "Is this seat taken?" I ask, setting my beer down and placing one hand on the empty seat beside her at our usual table.

"Depends on who's asking?"

Instant relief floods my body at her teasing tone. I wasn't sure what reception I'd get from her today. This I can work with. "What if it's me?" I flash her my signature grin, silently celebrating when a dazed look appears on her face.

"You can sit," she says, and I don't waste a second, sinking onto the chair beside her.

"Here." I hand her the drink I just bought her. "You drink pink gin and 7UP, right?"

"Thank you." She takes the drink from me, and our hands touch in the exchange, sending a scintillating electrical charge up and down my arm. I'm amazed at the things her touch does to me, and I can't wait to explore it more.

"Good set, bro." Ash leans across Viv for a knuckle touch. "When are we going to hear these new songs you're writing?"

"You're writing new music?" Viv's brows climb to her hairline.

I fight a smirk as I toy with the label on my beer bottle. "I'm our chief songwriter. What else do you think I do with my days?"

"Watch porn. Jerk off. Bang groupies," she drawls, and I crack up laughing.

I watch her watching me, and there's no disguising her interest. I hope that means she'll say yes when I ask her. Lowering my voice, I lean in a little closer. "You're staring." My thigh brushes against hers, sending bolts of electricity flooding through my body. I swear, if I don't get to act on this chemistry soon, I'm going to detonate from the inside out.

"You're kind of beautiful," she blurts, and my heart swells behind my chest.

"*You're* beautiful, and there's no kind of about it."

A pretty blush steals over her cheeks. "Thank you," she whispers, lowering her eyes.

"You act like no one's ever told you you're beautiful before, and I know that can't be the truth." Surely, in all the years they were together, my dick of a twin showered her with compliments? If he didn't, he's the biggest dickhead walking the planet.

She stares straight into my eyes. "I'm kind of not myself at the moment."

"I kind of want to do something about that." My lips kick up at the corners.

"You do?"

I nod.

"Why?"

I go with honesty. "I've never felt drawn to any woman from the first second I met them, like I have with you."

"You were an ass to me." She narrows her eyes a little.

"I was confused, and it scared the crap out of me. Still does." She devours me with her eyes as I take a healthy swig from my beer bottle, and my ego sure loves that even if the intensity of our attraction truly terrifies me. I cannot fall for this woman, and I fear it would be far too easy to do it.

How can I make her fall in love with me and not fall myself?

"That makes two of us," she replies with quiet sincerity before sipping her drink.

See? She feels it too. And I'm in awe of her. Her heart was pulverized but she's not letting it hold her back. That takes a lot of guts.

Falling in love with her would be effortless.

I fear I'm already halfway there.

Get with the program, dickhead. I shake myself out of it. I don't fall for women, not even when they're as special as the woman sitting beside me. I'm worrying for nothing. I'll fuck this crazy connection away, and when it's time for her to leave, I'll just pick up my old life without a care in the world. "Then I don't see what the problem is." I flash her another signature grin. "We can be scared together."

"You don't just want to fuck me?" she blurts.

Ash splutters, almost spitting her drink all over the table. That's what she gets for being a nosy bitch. Viv faces my sister while rubbing her back, and I slowly drink in every aspect of Vivien's appearance tonight. She's sexy as sin and sweet as honey, and I want to eat her alive. Placing my lips beside her ear, I admit one truth. "Trust me, there is no part of me that doesn't want to fuck you."

Panic is etched upon her face as she tries to pull away from me, but I wrap my arm around her shoulders, keeping her close. "Stop. Fucking. Running. I wasn't finished speaking."

"I kind of want to slap you right now," she says.

"And I kind of want to knock some sense into that beautiful thick skull of yours. So just shut up and listen."

She glowers at me like she's contemplating putting a bullet in my skull.

"You're sexy with a body to die for. I'm a horny twenty-year-old man with sex on the brain twenty-four-seven. Of course, I want to fuck you. I want to fuck you so hard you'll be feeling my cock inside you for days. But—" I hold her chin and trap her gaze in mine. "Listen up, Hollywood. This is the important part." I chuckle when her glare expands. I love seeing her feisty side, and I'm determined to push her buttons any chance I get so it comes to the surface. Viv is full of pent-up emotion, and I can't wait to see it overflow. "I also want to get to know you. I *like* being around you." It's not a lie. I love being with her. "Your presence calms me, and I just want to spend time with you."

Ash snorts, and Vivien elbows her in the ribs. I drink the rest of my beer, trying to leash my anxiety, while I wait for her to respond. She's not the only one being vulnerable tonight, and the fear of rejection is never far from my mind.

When she reaches out and touches me, I literally melt on the inside. The expression on her face as she strokes my arm is nothing short of miraculous, and I'm instantly under her spell. I want her to look at me like this for the rest of my life. Nothing else matters in this moment but her. I couldn't look away from her if I tried. It's as if we're the only two people in the bar, the only two people in the world. My heart swells with potent longing, and my fingers twitch with the need to hold her, cherish her, and worship her.

"I know that was hard for you to say," she says in a breathless tone.

"It was. This isn't me. I have no clue what I'm doing." *Isn't that the truth?* A strained laugh leaves my lips. What was I just saying about not falling for her? With one look, I'm putty in her hands. I'm

236

beyond terrified. There isn't a word in existence to describe how absolutely petrified I am of doing this with her. At the same time, wild horses couldn't hold me back now. Even if I wanted to walk away or ditch my plan, I can't. I'm already way too invested. "But I'd like to try."

"What exactly are you saying?"

"Go out with me?" *Please say yes.*

"Like, on a date?"

My throat is dry, and my hands are clammy as I nod. *Please, please say yes.* As much as I'm afraid of feeling too much for Vivien Grace Mills, I'm more afraid of her rejection. Of never getting to touch her how I've been dreaming about touching her from the minute she appeared in my life.

I'm trying to prepare myself for the worst when she says, "Okay."

I stop breathing for a second. "Yeah?"

Her beautiful smile washes over me like a comfort blanket. "Yeah. I'll go out with you."

"Surprise. You're alive," I tell Vivien when we reach Killiney Hill, and I park my bike at the back of the car park.

"That was actually fun."

"Told ya!" I tweak her nose before helping her off the seat, and then I unzip my leather jacket to cool down after the ride.

"You love your band shirts," she says, checking out my U2 shirt while unzipping her jacket.

"I'm a rocker." I shrug. "And I like shirts." Removing my backpack from under the seat, I pray our picnic is still in pristine condition. I went to a lot of trouble making various sandwiches, and I hope they're still fresh. "Bono lives near here," I confirm.

"Really?"

"Yep. If it's not too late when we leave, I can drive by his place, if you like." I close the seat, smiling as I watch Vivien casually shrug. "I keep forgetting you're not bothered by celebs."

"One of the things I love about Ireland is how relaxed people are about fame. It's a refreshing change."

Slinging the bag over my shoulder, I take her hand and walk toward the path that leads up the hill. Warmth seeps into my callused palm from her much softer one, and fiery tingles spread across my skin. I'm amazed every time we touch with the extent of how deeply it affects me. "I hate the thought of fame," I admit, and we chat about it in more depth as we make our way to the very top.

Vivien has given me a lot to think about in relation to integrity, and she even talked a little about Reeve and his celebrity.

Her hand is still curled around mine as I lead her toward my favorite picnic spot in a little secluded area right by the edge of the cliff.

"Is this safe?" she questions, and I can't help laughing at the expression on her face.

"You really are a scaredy-pants, aren't you?"

She shoves her middle finger up at me, and I crack up laughing.

"It's fair to say I've led a more sheltered, less reckless existence than you," she says, and all my good humor fades, quickly replaced by familiar anger when I think of the privileged upbringing my twin has enjoyed.

Knowing Reeve got to spend his formative years with the woman currently holding my hand only adds to my rage. *Where is the fairness in all of this?*

"Did I say something wrong?" Her frown is immediate.

I pull her to a halt before we reach the edge, forcing a smile as I try to shake off my anger and recover my good mood. It's not Vivien's fault I was tossed to the side like garbage and denied the upbringing I should have had. "Don't mind me. I'm a moody fucker."

"I've noticed. At least you're self-aware. There's a lot to be said for that."

"Trust me, I'm well aware of all my failings."

After laying down the blanket, we sit down, side by side, and I unpack our lunch before quickly tucking in.

"This is delicious." She licks her fingers after demolishing a chicken and a tuna sandwich. "What deli did you get it from?"

I grin at the compliment. "Deli O'Donoghue."

Her eyes widen. "You made these?"

"Don't look so shocked. I have many talents." I waggle my hands in front of her face. "These hands are *very* skilled."

"They've had enough practice, I'm sure," she murmurs.

I brush some stray hairs back off her face. "Does my history with women turn you off?"

She waits a few beats before replying. "A little, if I'm being honest. But you can't change your past any more than I can change mine."

"Would you want to?" I'm thoroughly invested in her reply.

"That's the million-dollar question." She stares at the sea before cocking her head to one side and focusing her attention on me. "If I could erase the last couple of years, I would, but before that, everything was perfect. In a lot of ways, it's easier to cling to the hurtful stuff, to let my anger override my other emotions. It's easier to forget about the good times, but there were lots of good times," she quietly admits, brushing crumbs off her lap and keeping her head down.

"What's he like?" I ask.

She whips her head up, fixing her eyes on mine.

"I'm guessing everything reported isn't true," I add. I know the media love spinning shit, but they'll often take the truth and embellish it. I want to know how much of what's been written online is true. While I don't want to spend our first date talking about her ex, I'm curious for her spin on things. Vivien is most likely the person who knows him best, and I want to hear her opinion of him.

"It's not. Reeve isn't a bad person, and I know he loved me. I guess he just lost his way."

That's no excuse, and I'm disappointed she's making allowances for him. "That sounds like polite bullshit." Handing her a bottle of water, I work hard to restrain the anger waiting to surface.

"I need to believe he was manipulated and tricked into following the path he did, because the other reality is too hurtful. If he knew what he was doing, it means he didn't care that he hurt me, and that thought is unbearable."

Tears well in her eyes, and now I feel like a piece of shit. When she puts it like this, I get it. She's telling herself what she must for her sanity and survival, and I can't fault her for it. Sure, I'm doing the same. Ignoring the part where I'm going to deliberately hurt her because it upsets me every time I think about her being collateral damage. The only way I can do this is to avoid thinking of it like that, so it's hypocritical of me to criticize her for doing the same.

"I'm sorry. I don't mean to upset you." Sliding my arm around her shoulders, I pull her in tight as guilt slaps me across the face. When she rests her head against my shoulder, it feels like the most natural thing in the world to be sitting here with her like this. "I'm just trying to understand."

"How much of a basket case I am?" she says, half laughing, half crying.

"How badly he damaged your heart and whether there's any hope for an impatient asshole like me." The words come straight from my heart.

Her head rises from my shoulder, and she turns into me placing her arms around my neck. My heart is crashing around my chest wall, throwing shapes and jumping hoops. "He hurt me, but I'm not some fragile broken doll you need to walk on eggshells around."

I hold her face in my hands, hoping she can't feel how badly I'm trembling. Being this close to her is exhilarating but terrifying too. "I already know that, Viv. I just don't want to rush you when you're not ready. You'll need to set the pace because the very last thing I want to do is hurt you too."

"I think you're a liar, Dillon O'Donoghue."

I stop breathing. Panic surges through my veins at her words.

Confusion paints her face as she examines me, easing back a little. "Remember, we're going to be scared together."

My anxiety fades as I realize I'm overreacting. She didn't mean anything in particular. Her soft lips hit the edge of my mouth, and my dick instantly stirs behind my jeans. Her scent swirls around me, and warmth from her body seeps into my bones, eviscerating the last trace of my paranoia. Leaning into her is instinctual, and we're so close it would take nothing to kiss her, but she's got to make the move.

"You wave that asshole flag around, wearing it with pride, but I'm onto you." She smiles while tweaking my nose. "You do it to keep people away. To stop yourself from feeling. I recognize the signs, so don't try to deny it. But it's not who you are. Underneath that façade hides a different man. One I really want to get to know."

It's scary how quickly she's burrowed underneath my walls and figured part of me out. It should be enough to send me running in the opposite direction, but it doesn't. I like that she's seen part of me and she's still here. She isn't aware of all my flaws, but she knows enough, and she's still interested. That revelation does something to me. My hand lowers to her hip. "I've told you things today I haven't fully shared with anyone. You're already getting under my skin." My eyes drop to her tempting mouth.

I want to kiss her so badly.

I need her like I need music.

"You're getting under mine too," she whispers, pressing herself all up against me as her eyes fixate on my mouth. "Kiss me." Confidence radiates from her tone and her expression, and it's sexy as hell. "Kiss me like you'll die if you can't taste my lips."

She had me at *kiss me*. Hell, she's had me long before that, but I can't help laughing at her melodramatics. "You English students." I shake my head as anticipation replaces the blood flowing through my veins.

It's happening.

I'm going to taste her again, and this time, it won't be a fleeting kiss.

I know I'm, *we're*, on the verge of something monumental. We can't share the chemistry we do and this not be spectacular and mind-altering. My heart is thumping like crazy as I remove the tie from her hair, and it falls in gorgeous soft, thick layers around her face and shoulders. "Are you sure this is what you want?" I examine her face carefully as I weave my fingers through her silky hair. I don't want to fuck this up or have her feeling pressured into this before she's ready. It'll kill me if she says no, but I'm determined to do this right.

"Oh my god. Just kiss me already."

I'm smirking as I pull us back from the edge, to be on the safe side. And then I'm smiling so wide it feels like my mouth might split my jaw apart. My heart is fit to burst as we move together, and our lips meet in the most perfect kiss. I've never experienced anything like this soft, passionate, sultry blending of lips and minds. I'm in no rush, enjoying savoring the taste of her perfect mouth as we slowly get acquainted.

Vivien is pressed close to my body as we kiss, holding on to my shoulders like she's afraid I might disappear if she's not holding me tightly. When her fingers wind into my hair and she moans into my mouth, I'm completely undone. My tongue slips between her lips, and I groan as I explore her exquisite mouth. My dick is jerking against the zip of my jeans, eager to slide between her soft thighs.

I lie down flat on my back and pull her up over me so she's straddling my hips. My arms band around her back, keeping her safe as our kissing turns more frantic. Gone are the first soft sensual kisses, replaced with heated kisses that still aren't enough. My cock is rock hard now, and there's no way she's not feeling it. I almost come on the spot when she pivots her hips and grinds down on me.

"Jesus, Viv." I suck on her earlobe. "What the fuck are you doing to me?"

"Less talking. More kissing," she rasps, and I chuckle as I leave a trail of hot kisses along her neck and across her collarbone.

Then my mouth is on hers again because I can't get enough of it, and we're passionately kissing and grinding against one another, and it's the best intimate encounter of my entire life.

I was wrong earlier.

This isn't just spectacular and mind-altering.

It's life-changing.

No matter what happens from this point on, Vivien will leave me irrevocably changed.

It's one truth I can't deny.

Chapter Thirty-One
Age 20

My fingers fly across the page, the lyrics coming to me easily as the melody plays out in my head.

"Damn, that's good," Jay says, hovering over me as he reads the words I've written down.

I look up at him, wondering when and how he snuck into my bedroom without me noticing. "It's not finished." I snap my notebook closed, feeling territorial over these lyrics.

My best mate flops down on my bed beside me. "She's your Yoko Ono."

I swat him with a pillow. "Fuck off with that crap."

"You can't deny the truth. You had writer's block for months, and from the second Vivien showed up, you've been writing up a storm. It's your best work, Dillon."

I lean back against my headboard, reaching for my smokes on autopilot. "I won't deny she's inspiring me, but don't call her that. Yoko Ono was the bomb that detonated The Beatles. Vivien could never be that."

Jay smirks. "Defensive much?"

"Fuck off."

"It's cool, mate. I like her for you." He props up on one elbow. "I never thought you'd have a girlfriend before me. You were always destined to be the eternal bachelor."

My fingers wrap around my lighter, stalling just as I'm about to light up. "Vivien is mine for now, but it won't last." I toss the lighter and smokes back on my locker. I want to quit, and I've got to start breaking the habit.

"Wow, does she know you've already written off your relationship?"

"I'm being pragmatic." I glance at my watch as I swing my legs onto the floor. "She's returning to L.A. at the end of the summer."

"Maybe."

I stand and stretch my back out. I've been holed up on my bed all day writing lyrics, and I'm a little stiff now. "There's no maybe about it."

"She might change her mind."

"I don't want her to change her mind." I level him with a sharp look. "I'm not long-term relationship material, and we both know it. This will be fun while it lasts. Then she'll go home, and I'll go back to how things were."

"Sounds so easy." He climbs to his feet and claps me on the back. "Hope it all works out for you, lad."

"Sorry, how much?" I'm sure my incredulity is evident in my tone as much as the disbelief is written all over my face.

"Eighty-five euro," the woman behind the counter in the florist's says.

"For twelve fucking roses? Are you shitting me?"

I have lots of plans for things to show Vivien this week, and I can't afford to do all of them if I blow this kind of money on a bunch of flowers, at least not without making a considerable dent in my savings.

"That's what they cost." She folds her arms and purses her lips. "Are you taking them or what?"

I grind my teeth to the molars, beyond pissed off. "I'll leave them."

"Cheapskate," she murmurs under her breath, and I glare at her as I stomp out of the shop.

I'm fit to kill someone as I storm down Grafton Street, trying to push the images of those roses Reeve sent her from my mind. There were at least thirty in that bouquet, and it enrages me he can buy stuff for her on a whim and I can't.

I recall the shite Aoife said that first night Viv showed up, and her words actually help. Aoife got it all wrong. Vivien isn't the kind of girl who demands expensive things. Far from it. She's generous with her money, but it's never extravagant, she never brags, and she usually doesn't want to draw attention to it.

Vivien seems to appreciate the little things I do for her, like washing her shirt, making sandwiches for our picnic, and showing up yesterday with ice cream and wine and cooking her dinner when she was feeling low.

We fed one another ice cream, in between kisses, and it was so fucking hot. I'm addicted to her lips and the way she feels under my hands. I didn't even mind enduring *The Notebook* again because she kept me distracted. Just holding her and spending time with her soothed my soul. She fell asleep before me on the sofa, and I snapped a few sneaky pics because she looked so fucking beautiful. I might have stared at those pics one or a thousand times today.

It took huge effort to remove myself from her gaff last night after Ash woke us up because I could barely tear myself away from her. I didn't want to go home to my empty bedroom, and I've been dying to see her all day. Which is why I'm planning to show up outside the gates of Trinity tonight to take her to dinner. I've been suffering withdrawal symptoms all day, and I refuse to go any longer without seeing her.

There's a nice Italian place just off Dame Street that is good quality food and reasonably priced. I walk into Spar, trying not to feel like a worthless sack of shit when I buy a bunch of cheap lilies. Hopefully, Vivien will appreciate the gesture more than the expense.

"What are you doing here?" Vivien asks when she finally appears thirty minutes later. I've been freezing my bollocks off waiting for her. Ash said her last class ended twenty minutes ago, but she was obviously held up. Although she's all bundled up in a coat and scarf and I can't see much of her, she's still a sight for sore eyes. The tip of her nose is red, and her cheeks are flushed, and though her hair is pulled back in a ponytail and she has no makeup on, she's still the prettiest girl I've ever seen.

"Waiting for you, Hollywood," I confirm. "I'm taking you to dinner." Out of the corner of my eye, I spot Cat frowning, but I ignore her, keeping my focus on my girl. Gulping over the lump in my throat, I hand the flowers to Vivien. "These are for you." I shove my hands in my pockets to stop myself from grabbing her like I want to.

All my anxiety disappears the instant her face lights up. Viv buries her nose in the petals. "I love them. Thank you." She leans up, pressing her mouth to my ear. "You're always so thoughtful. It means a lot," she adds before brushing her lips against mine.

That's all the invitation I need. My arms band around her automatically, and I yank her against my body, clasping her cold cheeks in my cold palms and kissing her passionately. Something settles inside me the instant our lips collide, and I take my sweet time exploring her mouth.

We're both panting when we break apart.

"Wow." A happy smile spreads across her swollen lips. "Can't say I mind your history with women when you kiss me like that." She loops her arm in mine. "I'm happy to reap the benefits of your experience."

"I haven't enjoyed kissing any other woman as much as I enjoy kissing you," I truthfully reply, snaking my arm around her shoulders.

"Spoken like a true player." She rolls her eyes playfully.

"It's the truth." I gently squeeze her hip. "You're one of a kind, Hollywood."

She beams up at me, and warmth floods my body. We stare at one another, and that potent chemistry kicks into gear, charging the small gap between us. My eyes land hungrily on her mouth, and I want to spend the evening kissing her.

"I guess I'll see you tomorrow, Viv," Cat says in a pissy tone, folding her arms and wearing a grumpy look. *How is she still here?* Any normal person would have slunk off the second we started kissing. I've always thought there's something not quite right about Ash's friend. Cat was actually in my year in school, and Ash only got friendly with her during sixth year. She's come on to me a few times, but I've always turned her down. She's pretty enough, but she does nothing for me, and I'm wary of her intentions. Ash says I'm being paranoid, and she seems to like her, so I guess that's all that matters.

Still, this right here is not normal behavior.

Cat's intervention breaks the spell, and Vivien drags her gaze from mine. I'm getting sick of other women coming between us.

"Yes, of course." Viv leans over and hugs Cat. "Have a nice night."

"Bye, Dillon."

"See ya, Cat." *Good riddance.*

"So, where are we off to?" Viv asks, securing the flowers in the crook of her arm after I take her bag and sling it over my shoulder. "A nice Italian place I know. The food is good, and it's only a ten-minute walk."

"Sounds good. I'm starving."

Her face is fucking glowing as she looks up at me, and I can't resist kissing her again. She tastes like heaven on my tongue, and I don't think I'll ever get enough of her. I meant what I said. I've never experienced kissing like this before. It's as if her lips were made to slot perfectly against mine. It takes all my willpower to pull back after a couple of minutes, but if we keep going, it'll escalate, and we're likely to be arrested for public indecency.

"If you keep this up, I'm going to melt into a puddle on the sidewalk."

I chuckle as I tuck her in close and steer her forward. "You're in Ireland now. It's a *path*, Hollywood."

"Okay. I'm going to melt into a puddle on the path if you keep that up," she says in the worst Irish accent.

I snort out a laugh. "I see your mother's talent wasn't passed down," I tease as we maneuver around people, making our way towards Dame Street.

She slaps my chest. "That was mean, but I concede. I'll leave the foreign accents to my mom." A shroud of sadness ghosts over her.

"You miss her." I hold her closer, the need to comfort her instinctual.

"I do. I miss Mom and Dad. Audrey too."

"You're very brave, Viv." I brush my knuckles across one cheek as we stand at the pedestrian crossing, waiting for the lights to turn green. I pull her flush against my front. "It took guts to fly halfway round the world on your own. To start over in a new place, a new college. They must be so proud of you."

"They're always proud of me." She links her fingers through mine as the lights change, and we break our embrace. I keep a firm hold of her hand as we cross the road. "I'm so lucky they're my parents. They always have my back, and they support me one hundred percent. I talk to them several times a week, but it's not the same."

"They must miss you too."

"They do, but they're coming over in July, and we're going to travel around a bit." She bites on the corner of her lip, looking sheepishly at me.

"What?"

"Nothing."

Dillon

"Hollywood." I drill her with a stern look as we turn the corner and head towards the restaurant. "Out with it."

"This is probably premature, but I was thinking maybe you could come with us? Ash is coming too."

A knot forms in my stomach. "We'll be busy with the band in the summer, so I'm not sure I could get time off."

"Oh, of course." Her cheeks stain red, and she averts her eyes.

I pull her to a standstill just outside the restaurant. "Hey." I tip her chin up with one finger. "I'd come if I could." If I wasn't afraid her parents know Reeve is a twin and they might spot a resemblance. But what I said about the band is no lie, and it would probably be impossible anyway. "And I promise I'll take you to places on days when we don't have gigs. I already have a list of things I plan to do with you."

"Oh, you do now, do you?"

I'm glad to see the smile back on her face. "You have a one-track mind, Hollywood." Yanking her into my body, I grind my hips against hers. "Not that I have any issue with it," I add before my lips descend.

Chapter Thirty-Two
Age 20

"Thank you for taking me. I loved it." Viv wraps her arms around my neck as I crowd her against the door to her apartment.

We've spent every night this week together, and I can't get enough of her. "I like showing you my country, and I love that you're so interested in our culture and our history." My hands land on her slim hips as I lean down and glide my lips against hers.

Kissing her will never get old.

Her mouth is like a drug to me.

A contented sigh slips from her lips, and I grasp the opportunity, sliding my tongue into her mouth. Our mutual groans are like a shot of liquid lust charging through my veins, and my grip on her tightens as I pivot my hips, pressing my semi against her stomach. Her breathy moan is my personal aphrodisiac, and my kiss turns demanding as my hands gravitate to her arse and I knead her firm cheeks.

I react fast when the door opens unexpectedly, wrapping one arm around her back and keeping her body pressed tight against mine as I use my other arm to cling to the door frame so we don't fall to the ground.

"Fucking hell. Could you two not maul each other *inside* the apartment?" Ash's tone carries no heat, only the usual joy. She's beyond excited I'm going out with her best friend.

"Whoops." Vivien giggles as I straighten us up. When she attempts to separate our bodies, I fix her with a glare and keep her pressed all up against me.

"Are you heading out?" I ask my sister as I maneuver Viv and me inside.

"Nah." My sister dangles a rubbish bag in the air. "Just doing a rubbish run. I went to the pub for a bit earlier. I just got home."

"We were at Trim Castle," Vivien explains, resting her head against my chest. "It was amazing."

I press my lips to her hair, inhaling the familiar fruity scent.

Ash leans against the doorway. "You went all the way to Meath on the bike?"

"I have the windswept hair to prove it," Viv jokes, snuggling in closer.

"Hollywood loves my bike now." I love having Vivien behind me on the open road. The feel of her slender arms around my waist and her back smushed up against me is my favorite new feeling in the world.

I'm turning into a right sap, going to bed every night this week with a goofy smile on my face.

"I'm converted," Vivien admits, and I cradle her in my arms, dotting kisses into her hair.

Ash's face softens as she looks at us. "You two look so good together."

"So you've said a time or a hundred." I arch a brow.

"I'm just saying you're so natural with one another. Like you've been together years, not just a week."

Technically, it's only a week tomorrow, but who's counting? The truth is, I agree with my sister. I'm more comfortable around Vivien than I've ever been with any woman who isn't a relative. I have no experience with relationships to know if this is the norm or unusual, just that it doesn't feel forced or unnatural. It's the best feeling in the world.

"Ash is right." Viv smiles shyly up at me. "You're an amazing boyfriend, Dillon. No one would ever know you've never done this before."

My mouth is on hers in an instant, and I devour her lips as Ash chuckles, sliding past us and out the door.

"Oh, Dillon." Vivien swoons in my arms when we break our lip-lock. "I could kiss you forever and never get tired of it."

"Is that right?" I grin as I sweep her legs out from under her and toss her over my shoulder.

"Dillon! What're you doing?"

Swatting her delectable arse, I stride down the hallway and into the living room. "Making you dinner," I explain, dumping her gorgeous butt on the sofa.

"No way." She hops up super quick. In a lightning-fast move, she pushes me down on the sofa and pins me in the chest with one hand. "You and Ash cooked last night, and you've been taking me out all week. It's my turn to look after you."

"Ordering takeaway is cheating, Hollywood."

She jumps on my lap and tugs on my hair. "Who said anything about takeout?"

"Take-a-way," I enunciate the words as I squeeze her arse cheeks. I love pushing her buttons when she comes out with all her Americanisms even if they're adorable as fuck.

My dick is hardening again, twitching with the need to drive inside her sweet cunt.

Abstaining is new for me. Usually, when I want to fuck a woman, I just do it. But this is different, and though I'm dying to fuck Viv, I'm also happy with kissing and groping until she's ready to take that step. I know it's a big one for her. I suspect Reeve has been her only lover, though I could be wrong. I'm not sure what went down at that college frat party last year or if there was anyone before they became more than friends. I have made it a point of not talking about her ex this week. I want her to forget all about him, and bringing him up repeatedly won't serve any purpose except curiosity and to rile me up.

"Yes, yes, asshole. I'm aware of the differences." She tugs on my hair harder as I laugh. I love that she calls me out on my bullshit. Placing her hands on my shoulders, she leans down and kisses me. "I'm not a great cook, but I can cook a few things decently. I made lasagna first thing this morning before I left for class. I just need to pop it in the oven and make some garlic bread."

"You must have been up early." I wind my fingers through her tousled hair.

"I was." She kisses the tip of my nose before sliding off my lap.

I pout. "I'm not that hungry." At least not for food. "Get your sexy arse back here."

"Nope." She plants her hands on her hips and pins me with a challenging stare. "I'm making you dinner. You'll stay right there and let me spoil you for a change."

"You spoil me just by breathing." The words glide out of my mouth uncensored.

Tears fill her eyes, and I sit up in alarm, wondering what I've done to upset her. "For a self-professed novice, you sure are a diehard romantic, Dillon." She flings herself at me, and my arms suction around her warm body. "You make me happy," she whispers, hugging me close. "I didn't think it would ever be possible again."

"You make me happy too." I bury my face in her neck, inhaling the delicious scent emanating from her skin.

Vivien is so real. There are no pretenses. She speaks her mind, and she wants me for *me*. There is no other agenda. She seems to love being with me as much as I love being with her. It's the most exhilarating feeling.

She lifts her head, staring deep into my eyes. My heart is going crazy, and butterflies swoop into my chest the longer we stare at one another. "You're so hot, Dillon." She peppers kisses along my jawline. "And so thoughtful." She cups one side of my face. "Thank you for this week. It's been incredible."

I lean into her touch. "You don't have to thank me. I told you I love spending time with you, and I meant it. This week has been special for me too." Turning my head, I press a kiss to her palm.

"I know you're not used to taking things slow, and I—"

"Do not apologize, Vivien." Clasping her hips, I lift her onto the sofa beside me. I can't have a serious conversation when she's straddling me. I cup her stunning face in my hands. "I told you we'll go at your pace, and I'm perfectly happy with that. I never want you to feel pressured. I'm fine to wait." I press a kiss to her brow, just needing to be touching some part of her all the time.

Tears pool in her eyes again as she threads her fingers in mine. "It's not that I don't want to because I really, really do." She kisses me softly on the lips. "I'm so into you, Dillon. One touch and I want to strip my clothes off and impale myself on your cock."

"Holy fuck, Hollywood." I rub my aching dick. "Are you trying to torture me or what?"

A tiny giggle filters into the air. "If it helps, I'm torturing myself too." She sits up on her knees and leans into me. "I want you bad, Dil, but we're still new, and when we fuck, I want it to be for all the right reasons."

This girl. She slays me. "I'm cool with it, Viv. Don't sweat it."

"It's a big step for me, and I want to ensure I'm fully onboard with it before we go there. I don't want my ex to come between us."

"I don't want that either."

"When I have sex with you, I want to be all in with nothing in the way. Does that make sense?"

"Absolutely." I don't like the potential of my twin coming between us like that, but she wouldn't be the person I know her to be if she didn't feel like this. "And for the record, I like that this is new for both of us. What we have is different than anything I've experienced before. I don't want to rush into sex either. I want it to be special between us, and I know it will be as long as neither of us are forcing it."

She slides back onto my lap. "How have you never had a girl-friend before, Dillon? I just don't understand it."

"It's pretty simple." I run my thumb along her lower lip before lifting my eyes to hers. "I was waiting for you."

"How did Aoife take the news?" I ask Jay as we wait to go onstage at the Trinity Ball. After Aoife threw a hissy fit a couple of weeks ago when Jay told her she wasn't invited to come with us tonight, he decided it was time to cut her loose once and for all. Conor has no issue with it either, and I've been wanting to sever ties for some time.

"She was upset, but she's promised to be cool about it as long as we don't mind her hanging around Whelans and Bruxelles. She still wants to support Toxic Gods even if she's no longer warming our beds."

"I hope that's the truth. If she causes trouble, she's barred."

"She has stayed away from Viv after you spoke to her," Jamie reminds me.

"Because I made it very clear what would happen if she continued that bullshit."

I was fuming when Ash and Viv told me how Aoife was treating Vivien when my back was turned. I promised Viv the band groupies wouldn't be an issue, and I intend to stick to my word. I want Vivien to feel comfortable when she's with me, and no woman is going to make her feel less than on my watch.

"How is Viv? She didn't seem too upset about the pictures."

We were in the middle of our soundcheck when Jay showed me the pictures on *OK Magazine*'s website of Reeve fucking around with Saffron Roberts in Mexico. I know they are splashed all over the print editions in the shops because Ash said that's how Viv learned of their existence after I called my sister to give her a heads-up.

My twin is such an idiot, and he deserves to lose Vivien forever.

"She's grand." I was expecting her mood to be low and maybe

some tears, but I'm glad to have been proven wrong. I think Vivien has turned a corner, and I'm happy for her. She didn't deserve the way he treated her, and now she's fully exorcised Reeve from her life, the path is clear for me. "He's a free agent now, and in a weird way, I think it's given her the closure she needed."

I don't tell my mate Viv told me she's ready for sex because it's private between her and me. She let me eat her out a few nights ago, and she sucked my dick, and all I've been thinking about since is how utterly stunning she is naked and how incredible she felt coming against my lips. It was hands down the best blowjob of my life, and I know sex with her is going to be out of this world. My cock has been straining against my zip ever since she pulled me aside a few minutes ago and told me she wants to ditch the after-parties later and go back to her place to fuck the rest of the night away.

I am dying to feel her tight cunt hugging my hard dick.

I have never wanted to fast-forward time as badly as I want to fast forward it tonight.

"She loved her presents. You were worrying for nothing." Jay slaps me on the back.

I might have had a little existential crisis over what to buy my girl-friend for her twentieth birthday. "It's hard to buy birthday presents for the girl who has everything, especially when I'm on a limited budget." She seemed to love the Claddagh necklace and the photo album I bought her, and Ash said the breakfast I sent to their gaff was well received. My sister was a little cagey on the phone this morning, and I know she lied when I asked her what Reeve sent Vivien. Maybe it's best I don't know. I don't want anything ruining tonight especially not my twin.

"Dil, you need to let go of this shite. So what if she has wealthy parents and more money than you? Viv doesn't give a crap about that, and you shouldn't either. She likes you for you, mate. It's not about what you can or can't buy her."

I wish it was that easy. It's hard not to compare myself to my twin and difficult not to feel inferior when he can buy her the world and all I've got to give her is a part of myself. Maybe if I was being fully honest with her and all the secrets and lies were out on the table, it might be easier to disregard the vast differences in our upbringings and our bank balances.

But that's an impossibility when I've pledged to use her for my own gain.

Even if I wanted to change my mind and fess up now, it's too late.

It will seem like another betrayal to her, and I'll lose her anyway.

I doubt she'll like me very much when she realizes she doesn't really know me at all.

Chapter Thirty-Three
Age 20

"Hurry, Dillon," she rasps, collecting her hair in one hand and lifting it so I can access the back of her dress. We tried and failed to find a taxi, racing home on foot, desperate to be together. It's been a long day and night, but I've never felt more awake.

I think I'll die if I don't get to fuck her ASAP.

"I'm trying. Could you have made these buttons any smaller?" I curse a few times as I grapple with her dress, and she giggles. The sound of her happiness does weird things to my insides as I fumble with these fucking stupid buttons. "Done," I say a few seconds later, watching with my tongue hanging out of my mouth as she shimmies out of the gorgeous dress she designed and made especially for the ball.

When she turns around, wearing only a blue lace thong and high-heeled strappy silver sandals, I almost come apart on the spot. She is so incredibly intoxicating. So beautiful laid almost fully bare before me.

I will never get enough of this view.

"Fuck. Look at you." My gaze roams leisurely and sensually over her tempting body, and I watch her nipples perk up under my attention with smug satisfaction. She's equally as responsive as I am. It doesn't seem to take much for either of us to be primed and ready to go. One heated look or one soft touch is often enough to ignite that flame.

"We need to capture this moment." I want to freeze-frame this moment so I never forget it. I grab my phone. "Can I take a photo?"

She looks unsure, and I can guess why.

"I promise I won't show it to anyone. This is just for me." It's no word of a lie. I never want anyone to see her like this. She is *mine*, and this is only for me. "Ammo for the spank bank," I add as I rub my erection through my trousers. I'm so turned on I'm liable to explode at any moment.

"Okay, but from the neck down."

If that's what she needs to feel comfortable, it's fine by me. I take the picture, drop my phone, and stalk forward, frantic to touch her. I'm all over her the second I reach her. I play with her nipples as I kiss her neck and along her jawline, and my dick is twitching behind my boxers, begging to be let free. "You looked like Hollywood royalty at the ball," I admit before sucking one taut nipple into my mouth. "Tonight, you're my queen."

"You're wearing too many clothes," she grumbles, clutching my shoulders. "Strip for me, baby."

I fix her with a challenging look. "Undress me." Lowering my hands from her body, I straighten up and wait to see if she'll rise to the occasion.

"Gladly," she says, not disappointing me. Her hands are all over me in a flash as she starts undressing me. I shiver all over when her fingers trace lightly over the tattoos on my arms and my chest. Her touch sets me on fire, and I jump a little when she turns her attention to the scorpion inked across my back. "This is gorgeous. Does it have any special significance?"

How do I answer without outwardly lying to her? She massages the knots in my shoulders while I compose my reply. "The scorpion represents a lot of things that have meaning to me."

"Like what?" she asks as her hand travels to my crotch and she slowly tugs the zip down.

"Determination, rebirth, resilience."

"I like it," she whispers, moving to my front. "I love all your ink." She yanks my trousers and boxers down, and my erection springs free. "That's not all I love." Her wicked grin as she drops to her knees has precum leaking from my crown.

"You look good on your knees." I grab her head and guide her mouth to my cock.

Keeping one hand on the back of her head, I grope her perfect tits with my free hand as she licks the salty liquid at the tip of my dick. I stifle a groan when she slowly takes me into her mouth, the feeling exquisite, beyond anything I've ever felt before. Her mouth is my kryptonite. If she wants to control me, all she needs to do is wrap her lips around me, and I'm a goner.

"Touch yourself," I command, driving slowly in and out of her hot mouth.

Her fingers slip into her knickers, and I thrust harder.

"Push two fingers into yourself," I instruct, and she obediently complies. "Work them faster." She is so damn sexy. She has no clue. "Fuck, yeah." I pick up my pace, thrusting into her harder and faster, and the only sounds in the room are my contented groans and the sucking noises she's making. "Enough," I demand, needing to stop this while I can. I pull out of her mouth with a loud pop. "I want to come in your pussy after I eat you out."

Tossing her on the bed, I rip the thong from her body, and launch myself on her pussy, using my tongue and my fingers to work her real good. My cock is straining and jerking as I dry hump the duvet while I feast on her cunt, staying with her through her orgasm. Then I roll a condom on and prepare to meet my maker.

"Are you still okay with this?" I ask, wanting to make sure she's not having second thoughts. As much as it would kill me to pull back now, I know this is a big deal for her, and I want her all in. I want her looking at *me*, seeing *me*, feeling *me*, when I fuck the living daylights out of her and alter her world forever.

"Yes. Hell yes. Fuck me, Dillon. Do it now."

"It would be my pleasure, Hollywood." My fingers coast over her legs as I spread her thighs wide and settle between them. I lift her legs over my shoulders and drive two fingers into her wet cunt. She's soaked, and it's the biggest turn-on knowing I did that to her. "Tasty," I confirm after licking her essence from my fingers.

No woman has ever tasted so sweet.

Keeping my eyes locked on hers, I drive inside her in one fast thrust, pushing all the way to the hilt. Fuck. Me. She feels incredible squeezing my dick. "Jesus, you're so tight." I don't move for a few beats, letting her body adjust to the feel of me. Then, I bend down and kiss her passionately while I start moving in and out of her wet warmth.

I pick up my pace, fucking her hard, shoving my cock deep, needing to feel every part of her. The sounds coming from her are music to my ears, and she's panting and writhing as I slam into her harder and harder, loving the feel of my piercing dragging along her hot smooth inner walls.

"Harder, Dil," she rasps, lost to ecstasy as I ram inside her like a wild beast. I straighten my back, positioning her legs a little higher, and gyrate my hips, hitting her at a different angle. Then I pound into her like a madman. Sweat rolls down my back as I grip her legs tight and pivot into her over and over, hitting deeper and deeper each time.

"Yes, fuck, yes, Dil, keep doing that."

Sweat beads on my brow and my chest as I work her over good, slamming into her tight body repeatedly, letting pleasure roll over my body in blissful anticipatory waves.

There's a level of intimacy between us that's always been missing for me in past encounters. I'm fully aware of the woman lying underneath me—highly tuned to her raspy breath, every scintillating move, and every seductive moan and whimper leaving her swollen lips. I'm focused on responding to the clues her body is offering, ensuring she's happy and I'm giving her maximum pleasure. I want this to be as special for her as it is for me. Sex has never been like this for me. I want to live inside her and always feel this.

Vivien screams when her second orgasm hits, her body arching and thrusting as she succumbs to the ultimate high. Flipping her over onto her stomach, I yank her arse up and shove her thighs apart with my legs. Then I ram into her again, quickly losing myself to the feel of her body worshipping mine.

Vivien is moaning and screaming, pushing back eagerly to meet my thrusts as I drive into her continuously. My fingers dig into the flesh at her hips as a familiar tingle starts at the base of my spine and my balls tighten and lift. As I hammer away, my climax peaks, and I explode inside her. I almost black out as I shatter in the most indescribable way. I keep thrusting until I've released every drop of cum into the condom, and then I collapse on the bed, holding her against me as I spoon her from behind.

Our slick, warm skin meets in the perfect marriage as we take a few moments to come back down to earth. Brushing her hair aside, I kiss and suck on her neck, almost afraid to ask this question in case I've let her down. Finding my balls, I eventually ask, "Well, Vivien Grace? Did I live up to my promise?"

She turns around, spearing me with the most glorious smile. A satisfied expression rests easily on her face as she caresses my cheek. "Yeah, baby. You definitely did."

"I can walk," Vivien protests when I lift her from the bed a few hours later. I've lost count of how many times we've fucked. All I know is I'm insatiable and every time is better than the last, if that's even possible.

A chuckle tumbles from my chest. "I must be doing a shit job if that's the case." I set her arse down on the bathroom counter, laughing as she shrieks when the cold marble hits her overheated skin. "I'm gonna keep fucking you until you physically can't walk. I won't accept anything less."

"Baby, you're gonna fuck me to death if we keep going." She drops her head to my shoulder. "I can't believe I'm gonna say this," she adds, peeking up at me with sleep-heavy eyes. "But no more. You are a sex god among men, Dillon, and I am a hungry slut for your cock, but no more tonight. I need sleep, babe."

"You sleep, and I'll fuck you," I joke.

She lifts her head. "You like that?"

Sweeping knotty strands of hair back off her beautiful face, I say, "Never tried it, but I think I'll like everything with you."

Her lips tug up at the corner. "You're kinky."

I shrug as I rummage around in her bathroom press. I don't really want to get into all that right now. I'm not sure how she'll feel with the stuff I've done with others, and the last thing I want her thinking about is the things she's done in bed with my twin. "I like to be adventurous, but I'm not into hardcore stuff unless you are, and I'm down to try anything once."

"I don't really know," she says as I remove a tube of plain aloe vera gel and a clean facecloth from the press.

I lightly cup her face. "We can try anything you want, but I know you're tired now. Let me take care of you, and then we'll snuggle and go to sleep. I wasn't serious about the sleep fucking thing," I add before gliding my mouth against hers. "Though now I'm thinking about it, and it's making me horny."

She wraps her arms around my neck. "I'm not opposed to you waking me up with your tongue, fingers, or cock in my pussy but don't try it tomorrow." Her brow puckers. "Or today, I guess. It must be almost morning by now." Yawning, she runs her fingers through the stubble on my cheeks, and I close my eyes, purring like a cat in heat. "I'm a little sore, and I think that's all my body can handle right now."

"I know, beautiful." I brush my nose against hers. "Go pee while I change the sheets."

"There's fresh bed linens in the hall closet," she calls after me as I walk out of the en suite bathroom.

While I haven't heard Ash come home yet, I don't want another lecture about flashing her, so I pull on my boxers and head out of Viv's bedroom to grab clean sheets, some water, and painkillers.

After I make the bed, I return to the bathroom, chuckling when I find Vivien dozing on top of the toilet seat.

"Hollywood." I press a kiss to the top of her head. "Let's get you cleaned up." She doesn't protest when I scoop her up and set her back on the counter on a towel this time.

"I'm so tired," she mumbles as I help her to brush her teeth and comb her hair. Then I wet the facecloth in warm water and clean between her legs. She winces a little.

"How sore are you?"

"I'm a little sore, but it's fine. It's nothing some cock-free sleep won't cure."

I tweak her nose and chuckle. "Hold on to the counter. This will be cold, but it'll help." I smear some aloe vera gel over my fingers and gently inch two inside her, pushing all the way up so I can coat her inner vagina with the calming gel.

She emits a little squeak, jerking on the counter. "Holy fuck, that's cold."

"Yep, but it'll soothe the burn." I lift my eyes to hers as my fingers move tenderly inside her. Her brows knit together, and I think I know where her mind has gone. "At least that's what Ash says. She's had thrush a few times, and she swears by this stuff. I was always running to the chemist to grab her some."

Her features relax, and her thighs widen, and I love she's trusting me with something so intimate. My gaze rakes over her body, surveying the light bruises on her tits, hips, and inner thighs, and the couple hickeys on her neck. Seeing my marks on her body does something to me. I feel like beating my chest and hollering from the top of my lungs, claiming her as mine.

I stall with my fingers buried inside her to kiss her softly. "All good?"

"Yes," she whispers, and a ghost of a blush creeps onto her cheeks.

"I like having my fingers inside you," I truthfully admit, and we both look down to where my fingers have disappeared inside her. "If it were possible, I'd just stay in bed with you forever, stuffing you full of my tongue, my dick, my fingers."

The color on her cheeks darkens. "You have such a filthy mouth."

I tilt my head to one side. "You complaining?"

"Not at all." She threads her fingers in my hair. "I like feeling you inside me. I liked everything you did to me tonight, and I want more."

"Good," I say, reluctantly withdrawing my fingers from her cunt. "Because I have so much I want to do to you and with you, Vivien Grace Mills."

Chapter Thirty-Four
Age 20

"**U**gh, that feels so good," Vivien says, lying face down on the bed as I straddle her naked body from behind and massage her tense back muscles.

"You're studying way too hard. Your shoulders are tied into knots, Hollywood."

"I want to get good grades," she mumbles into her pillow as my fingers work the kinks out of her back.

"You'll ace these exams, and you know what it means." Sitting back a little, I drizzle some of the massage oil into the crack between her cheeks. "Your arse will finally be mine." I've been dying to take her anal virginity since she told me she's never had a dick in her tight hole. Knowing I'll claim this first cranks my arousal to the max. She's understandably nervous, so we've been indulging in a little arse play in preparation for the big event, which Vivien has determined will happen after she finishes her exams.

Rubbing the oil around the edge of her puckered hole, I wish I could claim her here now, but my girl sets the pace. Always.

She lifts her head and looks back at me. "I'm still a little nervous, but I trust you."

Those words both excite and disgust me. "Have I ever left you feeling anything but good after we fuck around?" I sink the tip of my pinkie inside her arse.

A little gasp trickles into the air, and her face flushes. "I'm always floating on a cloud. You fuck me real good, Dil. Best sex of my life."

I'm gloating on the inside. *Something I'm better than you at.* In fact, I'd go all out and say I'm a hundred percent better at being her boyfriend than Reeve Lancaster ever was.

Pushing my little finger in a bit more, I lean down to kiss her on the mouth. "Then trust me on this. I will blow your mind. It'll be the ultimate post-exam high."

I toy with her arse for a few more minutes before cleaning up, and then I finish the massage and tuck her into bed while I go to the kitchen to make her some hot chocolate.

"Hey, broski," Ash says, looking up from where she's stacking the dishwasher when I enter the kitchen.

"Sick of me yet, little sis?" I tease as I pour milk into a saucepan and set it on the hob.

Since Viv and I started fucking, I basically live here now. Apart from our regular Friday night Whelans date, we haven't gone out much the past few weeks because Viv is studying. If I wasn't sleeping over, we wouldn't get to spend much time together at all. The band has picked up a regular mid-week gig at another pub in the city, and I still work the odd shift at Whelans behind the bar, so we're both pretty busy.

Viv doesn't want to stay over at my place, not even after I offered to buy a new bed because I figured she didn't want to sleep in it knowing she's not the first woman to claim a spot. Can't say I blame her. Doubt I could sleep in her bed knowing my twin or any other man had slept there first.

She's as territorial over me as I am over her.

I honestly can't remember a time I was this happy. It's all very domesticated, and I'm shocked at how much I'm loving just doing the normal mundane things with her. Going to sleep holding her in my arms and waking up wrapped all around her is like a balm for my soul. On the rare nights where I have slept alone at my gaff, I've felt bereft, like I'm missing an integral limb.

"Never." Ash snuggles into my side as I stir the warming milk. "You know I love having you here, and you make my best friend really happy, which makes me happy."

I wrap my arm around my pint-sized sister. "Viv makes me happy too."

Ash looks up at me with a soft expression. "I know, Dil. You're made for each other."

Yeah, I'm not touching that. I've given up feeling guilty for my agenda. I had to drop it and just let the chips fall where they fall because I was beating myself up every time I was with Viv, and she was picking up on it. It is what it is, and feeling guilty over it isn't going to make any difference. So, I'm pretending like it's not a factor. I'm treating this like a real relationship because it fucking is, and I'll handle the potential fallout later. Right now, Vivien Grace Mills is my world, and I'm not beating myself up for feeling happy. I'm soaking up all the feel-good emotions like a sponge, cherishing every moment and committing it all to my memory bank to draw upon after it's over and she's gone.

A pang hits me square in the gut while my heart lurches in my chest like always when I think about our inevitable end. I'm trying not to go there, but sometimes it's hard because I'm struggling to imagine going back to my old existence after she's gone.

"Going to tell me where you keep disappearing to?" I ask Ash, purposely changing the subject before I get depressed.

Ash slinks out from under my arm as I remove the box of Butler's Hot Chocolate from the press.

"He's no one important," she lies, avoiding eye contact.

I drop three of the yummy hot chocolate pieces into the milk and resume stirring the liquid.

"If you say so." I have my suspicions, but I'm saying nothing. When I first suspected Jamie and my sister might have rekindled whatever romance they had last summer, I was tempted to pull my best mate aside and rip into him. But I stopped myself in time. They're grown-ups, and Ash knows her own mind. If she's started something with him, she's gone into it with her eyes wide-open. *Who am I to interfere?* I've hated other women stepping in the path of my relationship with Vivien, and I'd be a hypocrite to do the same and deny them the happiness I feel.

If it's serious, I'll talk to Jay to ensure he's on the same page as her. But I'm not going to tell him she's off-limits anymore. I don't think I ever should have.

Ash takes three mugs out of the press, placing them on the counter. Her shoulders are rigid, and her lips are pursed, so I go easy on her. I'll wait for her to raise the subject with me. And perhaps I'm wrong. Maybe she's banging some other guy and I'm way off base. "How is studying going?"

The tension eases instantly from her shoulders. "Good. Viv and I have been studying together at the library, and I think we're well prepared."

"You're both going to nail it."

"Thanks for cooking dinner every night. It's a big help."

I shrug because it's not a biggie. "I like cooking for my favorite sister and my best girl. It's the least I can do."

She leans in and hugs me. "I love seeing you as a boyfriend. I knew all along you'd be the best, and you are."

I laugh while turning off the heat on the hob. "You were always going to be biased."

"Doesn't make it not true."

"He's not sending her stuff or messaging her anymore, right?" I ask, avoiding looking at her as I pour the chocolate milk into the three mugs.

"Dillon." Her tone contains censure. "We talked about this. I'm Switzerland. You need to ask Vivien. I'm not your spy."

Setting the empty saucepan down, I rub the back of my neck. "Sorry," I mumble as I retrieve the packet of mini marshmallows from the press. "I just don't like asking her about him, but I was wondering."

We sent him an intimate photo of us in bed the morning after the Trinity Ball. It didn't leave much to the imagination, and I hope it drove the point home. She's *mine* now. I need to know he understands that. Vivien hasn't mentioned anything to me in the weeks since, and she never talks about him anymore, which I hope is a good sign she's moving on, but I can never be fully sure.

Ash glances behind me before lowering her voice. "I'm not doing this again, Dil. We all agreed I'd keep my friendship with Viv separate to your relationship with her for a reason. But to answer your question, no, he hasn't contacted her, and he hasn't sent her anything. He got the message loud and clear."

"Good." I drop marshmallows on the top of the three mugs.

"Don't worry about Reeve." Ash rubs my arm before taking one of the mugs. "Viv is crazy about you, Dillon. You're the only one putting that big smile on her face every day."

I know, but for how long?

"This is too much, Hollywood," I say, shaking my head at the deluge of clothing bags littering the floor of her bedroom. It's mostly new stuff she bought herself today to celebrate the end of her exams, but a good few of the bags contain clothes she bought me.

"I told you I'm determined to introduce more color into your life, babe." She cops a feel of my arse. "You can't go around dressed like the Grim Reaper all summer long." Her soft giggle trickles into the air, warming every part of me.

Backing her up against the wardrobe, I cage her within my arms. "You'll pay for that." I dive in and drag my teeth along her earlobe. "What's wrong with all black? It's my signature look."

Her arms snake around my neck. "I love your signature look. Honestly, you'd look hot in anything. You are sexy as hell, Dil, and I'm horny for you twenty-four-seven." She grinds her pelvis against me, and predictably, my dick stirs to life. This is the way it is with us. We fuck at least twice a day. We can't get enough of one another, and I'm having the best sex of my life.

"I just like buying you things, and I wanted to thank you," she continues, kissing the corner of my mouth. "I couldn't have sailed through my exams without you. You cooked, cleaned, brought me drinks and snacks, escorted me to and from college, gave me the best freaking massages, and fucked me into oblivion so I got a good night's sleep." Her eyes turn suspiciously glassy. "You don't know how much your unconditional support means to me, and I'm struggling to find ways to show you, so don't get angry that I spent a little money on you." She chews on the corner of her mouth, looking nervous, and I know why.

We've had a few arguments over money. She got me added as a named driver on her rental car and refused to let me reimburse the additional cost. I always want to pay for her when we go out, and she doesn't like it, wanting to pay her own way or take it in turns, arguing she'd be like this with any guy and it's not just because she has more money than me. I know my hang-ups are tied up with my twin. But it's not like I can explain that to her or tell her how inadequate it makes me feel when I can't properly provide for her.

I hate feeling inferior to that prick, but being an ass isn't making me feel any better. Viv did something nice for me, and I'm acting like an ungrateful punk. She just finished her exams, and we have the whole summer together before we are forced to part. This is a happy occasion, a night to celebrate, and I'm determined to ensure she has a good time. Which means I need to let this go.

"I'm not angry, beautiful." I kiss her softly. "Thank you for buying me things. It's very generous, and I'm a lucky fucking bastard to call you mine."

She visibly relaxes against me. "I'm so lucky I met Ash. She's my best friend, and you're the best boyfriend a girl could ask for. I don't want you to think I take you for granted because I don't, Dillon." She stabs me with earnest eyes. "I'm lucky I get to call you mine. I still pinch myself most days to believe it's true."

Vivien does wonders for my self-esteem. I feel like I'm the best version of myself when I'm with her, and I don't even have to try. It's as effortless as breathing. Pulling her into a hug, I rest my chin on her head and hold her close, wishing I never had to let her go. She completes me, and I'm not sure I'll ever be whole again without her. If I could open myself up and tuck her inside, I would. "I never think that, and I don't do it for any reason except I like looking after you and I like making you happy."

"Well, you're really good at it, Dillon." Her hands trace a path up my chest, and she cups my face. We stare deep into one another's eyes, and my heart thumps wildly in my chest. That familiar electricity surges around us, enveloping us in a bubble. My arms tighten around her, and my heart swells to bursting point. I could stare at her all day. I love every single thing about her. Holding her in my arms is the best feeling in the world. "I love being with you, Dil, and I'm excited to spend the summer with you."

Unspoken words hover in the air, but neither of us will articulate them. *What's the point?* We both know the inevitability of our demise. Talking about it all the time won't change that fact, and I'm trying not to think about it too much because it'll only cast a shadow over the time we have left, and that'll defeat the purpose.

"We're going to have the best summer ever," I say, pressing a fierce kiss into her hair. That's one promise I fully intend to keep.

Chapter Thirty-Five
Age 20

"She's getting on my fucking nerves," I tell Jamie as I glower at Aoife across the table at Whelans. As soon as Ash and Viv got up to go to the bar, she turned her simpering gaze on me.

"Has she said something to Viv?" he asks before gulping a mouthful of his pint of Guinness.

I shake my head, gripping the edge of the chair in frustration as Aoife bats her eyelashes and fixes me with a flirtatious smile. "She's stuck to her word. She isn't giving Ash or Viv any grief, but I'm sick of her eye fucking me any chance she gets. It's bloody disrespectful to me and to Viv."

"Have her barred then." Jay shrugs, stretching his legs out under the table and crossing his feet at the ankles.

He sure has changed his tune. I arch a brow, surveying my best friend. He's happier than he's been in ages, and I'm convinced something is going on with Ash. I haven't been around our gaff much to confirm it, but I'm pretty sure he hasn't fucked any bird since the Trinity Ball. At least, he hasn't gone off with anyone after our gigs, and he's as much of a pro as me now at deflecting attention from the groupies. "You wouldn't care?"

"Nope." He pops the P. "I was done with her back in April."

I'm so tempted to pry, but I don't go there. It's not really my business. I'm waiting until one of them says something to me.

"I don't want to do that to her, but it's looking like it's my only option." I remember Aoife's heartfelt plea about how she doesn't have much besides the band and the scene in her life. I don't want to take that from her, but she's bringing this on herself.

"Do what you need to do, mate. I'm cool with it."

"Here, babe." Viv hands me a bottle of beer before depositing her pink gin and 7Up on the table and dropping back onto my lap.

Setting the beer down, I grab the back of her head and pull her face to mine. The instant my lips crash onto hers, everything settles in my world. She has no idea what she does to me, for me. She doesn't understand how she soothes every ragged, jagged, broken part of me just by her presence. My girl doesn't let me down, devouring me back with the same intensity and subtly grinding on my erection. I love how much she loves sex and how she's down to try anything in bed. She's every bit as insatiable as me, and we couldn't be any better matched. We just work, full stop.

"You were so freaking hot on stage tonight, Dil," she pants in my ear as she scrapes her nails back and forth along my scalp in a way she knows I love. "All I kept thinking the whole time you were up there is you're *mine*. Those girls can scream their lungs out and throw their panties at you all they like, but I'm the one you're coming home with." She nibbles on my earlobe.

"Always, Hollywood." I palm her arse. "I only have eyes for you."

"I know." Her eyes fill with emotion. "You show me all the time." She grabs my face in her small, soft hands. "You have no idea how happy that makes me or how sexy you are. You own that fucking stage, babe. You have this indescribable stage presence. I know the guys are disappointed nothing happened with that scout, but it's going to happen. You guys are too good for it not to. You're a bona fide rock star, Dillon, and you're going to make it. I feel it deep in my soul." She presses her palm in the middle of her tits.

"Your belief means everything to me."

"It's easy to believe in you. You're hardworking, and you have talent and determination oozing from your pores." She moves on my lap, and I groan as fresh need charges the blood flooding to my cock. She flashes me a wicked grin. "But it's more than that. I want only the best things for you, Dillon. I want to see you soar, and I'll support you any way I can. If there is anything I can do, any way I can use my contacts to help, you only have to ask."

My heart is pounding like crazy, and an unfamiliar feeling spreads across my chest, infusing every part of me. I don't have the words to properly express how much her encouragement and support means to me. "You've already done so much. Just knowing you want this for me is more than enough."

"Always, Dil. I'll always support your dreams." Viv leans down, sliding a sneaky hand between the gap in our bodies to grab my crotch through my jeans. "I fully understand how every woman wants you, but they can't fucking have you. You're mine, and I want you right fucking now."

"I love when you get all possessive." I squeeze her arse, uncaring who sees. I want every fucker in this place to know she's mine and I'm hers.

"It comes naturally," she says before her mouth slams down onto mine.

We ravage one another, and a chorus of catcalls and wolf whistles ring out along with calls to "get a room!"

"I've never fucked in a public bathroom," she purrs in my ear.

Hell yeah. I like where this is going. "Want me to rectify that for you?" I growl in her ear.

"Yes, please." She jumps off me so fast it's like a superpower.

I bark out a laugh as she pulls me to my feet, her eyes alight with wanton desire. I love seeing this side of Vivien when she lets go of her inhibitions and just lets her personality shine. Out of the corner of my eye, I spot Aoife scowling. I would never fuck my woman to prove a point to another, but this decision is already made, and if it drills the point home more directly to my ex-fuck buddy, then great.

More wolf whistles accompany us as I grab Viv's hand and escort her to the bathrooms, commandeering the accessible toilet before a group of drunken girls waiting in line nip in ahead of us. Vivien cracks up laughing as the girls pound on the door, but I quickly distract her, lifting her sexy dress and yanking her knickers down her legs.

Stuffing the red lacy underwear in my back pocket, I have zero intention of giving them back. They're going in my growing pile of stolen undies. It's a miracle Viv hasn't copped on to it yet, but if she has, she hasn't said anything. And if she thinks she's getting this pair back, she's another think coming. They're mine now. Besides, her dress is long enough to cover her, and she'll be parked right on my lap for the rest of the night, so it's not like she needs them.

Shoving my jeans and boxers down my legs, I roll a condom on and lift my girl in my arms. Flattening her back against the wall, I line up my dick and slam inside her in one fast thrust. Vivien screams, and the banging on the door miraculously stops. I keep one arm around Viv's back and one hand planted on the wall as I fuck her.

Viv's legs are wrapped snugly around my waist as I pound into her with potent need. Our lips clash in a battle for supremacy as we thrust against one another in perfect sync. It's as if we were made for one another. We fit perfectly together, and sex with her is always out of this world. I bite her tits through her dress, as she moans and whimpers on my cock, wishing the top was low-cut so I could pull it down to suck on her nipples and gorge on her velvety-soft flesh.

When I feel her tight walls squeeze my dick, I shove myself in deeper. "Touch your clit," I demand, pushing harder into her. "Come with me, Hollywood."

Two minutes later and we're both groaning and thrusting our way through mutual climaxes. Then I set her down, get dressed, and help to clean her up with some tissues.

Dillon

"That was so fucking hot." Vivien beams at me, and I love seeing her hair all mussed up from my hands and her lips all swollen from my kisses. Her chest is flushed, matching the stunning glow on her face. Her pretty brownish-green eyes are wide with euphoria, and she's wearing the biggest smile.

"Has my woman gained a newfound liking for public sex?" I quip, crowding her against the door as my fingers glide under her dress and I cup her pussy.

"I'm thinking I might have, and also you need to give me back my panties."

"Nope." I grin. "They're mine. I love knowing you'll be sitting out there, on my lap, completely bare. Prepare to be fucked to within an inch of your life by the time we get home." I nip on her ear as I release her tempting cunt and unlock the door. "And forget about sleep because you won't be getting any."

"Oh my god, Dillon!" Viv whimpers the next night as I eat her arse out on her bed. We spent all last night fucking, and after grabbing a few hours' sleep this morning, we stayed in bed watching movies and making one another come, only leaving the room to get food and drinks.

I pause what I'm doing, keeping my hands clasped on her arse cheeks and her spread out before me like the most decadent feast, to check in with her. "You doing okay, Hollywood? Any second thoughts?"

"No." She shakes her head, propping up on her elbows and looking at me lying on my stomach in between her thighs with her legs thrown over my shoulders and my fingers digging into her toned cheeks. "I want this. I'm excited, and it already feels so good."

The blush on her face darkens, and my heart melts. "It's okay to like it, beautiful. Lots of women do."

"I know. That's not it. I'm just amazed I'm so comfortable with this, but then I shouldn't really be surprised. You always take such good care of me."

It's not like it's a chore. Pleasuring my girl is my favorite pastime. "So, lean back and let me take your virginity because my dick's about to sprout wings and take flight if I don't bury it deep in your tight hole."

"You're ridiculous, but I love"—she stutters over her words and her cheeks turn impossibly red—"it."

My breath seizes in my chest. *Did she...was she about to say what I think she was?* My heart beats faster in my chest, but I force all such thoughts aside because now isn't the time. "Tell me if you don't like anything or if you want me to stop. You okay if I fuck you like this?"

"Oh, I thought you'd take me from behind."

"I can do that, but I'd prefer to see your face when I bury myself in your arse for the first time."

She covers her face with her hands, and I snort out a laugh before I drive two lube-slickened fingers into her arse. She cleaned up earlier, and I've been playing with her hole for a while now, wanting to ensure she's fully relaxed and prepped before I fuck her with my cock.

Vivien moans that sensual, deep, sexy, erotic sound that always does things to me, and I squeeze the tip of my dick to calm down. Then I resume fingering her puckered hole in between thrusting my tongue inside. Replacing my tongue and fingers with her vibrator, I stretch her for a few minutes until I'm happy she's ready to take me.

"So fucking wet," I purr when I thrust my other fingers in her soaking cunt. "You like me licking and fingering your arse, huh?"

"Dillon!" She covers her face with her hands again, and I chuckle.

"No hiding, Hollywood. I want to look right in your eyes when I drive my dick inside you."

I roll a condom on and apply tons of lube to my shaft before lining up at her glistening hole. Pushing her bent legs to her chest, I drool over the sight of both holes seeping with need. I worshipped her pussy for hours last night, and now it's time I lavish attention on her virginal hole. Precum leaks from my cock at the thought. "Fuck, Hollywood. I wish you could see yourself. You're exquisite, and I'm so turned on. I'll try to make this last, but I've literally never been this horny in my entire life."

"Good, now shut up and fuck me, babe, or I'll think you're all talk and no action."

"Feisty," I say, rubbing my cock up and down her crack. "I like it when you get all bossy and demanding. You're a kinky little slut, aren't you?" Leaning down, I plant a kiss against her pussy lips.

"Dillon, please."

"Please what?" I tease, rubbing my piercing around the edge of her tight hole.

"Please fuck my ass!" she screams, and it's a good thing Ash is out tonight and we have the place to ourselves.

"Very well, Hollywood." I push my dick in an inch. "Remember you begged for this." I take my time easing inside her, thrusting a little harder through the first ring of muscle. "Relax, beautiful." I lock eyes on her. "Watch my face and just let yourself feel me going where no man has gone before." My lips twitch.

She narrows her eyes before a giggle bursts free. "You're ridiculous. Your dick is partway in my ass, and you're cracking jokes."

"Just keeping it real, Hollywood. Now eyes on me."

The air shifts, and delicious tension wafts around us. "You are so sexy," I say as I push through her resistance. "You undo me, beautiful." I thrust fast, bottoming out, and she gasps. Leaning forward with my hands on her folded legs, I brush my nose against hers. "My dick is all up in your arse, Hollywood. I'm all kinds of excited." She rolls her eyes, but she's smiling. I kiss her lips. "All joking aside, you doing okay?"

"Yes. I'm good." Her eyes well up. "I've never felt closer to another soul, Dillon."

I know what she means. There's a level of trust doing this that is unlike anything else. "Same, beautiful," I whisper before I kiss her softly and without urgency. We kiss for a few minutes while I let her body adjust to me, and then I fuck her.

Boy, do I fuck her.

I can't hold back any longer. I'm more aroused than ever before, and she feels fucking divine. It's no surprise I'm already addicted to her arse, just like I'm addicted to every other part of this incredible woman.

Vivien stays with me, responsive and enthusiastic like always, as I slam in and out. The sensations flowing through my body are transcendental. As I rock into her, I watch her face, ensuring she's comfortable and in this with me. She doesn't let me down. Seeing the look of raw pleasure in her eyes almost undoes me. She's loving it, just like I hoped she would. I'm reading her body, watching for familiar signs, and when I see them, I rub her clit with my fingers and command her to come, watching in awe as she comes apart with my dick buried deep in her forbidden place.

I'm not long following her, spilling cum into the condom as I slide in and out, wanting to milk every drop of this experience.

Dillon

After, I cuddle her, and then we shower together, and I rub some aloe vera gel around her hole before we crawl back under the covers.

"Was it okay?" I ask when we're naked spooning.

She turns around, caressing my chin and pressing a light kiss to my lips. "It was amazing. You're amazing. I love everything you do to me."

I hold her even tighter, wanting to bundle her up and keep her in my arms forever. I didn't think it was possible, but this has brought us even closer. I've never felt more connected to another living soul, not ever, and I don't say that lightly. Emotions whirl inside me, but I refuse to untangle them. Not now. I just want to enjoy every second of this moment, already knowing this is a memory I'll never forget.

Viv falls asleep before me, looking like a goddess with her flushed cheeks, plump lips, and dark hair fanned out on the pillow. I stare at her for a long time, memorizing every freckle, every trickle of air that escapes her full lips, and tracing the subtle lifting of her chest with my eyes. My heart swells and swells until it feels like it might burst. She makes me feel so many things, and though I'm still terrified, my fear pales under the weight of everything else I'm feeling. Dusting soft kisses into her hair, I hug her close, careful not to wake her up.

I desperately want to grab a few pictures to capture this moment because she looks so satisfied and peaceful in sleep, but I can't force myself to break away from her, and it isn't long before I'm joining her in slumber.

Chapter Thirty-Six
Age 20

"Why do you have that goofy look on your face?" Ro asks after I collect my washing from the washer-dryer in the kitchen. I didn't want to leave Viv this morning, but I've run out of clothes, so I dashed back to our gaff to put on a wash and get changed. Ro and I will meet the girls at the usual place in Christchurch, and we'll all drive together to Kilcoole. Ma is expecting us for Sunday dinner.

"No reason," I lie. I'm not telling my little brother it's 'cause I'm deliriously happy. And not just because of the nonstop sex or the fact I took Viv's anal virginity last night. It's the combination of everything. Happiness just bleeds from my pores these days. It's impossible to be in a bad mood. I just float around the place all the time like a right clown.

"Can I talk to you?" Jay asks, wetting his lips and tweaking the tips of his faux hawk. It's a nervous tell, which is how I know this is serious.

"Sure."

"In private," he adds, and Ro flips his middle finger up.

"Some things are not for your ears, little O'Donoghue," Jay says.

Ro grabs his junk. "Suck my cock, Fleming."

"You're not my type."

My gaze bounces between them. "If you two clowns are done, let's talk. We're leaving soon."

"Okay. What's up?" I ask Jay a couple minutes later when we're safely tucked away in my bedroom. I start folding my clothes, placing them in my duffel bag as I wait for my best mate to fess up.

"I need to ask you something, tell you something. Fuck." Jay scrubs his hands down his face.

Poor fucker looks terrified, and I decide to go easy on him. "If this is about Ash, just spit it out, mate."

Shock splays across his face. "You know?"

"I've suspected."

His shoulders visibly relax, and he finds his balls, straightening up and projecting confidence. "I love her, Dillon."

I stop packing my clothes. "For real?" I scrutinize his face, inspecting his reaction.

"Yes. I really fucking love her. To be honest, I always have. I just never thought I'd have a chance. Cill got there first, and after that all turned to shite, you warned me off."

A sigh cleaves from my lips. I flop down on the bed. "I shouldn't have interfered though I'm not sorry I did. Ash wasn't in a good place after everything with Cillian." I snarl his name. I still can't think of that prick without feeling murderous rage. I've seen him a couple times in Kilcoole, and he's attempted to speak to me, but I always give him the cold shoulder. Hell will freeze over before I ever talk to that asshole again.

Jay sits down beside me. "I know, and I never would've tried anything." He eyeballs me. "You must think I'm a total prick if you think I'd make a play for her when she was clearly heartbroken."

"I think you were a horny prick who thought you could help."

He glares at me. "I still wouldn't have taken advantage of her!"

"I know you wouldn't." I clamp a hand on his shoulder. "I

shouldn't have cock-blocked you, but I was just trying to protect her. It wasn't really about you."

"Fuck off, Dil." His aggrieved expression pins me in place. "It was totally about me, and I get it. I've fucked around with lots of girls, and you want someone decent for Ash, but I swear to you, Dillon, no one will love her as much as I do because I really, really fucking love her." He thumps a clenched fist over his heart. "I'm done with other girls. Ash is all I want, and she seems to want me too, and I'm not fucking it up this time."

That confirms something definitely happened with them last summer. "What are you asking?"

"I want your permission to go out with her. Officially. I want to make her mine."

"I'm not the one you should be asking. You don't need my permission. You're both adults."

"You're a real fucking prick at times, Dil."

"Tell me something I don't know." I claw a hand through my hair. "I shouldn't have gotten in your way, and I won't stand in your way now. If you are who Ash wants, I won't interfere."

"Thank fuck." His face explodes with happiness, and I feel like a right cunt for denying him something he's clearly wanted for a long time. But I don't regret it. I don't think the timing was right for them before. I'm hoping it is now. Seeing my best mate and my sister happy together would be the icing on the cake.

"I'm happy for you, Jay." I squeeze his shoulder more firmly. "But you better treat her right. One false move, one fucking tear, and I'll lay into you worse than I ever laid into that prick Doyle."

"You don't need to worry. I'm gonna treat her like a queen."

"See that you do, mate." I stand, and he jumps up, grabbing me into a hug. "You're already family, Jay. Nothing would make me happier than if that ever became official."

"Oh my god, Dillon, stop!" Viv hisses, latching on to my wrist under the table and stalling my upward trajectory.

"I can't help it," I whisper in her ear, brushing the tips of my fingers against her bare thigh. "I need my hands on you like I need air to breathe."

Her features soften, and her guard lowers, and I don't hesitate to take advantage, pulling out of her grip and dropping my hand to her pussy. I manage to push her knickers aside and run one finger between her slit before she yanks my hand away.

"Fucking stop, Dil," she snaps, pressing her mouth to my ear. "You are not fingering me at your mother's dinner table. Stop this now, or no sex for a month."

I narrow my eyes as she digs her nails into my hand. "You wouldn't dare." Not when we only have ten weeks left before she's due to go home. Vivien loves sex as much as I do. She'd never last a whole month without it. Wrenching my hand from her grip again, I lower it to her thigh, keeping it stationary as we battle this out.

"Try me. I dare you." Her face carries considerable warning.

"Earth to lover boy," Shane barks, nudging me from the other side. "Get your paws off your woman, and pass your brother the spuds."

Vivien's blush is instant, and I should probably feel bad about it, but I don't. I will never apologize for being horny for my woman.

"Sorry." I smirk, giving her thigh one final squeeze before I concede and raise my hand to the table. I won't apologize for needing her so fucking badly, but I won't make her uncomfortable either. I'll just take her to the barn after dinner and fuck her brains out. Lifting the bowl with the potatoes, I pass it to Ciarán. "I get hugely distracted whenever my girl is around."

"We've noticed." Shane grins, and I brace myself for whatever shite is about to fly from his mouth. "Oh, how the mighty have fallen. I am going to enjoy giving you all the crap you gave me when I fell for Fiona."

"Stop teasing your brother," Ma says, smiling widely as her gaze dances between Vivien and me. I thought she was going to burst into song when I told her Vivien and I were officially going out. She's delighted and not just because Viv is Lauren Mills' daughter. Mum genuinely loves Vivien. "I think it's wonderful to finally see Dillon happy and in love."

My entire body locks up at her words, and panic is instantaneous. I stand and push my chair back. "I need a smoke." I kiss Vivien once on the lips. "Finish your dinner. I'll be back." I storm off without looking back at anyone.

My mind is a cyclone of conflicting thoughts as I stalk through the orchard toward our old play barn. I light up a smoke even though I've barely smoked any these past two months. I need something to take the edge off.

I'm not in love with her.

Ma is reading way too much into things.

And putting stupid notions in Vivien's head too.

Why the fuck would Ma say that? She knows Vivien is going home in August. And she knows I'm incapable of loving anyone. I haven't been able to tell my own mother I love her since I was a little boy, and she just throws that comment out there? I'm super pissed off with my family. Shane fucking started this with his teasing. *Why the fuck can't they just let me be?*

I puff away on my smoke as I near the old play barn, but it does little to ease my agitation.

Pushing into the barn, I'm accosted with a host of old memories and feelings, but that doesn't even distract me. I trail my fingers along the old leather sofa as my head battles with my heart.

After two more cigarettes, I finally calm down enough to go back to the house. I shouldn't have walked off on Vivien like that. I don't care what Ma thinks. She's wrong. I really like Vivien. A lot. She's amazing, and I love her company. But I don't love her. Only an idiot would fall in love with a girl he's using to get back at her ex.

Conversation trickles out the open back door as I near the house.

"Dillon has been fighting different demons his entire life," Ma is saying, and I sprint the last few feet as panic threatens to knock me on my arse. "We have tried to support him to the best of our abilities, to let him know how loved and cherished he is, that he's no different—"

What the actual fuck?!! "Ma!" I snap the second my foot hits the doorway. "Stop." I convey everything with a penetrating look, and I know she gets it. She's my mother. She fucking knows I don't like anyone knowing I'm adopted. She knows I hate talking about it. She doesn't need me to tell her not to tell Vivien the truth. She already fucking knows I wouldn't want that.

"Are we eating dessert or what?" I ask, working hard to maintain a casual demeanor when I'm like an overworked pressure cooker inside, rattling and shaking, ready to explode. Snagging two dessert bowls from the counter, I stride towards the table, thankful I was in time to stop Ma from dropping a bomb.

I eat my crumble and cream on autopilot, faking a disinterested look as I contemplate all my near misses. My contacts have fallen out twice in Viv's bed, and it's only my quick thinking that stopped her from discovering my natural blue eyes. Ro almost blabbed about my fake look one night at Whelans. I stopped him before he ruined everything, later taking my siblings and my band mates aside to tell them I didn't want Vivien to know because what's the point in getting into deep shit when she's leaving at the end of the summer? Thankfully, they bought the excuse, and no one has broached the subject since, but there's been a few moments that were definitely touch and go.

I really didn't think I had to say anything to my family about my adoptive status as they never bring it up in conversation, knowing it's a touchy subject. So, I'm enraged Ma went there. I know she probably thought she was helping, but she really needs to learn to keep her gob shut.

Dillon

After dinner ends, I escort Vivien to the barn where I dole out her punishment, slapping her nosy arse before fucking her hard and fast. She asks me again what happened when I was seventeen, and I deflect like usual. The sex helps me to relax, and I'm more chill exiting the barn than when I was entering it.

"Are you okay?" I ask, dotting tiny kisses across her face.

"I'm perfect." She snuggles against me, and I'm glad things are back to normal.

Pushing her against the wall of the barn, I crowd her with my arms. I press my forehead to hers and close my eyes. Her hands land lightly on my hips, and her touch grounds me. I feel the need to try to explain. "I know I'm not the easiest person to be with," I whisper, and it's the understatement of the century. "I know I'm a moody prick, and I have anger issues, but they're never directed at you."

"I know."

I reopen my eyes, shielding nothing, because I owe her for being a dick. "You make everything better, Viv." I clasp her face in my callused palms. "I never knew it could be like this, and sometimes I'm terrified beyond words."

"I get that." She presses a sweet kiss to my lips. "And it's okay to feel what you're feeling, Dillon. Just sometimes, I'd like it if you could let me in."

"I'm letting you in more than most people." I wish I could tell her everything, but it's too late now, and what *is* the point when she's leaving in two months? "I want to let you in more. Just be patient with me."

"I can be patient." Her arms wind around my neck the same time she presses her sexy body against me.

We both know time isn't on our side. I might not be able to give her all my truths, but I can give her this much. "You've come to mean everything to me, Viv," I whisper as we cling to one another. "It's happened so fast. Like lightning. I didn't think it would be like this, and it confuses me as much as it makes me happy." It's the god's

293

honest truth, and delving any further into it is a risk I can't afford to take. I peer deep into her eyes. "Does that make any sense?"

"It makes perfect sense." She kisses me, and it's full of emotion I can relate to. "I feel the same way too."

"I don't know where we go from here when—" I stop before I say too much. My heart is aching behind my chest, and it's like someone is stabbing me all over. "I just know I don't want to stop. I want to keep doing this with you. I—"

I'm cut off by the sound of a very distinct moan, quickly followed by a second one. Horror lays siege to me as I grab Viv's hand and haul her around the corner of the barn. Finding Cillian Doyle balls deep in my sister is the shock of the century. *What the fuck is Ash playing at?!* "You fucking bastard!" I shout, dropping Viv's hand and racing toward them.

Grabbing Ash's cx, I go to town on him, pummeling him with my fists. He lets me at first until he sees my determination and starts fighting back. But he's no match for my aggression. I swore to myself if Cill ever came near my sister again I'd kill the fucker, and right now, I think I could.

Cillian lands a few punches to my face and my stomach, but I'm lost to blood lust, pounding him into the ground until Vivien kisses me, dragging me from my murderous rage. When Cillian shoves her and she falls to the side, I'm ready to kill the prick.

Helping Viv to her feet, I shove her behind me and face off with my ex- best mate. "You cheating cunt! You stay the hell away from my sister, and if you ever touch my girlfriend again, I'll fucking kill you!" I roar.

"You're a crazy bastard, O'Donoghue." Cillian sways on his feet, spitting blood onto the ground. Lifting his shirt, he dabs the blood on his face with the hem "I let you have the first few punches because I deserved those, but you don't get to threaten me, asshole. Your sister wanted it. I've done nothing wrong."

"Except cheat on your wife," Viv says in a clipped tone.

"This is nothing to do with you." Cillian jabs his finger in her direction. "Butt out."

I lunge for him and grab his shirt, ready to go another round with him. How fucking dare he speak to my girl like that!

"Let it go," Viv says. "This ends now."

"Like fuck it does," Cillian yells. He waves his finger in my face. "I'll have you arrested for assault, you prick." He hugs his stomach, wincing in pain, and I hope it means I broke a few ribs.

"I'll have you arrested for trespassing," Ash shouts, finally finding her voice.

Vivien steps right up to Cillian, wearing the fiercest expression on her face. "You will not press charges against Dillon. If you even breathe a word of what happened here today, we will go straight to your wife and your parents and tell them you've been stalking Ash for months and you forced yourself on her today when she was stoned and incapable of pushing you away."

She's magnificent, and I'm in awe of her. It's a despicable threat. One I know she'd never follow through on. Not after the things she endured. But fuckface doesn't know that.

"That's bullshit," he splutters. "No one will believe you."

Viv thrusts her mobile phone in his face. "I recorded you," she lies. "Whatever the circumstances, it shows your wife you were cheating on her. And if ruining your marriage isn't enough, I'll ruin your fucking career too. I'll email this to your boss. I'll post it on social media. I'll destroy your reputation."

I want to rip her clothes off and worship at her altar for eternity. She's incredible, and I'm so fucking hot for her. No girl has ever gone to bat for me like this, with the exception of my sister. Viv's loyalty is a thing of beauty, and my heart mushrooms behind my chest. I can't believe she's stood up to him like this for Ash and me. She can't know how much it means to me.

His eyes narrow suspiciously. "Who are you?"

"I'm your worst fucking nightmare." She takes another step

towards him, leveling him with a warning glare. "Don't fucking push me, Cillian. I can ruin your life like that." She clicks her fingers.

"You're all fucking mad," he snaps. "And you two are a match made in hell." He points between me and Vivien.

I take that as a massive compliment.

"Leave," Viv demands. "Don't say a word about Dillon or Ash. Not if you value the life you've got."

"Crazy bitch," he mutters, and I see red again. Before I can throw myself at him, Ash and Viv are dragging me back.

"Well, that was fun." Viv's tone is laced with sarcasm as she looks between me and Ash. "We should do that again some time."

"Bloody hell." I crush her against me. "Is it wrong I'm turned on right now?" Nothing gets me hotter than my girl jumping in to defend me.

She was fierce, and I'm melting into a puddle at her feet.

As long as I live, I'll never forget the way she had my back today. There aren't many people who have done that for me, and she's just earned my undying loyalty for life.

Chapter Thirty-Seven
Age 20

V ivien is so engrossed in her book she hasn't realized I'm indulging my inner paparazzo and snapping tons of pics. She's curled up on the sofa in her place, wearing a cami top and leggings, with her feet bare and her hair up in a messy bun. There isn't a scrap of makeup on her face, and her skin is flawless perfection where the sun highlights it through the window. I wonder if the blush staining her cheeks is from the heat of the sun or whatever filth she's reading. Ash has been loaning her some of the smutty romance she reads. Not that I'm complaining. I'm more than reaping the rewards.

My girl looks a little overheated. I should do something about that. I'm smirking to myself as I shove my phone back in my pocket. I tiptoe in my socks to the kitchen, slowly and carefully opening the freezer part of the fridge. Sticking my hands inside, I wait until they're nice and chilly, and then I creep back into the sitting room. My little American beauty hasn't budged. Viv is thoroughly sucked into whatever she's reading, and she doesn't hear me approach from behind.

I move fast, sliding one cold hand down the front of her cami and under her bra cup, fondling her boob and tweaking her nipple.

"Dillon!" She screams, instantly dropping the book and trying to pry my hand free. "Your fingers are like icicles!"

Driving my free hand down the other side of her top, I grab her other tit, giving it the same treatment. "You looked hot, Hollywood. Thought I'd help you to cool down." I grope her tits and grind my hips against the back of the sofa as I instantly harden.

"You're an asshole."

Removing my hands, I throw myself over the back of the sofa, landing beside her. "Yep." I draw the word out as I slide the straps of her cami and bra down her arms, freeing her magnificent tits. "But I'm *your* asshole." My lips descend on one boob as I grope and fondle the other.

A breathy moan leaves her lips. "What time does Ash's shift finish?"

"She's on the late shift," I confirm in between sucking her nipple. "She won't be home for hours."

"Oh god, Dillon. I need you." She reaches in between our bodies and grips my dick through my tracksuit bottoms.

"I know what you need, babe." I hop up, chuckling at her frown. "Strip, beautiful. I'll be right back."

Tugging my T-shirt off as I race into the kitchen, I toss it on the tiled floor and snatch the chocolate chip ice cream from the freezer. I pop it in the microwave for a few seconds to soften it a little before rejoining my sexy naked girlfriend in the living room.

Vivien is sprawled out on the leather sofa on her back with her thighs spread and her fingers between her legs. "I started without you." She smirks at me as I quickly remove my socks and bottoms, kicking them away.

"Fuck, that's hot." Kneeling between her open legs, I stare at where her fingers are disappearing into her glistening cunt. "You're fucking soaked, beautiful."

"It's the book," she pants, looking at me with flushed skin and desire-laden eyes. "The heroine was being nailed by three hot bikers, and boy, did they know what they were doing."

"Bullshit." Wrenching her fingers out of her cunt, I raise her hand to my mouth. "It's *me*. Always *me*." I lick her juices off her fingers, and my cock twitches, dying to dive into her welcoming warmth. "I'm the only one who gets you wet, Hollywood, and I'll never share you, so put all ideas of foursomes out of your mind 'cause it'll never happen."

"Prove it," she challenges, waggling her brows.

"Oh, baby, I fully intend to." Flipping the lid on the ice cream tub, I sink between her legs.

"What're you doing?" She props up on her elbows, staring at me curiously.

"Eating ice cream." I flash her a flirty grin. "From your pussy." Her eyes widen around a gasp. "I'm going to cool you down before I heat you right back up." I scoop ice cream from the tub with two fingers and shove it into her cunt. Vivien screeches, attempting to wiggle out of my reach, but I keep one arm tight against her hips holding her in place as I drive my tongue inside her, and I almost come on the spot when I taste her juices mingling with the decadent chocolate goodness.

"Fuck me," I say after I've licked it all up. "I've just found my new favorite hobby."

"You're so dirty, Dillon," she rasps, watching with a heated stare as I scoop more ice cream up and slowly coat her inner walls with it.

"You love it." I smirk as I lap at her chocolate-covered folds. "And I'm nowhere near done with you yet."

"Have you ever done that before?" she asks a couple of hours later after we've finished eating ice cream off one another and fucking. We're freshly showered and lying on the sofa, draped around one another.

"Eat ice cream out of a woman's cunt?"

She lifts her head from my chest, turning to face me. My arm tightens around her back, keeping her tucked in close. "Yeah." She nibbles on her lip, and I see the anxiety flaring behind her eyes.

"Never," I truthfully reply. "I've only done that with you." I kiss the tip of her nose. "Hottest sex ever."

The relief is obvious on her face. "Every time we have sex, I think it can't get any better, but it always does. I don't think I'll ever get enough of you fucking me. Even when we fuck two or three times a day, it's still not enough. I always want more."

My chest swells with masculine pride. "Snap, Hollywood. I always want you. Why do you think I have such a hard time keeping my hands off you?"

She rolls her eyes while fighting a smile. "Here I thought it's because you love groping me in public and marking me as yours."

I quirk a brow. "Are you complaining?"

"Hell no. I love when you get all possessive and the grabby hands come out." Her eyes narrow a little. "Though I draw the line at public groping when we're with your family, but otherwise, I have no issue with it."

"I want to murder every man who looks at you," I admit. "Sometimes, I even want to throttle my own brother." For the most part, Ro has gotten over Viv. But on odd occasions, I see his look lingering, and I don't like it.

"Don't hate on Ro. He doesn't want me like that anymore."

The jury is out on that one, but I'm not arguing with her over my little brother.

With the tip of her finger, she traces circles on my chest, following the ink patterned on my skin. "Has sex always been like this for you?" Vulnerability is back on her face as her eyes lift to mine.

"No." I shake my head as I give her another truth. "Before you, sex was always about an instant release and nothing more. It was fleeting and never memorable."

"How many girls have you been with?" she blurts.

"I haven't kept count, and I'm not sure you really want to know."

She looks away, and in this moment, I hate I've been such a

hound. "Hey." I tilt her chin up with my finger. "None of them meant anything. You mean everything."

"Sometimes, I don't understand how I can keep you satisfied when I'm much less experienced than those other girls."

"Vivien." I sit up against the arm of the sofa, pulling her with me. I reposition her so I'm cradling her in my arms. "You satisfy me completely, and no one compares to you. No one." I drill her with a sharp look, hoping to embed that truth deep. "Where is this coming from?"

She shrugs, resting her head in the crook of my neck. "Don't mind me. I'm due for my period, and I get a bit mopey."

I make a mental note to check we have Nurofen and Epsom salts. Vivien suffers badly with her periods, way worse than my sister during her time of the month. I hate to see her in pain and want to do whatever I can to help.

"Can I ask you something?" I rub a hand up and down her arm.

"Of course." She plants a featherlight kiss to the underside of my jaw, and I shiver all over.

"You don't have to answer if you don't want to, but I was wondering if you've had sex with anyone else besides me and your ex." I must be a glutton for punishment because why the fuck would I open up this conversation?

"No," she quietly replies. "I've only been intimate with both of you."

I swallow thickly over the lump in my throat, not wanting to ask this question but needing to at the same time. "Was it like this with him too?"

Tense silence bleeds into the air, and I instantly regret asking it.

"No," she whispers after a few silent beats. "It wasn't like this. It was different. Special in a different way."

"Oh." My stomach drops to my toes.

"Dillon." She lifts her head and clasps my face. "What we have is purely ours. I've never had this with him, but don't ask me to compare my relationships. Each was different." She peers deep into my eyes.

"I'm not going to lie and say my past didn't mean anything. Reeve was a huge part of my life, and he took a lot of my firsts. As much as he hurt me, I won't trash the good memories or rewrite history, but you have nothing to feel jealous about because I'm with *you*. I'm crazy about *you*, Dil. I can honestly say I don't think I've ever felt this alive or this happy, and a lot of that is down to you."

I shouldn't feel such crushing disappointment. Of course, I can't erase her memories of him, and a few months with me isn't comparable to the years she spent with him, but I guess there was a part of me that hoped I meant more.

It's stupid, and I brought this on myself by asking the question in the first place.

"You're upset." Emotion pools in her eyes. "I'm sorry."

"Don't apologize." I clear my throat and force a smile. "I know I can't compare with all you shared with him. A few months is a blip compared to years with someone."

She vigorously shakes her head. "No, Dil. Don't do that. Don't dismiss what we have because it means the world to me." She kisses me softly. "You mean so much to me. You've spoken about the intensity of our connection and how it scares you, and honestly, I feel that too because it's intense in a way I have never experienced. And whether it's months or years, it doesn't matter." She puts her hand over her heart. "I know what I feel in here, and it's deep and true. If anything, what we have means more because our connection has been powerful from the instant we met, and it's only strengthening the more time we spend together."

The air charges with unspoken words, and it's not the first time lately we've found ourselves in this place.

"In case you haven't noticed, we basically live together, and I never had that with him." She caresses my face, and the look on her face is nothing short of absolute love. *Can I dare to dream it's true?* We're both holding our cards close to our chests, for obvious reasons. "You can't compare them because they're not comparable."

"I'm sorry if I ruined the mood."

Her fingers thread through my hair, and a deep sense of contentment settles in my chest. I love her fingers in my hair and the way she massages my scalp. "Never be sorry for speaking your mind and sharing your feelings, and you didn't."

"You don't do anything to make me feel like this, but sometimes I can't help feeling like I'm constantly in his shadow."

"You're not, Dil. You're your own person, and I see *you*." Her lips open and close, and I will her to say it because right now I'm selfish enough to need those three little words. But she traps them inside, the same way I do. A few seconds later, she climbs off my lap. "I have something for you. Stay here."

I lean my head back as she runs off to the bedroom, contemplating how it's possible to feel both elated and deflated at the same time.

"I made something for you," she says, materializing in front of me. Her hands are clasped behind her back as she chews on the corner of her lip in a nervous tell.

"Okay."

"I wanted you to have a special notebook for writing your songs." She hands me a thick book with a crushed red and black velvet handmade cover. Our logo—the one Ash designed with the skull and serpent—is embedded in the front, and my name is etched on it too.

I'm speechless.

My heart is hammering inside my chest, swelling and swelling with so much emotion.

"It's a songwriting journal." Viv wipes her hands down the front of her leggings. "I got it in a store on Exchequer Street, and then I made the cover myself. If you don't like it, I—"

I jump up, grab her into my arms, and crush my lips to hers, pouring everything I'm feeling into my kiss. Viv clings to me, and my heart is pounding so loud it's a miracle she doesn't hear it. "I love it," I pant when we finally break apart. "I love it so much. I can't believe you made this for me."

"Really?" Hope blazes in her eyes as she fists a hand in my shirt.

"Yeah, Hollywood. It's the best present anyone's ever given me. It's right up there with the special edition Stratocaster I told you about."

"Well, it's not a limited-edition guitar but I'm glad you like it."

I lift her up, and her legs automatically wind around my back. "I don't have words to describe how much I love it, but perhaps I can show you," I promise, leading her into the bedroom where I spend the rest of the night trying to convey everything it means to me.

Chapter Thirty-Eight
Age 20

"Nervous?" Jay asks, trying—and failing—to smother a grin.

"I'm shitting bricks, mate." Wiping my clammy hands down the side of my black suit trousers, I will my racing heart to calm down. If I don't get it together, I'm liable to forget the lyrics to my own bleeding song.

"She'll love it, Dil. She's been wearing heart eyes all day." Jamie chuckles. "Ash was crying in the church. What is it with women and weddings?"

"You've got to admit it's been emotional." Shane and I have had our ups and downs, but watching him marry the love of his life with their daughter a big part of the day has tugged at my heartstrings. Then Ciarán's speech had us all cracking up and welling up in equal measure. Ma has been beaming like a proud mother hen all day. It's been a great day, and now the party's in full swing in the large ballroom of the County Wexford hotel.

The band Shane and Fiona hired for the night announce they're taking a short break, and it's our turn to play a few numbers. We've been rehearsing our new song for weeks, and we've nailed it, so I hope I don't fuck it up. I've never been so nervous getting up on a stage.

Shane introduces us, and we start off with a crowd-pleasing tune from Coldplay before moving on to one from The Script and then a couple of other well-known songs. The crowd are loving it, and most every guest is up dancing.

My eyes have been laser focused on Vivien the entire time we've been up here. She's a vision in a gorgeous purple strapless dress that accentuates her figure beautifully. Pride fills my veins seeing her wear the Claddagh necklace I bought her for her birthday, and she's wearing understated diamond stud earrings and a row of silver bangles on one wrist. Everyone has been complimenting her on the bridesmaid dresses, and I love seeing her receive the acknowledgment she deserves.

Viv is very talented, and she whipped the dresses up in no time. She refused to take any money from my brother or his fiancée, insisting they were a wedding present, even though she chipped in with me to buy them a set of Waterford Crystal wineglasses. She's as generous with her time as she is with her money, and all day I've been overcome with emotion any time I look at her.

Having her share today with me is super special. I've loved having her by my side.

Fiona included Viv in their morning hair and makeup session, and she looks sensational. Keeping my hands off her has been an exercise in self-control, though we did sneak a quickie in when we were checking into our room. My eyes gravitate to hers again as we bring our current song to an end.

Waves of glossy dark hair hang down her back, and the front part of her hair is braided like a hair band. Her makeup isn't caked on like some of the female guests, Viv having favored a more natural look that emphasizes her stunning looks.

She's been smiling nonstop today, and it's carried over to the dance floor as she laughs and dances with Ash, Fiona, Susie, Cat, and little Chloe. My niece looks adorable today in the dress Vivien made for her, and she's clearly a fan, following my girl around any chance she gets.

The song ends, and I clear my throat, gripping the mic as my eyes land on Vivien. Ash has moved them up to the front because she knows what's coming next. "This next song is one of our own. It's called "Terrify Me," and I wrote it for, and about, my girl." Oohs and ahhs ring out around the room as I watch Vivien's eyes pop wide. "This is for you, Vivien." Drawing a brave breath, I strum my fingers along my guitar and open my mouth to sing. As I perform the song in public for the first time, my gaze never leaves my girl, and I pour my heart and soul into every word.

The crowd goes insane when we finish, and we jump down off the stage to shouts of congratulations and multiple back slaps. But I have singular vision, and I don't take my eyes off my girl until I'm in front of her, gently pulling her out of Ash's arms and into mine. "Hey, Hollywood." I hope she doesn't notice how badly I'm shaking.

"Dillon." A few tears leak out of her eyes as she holds on to my arms and leans in to kiss me. "I can't believe you wrote a song for me. It's beautiful. I love it, and you're so incredibly talented. All of you are." Her voice cracks, and a little giggle rips from her lips. "Sorry, I'm a bit of a basket case right now. No one has ever done anything like that for me before. I'm blown away." Flinging her arms around my neck, she kisses me hard on the lips as the wedding band return after their break. "Thank you."

"I'm so happy you like it. Don't mind admitting I was sweating bullets up there," I say as we sway in time to the music.

"You had nothing to be nervous about. It's an incredible song."

"You sure you even heard it?" I tease, pulling her close as we dance. "You looked a little dazed."

"Dillon, I don't think you understand how big of a deal that is for me. You just basically stood up there and told all your family and friends how you feel about me." A choked sob erupts from her mouth. "It means everything to me," she whispers as I pull her head down to my chest and hug her close.

"You mean everything to me, Viv."

We don't speak for the rest of the song, and no one disturbs us, leaving us to hold one another and dance. Beside us, Jamie and Ash are locked in a similar embrace. Jay and I nod at one another, both looking like the smug bastards we are. I've never seen Ash so happy, and any fears I had about those two were unfounded. They are like two peas in a pod, and I'm glad to be proven wrong.

Out of the corner of my eye, I spy Ma talking to Uncle Eamonn's wife, and they're both looking over here with big smiles. I imagine Ma is already planning a double wedding. Pain settles on my chest as that thought drops into my head, but I push it aside, determined not to sink into my darker emotions today. Time with Vivien is dwindling, and I get a sick feeling in the pit of my stomach every time I think about our imminent separation.

When the next song starts, I wonder if my best mate requested it for me or if it's a coincidence. I need to be alone with my baby for this. "Dance with me under the stars?"

Viv nods, looking a little dazed, and I can relate. Today has been magical in more ways than one, and it's all a bit surreal. Taking her hand in mine, I lead her outside to the small courtyard, purposely leaving the double doors open so we can dance to the song.

I pull her into my arms, holding her flush against my body, and start dancing.

"What song is this?" she inquires.

"It's an older song by a group called Savage Garden. The song is "I Knew I Loved You." It's always been a favorite of mine." I peer deep into her eyes. "Especially now." My heart is banging on my chest cavity, shouting the truths I've tried so hard to hide.

I sing to her, maintaining eye contact the entire time. Every word could have been written by me for her. My heart soars and dips as I shield nothing, letting my truths run free. I swirl her around, pulling her back in close every time, needing to touch her as I finally admit it to myself. From the way her gorgeous eyes swell with unadulterated raw emotion, I think she's admitting the same things to herself.

Dillon

It truly feels like I've been waiting for her all my life.

Vivien Grace Mills *is* the missing piece, and she completes me in every way.

She is my home. She is my future.

I must have dreamed her to life because how do you explain how we came to find one another? I'm aware it's crazy, but I believe it is fate.

This wasn't the way I planned it, but I'm done living in denial.

I love her.

I love her so damn much.

Rain drops from the sky, getting heavier as we dance and I sing, but I don't feel it because all I feel is undying love for this beautiful woman in my arms.

She is it.

My one and only.

I don't know where that leaves me, us, but there'll be time to freak out tomorrow.

Right now, as the heavens open, pummeling us with heavy rain that sticks our clothes to our bodies and our hair to our faces, all I care about is the love replacing the blood flowing in my veins.

I barely register the song ending, twirling her again and again as I let myself feel it all. Happiness invades every nook and cranny of my being as she tilts her head up to the sky and laughs. Her obvious joy is intoxicating, and I just want to love her until the end of time.

Reeling her close, I band my arms around her, never wanting to let her go.

She's mine, like I'm hers. It's the only truth that matters.

My heart spins wheels as our gazes connect, and the intensity of our chemistry surrounds us in a protective bubble, blocking the outside world. The strength of the feelings swirling inside me almost knock me off my feet. I can scarcely breathe over the messy ball of emotion clogging my throat. I look at her, pouring it all into my expression and the possessive way I'm touching her, willing her to see me and feel me. To know the totality of my heart. To understand she owns it fully and completely. That there will never be another for me.

I was stupid to think I could protect my heart.

She's owned it from the very start.

And I don't regret it.

We move as one, and the instant our lips collide, I know I am hers in every single way. Vivien Grace Mills, my beautiful, brave Hollywood, has smashed through the walls protecting my heart, reached a hand inside, and claimed my love for all eternity.

Chapter Thirty-Nine
Age 20

As I sit on the deck of Conor's grandparents' holiday home in Brittas Bay, I wish the rest of the summer hadn't gone by so fast. Our time together is almost at an end, and I'm not ready for it.

Viv and I crammed so much in these past few weeks. Camping, swimming, biking, and hiking. Sneaking up Bray Head at night to fuck against the cross. I still get horny thinking about it. Spending three amazing days at Longitude with all our gang, indulging my joint loves—Vivien and music. In between gigs with Toxic Gods, Viv and I traveled the length and breadth of the country on my bike, visiting tons of the main tourist attractions, like the Cliffs of Moher, the Blarney Stone, and Newgrange. We've been inseparable, spending every spare moment together. Viv came to all our events and practice sessions, and she's now as big a cheerleader as Ash is.

Her delight when another A&R scout from a big label reached out was obvious in the extreme. Unlike the last guy who contacted me and then ghosted us, this guy is super enthusiastic, getting back to me within a few hours of sending him our EP and other demo tapes.

He's coming to Ireland in three weeks and plans to catch one of our shows. He sounds really keen, and my brother is practically busting a nut he's that excited. It feels like it might actually happen for us now, and I'm a little conflicted over it.

We haven't found an experienced manager, though we did meet with a couple guys Ash found. None of us liked either of them, so we've decided to just go it alone for now and see how things pan out.

I'm excited but nervous about the potential outcome for a couple different reasons. And to be honest, most of my headspace is occupied with my girl. My head has been a mess since I admitted my feelings to myself.

I love her.

I truly fucking love her.

I'm completely and utterly head over heels in love with my Hollywood, and I don't know what to do. I can't even talk to anyone about it because no one knows my truths. I'm in bits, though I'm able to forget about it when I'm with her and just focus on the here and now. But the instant we're apart, it's all I can think about.

I missed her like crazy the week she spent in Cork and Kerry with her parents, Audrey, and Ash, and it's a taste of what's to come. Vivien and I argued a lot in the run-up to her parents' trip. She understood my band commitments meant I couldn't leave Dublin for a full week, but she didn't understand my refusal to come for lunch at her place, especially when Ma was going to be there. I felt like total crap telling her I didn't "do" the parents thing. It's utter horse shite. If they were any other parents, I'd have been bending over backwards to meet and impress them.

But meeting Vivien's famous parents was too risky. Viv's mum was best friends with my birth mum, and our fathers are golfing buddies. They must know Reeve is a twin. They probably also know that *Rhett* was adopted by an Irish couple. Although I've changed my look, that doesn't mean they might not join the dots where their daughter hasn't.

Sometimes, I see Viv looking at me curiously, and I wonder if I have any of the same mannerisms as her ex. She never questions it. *Why would she?* But her parents might as they have the background knowledge Viv doesn't.

I agonized over it for days when she first asked me to come to lunch, but I just couldn't risk it. If Vivien learned the truth from anyone but me, it would definitely spell utter ruination for our relationship. *Who am I kidding?* Even if I had the balls to confess, our relationship would still be over. She would never believe me now if I told her I don't give a crap about getting revenge on my twin. All that matters now is her.

I'd give up everything if I just got to keep her.

I don't need fame or money.

I just need her.

I have wanted to tell her I love her so many times since the wedding, but the words refuse to leave my tongue. I'm out of practice saying them, and I can't get them out of my head.

Maybe it's for the best.

She'll never forgive me.

How ironic that I set out to decimate Reeve's heart yet it's my heart that will be left shattered when she gets on that plane and goes back to L.A. I have no doubt he'll be lying in wait for her, ready to swoop in and pick up where they left off.

I clutch the mug of now cold coffee in my hands, gripping it so tight it's a miracle it doesn't break. I feel sick. I want to reset time. To go back and do it all differently. But I don't have a time machine, and what's done is done.

I got steaming drunk last night after she sang "She Moves Through the Fair" for me. Jamie said she was practicing it for ages, wanting it to be perfect. She sang like an angel. She *is* an angel. *What am I going to do without her?* How can I go on with half a heart because I sure as fuck know mine will not function properly without her in my life.

Do I take a risk and spill my guts? Put it all out on the table and beg for her understanding and forgiveness? Or do I just beg her to stay because we love one another and this connection we share is too strong to walk away from? Could I be that selfish to ask her to stay when she doesn't know the truth? I'm scared to answer that question because I'm just desperate enough to do it. I've even considered asking her to marry me, but I've got nothing to offer her, and I couldn't let her tie herself to me without knowing the truth. I'm a conniving prick but not that big of a one.

"You're in pain," Conor says, easing through the sliding doors wearing black shorts and nothing else.

"It's that obvious?" I ask, staring out at the sea in the near distance as my introspective bandmate takes the empty wicker chair alongside me.

"Only to those who know how to recognize it."

He offers me his joint, but I shake my head. It's tempting, but my head's already a mess. Getting stoned won't help.

"She's leaving soon. I don't think I'll survive it."

"Don't let her go, mate."

"It's not that simple."

"It's as simple as you make it."

"I wish that were true." I could have made that my motto at the start, but I didn't, and now I'm dealing with the consequences.

He clamps a hand on my shoulder. "You'll figure it out. You always do."

This time, I don't have faith in my ability to un-fuck the things I've fucked up. If I tell her the truth, she'll go running straight to my twin, and I'll have sent her back into his arms heartbroken and hurting like I thought I wanted all along.

That is the last thing I want now.

I don't want to send her back at all.

I want to hold on to her tight and never let go.

"I've fucked up real bad this time, Con." Setting my mug down on the wicker coffee table, I bury my head in my hands.

"Remember we're all fuckups, Dil, in our own way, and bad situations don't always end up so bad." With those parting words, he gets up and leaves.

I don't know how long I sit out there before Viv finds me.

"Hey." My spine locks up at her soft seductive tone. She drops into the seat Conor vacated as I look at her. "Are you okay?"

It hurts to look at her. The pain eviscerating me on the inside is so extreme I wonder if this is what a heart attack feels like. I look away, resuming staring at the sea. "I'm fine," I lie.

"Dillon. Please look at me."

I don't know if I can bear it, but I can't ignore her either. Slowly, I turn my head and stare into her beautiful face. Concern is splayed across her features. "What is it? What's troubling you?"

"I'd have thought that was obvious, Viv."

Her tongue darts out, wetting her lips as she nods. She hands me a hot cup of coffee. "Are we going to talk about it?"

"What's the point?" I nurse the mug in my hands, willing the heat to seep into my chilled bones. My heart aches when she rests her head on my shoulder. *How am I going to live without this?*

"I hate this."

"Me too." I link our fingers, and we're both lost in thought as we drink our coffee and stare at the sea.

Tension is palpable in the air, so pungent I can almost taste it.

"You said some stuff last night," she says sometime later just as we put our empty mugs down.

My panic is immediate, and my entire body locks up. I was completely locked last night, and I don't remember much after she sang except holding her on my lap and touching and kissing her in between knocking back far too many beers. *What the fuck did I say?* Butterflies multiple in my chest, and my mouth turns dry.

"You don't remember?"

I shake my head, trying to calm down. If I'd said anything damaging, she wouldn't be looking at me with compassion. She'd be glaring at me like she wants to claw my eyeballs out and feed them to me. I doubt she'd still be here if I'd blurted the truth. She'd have run a

315

million miles away from me by now. Rotating my shoulders, I attempt to lessen the tension cording them into knots. "What did I say?"

"That you had something to tell me but you were scared."

"That's all I said?"

"You mumbled some other stuff that didn't make sense."

"It's nothing." Releasing her hand, I climb to my feet, needing to get out of here because it feels like I can't breathe, and I don't want to fall apart in front of her. "Don't take this the wrong way, but I just need a little space right now."

She looks miserable, and guilt has a vise grip on my heart. It seems I'm not done fucking things up.

"I'm going for a walk. I'll talk to you later."

I don't look back as I walk off, struggling to draw enough air into my lungs. When I reach the sand dunes at the back of the beach, I throw up, heaving until there's nothing left in my stomach. Then I wander off the beaten track, staying away from the busy beach, as my thoughts attempt to strangle me. Back and forth I go, debating the pros and cons of my options, until I feel like screaming.

I wish I could tell Jamie. I'm sorely tempted to because I need his help. But I can't pull him into this. It would set off a whole chain reaction of things I'm ill-equipped to handle.

I've been walking for hours when I finally make the trek back to the house. Ash has been blowing up my phone, but I've been ignoring her. Like I've ignored Vivien's messages.

My heart is splitting down the middle, and I don't want to face either of the women in my life.

I know what I need to do, but I don't know how to make peace with the decision I've reached.

I can't tell her.

Vivien can never know.

Either way, I will lose her, but at least this way she won't be aware of my betrayal. I know it's still gonna hurt her. But not as much as the truth. She'll never believe me when I tell her I fell in love too. That none of the other stuff matters anymore. Only she does. But my words would fall on deaf ears. She wouldn't be able to see past my manipulations.

I'm damned if I do and damned if I don't.

So, I'll take the path of lesser evil.

And hope I can somehow survive when the darkness descends, threatening to bury me under a mountain of rubble I created.

Chapter Forty

Age 20

I spend the next four days holed up in my bedroom, writing, internally screaming, and ghosting the girl I love. I can't eat. Can't sleep. Can't stop my brain from obsessing over Viv. It feels like I'm running on empty, and that hollow void is back, sucking all the happiness I'd previously felt and locking it deep down inside where I can't reach it.

I remember now. I remember whispering those three little words when I was drunk. She can't know how big of a deal it is that I said that. She doesn't know how hard it is for me to let people in. To let them love me and love them in return. But it happened with her without me even realizing. Which is how I know we are meant to be.

I love her.

I whispered my truth, and I can't remember if she said it back or not. She never mentioned any of this on Monday morning when we last spoke, and that tells me all I need to know.

Hope is such a cruel, fickle emotion. Deep down, there was a part of me hoping she'd make the decision. Praying she'd stay without me having to ask. But her failing to mention I told her I loved her puts the final nail in the hope coffin. We don't have a future. I can't conjure it into being no matter how much I've fantasized about sharing my life with her.

If she felt the same way, she'd have told me. She'd have already made plans to remain in Ireland. Vivien has done the opposite. Lining up a new apartment with Audrey close to UCLA and signing up for a dress design course at night are not the actions of a woman desperately in love.

In her head, she's already said goodbye to me and our relationship.

That realization about killed me, so I took the coward's route, and I've been avoiding my girlfriend, choosing to start the breaking and grieving process now. I'm not proud of myself for hurting her like this, but I'm trying to do what I think is best.

At least it's plenty of ammunition for my muse. I'm writing up a storm. No idea if any of it is useful, but at least it's helping me to vent.

The instant I see her face from the stage during our set at Whelans Friday night, all my resolve goes out the window. Fuck. *How could I have stayed away from her this week?* One look at her beautiful face is like being sucker punched in the heart and the cock. *I need her.* I need to hold her in my arms. Smell her familiar scent. Allow the feel of her soft womanly body to ground me and soothe all my jagged edges. Let her words comfort me.

It takes colossal willpower not to ditch the show to go to her. Pain is transparent on her face as we lock eyes the entire time I'm performing, and I hate myself for doing that to her. *What the fuck was I thinking?* I've just wasted precious days when I could have been loving her and showing her all the reasons why it's not too late to change her mind and stay.

I'm willing to give everything up for her. I've done a lot of soul-searching lately, and I'm wondering how much her decision to go home is tied into what might potentially happen with Toxic Gods.

Vivien lost Reeve in pursuit of his dreams. *Is she scared the same thing might happen now? Is that what's holding her back?*

I don't give a flying fuck about this A&R guy. I don't give a fuck about the band. I'll give it all up in a heartbeat if that's what she needs. I wouldn't even feel guilty because I'm that fucking selfish when it comes to the woman I love. My dreams mean fuck all when it comes to her happiness.

Jamie joked Viv was like Yoko Ono, and I swore she wasn't. Yet here I am, prepared to walk away because of her. It's irony at its finest.

I sing every song for her, wanting Viv to see she's more important than the music. The crowd go wild when we debut "Terrify Me." I dedicate it to her. Not by name. I still don't want her to be a target, though it's foolish to believe any of our regular fans don't know who I'm talking about. Viv has been glued to my lap and my lips for months.

The instant our set is done, I hand off my guitar, jump offstage, and stalk toward her. I pull her into my arms, feeling like the biggest prick in the world when a sob rips from her mouth. "I'm sorry, Viv. I didn't mean to abandon you all week. It just hurts."

"How do you think I feel?"

"I can't bear the thought of you leaving. It's killing me inside."

"So, you thought you'd ghost me all week and start the breaking early?"

Yep, 'cause I'm an idiot. I pull her aside where it's more private. "I don't know how to process this. It wasn't intentional. I was just all up in my feels, and I shut myself away, pouring my emotions onto the page." I caress her gorgeous face. "I thought it might be easier to go cold turkey, but I was wrong. I'm sorry. I'm no good at this stuff."

Her palms clasp my face. "No one is, Dillon. There is no rule book for this kind of thing."

"I want to rewind time and do things differently."

She lifts a brow. "Why would you say that? I wouldn't change a single thing about our time together except it'd be nice if you didn't give me emotional whiplash so much. But I know that's part of your charm. Part of who you are."

I love how she understands me and loves me, flaws and all.

"I'm going to make it up to you. We're going to have the best few days. We still have time."

The next few days are spent locked away in Viv's apartment, avoiding the outside world. Ash is staying with Jamie to give us privacy. There's an obvious desperation to the way we cling to one another as our time dwindles like sand disappearing in an hourglass. We fuck like savages, and it's pretty much nonstop when we're not talking or eating. I can't bury myself deep enough inside her, though it's not from lack of trying.

Pain, anger, and frustration are constant companions when I lie in her bed at night, cradling my sleeping beauty in my arms, while trying to find a resolution to this nightmare.

I still don't know the answer even though it's our last night together, and I'm officially all out of time.

"Come with me," I say on Sunday evening, pulling my girl off the sofa and guiding her into the bathroom where I have a bath waiting.

"What is this?" she asks in a strangled voice, staring at the rose petals drifting across the surface of the bath. Relaxing music is playing in the background.

"I have plans for us tonight. I kicked Ash out. I'm commandeering the kitchen, and you're to get your beautiful self in the bath and relax."

Ash wanted to join us for dinner with Jay, and I know it was selfish of me to tell her no, but this could be my last night with Vivien, and I'm not sharing her. Ash's relationship with her will continue, albeit it at long distance, but she'll still get to have Vivien in her life. I won't. Once she gets on that plane tomorrow night, I'll most likely never see her again.

"Jesus, Dillon. Are you truly trying to destroy me?"

A tear rolls down her cheek, and I capture it with my thumb. "Time is running out, Hollywood," I whisper, like speaking the words is blasphemy. "I want our last night together to be memorable."

Toxic Gods has a booking tomorrow night, and I'm sick we can't get out of it. I tried, but Bruxelles said they'll ban us for life if we're a no-show, and I can't do that to the guys.

"Take your time in the bath, and then get dolled up. But you're to stay in your room while I set things up. I'll come get you when I'm ready." I hand her a glass of prosecco, wishing my budget stretched to champagne.

Vivien wears her heart in her eyes as she stares at me with so much love and adoration my knees almost buckle. Her mouth opens and closes, and I will her to say it, but that's not what comes out of her mouth. "Thank you." She kisses me sweetly, and my heart physically hurts. "You're the best."

Remaining outside the bathroom for a few minutes, I drop my head to the closed door and squeeze my eyes shut when I hear her quietly crying. I get no comfort knowing she's in agonizing pain too. We've both been melancholy today. Quiet and locked in our own thoughts as we cling to one another with a desperation that can only be born from true soul-deep love.

Why did I deceive her?

Why did I refuse to see what's been there right from the very start?

If I hadn't lied, this would all be so different.

I hate myself so much as I tiptoe away from the bathroom, immersing myself in cooking while my heart cracks and breaks irreparably.

Chapter Forty-One
Age 20

When I have everything set up on the roof, I collect her from the bedroom and try not to drool all over her when I see how pretty she looks. I keep my hand over her eyes as I lead her upstairs. "Don't peek," I command even as she spreads her fingers and tries to sneak a look. It's the only thing to bring a ghost of a smile to my lips today.

"I'm not."

Little liar!

Positioning us in front of the small open marquee, I whip my hand away. "Surprise."

"Dillon," she whispers. Her wide-eyed gaze soaks up our pop-up restaurant for the evening. Colored string lights decorate the interior, and the floor is covered in a myriad of vibrant patterned beanbags and large cushions. In the center is a low glossy black table set with candles and silverware. Incense wafts through the air from a few diffusers I set up around the space. In the corner, a narrow rectangular table holds our plates and covered silver platters of food.

"Do you like it?" I ask over the lump in my throat.

She grabs my arm and smiles. "I love it. This is amazing." She blatantly eye fucks me as her gaze roams me from head to toe, and I'm glad I decided to dress up for the occasion in a black shirt and trousers. "As are you." She kisses me passionately. "You look so freaking hot."

Escorting her inside, I kneel to take off her shoes so she can sit comfortably on the large cushion in front of the table. "I cooked an Asian-themed meal, so I thought we could eat like this." Nerves fire at me from all angles as I hope I didn't fuck this up. If this is the last night we get, I want it to be super special. I want her to remember this night for the rest of her life as I already know I will.

She kisses me again. "This is fantastic. Thank you for going to so much trouble."

After we eat, Viv sips from her glass of prosecco while I play my guitar and sing to her. Her attention is laser focused on me, and I feel her gaze like a physical caress.

Saying I need to go for a piss, I sneak into her bedroom, dropping rose petals on her bed and lighting candles I strategically place around the room. The knot in my stomach grows tighter as I maneuver around the cases stacked against the wall, but I try to push the physical reminder aside.

Vivien attacks me when I show her the room a little later, ravishing my mouth and biting my lip as she pops the buttons on my shirt. My cock is rock hard when she wraps her slender fingers around it. We don't speak as she fully undresses me and lowers to her knees, sucking my cock deep into her throat. My fingers toy with her hair as she blows me, and I'm struggling to contain my emotions as I watch her pleasure me.

But I don't want to come in her mouth. I want to come buried so deep inside her she'll always feel me there. I lift her up gently, kissing her firmly and worshipping her with my tongue while lowering the zip on her dress. When it falls to her feet, I scoop her up and carry her to the bed, wasting no time divesting her of the rest of her clothes.

When she's lying naked on the bed, I take my time kissing and caressing every inch of her beautiful body until she's writhing and moaning and whispering my name.

These past few days, we've been like crazed animals fucking bareback and clawing at one another in desperation. I'm not feeling that now. Now, I want to adore her like the queen she is and ensure she knows how much I treasure her. Vivien feels different under my fingertips and my lips tonight. Her skin feels softer, more fragile, more precious. When our eyes meet, emotion radiates from her eyes, triggering mine.

When I've worked us up enough, I part her thighs, holding my cock at her entrance as I look at her, wanting to memorize how she looks and feels in this moment. Nudging her nose with mine, I move my lips to one corner of her mouth and then the other, kissing her tenderly as I slowly push inside her.

I'm in no rush, wanting this to last forever. My thrusts are slow and deep. My kisses lingering and passionate. My touch reverent and sensual. My hands explore her gorgeous curves, skimming over her hip, along the plane of her flat stomach, and sweeping the underside of her tits. I gently knead her boobs before sucking her nipples into my mouth.

Silent tears roll down her face as I make love to her, and it kills me. I lap at her tears, but more keep coming, and I'm unraveling like never before. The tears streaming down my face are unstoppable as I roll my hips, feeling my release waiting in the wings, trying to stall the inevitable because I'm not ready for this to end.

But I can't deny reality any longer. All it will do is cause me more grief in the end.

"Viv." I press a hard kiss to her lips as I pick up my pace. "God, I don't ever want to stop feeling this."

"I know." She cries, throwing her arms around my neck and suctioning her legs around my waist. "This is the best feeling in the world."

We fall off the ledge together, staring at one another with red-rimmed eyes as our bodies fly, our hearts break, and our minds cry.

We don't move after we're ridden out our climaxes, staying locked together as we continue staring at one another. After I've fully softened, I pull out and lie on my side facing her, threading our hands together and pressing my chest to hers. Emotion is etched upon her face, and my feelings are a tsunami of epic proportions on the cusp of freedom.

I can't hold it inside anymore.

I can't let her leave without saying this to her face.

Without at least trying to change her mind.

"I love you," I say, pleading with my eyes for her to meet me halfway.

Her entire face crumples, and I see the truth written all over it even if she still hasn't verbalized it. "Don't leave," I add as fresh tears cascade down her face. "Stay," I whisper, silently begging and praying. I'll do anything, *anything*, to keep her with me. She's crying and shaking as her emotions scream for an outlet, and I'm silently coaxing her to be brave. Summoning the last vestiges of my courage, I press my lips to her ear. "Say I'm the one."

Please pick me.

Please say I'm enough.

Don't go back to him.

She stares at me through glistening bloodshot eyes, and I know what she's going to say before she utters the words. "I can't. I'm sorry."

Something vital dies inside me. Bit by bit, I come undone. Snatching each shattered piece, I shove it down deep into the void, so deep it's lost to the internal storm raging, locking my emotions up with it.

I tried, and it wasn't good enough.

Like always, I'm never enough.

I was a fool to think she'd ever choose me.

Dillon

How many times do I have to be rejected before the harsh reality is accepted?

I was always destined to live in my twin's shadow. To be less than.

She's made her decision, and fuck this, I'm out of here.

She has leveled me so completely I don't know if I'll ever be able to get back up.

I swing my legs out of the bed. "Then I guess that's it."

She sits up, looking thoroughly confused, which is a bit rich. "Please don't go. I thought you were going to stay tonight?"

Is she for real? She rejects me. Refuses to tell me she loves me even though I see it written all over her face, and she thinks I'm going to what? Stay here and fuck her all night so she gets her rocks off before she runs back to him? Not fucking likely.

A harsh laugh erupts from my throat as I get dressed. "Why delay the inevitable? We might as well do this now." Rage is immediate and intense as, semi-dressed, I turn to face her. I slide my feet into my runners, and whatever she sees on my face is enough to have her tugging the covers up under her chin. "It's not like you really care. If you did, you'd want to stay."

"I do!" She stands, hugging the sheet around her body. "I wish I could stay here with you. I swear I do. But it's not possible, Dillon."

"Anything is possible if you want it badly enough."

"That's not fair!"

"What's not fair is you making me love you and then leaving to go back to that prick!" I shout as I drown under the weight of the pain I'm feeling.

She steps back, looking wary. "That's not what I'm doing."

Her protests are worthless. I bet this was always her plan, and I'm the gobshite who fell for it. "Bull-fucking-shit." I let the full extent of my frustration and anger loose, narrowing my eyes and spitting out my next words. "You're pathetic. Crawling back to him after he's probably spent months fucking his costar."

"Reeve has nothing to do with this. He won't even be in L.A."

329

Has she always been this much of a liar and I didn't see it? I jab my finger in front of her face. "You can't even admit it to yourself."

"Dillon, my entire life is back in L.A. My classes are starting in ten days. I've signed up for an evening costume design course. I have taken out a lease with Audrey on an apartment near UCLA. My parents are there."

"You could transfer to Trinity permanently, but you never even tried, did you?"

"The thought did cross my mind."

I scoff. "Yet you did nothing about it."

Her nostrils flare as the truth stings. She's just mad I'm calling her out on her bullshit tactics. "Hang on here a second. You never gave me any indication until right now that you wanted me to stay! Do you think I'm a mind reader?"

"Cop the fuck on, Hollywood. We both know what we're feeling. Or maybe I was the only one who fell." I pull my lips into a tight line as I angrily fasten the buttons on my shirt, needing to get out of here ASAP.

"You know that's not true, and what difference would it make anyway, Dillon? You're not going to be in Dublin for much longer. The band will take off, and you'll go with them. You'll be gone for years, and there'll be groupies and women coming out of the wood-work, and I'll be pushed aside. We'd try to make it work, but it wouldn't. I know. I've already been there."

I fucking knew it! I knew this was behind her reluctance. It seems my twin is not done fucking with my life. Well, fuck him and fuck her! They don't get to do this to me! My jaw pulls taut with stress, and my hands ball into fists. I need to hit something. Preferably my twin's smug face. "Know one thing, Vivien. I am *not* Reeve Lancaster!" I shout. She folds her arms across her chest, hugging herself as she clings to the sheet protecting her body. "I would *never* cheat on you. *Never.*"

I stalk to the door, almost slumping against it. My body deflates as adrenaline ebbs and all my sleepless nights catch up to me. I turn

330

around to face her one final time. Let her know this before we go our separate ways. Let her go back to her safety net and forget how incredible we are together. Let her choose comfort and predictability over passion and loyalty. "I would have stayed for you, Vivien. I would have fought for you. No matter what happens, know it was real." Sadness slaps me in the face. "Goodbye, Hollywood. I hope everything works out for you."

Chapter Forty-Two

Age 20

"**Y**ou disgust me." My sister's pretty face contorts into a scowl as she glares at me before shooting daggers at the gold digger situated in my lap. Aoife paws at my chest, her fingers creeping upward to my neck. Before Viv, Aoife's touch used to turn me on. Now, she makes my skin crawl because the touch is all wrong. Too desperate. Too harsh. Not the soft loving caresses from the only woman who matters. A woman who has just poured her heart out to me in front of everyone. A woman who just bled her truths at my feet.

But it's not enough.

She's still leaving.

To go back to *him*.

Anger glides up my throat, and a muscle clenches in my jaw, the same way it always does whenever I think of Reeve Lancaster.

"More than that, you disappoint me," Ash continues, shaking her head sadly. "I know you love her, Dil. You can deny it until you're blue in the face, and I won't believe you. You love *her*. She loves *you*." Leaning down, she puts her face all up in mine. "Fight for her, for fuck's sake."

I tried, and it didn't work. Even if I were to run outside and chase her, it won't change a damn thing. Viv is still getting on that plane to return to L.A.

To return to my *twin*.

I asked her to choose me, and she rejected me.

It's over, and the sooner my sister understands that, the better.

"It was a summer fling, and we both knew it had an end date." I shrug, bringing my beer to my lips. "The only one who doesn't seem to get that is you." I swallow a healthy mouthful of beer, hoping the alcohol will calm the violent emotional storm brewing inside me.

"I never took you for a coward, Dil, but that's exactly what you are."

Aoife drops a line of kisses on my neck, and my skin itches like I've stumbled upon a bed of nettles. I need my sister to fuck off so I can get rid of the parasite on my lap. My gaze lifts to my best friend in silent communication.

"Ash." Jamie reaches for my sister, but she swats his arm away.

"I'm going after Viv," she tells him, "because someone has to make sure she's okay." She sends one last scathing look in my direction before storming off.

Aoife giggles at Ash's retreating back. "You're well rid of that stuck-up American bitch," she says, pressing her ass down on my flaccid cock.

I shove her off my lap, needing her the fuck away from me. Ro rides to the rescue, grabbing Aoife around the waist before she hits the deck.

"What the hell, Dil?" Aoife plants her hands on her hips, pinning me with an angry stare.

"Fuck off." I don't look at her as I spit the words out, bringing the bottle to my lips and draining the rest of my beer.

"I can tell you're in one of your moods, so I'll forgive you." She plonks down on my lap again.

"Are you fucking deaf as well as stupid?" I hiss, shoving her harder. This time, she lands unceremoniously on the ground, whimpering while fixing me with hurt eyes. "I don't want you. I've *never* wanted you. You were nothing more than a hole to fuck when I needed a release."

Ro helps Aoife to her feet, glaring at me. "Don't be an even bigger asshole. It's not fair to take this out on Aoife. You fucked this up. *You.* Not anyone else."

Jamie whispers in Aoife's ear, and she leaves, taking her three friends with her. "Ro." Jamie shakes his head. "Drop it."

"No, Jay. I won't drop it. He needs to get his head out of his ass and remember where his priorities lie."

Conor leans back in his chair, nodding in silent agreement.

"We have a real opportunity this time," Ro continues, "and he's not going to fuck it up for all of us."

An opportunity we wouldn't have if it wasn't for Viv. My brother seems to have forgotten that. "Don't hold back, bro. Say what you really think."

"You knew what you had with her was temporary, so stop acting like someone ran over your dog. You should apologize and end things amicably. Ash is right in that respect, but you have no right to be pissed at Viv for returning home when it was the plan all along."

He has no idea how close I came to giving it all up. How I was prepared to quit the band and stay by her side if she had told me she'd stay.

I love music. I love performing. I'm happy doing what we're doing, and it's enough for me because I don't want the nasty side of fame. I don't want my private life under a microscope, and not because the truth about my twin brother would most likely come out. Why can't the music be enough? We could make a comfortable living producing and streaming our own stuff. Playing local events. Building a loyal fanbase locally. But it won't be enough for Jamie and Ronan. Even Conor is champing at the bit at the prospect this A&R scout might want to sign us.

Going to America and making it big has never been my dream,

but I'll do it for the guys, for my brother, because there is nothing holding me here now anyway.

———

"What is she doing here?" I slur a few hours later, spotting Aoife standing a few feet away, scowling in my direction.

"Ro invited her." Jamie flops down beside me on the sofa. He hands me a beer, and I drain the last dregs of the one in my hand before tossing it on the carpeted floor. "You know your brother is a bleeding heart. Apparently, she was crying in the toilets at Bruxelles, so he took pity on her."

"I hope he's planning to fuck her because I'm never going there again." I pop the cap on my beer, glugging a few mouthfuls.

"You should go after Viv. It's not too late," he says, glancing at the time on his mobile phone.

"Nah." I scrunch up my nose. "Ro is right. It was always leading to this point."

"I'm calling bullshit." Jamie scrubs a hand along his stubbly jawline. "There is no shame in admitting you're hurting. I know you love her. We all saw it happening."

It wasn't supposed to go down like this.

I was going to steal *her* heart.

She wasn't supposed to steal mine.

But steal it she did. The plan was to make her fall in love with me and then break her heart so badly he got a shell of the woman he loved back. My heart was never meant to get involved, but she reeled me in before I even realized what was happening. She made me feel things I have never felt before. Love. Hope. Possibility. She made me believe I was worthy. That things could be different, and for a little while there, I believed in a future where we were together.

Yet it wasn't real. She was always preparing to return to him.

Now, I'm the one left nursing a broken heart while she swans back to that selfish prick.

Dillon

How does he do this? How does he always come out on top? I have never hated anyone as much as I hate Reeve Lancaster and his father. I hate them with a burning intensity that grows hotter and stronger with every passing day.

"What is that slut doing here?" Ash snaps, materializing in front of us an hour later. The party is in full swing now, and our small living room is bursting at the seams. Music thumps through the loudspeakers, almost drowning out the sound of conversation and laughter.

"Hello to you too, sister," I slur, swiping the joint out of Conor's fingers before he can lift it to his lips.

"I'm not talking to you," she hisses, pinning me with red-rimmed eyes as she crawls into Jamie's lap. Ash curls into a ball against her boyfriend, sniffling into his neck.

She has the saddest expression on her face, and pain presses down on my chest as the realization dawns. "She's gone."

"No thanks to you." Ash swipes at the dampness on her cheeks.

"It's nothing to do with me." I blow smoke circles into the air. "This was always the way it was meant to be."

She opens her mouth, and Jamie whispers something into her ear. A hushed conversation ensues, and they both glance at me as they debate something. Jamie kisses her, and a pang of longing for my girl hits me square in the face.

I force beer down my dry throat, needing to numb myself to all thoughts and emotions. Ash stares at me as she cuddles with her boyfriend, letting him comfort her, but her angry expression has been exchanged for something worse—pity. I pretend I don't notice, sitting there stewing in a mess of my own making, drinking and smoking to drown out my pain.

The rest of the night is a blur, and I don't budge from my position on the sofa, observing the party raging around me like an objective bystander. I'm vaguely conscious of Jamie and my brother carrying me up to my room at some point, and everything is a blank after that.

Muffled voices tickle my eardrums, attempting to lure me from

337

sleep, but I ignore them. Drums are pounding a new beat in my skull, and my tongue feels like it's superglued to the roof of my mouth. Someone prods me in the leg, but I play comatose, knowing they'll go away if I continue playing dead.

"Aarghhh!" I bolt upright as ice-cold water drenches my upper torso, waking up every single cell and nerve ending in my body. "What the fuck?" I shout, shaking droplets of water all over my duvet as I push wet hair back off my face.

"Get up!" Ash says. "We need to talk, and I'm done waiting."

"Fuck off, Ash." I glare at her through blurry vision.

"You can't speak to Ash like that," Jamie says. "She's only trying to help."

I rub at my eyes, and my vision focuses. Jamie and Ash are standing in my bedroom, leaning against the wall, eyeballing me with an intensity that scares me. "I don't need any help," I mumble, pulling myself up against the headboard.

"Said the blind man as he was standing on the edge of the cliff," Ash deadpans, pushing off the wall and perching on the dry side of my bed. "I love you, Dillon, but you're a stupid fucker at the best of times."

I open my mouth to protest, but she clamps her hand over my lips. "Nope. You're going to sit there and shut up. I've got shit to say, and I'm saying it. Besides, your breath reeks, and I'm about to pass out from the fumes." She passes me a glass of water and two paraceta-mol. "Take those." She twists around, looking at Jamie. "Babe, can you make coffee? Lots and lots of strong black coffee. We need to sober him up fast."

Jamie nods, walking out of my room. His feet thud on the stairs as he heads down to the kitchen.

I knock back the painkillers because my head is pounding and pain rattles around my skull, reminding me I completely overdid it last night. "Spit it out," I tell my sister, needing to get this over and done with.

"I won't pretend to know the exact inner workings of your

338

mind, nor am I asking you to tell me, but you're my brother, and I know you well enough to know part of what is going through that thick skull of yours." She grabs a towel from behind her, gently mopping the wetness on my face. "You love her. I know you do. Like I know it terrifies you to trust your heart to someone. I understand she hurt you, but she's hurting too. I should've knocked your heads together weeks ago and forced you to have a conversation about the future. You've both been skating around it instead of just talking."

"We did talk. I told her how I felt. I asked her to stay, and she said no."

"You sprung it on her at the last minute, Dil! You didn't even give her time to consider it before you stormed off all butthurt."

"She rejected me, Ash." I rub at the tightness spreading across my chest. "She was never going to choose me over him. She's been in love with him most of her life. A few months with me isn't going to change that fact."

"Dillon. Jesus." She crawls up beside me, wrapping her arms around my wet chest. "She broke up with him because he betrayed her. He let her down, and she might never be able to forget that. She came here to heal. She didn't plan to meet anyone let alone fall in love. But she did. She fell in love with *you*." She taps my chest directly where my heart beats sluggishly. "You caught her off guard when you asked her," she continues. "She's confused, and her past is compounding the situation, but it doesn't mean she doesn't love you like crazy because I know she does." Ash grabs my face between her small, soft palms. "She told you she loves you in front of everyone last night. Didn't that mean anything?"

Of course, it did. That took huge guts, something Viv has in spades. I know I should have chased after her last night, but I was already drunk and hurting too much to think logically. All I wanted to do was hurt her, so she'd know what it feels like.

"It did, but it's too late now," I say, spotting the time on my mobile. It's already seven in the morning and her flight left at four.

"She's already in the air. And I'm not sure her saying that changes anything."

"You won't know unless you fight for her." Ash scrambles off the bed as Jamie reappears, carrying a steaming mug of coffee. "Stay here. I've got something to show you." She disappears as my best friend hands me a coffee.

"What are you going to do?" he asks, lighting up a cigarette.

I shrug. "What can I do? She's gone now."

Ash returns, carrying a brand-spanking-new guitar case into the room.

"What's that?" Jamie inquires, walking around the bed.

"It's for Dil. From Viv."

I set my mug down on the bedside locker, taking the case from my sister's hands.

"Holy fuck." Jamie kneels on the floor as I remove the expensive Fender from the case. "Is that what I think it is?"

My fingers run along the curved edges of the guitar with reverence. "It's a sixtieth anniversary American vintage 1954 Stratocaster."

"That's good, right?" Ash asks.

I can barely nod over the lump in my throat. "Just under two thousand of these were manufactured back in 2014."

"They're collector's items," Jamie says, his eyes still out on stalks.

"I thought it was new." Ash shrugs, not understanding the significance of this gift.

"It basically is," I admit, knowing from looking at it that whoever she bought this off hasn't used the guitar.

"She engraved your initials," Jamie says, rubbing his thumb along the DOD etched into the glossy wood.

"Look at the strap," Ash prompts, and I hold it out, examining the custom-made Toxic Gods strap. My heart, swollen with so many emotions, slams against my rib cage. I can't believe Viv did this for me. We spoke about it one time. She knows my goal was to buy one of these at auction someday.

Dillon

"Bro. She must really love you to leave you this after how you treated her last night." Jamie pulls a drag on his cigarette before Ash swipes it from his hand, stubbing it out.

Shame washes over me for the first time, and I'm embarrassed at how poorly I treated Viv at Bruxelles. I let my pain take control, hurting the girl who means everything to me.

"I wasn't with Aoife," I blurt, eyeballing my sister. "I just did that to hurt Viv."

"I know, dumbass. It was a shitty move, and you hurt my best friend." Her eyes turn glacial. "I don't know if I'll ever forgive you for that, even if you do make things right with her."

I set the guitar aside, too guilt-ridden to test it out right now. "I don't see how. She's gone, and I missed my chance to fix things."

Jamie and Ash trade conspiratorial looks. My sister grabs my mug, thrusting it into my hands. "Drink."

"What are you up to?"

"Do you love Vivien, Dillon? No bullshit. It's just us three here."

"I do. I love her so much."

"Then get on a fucking plane and tell her that. Talk to her. Make her see she has options. That this doesn't have to be the end for you two." Ash's eyes blaze with determination. "I think she just needs to hear the words from your lips and she'll change her mind."

Ash isn't aware of everything. I wonder if she knew the truth if she would still want me to chase after her best friend. Going after Viv is risky as fuck, and there are no guarantees. This could all end badly and cause a shitstorm of epic proportions. She could take his side when she discovers the truth. "What if she doesn't?"

"You won't know if you don't try, but you've got to hurry. Reeve is going to try to win her back, and she's vulnerable now." Ash extracts her phone from her jeans pocket. "There's a flight leaving for LAX in four hours. Say the word, and I'll book the ticket."

Of course, he's going to try to get her back. I've known that all along.

Reeve Lancaster always gets what he wants.

341

Except this time.

Fuck it.

I'm not a coward.

I'm not a quitter.

And Vivien is worth fighting for.

It's time to man up and claim my woman.

He is *not* taking her from me.

I will fight him to the bitter end because I love her. I love her more than life, and she's worth risking everything.

With my mind made up, I wish I could click my fingers and be in L.A. already. I don't know how much a plane ticket costs, but I have some measly savings, so I can probably just about afford it.

"Don't worry about the cost," Ash says, as if she's a mind reader. "I'll get it, and you can pay me back when you make it big. I haven't paid rent all year, so I've managed to save a lot. I'll book you a plane ticket and a hotel room. Just say the word." Her finger hovers over a button on her phone.

"How will I find her?"

Ash flashes me a triumphant grin. "I have her US mobile number. You can call her when you get there and arrange to meet."

Ripping the duvet off, I swing my legs out of the bed. "Book it. I'm grabbing a shower."

Ash squeals, and I hope I'm doing the right thing.

"Pack my shit," I tell Jamie, knowing time is of the essence. "Enough for a week."

"A week?" He lifts an eyebrow. "Don't forget the scout is coming to see us perform in ten days."

"I need some time to work through things with Viv, but I promise I'll be back in time for the event."

Chapter Forty-Three
Age 20

avigating my way out of LAX and finding the shuttle bus to my hotel is challenging because the place is ginormous, but eventually I find myself on the right bus, nabbing a window seat at the back. Thank fuck, I managed to sleep off my hangover on the plane, so I'm not feeling too bad, despite the change in time zone, climate, and culture. My nose is pressed to the glass as we leave the airport, heading for downtown L.A.

Viv wasn't joking about the traffic, and it takes forever to reach my hotel. After checking in, I grab a quick shower, order some room service, and map out what I want to say to her.

I've got to lay it all on the line. That means coming clean about everything—Reeve, Simon, my initial plan, and how I ended up falling completely and utterly in love with her to the point I know she's the only woman who will ever own my heart. I know it might mean losing her for good, because she's going to be pissed, but I can't beg her to come back to Dublin with me if she isn't privy to all the facts.

It's a huge risk, because she'll want to run straight to Reeve with the truth, but she deserves to know he's been lying to her too. She deserves to know what kind of man she's been in love with all these years. I hope the fact I've come all this way will help. That she'll see how important she is to me and how sincere I am about never keeping secrets from her again. I'm even willing to set aside my vengeance for her. If she agrees to be with me, I will drop all plans for revenge. Viv means more to me than getting even with my twin and my father. If she loves me as much as I love her and she agrees to spend her life with me, that is all I will ever need.

I know it's not black-and-white.

There's a lot of gray matter to trudge through, but she is all I want.

Nothing else matters except having her by my side, now and always.

Nerves fire at me and my palms are sweaty as I press dial on her number. Her voice mail automatically kicks in, confirming her phone is off. Maybe she's sleeping or it's out of charge.

Or she's already with him.

I rage at the devil on my shoulder, not needing his pessimistic comments right now. Viv wouldn't do that. Even though I was a total prick to her before she left, I know she loves me. She wouldn't run straight back into his arms because what we shared meant something to both of us.

I try a couple more times, but it's the same. Always sent to voice mail. Frustrated, I toss my phone on the bed, pacing the room as I contemplate leaving her a message. I decide against it. I'd rather speak to her in person so she can't duck out of meeting me.

I turn on the TV for something to do, instantly wishing I hadn't. All the color leaches from my face as I turn up the volume. Pain slices across my chest as the image of Reeve with Viv fills the screen. They are on an apartment balcony, and he's holding her in an intimate embrace, his chest to her back. The photo only shows from the waist up, but it's obvious they are naked. Reeve's arm is wrapped around Viv's bare breasts, and he's nuzzling into her neck, kissing her.

She's clinging to his arms, smiling like she hasn't a care in the world. Like she wasn't in my arms mere hours ago. Like she didn't just leave me behind in Ireland. She shows none of the emotion I saw in her eyes yesterday when she was telling me she loved me. I don't even look like a distant memory. I'm like a speck of dust that's there one minute and gone the next.

Pain eviscerates me on all sides, and I drop to my knees clutching my aching heart as tears sting the backs of my eyes.

The image changes to a live feed, and a reporter thrusts a mic into Reeve's face as he emerges from a high-rise building. "Reeve! Is it true you are back together with Vivien Mills?" a pretty blonde reporter asks, claiming his attention. "Is the photo from earlier today proof you are in love with your childhood sweetheart again?"

"I've always been in love with Viv," Reeve says, stopping to talk to her. He pins her with a wide disarming smile, and he's practically glowing. A swarm of reporters crowds around him, and camera flashes go off in his face. "I never stopped loving her, and I never will. She's the only woman for me." He stares pointedly at the camera, and I want to wipe the superior look off his smug face. "Nothing or no one will ever come between us again." He might as well be saying it directly to my face because I know this message is directed at me. "She's back in my arms, exactly where she belongs. Where she's going to stay."

I throw the remote at the screen, cracking the glass, as rage infiltrates my veins, replacing the blood flow. Anger unlike anything I've ever felt before races through me, and I tear through the room, ripping pictures off the walls, tossing the furniture around, destroying the curtains and bedding, and throwing anything that isn't pinned down at the walls and the windows. I can't see anything over the red layer tainting my vision and the angry tsunami sweeping through my insides, obliterating everything in its path.

I'm still in a monstrous rage when security enters my room and I'm hauled outside the hotel in handcuffs. I lose my shit in the back of the police car as they take me to the headquarters of the Los Angeles Police Department and throw me into a cell. Fury continues to pummel my insides even as the mad adrenaline rush leaves, and my exhausted body slumps against the bench. Vengeance returns, a million times stronger than before, and I know what needs to be done.

I am such a fool, and Viv has played me for a right idiot.

She never had any intention of staying with me. She waltzed straight back into his arms—into his bed—only hours after being with me. *How could she do that? Did I mean so little to her that she could fuck me and then fuck him without any remorse or guilt?* Because I saw zero regrets on her face in that picture. She was basking in his possessive adoration, like I no longer existed.

The walls around my heart harden along with my resolve.

Simon and Reeve are no longer the isolated entries on my shit list. I've now added Hollywood to the mix.

She will pay. They will all pay for treating me like I don't matter.

The seriousness of my situation hits home when I let my mind wander, and I realize how badly I've fucked up. It's quite likely I will be kicked out of the US and forbidden from ever returning. We can kiss our music dreams goodbye if that happens. I wouldn't care except it will devastate the guys. They are banking on things working out with this A&R guy, and I won't be the reason things fall apart. I need someone with clout in this town to make this go away, and I know just who to call. My mind churns ideas as I align both goals. It will take longer to achieve if I do this, but it's the only way.

Standing, I grip the cell bars, shaking them to get the attention of the woman behind the counter outside. "I want my phone call." I've watched enough US police dramas to know my rights.

Ten minutes later, I'm sitting in a small interview room while the surly cop rummages through my duffel bag. "This?" he asks, holding the wrinkled brown envelope in his hand.

"Yeah. See that number written on the top? That's the number I need." Thank fuck, I thought to stuff the old NDA into my bag before I left home. I've held on to it all these years because I knew there might come a day when I'd have to sign it. Some sixth sense told me to bring it with me, and now I know why. It's the leverage I need to get myself out of this mess and begin to put a new plan of revenge in place.

The cop picks up the handset and gives it to me. I punch in the private number, holding the phone to my ear as I wait for him to answer.

"Simon Lancaster," he drawls, arrogance dripping from his tone.

"I'll sign it on two conditions," I say, knowing he already knows who I am. "I want five million dollars, and I need your help to extract me from a situation."

Part Three
POST VIVIEN

Chapter Forty-Four
Age 20

"Follow me," a tall, thin man with cropped gray hair says after the cops release me into his care at the station.

"Who are you?" I'm not budging an inch until he explains who he is and why exactly he's here.

Removing a business card from inside his suit jacket, he hands it to me. "Gregory Lucas. I'm a colleague of Carson Park."

Flipping the card between my fingers without looking at it, I stare blankly at him, having no clue who that is.

"Mr. Park is Mr. Lancaster's attorney. Carson is out of state on business, so he asked me to look after this situation on his behalf."

Figures my sperm donor would send the hired help to deal with me. Not sure why that makes me so mad. It's not like I ever want to see that prick again. "What's the plan?" I'm not going anywhere until I understand how this will play out.

"I have a car outside. We'll go to my office to sign the paperwork. My assistant is booking your flight home as we speak. She's also smoothed things over at the hotel, paid the bill, and covered the damages. The cops won't press charges against you, and all record of your arrest has been wiped as if it never happened."

A shudder works its way through me. I always assumed Simon Lancaster was powerful, but the fact he can do all this tells me I was right not to challenge him. To let his offer sit until I needed it for leverage. I refuse to be grateful to the asshole, but I'm relieved my fuckup won't impact Toxic Gods' future. Right now, that's all I've got in my life, and I need it.

"Okay."

He arches a brow, but if he expects me to thank him, he can think again. He's being paid to do this, and I'm selling my soul in exchange for making this go away.

I'm thanking no one for shit.

The ride to the prestigious office building in downtown L.A. is long only because traffic is at a virtual standstill. I don't know how anyone lives in this city, though I expect I'm about to find out. My mind is tossing ideas about how to use the five million and how to explain it when I return home. I'm purposely not thinking about Viv because it'll only piss me off all over again. Betrayal is like a dagger gliding between my ribs, embedding deep inside, the blade piercing my heart, causing me to slowly bleed out. As I stare out the window, suffocating inside, I try to round up all my feelings for Vivien Grace Mills, toss them in a lockbox, and throw away the key.

At the office, I accept the offer of coffee and settle down to read the contract pushed across the desk to me. "You are free to seek your own counsel," Mr. Lucas says. "In fact, I highly advise it. While the paperwork has been drafted with your specifications in mind and it's a standard NDA in all other regards, it's wise to have a legal professional review them on your behalf. I can recommend a couple of people if you like."

It's probably smart, but I'd be an idiot to take his recommendation. No doubt the people he's referring to are friends, and they won't be acting in my best interests. I could find someone myself with a bit of internet research, but it'll delay things, and I want to get the fuck out of here ASAP. I'm desperate to get home so I can lick my wounds in private. "I appreciate the advice, but I'll pass. I want time to read this thoroughly." I'm no legal expert, but I'm not a dumbass. I'm not signing shit without reading it fully.

"Of course. Take as much time as you need. Let me know if you have any questions."

He works away on his desktop computer as I take my time reading over the document. A lot of it is legal jargon, but with the help of Google, I decipher it. Everything I've asked for is included, but there's one thing I hadn't thought to specify. "This needs to come out." With my finger, I underline a part at the end of the document. "I didn't agree to never step foot in L.A., and it's not something I can concede."

He schools his face into a neutral expression as he looks at it. "I'm not authorized to make changes. I'll need to contact Mr. Park."

"Then contact him."

His pretty assistant escorts me out of his office and into a small meeting room, flashing me flirty looks the whole time. "Can I get you anything, Mr. O'Donoghue?" Licking her lips and eye fucking me from head to toe, she's not disguising her interest.

"Another coffee would be good."

"Are you sure that's all?" Her eyes zoom in on my mouth, and wow, are all the women in L.A. this forthright?

I quirk a brow and stare at her without replying.

"I can order some food for you if you're hungry." She's quick to backtrack at the expression on my face.

Briefly, I consider locking the door, slamming her up against the wall, and fucking her. There's nothing stopping me now. It sure as fuck didn't hold Vivien back. Maybe I should bang this slut to get over the bitch who has taken a sledgehammer to my heart. But even the thought of touching anyone else makes my skin crawl and my stomach twist into painful knots.

"I'm not hungry." I can't stomach food either. "For food or anything else," I add when she still lingers.

Her cheeks stain red, but I don't give a fuck if she's embarrassed. She should be. *Isn't she supposed to be a professional? Does she hit on every young guy who comes into the office?* She looks young too. Probably only a couple years older than me. Fresh out of college is my guess. I doubt she'll last long in the legal profession if this is how she plans to conduct herself.

"Okay. Let me know if you change your mind," she says, deliberately sashaying her hips as she walks out the door.

She's got balls. I'll give her that.

I bark out a laugh, thinking of how Ro hit the nail on the head about Hollywood women that first time Viv came to Sunday dinner when we were all discussing it. My mood instantly sours as images of Viv flood my mind without invitation. We had our first kiss that day out in the orchard. Swallowing thickly, I lean my head back and close my eyes. Pain accosts me like a battering ram, pummeling me from all sides. The ache in my chest is so severe it feels like I can't breathe.

Burying my head in my hands, I try to bat all thoughts of Vivien and Reeve from my mind, but it's impossible. The image of him cradling her naked body on that balcony burns behind my eyes. I doubt I'll ever be able to dig it out of my mind. *How could she do it? How could she run straight from my arms into his?*

I know I was a shithead in the pub. I was deliberately cruel and vindictive, but she *knows* me. Vivien knows how I operate. She knows I didn't mean it. That I was lashing out in pain. *So, how could she do this to me? Was she playing me all along? Did she know who I was from the start and my initial thoughts were spot-on? Was Simon behind all of this?* He is getting what he wants, after all, and it's my Hollywood who has driven me to this point. If I accept that's the truth, it means everything was a lie. That she was acting the whole time, and I don't think she's that good of an actress despite who her mother is.

Ugh, round and round it goes in my head, attempting to drive me crazy.

After the flirty secretary returns with my coffee, I drink it slowly in a daze, fighting a losing inner battle. Right now, I wish I could click my fingers and be home. I want to crawl under my covers and sink into oblivion. Resting my head on my arms on the table, I wish I could rip my shredded heart from my chest so I don't feel this gut-wrenching ache any more. I have never felt pain as excruciating as this before, though the way I felt after Ash tried to kill herself comes close.

Hurt spears me on the inside, and I want to curl into a ball and slowly die. I wonder if this is how Ash felt after what Cillian did. For the first time, I understand fully how she wanted it to stop. I'm only living with this torment a short while, and it's already unbearable. Not that I'd ever contemplate ending my life. I would never give the Lancasters the satisfaction or ever put my family through something like that again, but I have a greater understanding of how Ash came to do it now I'm experiencing similar heartbreak.

Eventually, I'm escorted back to Mr. Lucas's office. The older man holds out the phone to me. "Mr. Lancaster would like to speak with you."

A muscle clenches in my jaw as I take the phone. "What?" I snap.

"Watch your tone," he grits out. "Or the deal is off."

"Fine by me. There are other easy ways of making five mil in L.A."

My threat lingers in the air as silence greets me for a few beats. "That clause is nonnegotiable." His cold tone forces the temperature in the room to plummet even through the phone.

"Then the deal is off." I raise his cold tone with a glacial one. "I'm signing papers which forbid me from ever approaching Reeve or talking about the Lancasters. I'm aware of the consequences if I break it. Whether I'm in L.A. or Dublin doesn't make a blind bit of difference. I can't, and won't, go near your precious son. My signature ensures it, so you don't need that clause."

"Why is it so important?"

I ain't telling him jack shit about the band or our plans. I don't trust he won't try to fuck things up. "I won't have my movements restricted. I'm signing away enough. You want me to stay away from you and Reeve, and you've got it."

Mr. Lucas's neutral exterior cracks for a split second. Compassion splays across his face, mixed with a little anger, and I decide I like him.

The sperm donor releases a frustrated sigh before conceding. "You sign that contract now, boy. No delays and it's a deal."

It feels good to have backed him into a corner. To have safeguarded Toxic Gods' future. "When will I get my money?"

"The funds will be transferred to your bank account as soon as you sign on the dotted line."

"Fine." Handing the phone back to Mr. Lucas, I lift the pen and scribble my signature in all the places he has marked with a sticky note. He talks in a hushed tone to the prick before hanging up. Then I watch as he transfers the money via an online banking portal.

Business concluded, I grab my duffel bag and stand.

"Here's your passport, boarding pass' and some cash for the airport," he says, handing over the documents. "I have a car outside waiting to take you to LAX."

"Thank you." I thought I'd feel lighter finally drawing a line under the Lancaster drama, but my heart feels like it's been dragged through my body like a sinking ship.

"There's no need." He clamps a hand on my shoulder. "Good luck to you, Dillon."

As I wait in the business class line to board the plane, I send a link to a newspaper article about Vivien and Reeve to Ash and tap out a quick message before turning off my phone.

Wasted trip. I'm coming home.

Chapter Forty-Five
Age 20

"He won't talk to me either," Ash says to Ma in a low voice, but she's not quiet enough. "I've tried. He's been like this for the past two weeks ever since he came back from L.A."

I don't bother confirming I can hear them talking about me because it takes too much effort to open my mouth and speak. Lifting my glass to my mouth, I take another large gulp of my beer. My family know I went chasing after Vivien, only for her to make me a laughingstock in front of the entire world.

Celebrity Land is giddy at the prospect of Hollywood's Golden Boy reuniting with his childhood love, and it's all I fucking see when I open social media or walk past magazine shelves in shops. The same media who hounded and humiliated Vivien have done a three-sixty, and now they can't get enough of Hollywood's new potential IT couple.

Ironically, it helps me to relate to what Vivien went through on a deeper level. It's no wonder she flew thousands of miles away to escape it. I'd do anything to get away from the continual onslaught. I should be angry. I *have* been angry, but mostly I'm just fucking gutted and drowning under a mountain of self-loathing. I've lost her, and I don't know how I'll come back from that.

I should have done everything differently.

If I had, she'd be here with me. Not back with *him*.

I hate Reeve Lancaster even more than I did before, and I know I signed that NDA, but some day, somehow, I will make him pay for everything he's taken from me.

"Leave him be," Shane says. "If Dillon doesn't want to talk about it, that's his choice." He squeezes my shoulder in quiet support, and I'm grateful.

"We're here if you need us, Dillon." Ma reaches over to pat my hand. "And you should eat. You look thin."

"I'm not hungry." My appetite disappeared about the same time Vivien did. My heart hurts, same as always when I think about her. Pushing my uneaten plate away, I take another swig of my beer and mentally count down the hours until I can go home and lock myself away in my bedroom.

After dinner is over, I head out with Shane and Da, spending a few hours working on the farm. My brother and my dad don't pester me, and I appreciate it. Pounding my frustration out via manual labor helps but not much.

Back at the farmhouse, I walk ahead of Ash and Ro as they say their goodbyes.

"Dil." Ciarán pulls me into a hug. "I'm here if you need me."

I nod, falling into his hug and letting him clap me on the back.

"I hate seeing you like this," Ma says, fighting tears as she clings to me. "Please take care of yourself."

"I'm fine," I manage to croak out.

"No, you're not." She grasps my cheeks in her hands. "And it's okay not to be. Just don't bottle it all up, Dillon. Please."

I nod again, though I'm in no state to promise my mother anything. I have zero experience dealing with personal heartbreak, and I'm clinging to the edge of my sanity by my fingernails.

Jamie sits in the passenger seat while Ro and I hop into the back seat as Ash drives us back to the city. Closing my eyes, I lean my head against the window. Even being in this car is hard. I'm used to being the one behind the wheel with my pretty American beauty bouncing in the seat by my side. But it's Ash's car now. Viv left it for her, which was super generous.

I suppose it's proof their friendship was legit, though it could be the opposite. If Vivien always planned to return to Reeve, she'd know it would spell the demise of her friendship with Ash. Maybe the car was a peace offering. A way to ease her guilty conscience for doing my sister dirty.

Who knows? My mind still flits from one extreme to the other, and I can't decide whether all of this was premeditated or not. It's confusing as fuck, and it's tearing me apart. Pain slams into me like a tidal wave, and if I wasn't sitting down, I'd have fallen over. I bend over, clutching my head in my hands, as I struggle to breathe through the pain. It's like this sometimes. Crashing into me all of a sudden, knocking me flat on my arse.

"Everything will be okay, Dil," Ro quietly says as Jay and Ash talk privately in the front. "Wait and see. After this A&R guy sees us on Friday, it's all going to happen. You'll forget about her once the band takes off."

I know he means well, and though he's often wiser than his years, he's showing his age and immaturity now. "I'll never forget her," I grit out, straightening up. Opening my eyes, I drill him with a pointed look. I told everyone the day I came back that I didn't want to talk about Vivien ever again. That she's Voldemort. But my brother and sister seem determined to prolong my agony, and I'm getting sick of them bringing her up. *How can I move on if people keep fucking talking about her?*

Indecipherable emotion flits across Ro's face before he looks away, staring out his window.

"Can we talk?" Ash asks when we pull up to the curb outside the apartment I now share with Ronan and Conor. Ash and Jamie moved into a one-bed studio a few days after Viv left.

"No." I climb out of the car. "Thanks for the lift."

"Dillon!" My sister's concerned plea follows me as I stride across the path and into the building.

I've only just settled on my bed with my new Fender and my notepad, ready to lose myself in music, when Ash bursts into my bedroom like a charging bull. "That was fucking rude, Dillon!" She slams the door shut, and the walls rattle with the impact. "And I'm done with this crap. We're talking about this whether you like it or not."

"I'm not talking about her," I repeat, strumming my guitar. "There's nothing to say."

"There's everything to say!" Her voice cracks as she climbs onto the bed beside me with tears in her eyes. "Now I know how you must have felt when I shut you out. I'm sorry I did that, and trust me, it didn't help locking all my feelings up inside and trying to pretend like I wasn't dying a thousand different deaths on the inside." A sob filters into the air, and I set my guitar aside and pull my sister into my arms.

"Don't cry, Ash. Please." My voice sounds as choked as I feel. "You know how it kills me."

"Like it's killing me to see you like this," she sniffles, burying her face in my chest.

My arm tightens around her. "It hurts, Ash," I whisper. "It hurts so fucking much."

She squeezes me tight. "I know, bro. I know." Air huffs out of her mouth. "She's still not answering my calls or texts."

I hate that Vivien appears determined to cut Ash from her life too. She always promised she wouldn't do that. Vivien hasn't just let me down; she's let my sister down too. "She played us, Ash. My guess is this was always her plan. She was never going to stay here. She was always planning to go back to him, and she knew that would mean the end of your friendship too."

"No, Dil." Ash rubs at her red-rimmed eyes before propping up on one elbow. "I refuse to believe that. I know Vivien." She places her hand on my heart. "You do too. She didn't plan this. You didn't see her after that last night in the pub. She was devastated, Dillon. She threw up and everything. Her heartbreak was written all over her face."

"Her mother is one of the best actresses in the world, Ash. Who's to say she wasn't acting too?" I don't really think she had it in her, but I'm questioning everything I thought I knew about her now.

"To what end, Dil? What the fuck did Viv have to gain by playing us?"

I considered asking Simon outright on the phone that day. But if he put Vivien up to this, he'd never admit it. "I don't know," I lie. As far-fetched as it seems, I have considered this was some plan concocted by the three of them. That they sent her here deliberately to seduce and destroy me. To eliminate me as a threat to Reeve Fucking Lancaster. *How else would she end up back in his arms the instant her feet hit Californian soil?* "But it's obvious she doesn't want to explain it to you."

She nibbles on her lip, staring off into space for a few seconds. "I know those balcony pictures seem damning, but it could've been staged that way." She stares me in the face. "You know the kind of media shite she had to deal with previously. All they seem to do over there is manipulate situations to their advantage. I warned you Reeve would make a play for her. That's what I think this is."

"You're too smart to be this naïve." I sit up against the headboard while Ash sits cross-legged in front of me. "She fucked him, Ash." Pain scorches a blazing trail up my throat, singeing my words on the way out. "She didn't give a flying fuck about me if she could do that because I can't even think about laying a hand on another woman without feeling sick."

"They have a lot of history, and he was her best friend before he was anything else. I didn't say anything to you before because I didn't want to upset you, but Audrey and I butted heads a lot that week we spent with Viv's parents on holiday. She was purposely mentioning Reeve and dropping all these hints that he was working hard to make things up to her."

Anger is a red-hot poker stabbing me in the eye. "You should have fucking told me!"

"I was supposed to be Switzerland, remember?"

I snort out a bitter laugh. "You're more like South Vietnam, Syria, and Afghanistan all rolled into one."

"She hasn't abandoned me."

"Then why isn't she calling you back?"

"Because she's embarrassed and heartbroken. She thinks you don't want her and you're shacked up with Aoife most likely."

"All things related to me. She promised your relationship wouldn't be impacted by ours. She. Lied." Tension tightens my jaw.

"Gawd, it's all such a mess." Ash flips onto her back, staring at the ceiling. "I just know she didn't come here with an agenda, Dillon. She didn't come here expecting to find love, but she did." She locks eyes with mine. "She loves you. Like really fucking loves you. I know it's true. She wasn't lying about that."

"If she loved me, she'd be with me right now. But she's not. She's with him."

"There is nothing on social media to confirm that. Those pics are the only pics of them since she returned to America. I'm telling you all is not as it seems."

"It doesn't matter. She chose to return to L.A. which is as good as saying she chose to return to him. She's gone. I've lost her. The end."

Ash sighs and rolls over onto her stomach. "I wish you'd gotten to speak to her in L.A. If you'd looked her in the eye and asked her, you'd know the truth."

Pain presses down on my chest, compressing my lungs and making it hard to breathe. I squeeze my eyes shut.

"Oh, Dil." Ash hugs me. "I wish I could take all your pain away. I wish I knew how to fix this."

I draw air deep into my lungs and push past the pain. "There is nothing to fix, Ash. Viv and I aren't together anymore. Technically, she hasn't even done anything wrong. I pushed her back into his arms with the way I behaved that last week. That's all on me. I'm the one who has to live with the consequences. You shouldn't be paying any price. That one's on Viv." I press a kiss to her brow. "I'm sorry you've lost your friend."

"I haven't lost her yet," she quietly says, but we both know the truth. "And you know if it was a choice, I'd choose you. The same way you have always chosen me."

"You have Jay now. You should always choose him."

"You're my brother, Dil. I'll always have your back." She kisses my cheek. "I won't ask you about her again, but I want you to promise you'll come to me when you have bad days. Let me help. Even if it's only to give you a hug or make you tea."

"I'll try. That's as much as I can promise."

Chapter Forty-Six
Age 20

"This is happening. This is really fucking happening." It's hard to remain detached when faced with Ro's excited tone and ecstatic smile, and I'm grinning alongside Conor and Jamie. Dave—the A&R guy—has just left Whelans. After watching our full set, he hung back to talk to us. He was almost as giddy as my little brother, repeating how much he loves our sound, our look, our story, and how he thinks we'd be a perfect fit. He made a couple of initial calls, and it's looking like Capitol Records want to sign us.

I'm still in a bit of a daze. It all feels surreal.

"We need to make plans," Ash says, placing a tray of vodka shots on the table. "Like Dave said, these things take time to line up and nothing is guaranteed until we have a signed contract. But he seems genuinely interested, and I don't think he'd have said those things if he wasn't confident he can push this through."

"I think we should move to L.A. now." Ro lifts a shot glass in front of him.

"I agree," Ash says. "We need to get out there and hire a manager pronto. Holiday visas are good for three months, and that should be enough time to find a manager, sign a contract, and organize long-term visas. I presume the label will help with that."

"We have the money now to do it. It's all falling into place." Jay is grinning as he looks at me. "Thanks to you." He nudges my shoulder. "We'll pay you back for everything once the money starts rolling in."

"Don't talk daft." I accept a glass from Ash. "I won this money on the lottery. I told you it's for the band." I hate lying, and I'm only able to appease my guilt knowing the money will go toward Toxic Gods' future. We've already bought all new equipment, guitars, and a top-of-the-range drum kit for Ro, and we used some of the funds to pay for studio time to record a few new songs I've been working on with Con.

The only good thing about heartbreak is the endless songwriting material. My muse is on fire, and I'm writing nonstop around our other commitments. Music distracts me from thinking about Viv, and I'm immersing myself in the band. Falling into bed exhausted after pulling a long day writing and playing is the only way I can sleep at night. Otherwise, I'm tortured, tossing and turning all night, as everything I've fought to avoid during the day haunts me in the silent nighttime hours. My appetite is still nonexistent, and I'm drinking way more than I should, but I'm coping the best I can.

"I know you won't want to hear this, and don't rip into me for saying it." Ro glances nervously at me. "But it's like you were meant to follow her to L.A. to win that money and help secure our future."

Without waiting for the others, I knock back my shot and try to avoid looking at my brother so I don't throttle him.

"Ronan." Ash's warning tone shuts him up.

"A toast," Ash says, handing me another glass. Just as well she bought extra shots. "To Toxic Gods!"

"Toxic Gods!" we chorus before knocking back our drinks.

"I've always known you were destined for greatness," Ash adds, fighting tears. "You're going to be as big as U2. I just feel it in my bones."

"Steady on, love. Don't go putting that kind of pressure on us." Jamie pulls her down onto his lap. "I'm already shitting it."

"Same," I truthfully admit for a whole heap of reasons.

"You'll be in the same town as her," Ash bravely volunteers. *Didn't she just warn Ro to keep his gob shut?* Honestly, I just can't with my family sometimes even if I know it's coming from a good place. "You could go talk to her."

"Won't be happening." I drain the rest of my beer and stand. This conversation ends now. I'll not have thoughts of Vivien with my prick twin ruining our celebration. "Anyone want anything at the bar?" Con and Ro bob their heads, and I stomp off, ignoring my sister's question. So much for promising she wouldn't bring her up. It hasn't even been a week.

I'd be lying if I said the thought hadn't crossed my mind. Right now, I'm still devastated at her betrayal, but I don't know how I'll feel in time. As much as I want to despise her, I can't. I love Vivien too much to hate her, and I can't ignore the part I played in this mess. I know I'm not blameless either.

I miss Vivien so goddamned much. She is so ingrained in every aspect of my life it's hard to go on without her. I miss her laugh. Her playful teasing. Her incessant chatter as she fills me in on her day when we cook side by side. I miss snuggling with her on the sofa while I pretend to watch a movie. I miss looking out at the pub crowd and seeing her proud face. I miss the feel of her slender arms wrapped tight around me on my bike. I miss counting the tiny freckles on her nose and playing with her hair. I miss the sounds she makes when I'm driving her out of her mind with pleasure. I miss going to sleep beside her and waking up with her limbs all entangled in mine.

At night, I listen to the soundtrack of our summer while I flick through the multitude of photos I have of her on my phone. I usually fall asleep with tears clinging to my lashes. Waking up to an empty bed feels like losing her all over again every morning. Most days, I literally have to drag my lovesick arse out of bed because the temptation to stay under the covers and succumb to my heartache is almost too much to overcome.

My mind replays all the highlights of our time together. Despite my protests to the contrary, I struggle to believe it was all a lie. She loved me. I know she did. The same way I love her. She's the best thing that's ever happened to me, and I can't believe she's gone. I can't believe I fucked this up so spectacularly.

"Hey, Dil." An annoyingly familiar voice yanks me out of my inner monologue as I stand at the bar.

Aoife presses into my side, putting her hand on my arm. "How are you?"

"Never better," I lie, plastering a fake smile on my mouth as I pry her hand from my arm.

"You don't have to lie to me."

The sympathy on her face irritates me to no end. The same way all the finger-pointing and hushed whispers has in the aftermath of Vivien's departure. Since those pics of her with Reeve went viral, everyone on the scene now knows who she is and how she left me behind for a rich Hollywood star. The groupies are hitting on me left and right, desperate to reconnect now I'm single again. But I have zero interest in any of them, and I've rejected every advance.

"I'd feel like a complete fool too if some bitch had played me like that," Aoife continues.

"Don't call her that," I snap before leaning in and giving my order to the barman. I deliberately don't order Aoife a drink. She's been sniffing around me constantly since the night Viv left even though I was a complete asshole to her and treated her like shite. *Has she no self-respect?*

"How can you defend her after what she did to you?" Her eyes harden as she folds her arms around her chest and stares at me. "She showed up here professing her undying love and then went home and fucked her ex like you never meant anything to her. She was lying the whole time! That bullshit act she put on proves she's her mother's daughter. You should be super mad. How dare that fucking slut treat you like that, and for the record, you're way sexier than Reeve Lancaster."

No way am I letting her think that crap about Vivien. "Viv never lied. I've known all along who she is and who her ex was, like I've always known she was going back to L.A. at the end of the summer. Vivien hasn't done anything wrong. We broke up, and she's free to do what she wants." It kills me to say those words, but I won't have Aoife spreading bullshit about her to further her own agenda.

"You're unbelievable, Dil." She shakes her head as predictable tears well in her eyes. "I've been nothing but loyal to you for so long, and you treat me like trash! I love you!"

"Bullshit. If you loved me, you'd never have fucked my friends. You love the scene and the bragging rights." Ash was right all along about Aoife, and I was an idiot for not seeing it.

"You're so wrong, Dillon. Have you any idea how much you've hurt me?" A few tears spill out of her eyes and roll down her cheeks.

I barely resist an eye roll. *How did I ever put up with her dramatics?* She's fucking exhausting. "Do I look like I care?"

"You should, you prick."

She's bristling with rage now, and I'd like to say I care, but I really don't. I just want her out of my face.

Her nostrils flare as she spews the rest of her poison. "As soon as Miss Stuck-up-her-own-arse Yank shows up, you ditch me for her like I never existed, and I didn't call you out on it. I loyally stood by, waiting for the bitch to fuck off, and when she does, she shits all over you, and you fucking defend her? Why the fuck would you do that?"

"Because I love her!" I hiss in her face. "I love her, and I won't let you or Breda or any other skank disrespect Vivien by spreading lies."

"Skank?" Her eyes narrow dangerously.

I pay the barman and slide the tray off the counter. "If the shoe fits, Aoife."

"Fuck you, Dil."

"No thanks. I'd rather cut my dick off than put it anywhere near you again."

Her hands ball into fists at her side, and I do believe she wants to punch me. Maybe she's finally got the message that I don't want her. Never have and never will. "I hope you never get her back. I hope she marries him and leaves you to rot because you deserve it." She waggles her finger in my face. "And I lied. Reeve Lancaster is way sexier than you."

"Get the fuck out of my face, slut."

She smirks. "The truth hurts, huh, Dil?"

"Not as much as being fucking barred will," I retort, loving how her face drops as realization dawns.

We might be leaving for America soon, but I'll make sure Aoife gets what's coming to her before I go.

No one gets to insult Vivien and get away with it.

At least not on my watch.

Chapter Forty-Seven
Age 20

"Pinch me." Ash thrusts her arm out as she surveys the outdoor area of our new rented house in the Hollywood Hills with awe-widened eyes. "We have a fucking pool, jacuzzi, and outdoor kitchen, Dil." Her eyes are twinkling as she looks up at me. "What even is this life?"

I press a kiss to the top of her head. "I know. It's fucking insane."

"I'm so glad to be out of the hotel and to have our own space."

"Same. It was getting claustrophobic even if we were largely only sleeping there."

We stayed in a hotel for a few weeks when we first arrived in L.A. But after there was a bidding war for us—with several top labels vying for our commitment—we signed with Capitol Records and promptly started looking for a suitable place to rent.

We were offered a decent advance for a six-album deal, but we turned it down on the advice of our new agent-slash-manager, Frankie, and our new lawyer, Ted. Frankie explained how the only guarantee was our first album. After that, the label has the option of producing and distributing any future albums, meaning we could be tied to them for years if our first album is a big success. With current streaming and distribution options, we might want to go it alone after we establish a name for ourselves. It was sound advice, and we renegotiated a three-album deal with no advance and as much creative control over our image, our music, and our schedule as is possible with these types of contracts. Our lawyer more than earned the hefty fee he charged us.

We learned all upfront payments might be paid by the label, but they come out of our future share of the royalties, the same way an advance would. Thankfully, we have the Lancaster millions to cover us until royalties start coming in. Apart from the new equipment we bought and the studio time we paid for back in Dublin, our only other expenses were flights, hotel accommodation, food and drink, and legal fees. Up until we signed a twelve-month lease on this place a few days ago and bought motorbikes and cars. But there will be no other big spending unless something crops up.

Ash has taken full control of our finances. We trust her more than we trust ourselves with the money. She's going to hire a housekeeper and a PA, and the label provides a publicist. Ash will act on our behalf, carefully vetting our options to ensure whoever is appointed is the best fit.

The two-year contract we signed with Frankie Freeman includes provision for Ash to be mentored by him. It cost us an extra five percent in commission and an agreement to pay him an exit bonus when the contract ends, should the band sales and royalties exceed a certain threshold. But it was worth it to know we'll have full control of our careers in the future under Ash's stewardship. Frankie is already treating Ash like his daughter; my sister having charmed him in record time.

Ash is going to be every bit as busy as we are between learning how the industry works, attending business meetings, managing our finances, paying our bills, and attending online classes. She's determined she still wants to get her degree, so I hope she's able to juggle everything. The label is already talking about a tour the year after next if everything goes well, so I'm not sure how viable it will be for her to do post-grad studies when we hit the road, but she says she'll cross that bridge when she comes to it.

"I can't believe we get to live in a mansion like this." Reverence fills her tone as she looks all around.

"It's surreal for sure," I agree, needing to pinch myself too. It's only been seven weeks since we landed on US soil, and so much has happened in that short space of time. It's been hectic. A blur of meetings and performances, signing paperwork, organizing long-term visas, and making plans. All the important things are in place now, and we can get settled in our new routine.

Come Monday, we start recording our album at Capitol Studios, which is in the Capitol Records building. One of the benefits of this gaff is its proximity to the label. A thirty-minute walk or a five-minute bike ride is all it will take between both places. I couldn't stomach the thought of sitting in that bullshit traffic every day. A ton of iconic music venues are on our doorstep along with top-notch restaurants, bars, and clubs. So, as locations go, it doesn't get much better than this. It's a quiet, private retreat only minutes from the hustle and bustle of L.A. life.

Our new home is a palatial Tuscan-inspired five-bedroom house costing a small fortune every month. I'm putting Lancaster's money to good use for sure. Dave, who is now our official A&R rep at the label, managed to secure us a decent discount seeing how the owner is signed to Capitol Records too and he's overseas for a year on an international world tour.

"We're living the dream, baby." Jay comes up behind Ash, throws her over his shoulder, and takes off racing around the large patio area in front of the infinity pool.

"Don't you dare, Jamie Fleming," she shrieks as my best mate moves closer to the water. "I'm warning you, there'll be—"

Whatever she's about to say is cut off when Jay jumps into the water, fully clothed, holding her tight to his chest.

"This place is sick!" Ro comes bounding down the steps, sporting a giant grin. "We have a proper home gym, a games room, cinema room, and a fucking wine cellar! And get this." Ro's face glows like a little kid on Christmas morning as he materializes beside me at the railing.

I've been admiring the stunning view of the city laid out before us from our Hills hideaway, trying not to think of how close I am to the love of my life or wondering if any of the structures in the distance are UCLA. From my research, it's less than a thirty-minute drive from here, traffic notwithstanding.

"All the bedrooms are en suite with massive rainforest showers, fireplaces and sitting rooms, huge walk-in wardrobes, and their own terrace with outdoor furniture," my little brother rambles on, unaware of my inner turmoil.

To be so close to her and yet still so far is a killer.

"I swear the kitchen is the size of our entire house back home, and there's a separate dining room and two huge living rooms. I just sent a video to the family group," Ro adds, practically vibrating with glee.

Pulling him into a playful headlock, I mess up his hair. "Wait until you see the home recording studio."

"What?" he yells, punching me in the gut as he wriggles free. "Are you kidding me? If you're joking right now, Dil, I'll fucking kill you." He swipes hair back out of his eyes.

I chuckle, loving seeing my little brother so happy.

If he only knew how close I came to walking away from all of this for her.

What a dumbass move that would've been.

"I'm not joking. You do know who this house belongs to, right? Of course, there's a recording studio." I point at the outbuilding beside the guest house at the far right of the property. "It's in there."

He moves to run off, but I grab the back of his shirt. "Did you break the news to Ma about Christmas?"

He bobs his head before swatting my hand away. "She was actually fine with the plan, and the others are excited. They can't wait to spend Christmas in L.A."

Dillon

Our first album is due to be handed in at the end of February, so there's no way we can fly home for Christmas. The three-bed guesthouse made softening the blow easier. We talked to Con and Jay first. Con's grandparents said they are too old to travel all this way, and Jay isn't speaking to either of his parents right now, so neither of them had any issue with us offering the guest house to the O'Donoghues to come visit next month.

It'll be nice to have them here. I know Ma is worried about us being so far away. Hopefully, seeing our setup and how we've surrounded ourselves with good people will help to put her mind at ease.

"Come on." Ro tugs on my elbow. "Give me a tour of the recording studio unless you want to stay for the show." He smirks as he jerks his head toward Jamie and Ash. My sister and best mate are now lip-locked and wrapped around one another, looking like they're seconds away from christening the pool.

A pang of longing creeps around my heart as pain mushrooms in my chest. Viv should be here with me. That should be us in the pool, ready to tear our clothes off and get lost in one another. I avert my eyes, drawing air deep into my lungs as I rub a hand over the pain spreading across my chest. I hate I can't look at my sister's happiness without being reminded of everything I've lost. I'm happy for Ash and Jay, and I loathe feeling like this.

"Good call." My voice sounds flat to my own ears as I ignore the sounds coming from the pool and follow my little brother.

Tears prick my eyes as I toss and turn in bed, tired, frustrated, heartsick, and fed up of feeling like this. "Ugh." I throw pillows across the floor before I sit up against the headboard, giving up on sleep because it's clearly not going to happen tonight. Flicking my bedside lamp on, I scrub my sore eyes and sigh. It's not getting any easier. It's been over three months since I last saw her, and the pain is only getting worse.

I don't know how much longer I can go on pretending everything is okay during the day and falling to pieces at night. As much as I'm loving being in the studio with our new producer and engineer and fucking stoked at how incredible this album is going to sound, it's only a distraction, not a cure.

I thought I grew up with a void in my heart, but that was nothing compared to the giant gaping hole that is now permanently clawing at my chest.

I need her.

I miss her.

I love her.

Tears come unbidden. I can't stop them. They just leak out.

Opening my phone, I scroll through my photos of Vivien through blurry eyes as I cry.

The pain is indescribable.

It feels like I'm slowly dying inside without her.

"Dillon." The voice is accompanied by a light rap.

What's Jay doing up at four in the morning? Or maybe I don't want to know.

"I'm awake," I call out, sniffling and swiping at the moisture under my eyes.

Jamie enters my bedroom, and the door softly shuts behind him. "I was on my way back from getting water when I heard you." He perches on the edge of my bed, his gaze sad as his eyes drop from my tearstained face to my phone. I don't even have the energy to shield it from him. "It's not getting any easier."

I like that he doesn't phrase it as a question. I shake my head. "If anything, it's getting worse."

"I'm so fucking heartsick for you, mate." Grasping the back of my head, he presses his forehead to mine. "I never saw it turning out like this. She should be here with you."

"I fucked up, and now I'm paying the price." We break apart, and I grab a pack of tissues from my locker and blow my nose.

"Why aren't you fighting for her?"

"What's the point? She's with him."

"There is no evidence of that. Ash has been stalking both their socials and the general media, and there are no pics, no videos, no sightings of them together."

"He's away filming," I say, confirming I've been doing some stalking of my own. It's a hideous obsession, but I'm like an addict, and I can't stop. "And her accounts are still inactive. She hasn't posted anything. She's not in any of Audrey's posts either, which is clearly deliberate."

"That's explainable after the way the media hounded her last year. It sounds like you're trying to find excuses instead of tackling this head-on."

Jay isn't mincing his words now. "She fucked him the second she returned, Jamie. Given their history, I doubt it was a one-night stand."

"Jesus. I should slam your head into the wall to knock some sense into you. We don't know she did that for sure, and even if she did, it doesn't necessarily mean she's back with him. They might have history, but that was before you."

"If that's true, why hasn't she sought me out? Our signing was reported in the media. We've been papped a few times going in and out of the studio. With her connections, she must know I'm in L.A. If she wanted me, it wouldn't take much to find me."

"I forgot how stubborn you are. You're making a lot of big assumptions, Dil. The truth is, you don't know what she knows. Maybe she's aware you're here. Maybe she believes Aoife is here with you. Perhaps she thinks you don't care because you haven't looked her up. She doesn't know you chased after her. There are too many variables, O'Donoghue. The only way to know is to fucking talk to the girl!"

He's talking sense, but fear is holding me back. *What if I'm too late? How will I cope if she looks me in the eye and tells me she doesn't love me anymore?*

Air blows out of his mouth. "I know this might seem harsh, but you need a kick up the arse, mate. This isn't the Dillon O'Donoghue I know. That motherfucker would not let anything stop him from going after what he wants."

"I don't think I can handle her rejection a second time." I finally admit the truth.

"You can, and you would." A stern expression crosses his face. "Find your fucking balls, Dil, and go see her. At least you'll have closure, one way or another, instead of existing in this limbo state. We are on the verge of achieving our wildest dreams, and you can't fully enjoy it because you're too preoccupied with her." He holds up his hands when I open my mouth to protest. "Not that I'm complaining. The new stuff you're writing is exceptional, but I hate seeing you like this. We all do."

"Guess I'm not fooling anyone, huh?"

"You don't make it obvious, but we know you, and we fucking care. I'm saying this now because I fucking love you." He slaps a hand over his heart. "When you hurt, we hurt. Don't ruin this experience because you're pining for her. It's time to stop licking your wounds and go do something about it. You wouldn't be my best mate if you didn't."

Chapter Forty-Eight
Age 20 to 21

This was a mistake. I should go before she shows up and sees me. But my feet remain rooted to the ground within the small cluster of trees I'm hiding behind. Vivien's apartment building is across the road, and I have a perfect vantage point from here. Luckily, Ash already had her address, and a bit of sleuthing on my part coughed up Viv's schedule, so I know her last class of the day finished twenty minutes ago, and I'm hoping she'll show up soon. It's not that far of a walk from UCLA to here.

The entrance to the apartment building is protected by a keypad, and the front desk area is manned by round-the-clock security personnel, according to their website, so I didn't even bother trying to get inside. I don't like the idea of approaching her outside as Westwood Village is a busy spot with tons of people coming and going all the time, but I don't have any other choice.

Though I'm not recognizable yet, I still took precautions, wearing a cap to hide my distinctive hair and sunglasses, which cover a good portion of my face. Back home, wearing shades when it's almost dark would be cringey as fuck. Over here, I fit right in with all the other pretentious dicks.

Rubbing my clammy hands down the front of my ripped jeans, I narrowly avoid the temptation to look at my watch again. Now that I've decided to grow a pair, I'm desperate to talk to Vivien. To find out if there's any hope left or if she's written me off completely.

Nerves fire at me from all angles as the clock ticks, elevating with each passing minute. By the time it's pitch-black outside, my shades are off, and I'm seriously considering going home. If I stay here much longer, I'll probably get arrested for loitering. I've only walked two feet toward my bike when she finally appears, rounding the corner with her American *bestie*.

If I wasn't so fucking anxious, I'd laugh at my own thought. Plenty of Viv's Americanisms rubbed off on me in the same way I think plenty of my Irishisms rubbed off on her. My breath falters in my throat as I scoot behind a tree and follow her movement with my eyes. My heart is ping-ponging around my chest, and butterflies are rioting in my stomach. My fingers twitch as electricity zips through my body like lightning. She still affects me like crazy.

As she walks under the lights at the side of her building, it's as if Viv just stepped under a spotlight, and I now have an up close and personal view. Pain is visceral as I drink her features in for the first time in months. Although she looks pale and there are bruising circles under her eyes, she still sucks all the air from my lungs. Fuck, she's so goddamn gorgeous. Her beautiful curves are hidden under an open coat and a shapeless baggy jumper. Paired with black leggings and black boots, it's an unassuming look that's totally her, but she still looks stunning.

Vivien clamps a hand over her mouth, and Audrey snakes her arm around her shoulders, hurrying them towards the front door.

Every nerve ending in my body cries out for her, and my feet move of their own volition, only slamming to a halt when I spot the large bulky male trailing the girls a few feet back. Astute eyes scan the area around the two women as they walk towards the entryway, and his body language confirms he's primed to swing into action at the first sign of danger. Shite! I'm going to lose her if I don't go now, but the obvious bodyguard has me second-guessing myself.

Who is he, and who hired him? Viv? Her parents? Reeve? Acid churns in my gut like sour milk, and I can only stare helplessly as Vivien and Audrey enter the building, closely followed by The Rock wannabe.

Fuck, fuck, fuck. Air expels from my mouth as I kick the bark of a tree in frustration, wondering what to do now. The chickenshit part of my persona wants to flee, but I'm not a coward. Jay is right. I've got to man up and talk to her. I'm striding across the road a few minutes later, having decided to announce myself to security and request they let her know I'm here and I'd like to talk to her, when a chauffeur-driven car pulls up to the curb. My instincts are on high alert, so I do a quick U-turn and dash back under the protective cover of the trees.

A guy in a black suit climbs out from behind the wheel and opens the back door.

Bile swims up my throat as a tall, toned figure gets out of the car, carrying a big box of what appears to be chocolates. Another man gets out the other side of the car, rounding the rear and waiting on the sidewalk. His broad frame and sharp gaze confirm his bodyguard status as he checks out the area while his charge ducks down, reaching for something inside the car.

When the guy pops back up, he's cradling a massive bouquet of flowers in his free hand. While his head is tipped down, he's wearing a cap and shades, and his features aren't easily identifiable, I know who he is.

Shock renders me frozen as I stare at my twin in the flesh for the first time.

Reeve straightens, looking around for a few beats, before his bodyguard says something to him. Anger locks my muscles up even tighter when I spot a few lilies perched between the purple roses in the bouquet.

Fuck him.

And fuck her.

I should have trusted my instincts from the start. Instead, I listened to my sister and Jamie and allowed hope to tentatively bloom in my heart.

But I was right all along.

She *is* back with him.

They're just playing it much smarter this time. Keeping it hidden to avoid the paparazzi attention.

Fuck this.

Those two manipulative assholes deserve one another.

I'm done.

As I stumble from my hiding place, I feel eyeballs following my retreating form, but I don't care if I've been made. I take off running, get on my bike, and hightail it out of there.

Dropping the bike off at our gaff, I avoid anyone seeing me and walk to the nearest dive bar where I proceed to prop up the bar for the night. Pain is my constant companion as I knock back whiskey like it's going out of fashion. I want to get blind drunk so I can blot out all the thoughts flitting through my head.

"Want company?" a woman with a sultry voice asks as the legs of the stool scrape across the wooden floor when she hops up beside me.

Whipping my head to the side, I can barely make out her features through my blurry eyes. "Depends," I say, signaling to the bartender to pour me another measure.

"On what?" A warm hand lands on my arm.

"On what you want." I rub at my tired eyes.

"Hmm." She props one elbow on the bar and perches her chin in her hand. "I suspect this is a test."

My vision focuses, and I get a good look at her. She's older than me but not by more than a few years. Pretty in that fake, manufactured L.A. way. Bottle-blonde hair, skinny as fuck with massive silicone tits and oversized glossy lips. She isn't a patch on my

Hollywood, and that's why I slide off my stool and grab her hand. "Not anymore." Images of Vivien and Reeve fucking have been assaulting my mind since I sat down in this shithole. I need to fuck that treacherous bitch from my mind, and now is as good a time as any to start.

Her smile is instant, her enhanced lips spreading over a dazzling set of perfect teeth. "Now you're talking my language."

Dragging her to the nearest single-door bathroom, I walk her inside and lock the door. She's on me like a rash, shoving me up against the door and grabbing my soft dick through my jeans as she stretches up to kiss me. The instant her lips touch mine, it's like being doused in a bucket full of icy water. Her touch is all wrong, and I instantly feel sick to my stomach. My skin is crawling like a thousand fire ants are throwing a party across my flesh. I'm not gentle as I push her off me, offering no explanation as I unlock the door and storm off. Tossing a few bills down on the counter, I leave my drink behind and stomp out of the place, feeling even more fucked up then when I entered.

Christmas comes and goes, and I enter fully into the party spirit, getting drunk whenever possible, purely to blot it all out. Vivien haunts me continuously unless I keep myself busy or distract myself with booze or weed.

Our no-hard-drugs rule is more important than ever before. Too many bands have fallen prey to rock 'n' roll excesses as soon as they make it, and we're determined not to get lured into the same trap. Only for our rule, I think I'd be falling down a more slippery slope.

This is a personal hell. One of my own making. However, my bandmates and my sister don't deserve to suffer the consequences of my poor decision-making, so I do my best to be present for the band, to try to hide my inner pain, only succumbing at night when I'm in bed alone with nothing to buffer me.

Our family thoroughly enjoy their visit. Though Ma is clearly worried about me, she bites her tongue. I do my best to fake it, but I don't think I'm fooling anyone. I can't remember the last time I had a full night's sleep, and I eat solely to fuel my body. I'm working out more than ever, and I joined a local boxing club. Though I regularly pound the bag and go a few rounds in the training ring with various blokes, nothing eliminates the raw ache that constantly eats away at me until it feels like I'm only a walking bag of bones.

The only thing that offers any respite is music. My addiction seeps out of me onto the page as I purge my emotions through song lyrics. I want to hate Viv for what she's done, but longing and pain are still my foremost emotions. I hate how much I still want her after everything she's done, but the truth is, if she rocked up here tomorrow and begged for my forgiveness, I'd take her back in a heartbeat.

I still want her, so fucking much, and it's doing my head in.

After I told Ash and Jay what went down in Westwood that day, neither of them have pushed me again. Ash has stopped ringing and texting her, and collectively, without articulating it, we're all relegating Vivien Mills to the past.

In January, I let the others drag me to a club for my twenty-first birthday where we all get completely shit-faced. It helps to block out thoughts of Vivien celebrating my twin's birthday with him. After another failed attempt at getting with a different woman, I have to face facts: Vivien broke me. Ruined me for all other women. Forget about fucking, I can't even kiss anyone.

I think I'm destined to be permanently alone. Pre-Viv Dillon was perfectly comfortable with eternal bachelorhood. Post-Viv Dillon is lonely as fuck and drowning in pain because the only woman he wants no longer wants him.

By the end of February, the album is done, and the label are ecstatic with the songs we've produced and practically frothing at the mouth in anticipation of launching us on the world in the summer.

It's early March, and we're at a giant meeting with the band,

Frank, Dave, Ava—our publicist—the VP of marketing, a few people from the marketing team, and one of the management bigwigs, brainstorming different things. This is stage one of forming a promotional plan to introduce us officially to the music scene. Currently, we're arguing over the band name. And surprise, surprise, my sister is the person fighting the hardest to keep Toxic Gods.

Always knew she was full of shit when it came to our name.

"The name fits, and they're already garnering attention online. All the old YouTube videos are racking up thousands of extra views by the day. We'll lose all that exposure," Ash proclaims.

"The name has negative connotations," the VP of marketing argues back. "Toxic suggests something unpleasant, something detrimental to one's health."

"And Gods suggests arrogance," some dick from the marketing team adds.

"Arrogance and rock star go hand in hand," I say, drumming my fingers on the table. My arse is numb from sitting in this chair for so long, and I'm on edge. I'm itching to put my gloves on and imagine my punching bag is Reeve Lancaster's face while I pummel it to oblivion.

"Not anymore," the VP says. "Times have changed."

Bullshit, but I don't bother arguing. I'm keen to end this effing meeting, not prolong it.

"I know you're concerned about losing any ground the band has gained," Dave says, speaking directly to Ash. "But what's come before really doesn't matter. This is a new start, a clean slate. I know you guys have support in Ireland," he adds, letting his gaze roam between me, Ro, Con and Jay. "But it means nothing here. Our team is the best at what they do. We only get one chance to make a first impression. The work we put in these next three to four months will make or break the band."

I like Dave. We all do. And I trust him not to feed us crap. He's our liaison with the label, and we'll continue to work closely with him while signed with Capitol Records. His career hangs in the balance if things go wrong, so I'm inclined to listen to him more than any of the others.

"We're on your side, Aisling," the VP says, pronouncing my sister's name all wrong, which pisses me off because Ash has told them repeatedly how to say it. "We have a vested interest in ensuring the band succeeds. We think they're one of the most exciting alternative rock bands to emerge in the last decade. Every facet of their brand needs to be nailed down tight before we launch, and I'm telling you now they need a different name."

Jay sits up straighter, leveling a look at the older woman Darth Vadar would be proud of. I smirk as I let him handle her. "It's not Aze-ling, it's Ash-ling."

"My apologies. I mean no offense."

"None taken." Ash warns Jay to pipe down with a subtle thigh squeeze under the table before swinging her gaze our way. "It's your call."

"I'm not attached to the name," Con says, gripping the arms of his chair tight. He's gone hours without a toke, and he's even more keen than me to leave.

"I like our name, and I hate having to let it go, but we'd be foolish to ignore the advice of the experts," Jay confirms.

"Plenty of bands have changed their name. I'm fine to go with something else," Ro supplies.

"Then it's decided," I say, not bothering to offer my view. It's pointless when there's already a majority.

"Good." The older woman looks relieved. "The team and I have come up with a list of suggestions," she adds, flicking a button on the fob in her hand, and a new page is projected on the wall-mounted screen. "You can, of course, suggest your own, but we need to agree on a name fast. Otherwise, it will hold up everything."

We debate the names at length, and none of us can agree on them. While a few are decent, none are quite right. The meeting is just about to break up—with the agreement we can take forty-eight hours to come up with our own suggestions—when it comes to me, birthed straight from my soul.

"Collateral Damage," I say, my loud voice booming around the room.

There's a pregnant pause as everyone stops, giving it consideration.

"It has negative connotations too," the pompous marketing dick says.

"Not in the same way," the VP argues as a lazy smile crawls over her face. "Toxic is poison, and that combined with the arrogance of Gods is too much, but Collateral Damage conveys power and influence. It's the unexpected reaction to the action. It carries gravitas." She positively beams at me. "I love it. It's perfect."

Well, okay then.

We discuss it a little longer before taking a vote.

And that is how Collateral Damage emerges from the ashes of Toxic Gods.

As I walk out of the meeting, I can't help laughing at the irony.

All along, I thought Vivien would be collateral damage. I never imagined it'd be me.

Chapter Forty-Nine
Age 21

id-March heralds the start of a four-month promotional onslaught to build hype for the band and our first release. Which everyone has agreed should be "Terrify Me." I wonder what Vivien would think if she knew how entwined she still is with the band. I'd love to be a fly on the wall when our song is released and she realizes it's the song I wrote for her. I wonder if she's told *him* who we are. Probably not, considering we didn't seem to mean that much to her after all if she could ghost us like this.

It helps that we're crazy busy during this time because there's little time to contemplate my heartache. It's a whirlwind of activity. Posing for photos for the album cover and magazine articles. Attending PR training and being coached on what to say and what not to say. Being interviewed by various reporters, including key players at *Rolling Stone* and *NME*. Appearing on radio and TV. Meeting with stylists to discuss and agree on our look. Filming the music video. Back in the studio, tweaking a few things. Working with marketing and PR on merchandise, video content for socials, and doing a few TikTok lives with key bloggers and influencers.

In the month before release, to further build buzz, we perform at ten small iconic venues in key states around the US, traveling on the label's private jet. It's definitely another pinch-me moment.

The marketing and PR teams have been working overtime organizing ongoing promotion and our calendar is full to the end of the year. An official band bio and press release goes out. Music journalists and influencers are loving our Irish roots and the story of how the band came together. Official social media accounts have been set up for the band, and we're gaining thousands and thousands of new followers every day, boosted by teaser clips of the song and background videos introducing us collectively and individually.

By the time "Terrify Me" officially releases, the anticipation is high, and the buzz is explosive. Radio airplay is insane from the second the song is published because the label has paid big bucks to have it played at the top of every hour to ensure our debut has strong mainstream coverage. Reaping the rewards of all our online marketing efforts, we instantly shoot to the top of all the digital streaming sites. Not long after, the Billboard Hot 100 reveals we're the number one bestselling song, and that day is the best day of my life.

Until it becomes the worst.

When Dave calls to break the good news, my immediate thought is I need to tell Viv. She helped to set us on this path, and not getting to share this journey with her guts me. Especially today of all days. Sadness threatens to suffocate me as my finger hovers over her number on my phone, but I put it away and force the melancholy aside. She made her choice. I don't get to share the highs and lows with her because she's no longer mine. The usual pain slams into me, but I work hard to stamp it out. I won't let today be overshadowed by my grief. It's been eleven months since I've seen her. It's high time I started letting go.

We spend the day doing interviews, and it's our first time properly understanding the enormity of our achievement as we are mobbed by screaming fans everywhere we go. Frankie swings into action, liaising with the label to provide a security detail, which is sorely needed after we get physically mauled leaving the Universal Studios lot where we were the top guests on a popular daytime show.

We performed live in front of a small studio audience before being grilled by the tenacious host who tried her best to pry into our love lives. Jamie refuses to hide his relationship status though they're not confirming he's practically married to Ash because he wants to protect her identity, to shield her from becoming a target. None of us have forgotten the things Vivien endured when Reeve's star ascended. The PR people only conceded because the rest of us are unattached.

Having to confirm my single status over and over is like repeatedly stabbing myself in the heart. But I play my part with gusto in case she's watching. I won't give either of them the satisfaction of knowing how wrecked I really am. Today is the culmination of a shit ton of hard work and determination and nothing is ruining it.

We're celebrating at a small party the label throws for us that same night when the news breaks. A few TVs are mounted on walls around the room, so there's no escaping it. All the blood drains from my face when the picture loads on the screen. A hush descends as everyone's gaze is riveted to the E-News report.

"Hearts are breaking across the world today as representatives for Hollywood actor Reeve Lancaster confirmed he is no longer a single man after marrying Vivien Mills two days ago in a hush-hush ceremony at one of L.A.'s most prestigious hotels. Vivien is the only daughter of actress Lauren Mills and her director-husband Jonathon. Both were in attendance at the wedding as well as Studio 27 CEO, Simon Lancaster, father of the groom, and a slew of other celebrities. *Vogue* won the exclusive rights to the wedding and a special edition hits newsstands tonight, but they have shared a few pictures as part of the official press release."

My heart ruptures in my chest as I spot Ash and Jamie dashing across the room to be with me. On the screen, Vivien is stunningly beautiful in a gorgeous white lace wedding gown. Her dark hair is up in some kind of elegant bun, showcasing her exquisite face. Sporting a glorious smile, she looks adoringly at her husband as they cling to one another with mere millimeters separating their faces. Bile churns in my gut as everything I've consumed today threatens to come back up.

"Dillon." Ash tugs on my arm. "Come with me."

"No." I can't tear my eyes from the screen even as the image slices strips off my already shredded heart.

"Please, Dil. I have something to tell you."

"No. No!" My voice cracks as the image changes on the screen, this time showing a picture of Vivien cradling a little baby boy in her arms while Reeve has his arms wrapped around them, smiling like his face might split in two he's so happy.

"The newlyweds also confirmed they welcomed their first child together, six weeks ago. They kept that a secret from all of us!" Her grating laugh barely registers as shock lays siege to every part of me. "Easton Elon Lancaster was born on June twelfth to the happy couple and..."

I tune the rest of what she's saying out, stumbling backwards as my legs buckle, attempting to go out from under me. Jamie grabs me before I fall on my arse, but it's not enough to protect the table behind me as I knock against it. Glass shattering, mixed with shocked cries, follows me out of the room as Jamie and my sister drag me away from prying eyes.

Another vital part of me dies in that moment, shriveling inside as the void grows larger, sucking all the light from my world.

Jay leads me into a smaller side room, where I fall to my knees and heave my guts up.

"Shite." Ash barks instructions to someone while I come undone on the floor.

When I've finished expelling my stomach contents, Jay and Ro lift me over to a sofa. Ash plies me with water while a staff member cleans up the mess I made on the floor. My sister helps to strip my soiled T-shirt off my body while I stare into space, rocking back and forth as my brain struggles to process the news I've just learned.

Dillon

Someone puts a fresh-smelling shirt on over my head while someone else cleans my jeans and my boots.

"I need an explanation right now," Ava says in a firm voice.

Lifting my eyes, I stare absently at her. Our new publicist is glaring at Ash, her stern expression demanding answers.

"I will explain it but not now, Ava. I'll call you later. We need to get Dillon out of here." She leans in, whispering something in her ear. "For now, can you get a car to the back entrance and ensure no one is outside to see us leave."

She married him.

She married my twin.

She married Reeve.

He won.

He fucking came out on top again.

He took her from me forever.

She will never be mine ever again.

I have lost her completely, and I want to curl into a ball and die.

These thoughts play on a loop in my head as the others get me safely out of the building and into the car.

Feeling eyes on me, I turn to look at my brother. A confusing mix of emotions is splayed across Ro's face. "I'm sorry, Dil," he whispers, grabbing my frozen form into a hug. "I'm so fucking sorry."

I don't know what he's got to feel sorry about, and I've already forgotten it by the time we get to the house.

Jay forces me into the shower, and when I return downstairs, Con and Ro have made themselves scarce. Ash and Jay quit talking the second I appear in the kitchen. "Don't stop on my account," I drawl, heading straight for the half-empty bottle of JD sitting on the island counter.

"That's not going to help, Dillon," Ash softly says.

"Trust me, it'll help," I snarl, unscrewing the cap and swigging straight from the bottle. I slam it down when I see the expression on her face. "Stop looking at me like that! Keep your fucking pity. I don't want it."

"Dillon." Jay snakes a protective arm around his girlfriend's shoulders. "I know you're hurting, but you can fuck off if you think I'm letting you take this out on Ash." He points behind me. "Sit your arse down. Ash made you a sandwich. Eat it."

I do as I'm told, slumping in the chair as the enormity of everything slaps me around the face again. My brain goes into overdrive as I eat on autopilot. "Could that baby be mine?" I ask before taking another bite of the sawdust sandwich. "The timing seems suspect." I'm remarkably calm as I discuss the thought that first came to me in the shower.

"I know you think she's done you dirty, but Vivien would not lie if that baby was yours, Dillon. She wouldn't do that." Ash claims the seat on my right, setting a mug of steaming coffee down in front of me.

"You're assuming any of us really knew her at all," I deadpan before swallowing the last of my food and reaching for the coffee.

"Do you know when she last had her period when she was with you?" my sister asks.

"Early August." I don't need to think about it. Everything about Viv is imprinted in my brain as well as my heart.

"Then I don't think it's possible. They calculate pregnancy from the date of your last period." Her hand lands softly on mine. "Her son was born in June meaning he was conceived in September, weeks after you last saw her. I'm sorry, Dillon."

Pain slams into me, and I shove my coffee away, reaching for the whiskey.

"At least we know now why she ghosted you, love," Jay says, taking the seat on my left. He drops two glasses onto the table, forcibly prying the whiskey from my hand. After pouring healthy measures into both glasses, he slides one to me.

"It makes sense, but what doesn't is her calling me now." Ash frowns.

Wait. My head snaps up. "What?"

"I didn't know if I should tell you." She knots her fingers on top of the table. "Viv's been calling and texting me the past week, asking if we could talk. I haven't picked up."

"Why not?"

"Because it's too late. The damage is done." She curls her hands around her mug. "You're my brother. My priority is you, and I'm fucking pissed at her for the things she's done. There's no going back even if part of me understands."

"She called to tell you she was getting married," I say, knocking back the whiskey and reaching for the bottle. "Probably to gloat."

"Come on, Dil. She wouldn't gloat." Ash scrubs her hands down her face. "She probably wanted to warn me. She must know the band has made it. That we're living in L.A."

"She's dead to me," I calmly say, chugging more whiskey. "I don't want to talk about her ever again. I don't want anyone in this house to ever mention her name. Tell Ava the bare minimum in case there is a need to do damage control, but otherwise, no one is to know." Swiping the bottle, I stand, my chair screeching across the floor. "I want to forget I ever knew the conniving bitch. I hope she's miserable with him." Anger comingles with pain as I vent all my fury. "I hope he keeps cheating. I hope she cries herself to sleep every night ruing the poor choices she made."

I sway on my feet as the adrenaline crash finally hits. Gripping the back of the chair, I add, "I hope she regrets abandoning me." Ash and Jay trade looks as I clutch the bottle to my chest like a lifeline. My jaw clenches. "And someday, when she least expects it, I hope karma comes for her."

Chapter Fifty
Age 21 to 24

A nger is my new best friend in the months after I discover Vivien married Reeve and had his baby. On the one-year anniversary of her leaving me, I finally kiss another woman, but it takes another year before I can fuck someone else. The whole time, I'm a writhing ball of rage. She's still my muse, still inspiring songs, but a lot of them during this time are full of the hate flowing through my veins. "Hollywood Ho," "The Regrets Club," and "Fuck Love" all top the charts the year I'm twenty-three, and I get immense satisfaction every time I hear them on the radio, wondering if she's listening right at this moment too. She's got to know they're about her. I hope they hurt. I hope they drive a stake through her heart the same way seeing her with him always does to me.

Our careers keep us super busy. Our first US tour is a massive success, and the following year, we embark on a world tour which lasts nine months. Con, Ro, and I enjoy the perks of fame, and nights after shows are spent partying, drinking, and fucking. It's all a blur, and none of it helps alleviate the constant pain in my heart.

Finding time to visit our family is challenging, but we make it back to Ireland at least once a year. Our brothers and parents have traveled to some of our shows, and we love giving them VIP treatment. Ash graduates with her degree and becomes our full-time manager. Frankie is satisfied with his golden handshake though unhappy to have to walk away from a band of our caliber.

The dough is rolling in now, and we're all independently wealthy. We're living our dream, and getting to perform our own music to sellout stadiums is the pinnacle of our careers. I love being up onstage. It's the greatest buzz, and I'm the best version of myself when I'm entertaining a crowd. Music soothes my soul. Yet I can't fully enjoy it because there's always something lacking in my life.

The others don't bring her up. After some of the songs I've written, they all believe I hate her. And I do. But I love her too, and the love in my heart far outweighs the hatred. I'm still not over her. I doubt I ever will be. I think I'll always pine for my Hollywood.

Jay is the only one who knows how fucked up I truly am. How I still watch Shane and Fiona's wedding video on repeat. How the songwriting journal Viv made me is my most precious possession, along with the Fender she gifted me. How I obsess over all the photos on my phone and wish I could turn back them to relive the memories all over again. Many nights, I've sat up late, pouring out my heart to my best mate when the pain almost becomes too much to bear. Ma would be happy to know I'm venting some of my emotions and not keeping everything bottled up inside.

Viv seems happy. They're photographed all the time, and I'm sick of seeing their smiling faces everywhere. I try to avoid stalking them on social media, but in dark moments, I fall down the rabbit hole, usually ending up a drunken mess after my heart is well and truly annihilated. Ash ensures there are no awkward run-ins, rescheduling events if they're due to attend, and so far, we've managed to avoid one another.

I regularly take supermodels and actresses to film premieres and industry events. Never the same woman twice, and I'm never interested in dating any of them. I usually fuck them, but the sex does little for me. It's a release and not much else. They all bore me. Every

398

single woman I've ever met fails to match the perfection that is Vivien Lancaster. Every other woman is a pale imitation.

The year I turn twenty-four, I buy my first house, and we settle in L.A. to work on our next album, all of us grateful to put down some roots after a few intense years of touring.

It's late afternoon, and we're laying down a new track when my latest mistake sneaks up on me.

"Hey, Dil."

Ava's smiling face greets me when I lift my head from my guitar and find her standing at the back of the recording studio at the Capitol Building. Tension brackets my jaw as I inwardly groan. Knew it was a bad idea fucking her at the awards ceremony last month.

For the past couple of years, she's made her attraction known though I've always denied her. Ash warned me not to shit where I eat. Should've listened to my sister instead of saying fuck it when I was locked at the awards after party and Ava propositioned me. She has been driving me nuts ever since even though I made it clear it was a one-and-done. "We're busy," I reply without even looking at her.

"I just need two minutes of your time. Andy said you're on a break."

Our sound engineer is an interfering little shit. "If this is business-related, you can talk to Ash." I drill her with a look. "If it's not business-related, I don't want to hear it."

The smile slips off her face. "It is personal, but—"

"Leave," I snap, the same time Ro says, "Dillon," in his usual warning tone.

"Butt out, little bro." I level him with a look as Con smokes a joint on the couch, the twitching of his eyes the only sign he's paying attention. Conor and I have spent a lot of time together these past few years. He never bugs me about shit I don't want to talk about, and there's a certain peace when it's just him and I together, sharing a joint, jamming, and shite talking about philosophy and spirituality.

"Please, Dillon. I just need—"

"I'm not interested in fucking you again!" I explode. "How many fucking times do I have to say it? I told you it was one time, and I did not sign up for this clingy shit. For fuck's sake, Ava, you've been around us for years. You've seen me screw my way through girls like they're a dying breed. Why the fuck would you think you're any different? You're nothing special, you're—"

Tears spill out of her eyes as she runs out of the room sobbing.

"You're the biggest asshole." Ro shakes his head as he twirls his sticks between his fingers. "Was there a need to be so cruel?"

"Yes," I grit out, twisting my neck from side to side to work out the kinks. "She won't stop calling, emailing, and showing up every chance she gets. I've tried letting her down gently, and that didn't work. Maybe now she'll get the message."

"She's a nice girl." Ro brings his sticks down on the cymbals, and a high pitched crashing shimmering sound ricochets off the studio walls. "You should try dating her."

"You know I don't fucking date." Setting my guitar down on the stand, I head to the fridge to grab a beer.

"I know you're wasting your life pining after a ghost. She's married, Dillon. You need to move on. It won't happen unless you try."

My hands are balled into fists as I swing around and glare at my brother. "Shut your face."

"I thought you'd be over it by now," he mumbles, laying his sticks down and standing. He drills me with a look I can't decipher. "Please move on, Dil. It's killing me seeing you like this."

"Fuck off, Ro." I pop the cap on my beer and knock back a mouthful. "We can't all be serial daters."

"At least I'm giving relationships a go. You can't go through life with a revolving door of casual fucks."

"Why the fuck not?"

"Because it's making you miserable!" His nostrils flare. "Would it kill you to take Ava out to dinner? Clearly, there's some attraction there. She's smart, pretty, sweet. She knows you're a jerk and somehow still wants you, and she works in the industry. You won't find a better woman."

"I have found better," I growl. "I had perfection, utter perfection, and I can't accept less. Ava is boring as fuck, and she was a shitty lay. I have zero interest in dating her. I'd rather chop my cock off than bang her again."

A shocked gasp, followed by heart-wrenching tears, greets my words, and my stomach drops. I lift my head in time to see Ava fleeing the studio for a second time.

Fuck. I didn't realize she'd come back, and neither did Ro or he wouldn't have started that discussion.

Ash rushes into the room and shoves my shoulders. "What the hell is wrong with you? You just destroyed her!" Steam is practically billowing from her ears as she stands before me wearing the angriest face I've seen in a long time.

"I didn't know she was there."

"Look on the bright side." Con blows smoke circles into the air. "I think she definitely got the message this time."

Ava quits the next day.

"She can't still be mad at me," I grumble to Jay a week later when Ash is still giving me the cold shoulder.

"She can and she is." He grabs a cold beer from the bucket on the table in the VIP section of the club we're in. It's become a regular Saturday night spot, and I usually end up going home with some bird.

"Ava leaving without working her notice created a mess," he adds. "Ash is still putting out fires."

"I thought she already had that other girl lined up as our new publicist, and she should probably be thanking me for forcing the issue." Ava worked for the label, and she served their interests first and foremost. Ava quitting gives us an opportunity to hire our own publicist, someone who will further our best interests.

"Jesus. Don't fucking say that to her. She's liable to throw you off the roof, and yes, *Dixie* has signed her contract, but she can't start for two weeks."

"Ash will smooth everything over; she always does."

"She's the best." The most nauseating, gooey, lovestruck expression materializes on his face.

I elbow him in the ribs. "Pussy."

Ro and I have been winding him up a lot lately over when he's going to propose. We all know it's coming. Those two are solid. They'll never break up. It's still hard sometimes being around them. It's a reminder of what I once had. What I could've had if things had worked out differently.

"Looking a little green there, lad." Jay prods my cheek, laughing when I swat his hand away.

"Move over," Ash says, throwing me a daggered look before shim-mying into the booth beside her boyfriend.

"You look gorgeous tonight, sis." I lean in and kiss her cheek. It's no word of a lie. During the working week, Ash dresses in power suits befitting of her authority. Weekends or when we attend industry events are her only opportunity to ditch the business attire and dress up. She looks a million dollars tonight in a short blue dress with skyscraper silver heels which elevate her tiny stature.

"Lick-arsing will totally work." Her tiny fist curls around my shirt before I can straighten up. "Apology accepted but keep your cock in your trousers with this new one, or next time, you can handle the shit show left behind." Ash had interviewed a few guys for the role, and I know she'd have preferred to hire a man, but Dixie was the only one we felt would gel with us, so she got the job.

"I'm done with blondes anyway."

I have a rule to only fuck blondes or redheads to keep as far away from memories of Vivien as possible, but it's not doing it for me anymore. Last night, I went home with a blonde I picked up at a local bar but ditched her halfway through the taxi ride when her mouth failed to raise even a modicum of interest from my cock. Watching her blonde head bob up and down was an instant erection killer. I can't do it anymore. Pretend like I'm not wishing they weren't a certain brunette, so I'm going to mix it up and see if fucking brunettes from now on will be the cure I so desperately seek.

But it doesn't help either. It only makes things worse.

A few hours later, I'm back in some up-and-coming actress's apartment, plowing into her from behind, imagining she's Viv as I fist her long dark-brown hair, pulling on the strands just the way my love liked. But the sounds coming from her mouth are all wrong as is the way she holds herself upright on all fours, not moving to meet my thrusts or writhing underneath me as I fuck her. She's going through the motions, just like me, and though I'm buried deep in the woman, in an act that should be personal and intimate, it's the complete opposite.

I've never felt more alone.

My hard-on dies an immediate death, and I pull out, disgusted with myself, with her, with life.

"What's wrong?" Her pout is instantaneous as she glances over her shoulder.

"We both know this isn't cutting it." I pull my boxers and jeans up my legs and tuck my soft cock away.

Yanking her dress down to cover herself, she moves up the bed, pulling her knees into her chest. Her lower lip wobbles, and I take pity on her. "It's all on me. My head is elsewhere tonight." I kiss her quickly, feeling nothing. "Good luck with your show. I'll look out for it." Only because Vivien is one of the writers, and yeah, maybe I flirted outrageously with her when I discovered that fact. As if Vivien would even care if some actress on her show fucked me. She clearly doesn't care. She ditched me years ago without ever looking back.

Which is what makes this all the more frustrating.

I don't go home, getting the taxi to drop me at Ash and Jay's place. I can't be alone right now even if both of them are probably asleep. I let myself in, surprised the alarm isn't on like usual at night. But it makes sense when I find Jay still up in the kitchen.

"Wasn't expecting to find you up," I say, removing my jacket and hanging it on the back of one of the chairs. A bottle of JD is resting on the table beside him, and his hands are curled around a half-empty glass. "Is everything okay?"

"Yeah, everything is perfect." The biggest smile crests over his face.

"What's going on?"

"Ash is pregnant."

My eyes widen as he just puts it right out there.

"Shite," he blurts. "She's going to kill me for blabbing, but I've been bursting to tell you since we found out last week."

"Why didn't Ash tell me?" Grabbing a glass from the press, I sit down beside my best mate. Guilt is instant at the thought of the additional stress I've landed on my sister's lap recently at a time when she should be stress free. I vow to find some way to make it up to her.

"She wanted to wait until the twelve-week mark when it's safe, apparently."

"I've no idea what that means, but this is amazing news." I grab him into a hug. "Congrats, man. I'm made up for ya."

"I'm over the moon." Tears fill his eyes. "I'm going to be a dad. I'm equal parts excited and scared."

"You'll be nothing like him," I reassure, knowing exactly where his head has ventured. I top up his glass before pouring whiskey into mine. "A toast," I add, raising my glass. "To baby Fleming."

"To baby Fleming." We clink glasses and swallow the amber-colored liquid.

"How come you're back so early? You give new meaning to wham, bam, thank you, ma'am." He snorts out a laugh.

"Wasn't feeling it." I shrug, deliberately downplaying it. This is a happy time for Jay, and he doesn't need my depressive arse dragging him down.

"Spill." He eyeballs me solemnly.

"Another time."

"Shut yer face, Dillon. This is me. Talk to me."

I open and close my mouth, knowing if I start it'll all just spew like lava. Jamie doesn't deserve that tonight.

"It's 'cause you went home with a brunette, right?" he coaxes, and the tenuous hold I have on my control snaps.

A shuddering breath flees my lips as I nod and prepare to drop a ton of verbal diarrhea. "There's something very wrong with me, Jamie." I grip the glass tight as my chin lowers. "I flirted with that actress only because she works on Viv's show, and when we got to her place, I wasted no time getting her on all fours and ramming into her from behind. I treated her like shit. Pretending she was someone else, and when she couldn't live up to that expectation, I just felt numb inside. My dick lost interest, and I couldn't get out of there fast enough." I rest my head on the table. "I don't like who I am anymore." Pain charges up my throat, garbling my next statement. "I don't like who I am without her."

"Oh, mate." Jay squeezes my shoulder. "I can't believe it's still her after all this time."

"It will always be her, Jamie. She is my one and only." My voice cracks, and it feels like my heart is rupturing behind my rib cage. "I don't want to live like this. Why can't I forget her?" I thump on my temples. "Why can't I get rid of her from here?" All the booze I've drunk tonight has exacerbated my emotional state, and I fall apart in front of my best mate. "Why is her face the first face I see every morning when I wake, and why does she still haunt my dreams? Why, Jay? Why?"

"I wish I had the answers, Dillon. I wish I knew how to help."

"I'm lonely, but I can't stomach the thought of fucking anyone else. Not anymore. It's doing nothing for me. It's only accentuating this ache inside me because none of them are her." I squeeze my eyes shut against a fresh onslaught of tears. "I love her, but I also hate her though I think I hate myself more."

"Maybe you just need more time."

"Maybe I just need a lobotomy," I semi-joke.

He pulls me into a hug. "It will get better. It's got to."

As much as I want to believe in those words, it's hard to buy into it because after more than four years I'm still every bit as heartbroken as I was the day I lost her.

Chapter Fifty-One
Age 25 to 26

A few months later, I check into rehab. Not for alcohol addiction, like the rumors are suggesting. I probably drink too much, but it's a choice, not an addiction. I need help but not to stop drinking. My head is still a mess over a woman I haven't been with in years, a woman who is married and lost to me forever, and it's starting to impact my career. I've had writer's block for months, and my mood is at an all-time low. It's time to tackle it with professional help.

The label are surprisingly supportive, deciding to release a mini EP with the tracks we've already laid down after I get out of rehab and push the full album out to next year. It takes a lot of pressure off my shoulders, and I'm grateful I can take this time to try to sort myself out.

Ash and Jay lost their baby, and it's been a difficult time even if they are now engaged and planning their future together. Ro's girl-friend is pregnant, and while I know my sister is happy for them, it serves as a permanent reminder of all she's lost. I've tried to support and comfort her, but it's hard to prop someone up when you're basically sprawling on the ground. Ash has Jamie, and he'll take care of her while I attempt to fix my head.

Rehab helps, but I've come to realize there is no permanent cure. Instead, I'm hoping the tools I've learned will help me to cope better in the future. The time away has done me good, and I'm feeling calmer and more in control.

Ten days after I leave rehab, we release our mini EP and travel around the US and Europe for a few months to promote it which helps to keep my mind occupied.

We return to L.A. in December, and Ro makes it back for the delivery of his little baby daughter by the skin of his teeth. Next year, we'll begin work on a new full-length album and prepare for a tour which will kick off the following year. In the meantime, we all enjoy a much-needed break over the Christmas period.

Though I attend lots of parties, I always return home alone. I haven't fucked anyone in months, and I have no plans to change that. I'm not interested in anyone else. And I find myself back at square one. Frustrated and pissed off to still be hung up on the one woman I can't have.

Anger flares again, and I begin strategizing how I can use my industry contracts to leak the news about the Lancasters. I'm done holding back. Fuck what my therapist said in rehab. He loved reminding me that planning revenge got me into this mess in the first place, constantly stating the only way to fully heal was to let it go. But he didn't get it. He didn't understand the torture my life has been these past few years or how I'll never get out from under it as long as the Lancasters continue to have the upper hand.

The only way I can move forward is to exact revenge, and I'm done waiting. It's time to stop obsessing and start planning.

A few days later, the Oscar nominations are announced, and we're on the list along with my twin. That prick seems determined to ruin every special occasion for me. Someone up there sure loves fucking with me. At least it means I'll get to see her in the flesh. There's no way she won't be there to support her husband, and she can't avoid me this time; I won't let her.

"You should go easy on that," Ash says, her face awash with concern as we sit across from one another in the limousine en route to the Dolby Theatre where the Oscar ceremony is taking place.

"You should mind your own business." I drill her with a 'butt out' look before I lift the bottle of JD to my lips again and take a healthy glug.

"Shut your fucking face, Dil, or I'll shut it for you." Jamie glares at me. "You're not taking your shitty mood out on my fiancée. Not after everything she's done to organize tonight."

Ordinarily, I love how my best mate rushes to defend my beloved sister. He always takes her side these days, and I only love him more for it. But tonight, it's just another thing that's grinding on my nerves. I've been in a pissy mood for weeks the closer we got to the ceremony. This is a big deal for the band. The Academy nominated Collateral Damage for the best original song, and I should be over the fucking moon.

Yet all I can think about is my imminent reunion with the woman who ripped my heart from my chest before pulverizing it to dust.

Fuck her and fuck him. Fuck them for ruining what should be a joyous occasion and something to celebrate.

"I'm worried about you," Ash adds.

"Worry about yourself," I say through gritted teeth. I open my mouth to hurl vitriol but stop before the hurtful words leave my lips. Tonight will be hard for Ash, too. Jamie is right. It's unfair to take this out on my sister.

"I'm sorry," I say before swigging from the bottle. "It's not fair to take my shitty mood out on you. I hate I'm in a shitty mood. If I could snap out of it, I would."

"Drinking yourself into a stupor won't help." Ash smooths a hand down the front of her silver-and-gold designer dress.

She ditched the pixie cut a few years ago, but she still wears her strawberry-blonde hair short, falling in sharp lines to her chin. The hair and makeup people did a great job, and she looks like she fits in with the snooty crowd. Unlike the rest of us degenerates. On this rare occasion, Jamie sided with the band, and we refused, en masse, to wear tuxedos tonight.

We're a rock band, and Hollywood can take us as we come or leave us.

However, the event has a formal dress code, and we were told, in no uncertain terms, they would refuse us entry if we showed up in jeans and leather jackets. It caused World War Three, and at first, we were adamant we weren't backing down, but ultimately, we did. For Ash. And our mums. They're getting a kick out of us attending the ceremony. So, we're all wearing penguin suits, under protest, and trying not to look pissy about it.

I didn't want to opt for a traditional tux, so I'm wearing a fitted black Armani jacket with silk lapels bordered in red and black trousers. For our performance, I'm wearing my signature black T-shirt, ripped black jeans, and my trusty scuffed boots.

"You look stunning," I tell Ash, wanting to make amends. It's not her fault the Lancasters will be here. I'm sure if she could've done something about it, she would have. But that prick is up for a best actor Oscar, and it's not like he's gonna be a no-show.

"And you're deflecting." Air whooshes out of her mouth as she leans back against the leather seat.

Jamie presses a kiss to her head, shooting me a warning look.

Conor stares out the window as he smokes a blunt, seemingly disinterested, but I know he's listening to every word. He didn't bring a date because he's in between girlfriends, and I didn't bring a date because I don't date. It's not worth the hassle. It's easy finding a willing body when I want to fuck, but like I said, even that's lost its appeal in recent months.

"Don't fucking ignore me, Dil," Ash hisses, leaning forward to jab me in the chest.

I return my attention to my sister. "If you're worried about my performance, don't be. I've been drunk onstage before, and I have never once fucked up or let the band down. And I'm not even close to drunk yet." For some inexplicable reason, drinking before we go onstage has helped my performance in the past. Go figure.

Ash pins me with a probing look. "You know what I'm worried about."

"Why do you think I'm trying to drink myself into oblivion?" I snap, dragging a hand through my white-blond hair.

"Give me some of that," Ro says, swiping the bottle from my fingers. "I could use a trip to oblivion myself."

Ash curses under her breath as she watches our younger brother drink the whiskey. "Drowning your sorrows in a bottle is not the solution, Ro."

"Clo is leaving with my daughter in ten days, and I don't know when I'll see either of them again. I'm fucking distraught, Ash, and right now, drowning my sorrows in a whiskey haze sounds like the perfect solution."

We have a new album to record and a few festivals to play in the coming six months, so Ro can't ditch L.A. for Wicklow like his selfish fiancée is doing. I'm not completely heartless. I know it's tough for Clodagh here with a two-month-old when she knows no one, but her parents and her sister have only just returned to Ireland after weeks in L.A., and she hasn't given it a chance. She is bailing before she even attempted to settle here.

Ro has bent over backwards for her. Buying her a house in Santa Monica so she has the beach at her fingertips. Installing an indoor pool, jacuzzi, and personal treatment rooms when she asked for them. Organizing a baby shower and inviting the girlfriends and wives of some of the crew and industry people we hang out with in the hopes

---

she could make new friends. Flying her friends and family in via private jet so they could surprise her. Purchasing supplies for the vegetable garden she said she wanted to grow, even though they all sit gathering dust in their garage.

I feel for my brother. I know this is not what he planned when he proposed to his pregnant girlfriend last year. He saw them building a future together, and it wasn't via a trans-Atlantic long-distance relationship.

I don't think they're a good match, but I haven't said it. It's not my place to interfere. I hate seeing my brother upset, and I'm trying to be there for him because I don't see how this will end well.

"You two are going to be the death of me." Ash shakes her head, but there is only sadness in her gaze. "This should be a joyous occasion. They have nominated you for an Oscar. A fucking Oscar." Her eyes latch on to mine. "Remember when we used to stay up until the early hours of the morning to watch the ceremony even though we had school the next day?"

"I remember." I hated the pomp and ceremony, the hypocrisy, and disgusting display of wealth and smug self-satisfaction. Still, I endured monotonous hours of "Live on the Red Carpet" and the long-drawn-out awards show purely for my sister. Ash loved dissecting the women's outfits and drooling over Hollywood's leading men. I usually spent the night trying not to give myself eye strain and combating a permanent headache.

"This is a big deal, and I want you to enjoy it." She folds her hands in her lap, pinning me with a familiar glacial look.

"I'd enjoy it if *she* wasn't there with *him*." Fuck, the whiskey is making me more talkative than usual. I'm pretty good at acting blasé and pretending I don't have feelings for her beyond loathing. It's all such a lie. Jamie is the only one who knows the truth, and it's the one secret he has kept between us.

"It's been almost six years, Dil. When are you going to let go of the hatred?" Ash asks. "I know she hurt you by running straight back to him. My heart ached for you, but it's in the past. Time has moved on, and you've got to let it go. She hurt me too, but life is too short to bear grudges. She's moved on. You need to move on, too."

"I don't want to talk about them. It's giving me a headache." I grab the bottle from my little brother and knock back a few mouthfuls as our car joins the line of limousines waiting to pull up in front of the theatre. Crowds line both sides of the street, monitored by LAPD's finest. Security is tight for the event, both inside and outside the venue.

"Fine. Have it your way, but I'm warning you both now to be on your best behavior tonight. Remember, your actions reflect on the entire band. When we step out of this car, you'll both leave your women troubles behind." Her sharp gaze dances between me and Ro. "I mean it." She snatches the bottle, daring me to fight her on it, but I just shrug and smile. She doesn't know I have a naggin of whiskey in my inside jacket pocket. "This is a special occasion, and nothing is going to dampen the mood. Got it?"

Chapter Fifty-Two
Age 26

My fingers twitch with a craving to slip the small bottle from my jacket and knock back a mouthful of whiskey. But I'm not brave enough to risk my sister's wrath. Cameras are filming as the VIPs take their assigned seats. The ceremony will begin shortly, and the security personnel have advised us to remain in our seats, so I can't even sneak out to the jacks.

The only thing worse than enduring hours of this bullshit from behind a TV screen is being forced to suffer it live with cameras watching your every expression and following your every move. Fuck plastering a fake smile on my face. I glare at the camera every time it comes near me and sneer at any asshole who attempts to look my way.

I'm not here to make friends in Hollywood.

I'm here for the band and Ash. Full stop.

Ash glances over her shoulder and then whips around, gripping my arm as she leans into my ear. "Don't look, but they're approaching. Just keep your cool."

"Don't worry. I won't punch him in public," I drawl, lowering my voice only because it would anger Ash if I didn't. I don't care if any of the surrounding pussies hear what I've got to say.

Ash inhales sharply as a vision in red sweeps by us. Reeve stops at the row in front of us to do some ass-licking. I know their seats are in the front row because Ash already confirmed we are eight rows behind them.

Should be interesting when we're up on that stage.

Viv can't escape me when I'm staring her in the face.

For years, on and off, I have tried to orchestrate a meeting at an industry event. At first, I did everything to avoid them in LA. But I'm a masochist. I want to torture myself by seeing them together up close. I want to torture myself by seeing *her* up close. My regular daydream was confronting her in front of her precious husband. *Does he know who I am?* He knows I exist, but did she ever tell him I was the man who held her together in Ireland after he shattered her spirit?

I'm guessing not, and I'm petty enough to want him to know.

Nowadays, whenever I see their names on an event attendance list, I add mine. Yet when I show up, they're never there. At first, I presumed it was a coincidence until I realized she was doing it on purpose. Ensuring there was no opportunity for us to meet face to face. Which answers my question.

Reeve *doesn't* know.

I wonder if I should tell him tonight.

Although it might be more fun to let her stew.

Ignoring Reeve, I stare at Vivien. Tension is evident in her shoulders as she faces the stage, with her back to us. It's probably not noticeable to most, but I know her. I know how to read her body language and she's definitely aware of me. I can't see her face from this angle, but she looks stunning in an unforgiving red silk and chiffon gown. It hugs her enviable curves and shapely arse. Her dark hair is up in some kind of elaborate bun, showcasing her elegant neck and the expanse of tan skin across her upper back and shoulders.

My heart leaps, craning toward her with abject longing, before remembering she's no longer mine.

"You're staring," Ash hisses, subtly digging me in the ribs.

"So?" I say, not tearing my gaze from my ex-girlfriend. I will her to turn around. To let me glimpse those gorgeous hazel eyes and see if they are more green or brown today.

"There are cameras," she adds, under her breath.

"I don't give a fuck." I drink Viv in, noting her stiff posture and the shuffling of her feet. Her head turns to look at her husband, and her side profile is in view. Her skin is as flawless as ever, the corner of her mouth offering a teasing glimpse of her lush mouth. A mouth I've never forgotten. I can still taste her on my lips. Feel the glide of her tongue dancing with mine. Still remember what her lips felt like wrapped around my cock.

I glare at Reeve's back as he takes her hand and slides his arm around her waist before guiding her to their seats. My gaze trails their every movement as my heart pounds against my rib cage.

"You've got serious issues," Ash whispers. "I really think you need therapy. It's not normal to obsess this much after all this time. Let your anger go, Dil. It's doing you no favors."

Ash doesn't get it because I've never told her the truth. In the early days, when I was a complete wreck after I returned from LA, Ash worried incessantly about me, so I downplayed it. Music saved me during that period of my life. Music was and is my therapy. I've run through the whole gamut of emotions since I lost Vivien, but one emotion has remained steadfast.

I love her.

I will always love her.

There will never be another woman for me.

If Ash knew, she'd probably have me committed. So let her think it's anger and loathing. It's better than the alternative.

My eyes remain glued to the back of Vivien's head the entire way throughout the ceremony. I wonder if she can feel it. Then we're called backstage, where Ro and I finish the naggin between us as we wait in the wings to perform. When it's showtime, we line up on stage as the presenter is announcing us. I'm not wearing a jacket because it's hot as hell up here under all the stage lights, so the ink on my arms is fully on display. I've gotten more tats over the years, and I wonder if she'll notice.

I belt out the lyrics while hugging the mic and working the crowd. Every second glance is in Viv's direction, and I can tell she's panicking.

Good.

Let her know what it feels like to live your life on edge.

She's so fucking beautiful; it makes my heart ache. Viv was always beautiful, but she's really grown into her skin and she's even more stunning than when we dated. A glow radiates from her face, despite the fear lingering behind her eyes. Small hands rest on her neatly swollen belly and anger flares in my chest. I knew she was pregnant as they announced it last week with a formal interview in *Vanity Fair*. But knowing and seeing it in the flesh are vastly different.

I wonder if it upsets Ash to see her former best friend pregnant like it did seeing Clodagh's pregnancy progress. That was a tough time for Ash and Jamie. They've only just come through it.

Knots twist in my gut thinking about *his* baby growing inside the woman I love. It reminds me of that harrowing time when I learned she'd married him and had his son. For a while, I thought her kid might have been mine, but the dates confirmed he was Reeve's. That was the trigger that sparked my anger, and I turned from a broken lovesick fool into an angry man hellbent on revenge on the woman who had wronged me.

I'm thinking all this as I give the performance of a lifetime, on autopilot, and I have the crowd eating out of my hand.

Well, not all of them.

I smirk.

Reeve watches me watching her as she dances in front of her seat, and I hope it's created some confusion. He looks like the quintessential Hollywood prick in his custom-fit tux with slicked-back hair and a smug grin on his face.

I hate looking at him and seeing my reflection.

I hate we share DNA.

I hate he stole the life that should've been mine and he keeps doing it.

Vivien flees halfway through because it's her usual avoidance strategy. My gaze trails her as she exits the auditorium and enters the hallway that leads to the bathrooms.

We finish our set to rousing applause, and I share a grin with Jamie. No matter what shit is going down in my life, I'm always happiest when I'm on stage. The only time I've felt happier is that summer in Ireland when Viv was mine. Back then, she usurped the performance high. The thought lingers and sadness mixes with longing.

I need to see her up close.

I need to look into her beautiful face and see those pretty eyes.

Maybe they'll hold the answers I've craved all these years.

On our way back to our seats, I detour to the bathroom and hang around in the hallway outside the ladies' restroom to confront the woman who haunts my dreams.

I want to know why she did it.

Why she ran straight back to him after professing undying love for me.

I love you, Dillon. I love you more than words could ever express. For as long as I live, I will never forget you.

But you did, Viv.

You forgot me the second your plane landed on Californian soil. The instant you raced back into his arms.

Pain rips through me like always. Her last words are imprinted on my heart and in my brain and I will die whispering them under my breath, even if they are the greatest lie she's ever told me.

Vivien emerges from the bathroom, stumbling and clutching her purse to her chest when she spots me. Fuck, she is spectacular. So fucking gorgeous. She takes my breath away, and the longing to cross the gap between us, pull her into my arms, and kiss the shit out of her is riding me hard, only adding to my torment.

A sob escapes her lips as we stare at one another. Emotion shines in her eyes, but I can't trust it's real. I drink her in, from head to toe, with hungry eyes, as I'm internally screaming and writhing in pain.

"Hey, Hollywood," I choke out over the messy ball of emotion in my throat. My fingers twitch with the need to touch her.

"Dillon," she whispers.

I push off the wall and walk toward her. Placing my hands on either side of her head, I lean in and close my eyes, soaking her up. Her familiar scent tickles my nostrils as her body heat seeps into my skin. I'm hanging by a thread, barely keeping my hands off her.

I have to remind myself she isn't mine to touch anymore.

She's pregnant—with her husband's child.

I was such a fool to ever let her go. If I could go back in time, I'd do it all differently.

I would never have let her get on the plane that night, and he wouldn't have had the chance to stick his claws in her again.

Everything would be different.

She'd be here with me tonight, and that baby in her belly would be mine.

I'm suffocating, dying inside all over again. My eyes open. I stare at her with my heart trying to beat a path out of my chest. "Vivien Grace," I murmur, peering deep into her eyes. "Still so beautiful." Electricity crackles in the tiny gap between our bodies and she's got to feel it too. This can't just be me.

She scrambles out from under me. "I've got to go."

Icicles form in my veins, replacing the blood flow as she reverts to form. "Run away, Hollywood," I shout after her. "After all, it's what you do best."

I stand rooted to the spot, unable to chase after her because I'm heartbroken all over again.

For a few seconds, I indulged the dream and forgot reality.

Dillon

But that reality is staring at me from the end of the hallway.

Reeve frowns as he looks over at me before wrapping his wife in his arms and escorting her back inside the auditorium.

I slump to the floor and raise my knees, burying my head in my hands as crushing pain stabs into me from every angle.

I think I'm destined to always live with this pain.

Because I can't cut her out of my heart, no matter how much I need to.

Part Four

VIVIEN FOREVER

Chapter Fifty-Three
Age 26

I feel nothing at first when the news breaks that Simon Lancaster is dead. For once, he did something to ruin a special occasion for the right twin. It feels long overdue. I let the dust settle for a few months, planning how I want this to play out before I contact Carson Park and tell him I want to meet my twin. I'm well aware the NDA I signed survives Simon's death, but the solicitor I consulted doubts it would hold up in a court of law as most NDAs have to include reasonable time restrictions and given that it's not guarding a trade secret it would most likely not be upheld. When Park readily agrees to reach out to Reeve, I take that as confirmation he is of the same opinion.

The day after Park confirms Reeve wants a meeting, I remove my contacts and change my hair back to its natural color. I'm as pale as a ghost as I stare in the mirror, more than a little freaked out by the resemblance. Although there are noticeable differences, and my ink and piercings give me a much edgier vibe, I still look way too much like my twin. I hate it and wonder how long I can keep this look before I thoroughly despise myself.

I'm too busy staring at my reflection to notice my sister come into the room.

"Holy fuck, what did you do?" Ash blurts, her eyes popping wide as she drinks in my drastically altered features.

"Thought I'd try out a different look." I don't look at her as I lie. This is all part of my plan to fuck with Vivien's head. I can't wait to see the look on her face when the realization dawns. My hair color isn't quite the same as Reeve's and I wonder if I should've asked Chris to add some blond highlights so we're an exact match.

"Let me see." Ash tugs on my arm, forcing me to turn around.

"You look so different without your signature hair."

I shrug before burying my hands deep in my pockets.

Creases line her forehead as she scrutinizes me.

"What?" I ask, gulping over the sudden anxious lump in my throat.

"Nothing. I—" She chews on the corner of her mouth. "I wonder what your fans will think."

Their reaction is not the one I'm most interested in.

A few days later, we're all having dinner at my place when Ash jabs her finger in my direction, her eyes blazing with self-righteousness as she practically vibrates in her seat. "I've got it!" Her cutlery drops to her plate with a loud clang.

"Got what, love?" Jay asks as concern instantly washes over his face. Ash's mental state has taken a battering this past year, and I love how protective my best mate is. He has jumped through hoops to support Ash through her grief when his own was considerable too. I'm embarrassed I ever thought he wasn't good enough for my sister. Jamie Fleming has more than proved himself, countless times, over the years.

"It's been bugging me ever since you took out the contacts and removed the hair dye." I can almost see the gears turning in her mind, and I sense where this is going. "I couldn't put my finger on it, but now I know."

"You're sounding crazy, just so you know," Ro mumbles, spearing a piece of chicken like he's murdering it. He's been very down since Clo took Emer back to Ireland. While he hasn't said much, I suspect things are not going great between them.

"You look like Reeve Lancaster!" Ash blurts, and I hope no one notices how all the color has just drained from my face.

"What the fuck, babe?" Jamie's gaze bounces between Ash's and mine, and I see the incredulity written across his face. He can't believe she's just said that.

I knew changing my appearance was risky. That my family might spot the resemblance or someone in the media might pick up on it. The latter is something that could work to my advantage; the former is definitely not. Ash was always the concern, and I need to nip this in the bud right now.

I can play this a few different ways. Get pissed off. Or laugh it off. I go for a mix of the two.

I crack up laughing. "Are you seriously trying to piss me the fuck off, Ash?" I say after I've stopped laughing. I'm desperately trying to quell the panic sluicing through my veins. Gripping the edge of the table hard, I lean forward, pinning narrowed eyes on my sister. "Why on earth would you even say that?"

"Don't tell me I'm the only one who sees the resemblance?" Her eyes bounce around the table.

Ro's brows knit together as he stares at me. "Now that you mention it, I can't unsee it." He sits back, rubbing a hand over his chin as he stares at me like I'm a puzzle he wants to solve. "You do look like him. Maybe that's why she was so drawn to you."

I instantly see red. I'm lunging for him before I've even processed the motion, sending plates crashing to the floor as I drag Ro across the table. "Take that back! You fucking take that back!"

Jamie wrangles me away from my little brother as Ash runs around the table to help Ronan.

"Jesus Fucking Christ, Dillon!" Ro hisses, brushing food particles off his shirt as he straightens up. "What the hell has gotten into you?"

"Drop it," Jamie barks. "I know you didn't mean it, but that was hurtful, Ro."

His face instantly drops. "Dil, I didn't mean it like that."

"Forget it." I shove Jamie off. "I don't fucking look like that prick, and this conversation is over."

No one brings it up again.

I'm a nervous wreck the night before I'm scheduled to meet my long-lost twin and his wife at their house, replaying scenarios on a loop in my head. No matter how this goes down, I need to keep my cool so I don't tip my twin off. This is a reconnaissance mission. Get in. Rattle them. Discover a few truths. Then retreat and plan the next stage.

As I wait in the living room of their house for them to appear, what I didn't anticipate is the raw anger which coats me in a blanket of rage from head to toe when confronted with the evidence of their happy family or the deep-seated pain I experience having a front row seat to everything I wanted with her without even realizing it.

The room is lavishly decorated, and I spot Vivien's input in the tasteful furnishings and fittings. Multiple framed family photos hang on walls around the room, each one tearing a fresh strip off my heart, especially the wedding and baby photos. Other frames house accolades Reeve has won, along with an award Vivien received for her writing on a TV show, and a few proudly display Student of the Week certificates given to Easton at his kindergarten. The floor-to-ceiling bookcase on one side of the room showcases a variety of different books and bound movie scripts. Biographies coexist with travel guides, historical tomes, romance novels, and children's books.

Turning my back on the evidence of their happy life, I stare at the playground outside the window as I attempt to wrangle my pain back into its lockbox. My breath hitches as the door opens behind me, and I turn rigidly still. My pulse pounds in my neck, and my palms turn clammy. Blood rushes to my head, and I warn myself to get a grip just as my twin clears his throat and then says, "Hello."

Here goes nothing.

Fixing my features into a neutral line, I turn around and face them. It's a miracle I don't lose my composure the second I see her. She's as beautiful as ever with minimal makeup adorning her flawless face, her long dark hair tumbling in soft waves over almost-bare shoulders, and her tanned skin glowing with vitality in a pretty dress with thin straps that highlights her much larger stomach. She was barely showing at the Oscars, but there's no denying she's pregnant now. As if sensing my thoughts, Vivien's free hand lands protectively on her bump while her other hand clings harder to her husband. I study her face, spotting confusion and then terror as the truth dawns.

As I walk towards them, I maintain my mask and keep my emotions on lockdown. I can't give anything away, or this will all have been for nothing.

Only when I reach them do I look at my brother. It's a lot like looking in a mirror. I've got a few inches in height on him, and I'm broader as well, but there's no denying we share the same DNA. Emotions slam into the walls I've built around my heart, shoving and pushing, desperate to break free, but I keep them locked up tight, hardening my heart and remembering the part Reeve has played in keeping me away. Frankly, I'm surprised he agreed to meet me, though he didn't really have a choice. Not if he wants to keep my existence a secret.

"I'm Reeve Lancaster," he says. "And this is my wife, Vivien."

"It's nice to meet you both," I lie. "I'm Dillon O'Donoghue."

Vivien almost collapses, and my every instinct is to rush to her side, but I'm forced to watch her husband fuss over her like a mother hen. Every time he touches her, I want to smash his annoying face into the wall.

"It's been a particularly stressful time for both of us recently,"

Reeve explains after getting Viv to sit down on the couch. Currently, her head is between her legs as she struggles to breathe, looking like she's on the verge of a full-blown panic attack. Guilt punches through my gut until I remember the part she's played in all this. "Stress isn't good for the baby, and I've been trying to get Viv to take it easy, but she's been worrying too much about me."

I swallow back bile and force the next words from my mouth. "Congratulations. This is your second child, right?"

A strangled sound emits from Viv's mouth, and Reeve rushes back to her side, suggesting she goes and lies down. I already know she'll refuse. There's no way she'll risk leaving me with him. It's blatantly obvious Reeve doesn't know I'm Vivien's Irish lover. I wasn't sure coming here if he knew, but their first reactions confirmed she hasn't shared that knowledge. It's hugely helpful he doesn't know. It will help me drive the dagger in deeper when the time comes.

Poor Vivien. I can only imagine the sheer terror she's experiencing right now.

"Why do I get the feeling I know you from somewhere?" Reeve asks, pouring me a coffee after their housekeeper deposited a tray and left.

"I'm the lead singer for Collateral Damage," I explain, accepting a mug when Reeve hands it to me.

"Yes! That's it. We saw you perform at the Oscars in February, didn't we, Viv?"

"We did." The smile on her face is as fake as her husband's obvious performance.

I've got to hand it to him; he's playing the part of the clueless twin to perfection. His eagerness and childlike hope is the perfect play. If I didn't know he was an experienced actor, I might even fall for the ruse. I'm wondering if he realizes I know he's known all along. *Is it possible Simon didn't tell him that part?*

"Congrats on your win, by the way. I loved your acceptance speech." It's a miracle I don't choke on those words, like it's a miracle

Dillon

I didn't puke all over the woman in front of me at the Oscars being forced to endure that nauseating speech.

Vivien is getting paler by the second, and she looks like she wishes the ground would swallow her whole. *What did she expect? That she could play me like that and there wouldn't ever be any consequences?*

Reeve continues with the charade, asking me questions about growing up in Ireland, and Viv shrinks further, pressing into his side, no doubt wishing she was invisible. Watching her clinging to him, touching him, and leaning into him for support buries the knife in my back deeper. It hurts watching them together like this, and I don't know how much longer I can sit here and pretend this isn't killing me. I've learned the things I needed to learn. Now I need to retreat and work out how to use it to my advantage. I doubt either of them will protest when I make my excuses and leave. To say things are awkward is the understatement of the century. It's clear they're both uncomfortable, and I draw some satisfaction from that.

Anger flares when Reeve offers me half his inheritance. *Is this how he intends to buy my silence?* Wow, he really is a chip off the old block. *How the fuck could Vivien have married this guy? Why can't she see who he really is?*

I lie and say I have to leave to meet the band because I need to get out of here before I say something I'll regret. Their son bursts into the room then, and I'm rooted to the spot watching his excited, inquisitive face. He's adorable, and he clearly loves his mommy and daddy. My walls crack, and the tenuous hold on my emotions is wavering. This is all too much, and it's time to leave. Until little Easton drops a bomb, revealing it's his birthday in *May*, not June, and I'm leveled all over again as I frantically recalculate the maths in my head.

Oh my god.

My dazed gaze drifts to Vivien, and I see the truth she's tried so hard to hide.

He could be mine!

It's a miracle my legs don't buckle.

Holy fuck. That little boy could be my son.

And I've lost years with him already.

Reeve's façade slips for a few seconds, and I see it then. The suspicion. The distrust.

Their reactions tell me everything I need to know, and though I'm in complete shock, I'm beyond enraged. Pain unlike anything I have ever felt before threatens to suffocate me, and I revert to form, lashing out and hurting Vivien with my words and my threats, before I finally make my escape.

Chapter Fifty-Four

Age 26

The hardest thing is keeping everything a secret from my bandmates and my sister. They can tell something is wrong. I've been agitated in the days since the reunion, unable to sleep or eat, and I'm barely functioning, running on empty.

All I keep thinking is Easton could be mine and pondering what it might mean if he is.

I arrive early at the medical laboratory just outside of Santa Clarita where the DNA testing will take place. I don't go inside, choosing to wait outside for Vivien to arrive. Technically, she doesn't need to be here. She could post Reeve and Easton's samples, but I knew she'd want to be here. She doesn't trust me. Pretty sure she hates my guts, and I can't say I wouldn't be the same in her shoes.

Every time I feel guilty for the way I've been treating her, I'm reminded she deliberately concealed her pregnancy and her son's real birthday, so I wouldn't find out. I know what she told me, but I don't believe her. It's obvious Reeve has really done a job on her. She fully believes every fucking lie that comes out of his mouth. I scoff at the notion he didn't know about me. Her claims that I'm the lucky one and Reeve was the unfortunate one only crank my anger to the max.

How fucking dare she insinuate he had it harder than me!

Nah, fuck that shite.

I should probably feel sorry for Vivien because Reeve has deceived her most all of her life, but I can't forget she's not entirely innocent either. Even if what they said about tricking the media into thinking Easton's birthday is later than it is is true, she still concealed her pregnancy from me.

I had a right to know. She openly admitted she didn't know who the father was when she got pregnant. She should have told me, but she only told him, choosing to cut me out entirely without any choice. I'm not sure I'll ever be able to forgive her for that even if she did try to do the right thing after Easton's birth by getting a paternity test done. She thought he was Reeve's because she didn't know I'm his twin.

Leaning against the gray brick wall, I mess around on my phone as I wait for her to arrive, absorbing some Vitamin D while I try to deny how excited I am to see her. It takes effort to pretend I don't spot her SUV pulling into the parking lot twenty minutes later.

I wait until she steps onto the path before I look up. She's pretty as a picture in a summery white dress that falls just below her knees. Slim legs fit neatly into a pair of off-white wedge sandals. Wavy hair cascades over her shoulders, blowing softly in the breeze. Like me, her eyes are concealed behind shades so I can't read her emotions.

I push off the wall as she stops in front of me, and we stare at one another without speaking. My heart is going crazy being this close to her. Everything about her is still intoxicating, and I have to imagine roots tunneling from my feet into the ground to stop myself from closing the gap between us and pulling her into my body.

I need to remember all the ways she has hurt me.

To remember she married him while turning her back on me.

Pain presses down on my chest, like usual, and now I want to be anywhere but here. Her presence sucks up all the oxygen, leaving me with the dregs. "You have the samples?" I ask.

She nods. "Let's just do this."

We enter together, and I explain who we are to the receptionist, and a few seconds later, the doctor I spoke to on the phone appears to escort us to his office.

She sits beside me in front of the doctor's desk. Heat rolls off her body, washing over me in comforting waves. It takes every shred of my willpower not to stare at her when she removes her sunglasses and folds her hands nervously in her lap. Shadows darken the curves under her eyes, and I know that's my fault. Guilt slaps me around the face, and I grit my jaw, staring at the doctor while trying to smother a bout of self-loathing.

The doc's eyes widen in surprise as he stares at her before clearing his throat and handing me an envelope. "The NDA has been signed by me and all the laboratory staff though there really was no need. We are always discreet. The nature of our work commands it, and our stellar reputation rests upon it."

Yeah, right. I'm taking no chances. The same way I took no chances with those we left behind in Dublin when we first made it, ensuring Aoife and a bunch of others signed watertight NDAs to guarantee they keep their gobs shut. "I'm sure you can understand the need for extra precaution," I supply.

"I can assure you both you have nothing to worry about. I am personally handling your case, instead of one of our geneticists, to ensure your confidentiality is protected." He offers us a tight smile. "As agreed, I will enter the samples under false names as an added safeguard," the doctor continues, his gaze floating between the two of us.

"Thank you." Vivien sets two small Ziploc bags down on the table. "The blue toothbrush is my husband's, and the smaller red one is my son's." Her voice cracks and my hand twitches with the need to reach out and comfort her. "Are you sure these will be enough to extract a DNA sample?"

"The DNA in a person's blood, saliva, hair, or skin cells is exactly the same. Toothbrush samples are commonly used for forensic test-ing, and it's no better or more or less accurate than a cheek swab or providing a blood sample, provided there is enough DNA on the sample," he confirms.

The doc comes around to me and swabs the inside of my cheek. "How long will it take to get the results?" I ask.

"Approximately ten days to two weeks."

Vivien visibly pales. "Can't you expedite it? We can pay more," she offers.

"That is as fast as we can deliver the results. This is not a routine paternity test. In order to determine paternity in cases of identical twins, we need to examine more than just the standard markers. There is no way it can be rushed."

"And you're sure you can conclusively determine paternity with these samples?" she asks.

He nods. "We will examine the entire genome sequence which will isolate at least a single mutation in one of the twin's genetics that has been passed on from father to son. The test will confirm which twin fathered your son."

She blushes, and it takes me back in time. "We'll await your call." I climb to my feet, barely resisting the urge to help her stand. "Thank you."

When we're outside, she tells me she needs to speak to me, walking off before I answer. Although, I suspect I know what she wants to say, I follow her across the car park and climb into the passenger seat of her car where we proceed to argue about her fucking husband. She wants to tell Reeve what's going on now, but I refuse, resorting to blackmail to ensure her secrecy.

If Easton is my son, I want to be there when she tells Reeve.

I want to see the look on his face when he realizes he's lost his son to me.

I want him to look into my eyes and see the love I hold for his wife and read my intent.

I want him to understand I'm going nowhere.

As soon as he fucks up again—and he will—I'll be waiting for Vivien with open arms, ready to be the man she needs me to be.

Dillon

I didn't fight hard enough for her all those years ago, and I'm not making the same mistake again. I might be crazy angry right now, but being around her again has only confirmed what I've always known. She's the love of my life, and I want her back. I know, in time, I'll find a way to forgive her for her sins, and we'll be happy together the way we always should have been.

Chapter Fifty-Five
Age 26

My hands are trembling as I hold the report, rereading the words through blurry eyes. *I have a son.* He's mine. Easton is mine. Mine and Viv's. The most indescribable joy swells my heart until it feels like it might burst out of my chest. Vivien and I created precious life together. I think I knew making love to her that last night that something magical was happening. Easton's excited boyish face resurrects in my mind, and I'm smiling as I dab at my happy tears. We made the most adorable little human, and I can't wait to hold him and shower him with love.

All I'm feeling in this moment is complete elation. Viv's deceit and the missing years don't matter. One-upping my brother fades into the background. Vivien and I have a son. He's ours, and I'm more determined than ever to win her back now.

I'm bursting with pride, and I wish I could tell Ash and Jamie. I want to tell them so badly I'm a daddy. I want to pick up the phone and tell Ma she's got another grandchild. I feel like shouting it from the rooftops so everyone knows.

But all in good time. Viv and I need to talk first.

Every unanswered call to Vivien chips away at my happiness

until all the negative feelings return to drag me down. I know she got a copy of the paternity report the same time I did, so she's purposely ignoring me. Too busy flapping over what this'll do to her precious husband, no doubt. I've been relegated to second place again, and I'm full of pent-up emotion I need to vent. So, I call the guys, and we enjoy a late-night jamming session in my home studio as I attempt to paper over the fresh cracks in my heart with music.

When Ash comes racing into the room a few hours later with tears streaming down her face, an ominous sense of foreboding washes over me. Watching the news report of Reeve's and Vivien's accident is a sobering moment. As is pacing the floor of the private waiting room at the hospital. I'm terrified she's going to die before I tell her the truth and before I can make up for all the hurt of the past few weeks. I'm full of self-loathing. Silently berating myself for fucking up again. I've put Vivien under enormous stress these past few weeks, and I'm ashamed of how I've treated her.

It's selfish of me to sneak back inside to see her after Lauren and Jonathon tell me to leave, but I need to see her with my own eyes. I need to apologize. To tell her I love her and I'm here for her and Easton. To convey how sorry I am she lost her little girl. I'm purposely not thinking about my twin because my feelings when it comes to his death are a clusterfuck of epic proportions. The envelope the detective gave me, with the stack of private photos, is weighing my pocket down. Reeve had someone follow us in Ireland, and I'm finding it hard to have charitable thoughts about my twin right now.

Entering Vivien's hospital room is the most selfish thing I could've done. I wish I'd realized it in time. She thinks I'm him. She thinks I'm Reeve. Until reality comes crashing down on her and she falls apart, hurling hateful words at me that I fully deserve. I break down in the hallway outside her room, and my best mate has to practically carry me to my car.

"Did you get any sleep?" Ash inquires when I materialize in her kitchen later that same day. They wouldn't let me go home alone, so we drove here from the hospital, all of us heading to bed to try to grab a few hours of sleep after pulling an all-nighter.

"No," I quietly admit, scrubbing my hands down my face as I stride to the coffee machine. It was impossible to sleep, no matter how exhausted I am. I just couldn't switch my brain off. There's far too much on my mind.

"Me either." She moves to the fridge, removing a carton of milk as I pour myself a coffee. "Jay is still snoring away. At least one of us managed to sleep."

"I've messed everything up so bad, Ash." I dump milk in my coffee and claim a stool at the island unit. "Vivien will never forgive me for the part I played in her husband's and daughter's death."

"You aren't responsible for that, Dillon. It was a tragic accident. Vivien was severely traumatized, and I doubt she'll even remember anything she said."

"It doesn't excuse my actions." I hang my head in shame.

"No, it doesn't. What are you going to do?"

I stare into space as I sip from my mug. I take a few moments to respond. "The temptation to bury myself at the bottom of a bottle of JD is enormous, but I can't fall apart now." My eyes are heavy as I fix them on her. "I have a son who needs me. A son who just lost the only daddy he's known, and I need to be strong for him. For Easton and Vivien." It's time to man up and come clean. To take ownership of the mistakes I made. I can't begin to fix them without accepting responsibility.

She links her fingers in mine on top of the counter. "They're going to need you."

"If she'll let me."

"She's going to need time and space. She's grieving an enormous loss."

"I know, but I need to at least let her know I'm here for her. That I'm not going anywhere."

Sadness splays across Ash's face. "She's not going to want to hear that now, Dillon, but I understand where you're coming from."

"I just called Ma. Told her to get Da, Ciarán, and Shane to pack a bag, that I'd send a plane for them. It's time I told everyone the truth."

Our family arrives a few days later with kids and wives in tow. I told Ma over the phone that Reeve is my biological twin brother, but I haven't revealed more than that. I need to tell them everything face to face. They've all seen the reports on TV and in the newspapers. It's all the media has been discussing for days. Some of the things I've read are disgusting. They can't even leave Vivien to grieve in peace.

My sisters-in-law take the kids out so I can talk to my parents and my brothers in privacy. Jay is here too. I took Conor aside the day after the hospital and told him everything. He didn't judge, just told me he was here for me, and I appreciated it more than he knows.

"What is going on, Dillon?" Ma asks when we're all settled in my sitting room with teas and coffees.

"I have things to tell you. Secrets I've been keeping for a long time."

"I can't believe Reeve Lancaster was your twin." Shane shakes his head. "Like what the fuck?"

"Did Vivien know?" Ma asks. "Did Vivien know who you were to Reeve?"

There are no rule books for this kind of thing. No way of sugarcoating it, so I don't. "No. She didn't know, and I purposely didn't tell her either."

Shocked silence echoes around the room.

"I'll fill in the gaps in a minute, but the other thing you need to know is I have a son."

Gasps and wide-eyed stares greet my announcement.

Emotion swims in my eyes, like every time I think of my child. "I only found out recently that Vivien's five-year-old son Easton is my biological child."

"Jesus Fucking Christ." Shane stands. "I don't know about you, but I need something fucking stronger than tea for this."

Jay and Ash organize alcoholic drinks while I tell my family everything. Simon approaching me at seventeen. Vivien landing in my lap like the perfect revenge plan. Falling in love with her only for her to return to my twin. The pain of losing her. The torment I've endured watching her with Reeve. Letting my anger take charge after Simon died and plotting against my twin and his wife. The horrible way I've treated Vivien in the past few weeks. The test confirming Easton is my son. Right up to the hospital and Vivien mistaking me for Reeve.

Ma is sobbing profusely by the time I finish, holding on to my father as she cries. Shane and Ciarán are speechless. Doubt it's ever happened to my older brother at any other time in his life.

"I wish you'd come to me," Da says. Pain underscores his words, and it radiates from his eyes. "I wish you'd let me handle that bastard." His pain quickly transforms. "How dare he hurt my son like that. How dare he blackmail you and make you feel less than you are."

"So much makes sense now," Ciarán says. Compassion is etched upon his face, and I'm not deserving of it. "He made you feel unworthy when he is the one who was unworthy. What kind of man, what kind of father, could do those things to his son? He's a prick."

"He's fucking lucky he's dead." Shane cracks his knuckles. "And that I left me shotgun at home."

"Don't make light of this," Ma chokes out.

"If you think I'm joking, Ma, you don't know me very well." Shane drills her with a look. "I want to dig that fucker up and piss on his bones for treating my brother like that."

"Stop," I grit out. "Don't do this. Tell me I'm a shithead. Tell me I deserve it all because of the things I've done. Don't feel sorry for me. I don't deserve that."

"You *are* a shithead," Shane says. "Don't mistake my feelings. I'm gutted for you, Dil. I can't imagine how I'd feel if the man who gave me life did those things to me. I hope Simon Lancaster is rotting in hell, but it doesn't excuse your actions. What you did to Vivien is disgusting, both then and now."

"I know."

"You were wrong to target Vivien, but you ended up paying the biggest price," Da says. "You lost her, and you've missed years with your son."

"I have, but I'm determined to make things right if she'll let me."

"Did you have any kind of relationship with Reeve?" Ma asks, taking a tissue from Ash and dabbing at her eyes.

"No." A muscle clenches in my jaw. "He was part of the manipulation."

"Oh, Dillon." Ma reaches forward, taking my hand. "Simon was a very evil man to have planted so many doubts in your head. Do you truly believe your twin knew and he wanted nothing to do with you? Do you truly believe Vivien could love and marry a man like that?"

"I've tried telling him, Ma," Ash says. "But he won't listen. He's convinced Reeve was in on the plan from the start. It doesn't matter what Vivien has told him. He refuses to believe it."

"What good does it do now? Reeve is dead. Even if I am wrong, it's too late. Reeve has displayed a lot of manipulative qualities. He was spying on us in Ireland, for fuck's sake!"

"You see the irony, right?" Ciarán asks, stretching his legs out in front of him.

"You're every bit as secretive and manipulative as Reeve was." Trust Shane not to mince words.

I want to argue, but I have no basis for disputing that view because it's true. *And you know what?* Maybe Viv is telling the truth. Perhaps Reeve wasn't acting at the meeting. Perhaps he didn't know until after his father died. Maybe that was Simon's greatest lie, forged to keep his twin sons separated forever, and I fell for it. I'm still struggling to figure out my twin and his motivations.

"I'm disappointed you kept so much from us, Dillon." Ma squeezes my hand. "You should have come to us when Simon approached you. I knew something happened that night at the boxing club. I should have pushed you harder to tell me what was wrong."

"It wouldn't have made any difference, Ma. I was never going to tell you." I knock back the last of my whiskey. "I was ashamed. I was hurting. I stupidly thought if I told you you wouldn't want me either."

"Oh, Dillon." Tears prick Ma's eyes again. "I feel like we didn't love you enough. Why else would you think those things?"

"No, Ma." Setting my glass down, I drop to my knees in front of her. "You loved me plenty even when I wasn't easy to love. The blame is on me. I was a stupid kid who focused on all the wrong things. I should have told you. Everything would have been so different if I had, but I can't turn back time. I can't change all the mistakes I've made. I've just got to try to make up for them and not make any more."

"You *have* made a lot of mistakes, Dillon. I'm still struggling to process all the secrets and lies. To understand how my son could lie to our faces and treat any woman the way you've treated that poor girl. But I also know you have the biggest heart and you've struggled with your feelings your entire life. I know you're not a bad person. We all know that. You're our son, our brother. We love you, and we're here for you. For you and Easton." A bright smile lights up her face. "No more lies, Dillon." Her expression morphs into a stern one. "No more concealing things from us. From now on, you'll tell us everything, and you'll let us help. It's nonnegotiable."

I bob my head. "I will need your help because Vivien is going to fight me every step of the way. She hates me, and I don't blame her."

"I don't think Vivien could ever truly hate you, Dillon," Ash says as I sit back in my seat and straighten up. "She loved you a lot. Those feelings were forcibly terminated, but they didn't die."

"That poor girl is hurting, and you'll need to be very patient with her," Ma adds.

"You can't railroad her," Shane supplies.

"Let her set the pace," Ciarán says, and his words take me back in time.

"I will be whatever and whoever she needs me to be, and she sets the timeline. I let her down before, and I won't do that again. I don't care what I must do to make amends, I'll do it. She might not know it, but Vivien needs me. Easton needs me. I failed my family once before, but I'm not failing them now. They are mine to protect and love, and I intend to do that every day from now until the end of my days."

Epilogue
Age 52

"What're you watching?" my wife asks, entering our living room in runners, yoga pants, and a slouchy top over a cropped bra top, clearly just arriving home after her regular weekly yoga class. Ash and Audrey attend the same session, and they usually grab a coffee afterwards. Viv's hair is up in a high ponytail, and there isn't a scrap of makeup on her face, but she's still the most beautiful woman in the world.

"Our movie." I press pause on the remote and open my arms in invitation. I need to hold my wife.

Viv drops her rolled-up yoga mat on the ground and crawls onto the sofa beside me, instantly curling into my side. My arms wind around her on autopilot. Her gaze roams to the giant wall-mounted TV screen, which is paused at the scene after Reeve's funeral at Vivien and Reeve's house, where we had the big meeting. Her probing eyes lift to mine. "Why are you watching that? We haven't looked at it in years."

I hold her tighter, pressing a kiss to her head, savoring the familiar smell and feel of her in my arms. "I've been feeling melancholy since Melody moved out." Our youngest starts UCLA in a few days. Her

447

brothers helped me and Viv to move her into her new dorm a couple days ago. She's the last one to move out of home, and we're officially empty nesters now. The house is so quiet even if I love having my wife all to myself again for the first time in years.

Viv rests her head on my chest, and I know she's listening to the rhythm of my heart because it's one of her favorite things to do. Deep down, I think she needs the reassurance my steady heart beat offers. It helps to ground her. "I know the feeling. Our babies are all grown up. They don't need us anymore." She sniffles, and I'm not surprised to see tears in her eyes when I lift her onto my lap, facing me.

"Our babies will always need us, Hollywood." I kiss her softly, and a deep sense of contentment sinks deep into my bones, like always. "I remember the time I discovered Easton was mine and then Reeve died. I stayed strong because I wanted to be there for you and our son, but I don't think I could have done it without the support of my parents and my siblings. They helped get me through it." I brush hair out of her eyes. "I was just thinking back to that time. It was the first time I truly leaned on anyone else. The first time I properly let my family in. Let Ma in. I was twenty-six, and I still needed my mother."

Our kids adore Vivien. They'll never stop needing her and loving her. Of that, I'm sure.

"I needed to hear that."

"I know."

"Something occurred to me this morning," she says, straddling my thighs.

"That we can have wild monkey sex, anytime and anywhere, now all the kids have flown the nest?" I quip, grabbing her toned arse in my hands. My woman is all kinds of flexible, thanks to regular yoga, and I'm always keen to bend her into lots of different positions.

She rolls her eyes and laughs. "Pretty sure we've had plenty of wild monkey sex with the kids in the house."

"We could build a sex room." My eyes widen at the prospect.

"You have sex on the brain," she teases, grinding on top of me.

"Seems like I'm not the only one."

"I thought for sure you'd want a lake with swans."

"That too." Grabbing her hips, I slide her back and forth on top of me, ensuring she feels my hardening length. I'm still so horny for my woman.

Heat flares in her eyes as she stares at me, and I get lost in her. She's still so fucking beautiful, growing old gracefully like my mum and mother-in-law. With the exception of a few laughter lines around her eyes, some gray in her dark hair, and slightly softer curves, Vivien hasn't changed much in all the years I've known her. She's still the most gorgeous on the planet. She cups my face. "You know I'll give you whatever you want because I love you and I like making you happy."

"I love you so much." Circling my arms around her, I hug her tight. "I love our life. You've made me so incredibly happy, Vivien."

We kiss slowly and passionately for a few minutes without any agenda despite my teasing. Sometimes, I just love hugging and kissing my wife, reveling in the intimacy we share. An intimacy that has lasted the test of time when plenty of other marriages have long since fallen by the wayside. "Love you, rock star," she says when we finally break our lip-lock. Emotion swims in her eyes as she cups my face. "What I was going to say earlier was I was thinking this morning about how I had Reeve in my life for twenty-six years and now you've been in my life that long too."

"I know, beautiful." I smooth a soothing hand up and down her back. "I'm always acutely aware of the years, months, days, minutes, and seconds we've spent together because I spent far too many of them without you."

"Still such a romantic," she whispers as tears fill her eyes.

"Do you still miss him?"

"I'll always miss him, Dillon, but it doesn't make me sad anymore. How could it when I have you and the kids and the most amazing life? I'm sad his life was cut so short, but I'm exactly where I was always meant to be." She kisses the tip of my nose. "Never doubt that you are the love of my life."

I haven't doubted it in a very long time. "I'm secure in our love." I brush my fingers across her cheek. "But I'll always regret I never got to know him. I'll always regret believing Simon instead of asking Reeve if it was true."

A pregnant pause ensues, and I guess we're both thinking how we might not be here now if that had happened. It's hard to admit you wouldn't change a thing about your life despite all the heartache and suffering—yours and others—because it seems like the most selfish admission even if it's also the most selfless. It's like saying we'd be okay if we'd never reunited. If Fleur and Melody didn't exist.

Things happen in life for a reason.

I fully believe that now.

"Reeve is at peace, Dillon. You should be too. Let go of your regrets, my love. I'm pretty confident he's looking down at the amazing husband and father you are, and it tells him everything he needs to know."

"Have you felt him at all lately?"

She shakes her head. "Not in years. Not since that awful night with Bodhi."

A shudder works its way through her as icy tentacles wrap around my spine. None of us like remembering that time. "He's in a great place," I remind her. "He's happy."

"I'm so proud of him. I'm proud of all our kids."

"Same. I don't think we can even take much credit. We lucked out. They're all such good, kind, compassionate kids."

"I miss them," she whispers, resting her head on my shoulder. "What'll we do with ourselves now they're gone?"

A deep chuckle rumbles from my chest. "Oh, Hollywood, I can think of plenty of ways to keep you busy." I nibble on her earlobe. "I'll give you a clue. Most all of them involve you on your back."

"That's a given, babe." She rocks on top of me, and my dick stirs to life again. "But I'm thinking we should do it. What you suggested."

Dillon

Excitement shoots through my veins. "Yeah?"

She bobs her head, and her entire face glows. "You're right."

"I usually am."

She rolls her eyes again. "We've worked our butts off for years with our careers and family, and we're still young enough to enjoy this stage of our life. Let's do it. Let's go traveling for a few years before we're inundated with grandbabies and extra responsibilities."

"How quickly can you hire someone to replace you at the foundation?" I ask while mauling her arse through her yoga pants.

"Quicker than you think." She smirks.

"Spill, Hollywood." My hand dips under her top, resting on warm skin.

"I asked Ria if she might be interested, and she's champing at the bit to take the role."

"That's a very smart move." Ria is Conor's wife, and she's worked in NGOs for years, most recently at senior management level. She's the perfect person to take over from Vivien at the foundation she runs in Reeve's name. It's important to her to leave the charity in trustworthy hands.

"She said she'd be happy to take over until we come back and then she's interested in a split part-time role with me or one of the kids if anyone shows an interest in getting involved at that stage."

"Sounds like a good plan, and I've spoken with Bodhi. He's happy to take on more responsibility at the label, and between him and the others, they can cover my shit."

Bodhi joined the CD label when he graduated high school, and he's never looked back. Meanwhile, Easton has ended up at Studio 27. He's working his way up the ranks and loving being a part of the movie industry from behind the camera. Both our girls are at college and still unsure about their futures, but they're young, and they have plenty of time to decide what they want to do.

Collateral Damage is pretty much retired these days though we never officially disbanded. We haven't ruled out making another album or getting back onstage. Viv and I have discussed setting up an annual memorial festival in aid of the foundation, and we might put that in motion when we return. For the past few years, myself and the guys have been happy running our label and helping new bands to make their mark on the music scene. I also write a lot for other artists, and my songwriting income vastly outweighs my non-songwriting royalties these days.

"When should we leave?" Viv pivots her hips on top of me, and I'm fully hard now.

"How about next month? I want at least a few weeks to enjoy doing nothing but feasting on you," I admit as I unclip her bra.

"You won't hear any complaints from me." In a flash, her bra and shirt are tossed on the floor.

"You're still so fucking perfect, Viv," I say, fondling her tits. "I'm so happy I get to live this life with you."

"Ditto, babe." She licks her lips as she gyrates on top of me while I grope her boobs. "This is the next part of our adventure together."

"Here's to the next twenty-six years," I say before sucking her nipple into my mouth.

One thing I know for sure is it'll never be boring.

I can't wait to begin.

THE END.

Threesome Bonus Scene: Ever wondered what might have happened if the twins hadn't been separated and they'd grown up together living next door to their dream girl? Step into an alternate fictional reality, where Dillon and Reeve are done fighting over Vivien, so they admit they love her and tell her she has to choose. But our girl has never been able to choose between them, and things quickly take a steamy turn...

Type this link into your browser to download your copy: https://bit.ly/DillonPWB

A Final Word from the Author

I'm all up in my feels as I write this because I can't believe this is the last book in my *All of Me Series*. (Excluding any spin-off romances I might write for Easton and Bodhi.) Cue the tears! I love every book I have written and I can never pick a favorite, but this series was extra special for me as part of it is set in my homeland of Ireland and even in my hometown of Kilcoole! Writing about places familiar to me was an extra special thrill.

I get fully invested every time I write a book, but never more so than this series. It had been brewing in my head for two years before I found time in my schedule to write it. I have never written books so fast! *Say I'm the One* is over 169,000 words which is A LOT, but I wrote the first draft in three weeks, and I didn't even change much during revisions because it came out pretty perfect the first time. That hasn't happened at any time before or since and I like to think something magical was taking place as I was conjuring this story to life.

I'm going to miss Dillon, Vivien, Reeve, Ash, Audrey, Alex, Jay, Ro, Con, and all the other characters I fell in love with.

I wasn't sure anyone would love this premise when I was writing it, but I just knew I had to get these words on the page and then share them with the world. I'm so grateful to all the readers who took a chance on this series, and for those of you who have stuck with it to the very end – thank you, thank you, thank you! The enthusiasm and passion you have shown these characters, and this world, is unlike anything I have experienced in my writing career to date. On difficult days, all I have to do is read some of your heartfelt reviews to feel better.

Like with Reeve's companion novel, I tried to create Dillon's point of view in a way that was fresh and offered new insights. I didn't want to just repeat the same scenes told from a different perspective. I wanted to show you the stuff you didn't see in *Say I'm the One*, and I hope I have delivered. This book is mostly brand-new scenes. Any original scenes were included for flow or because readers in the spoiler group on Facebook asked me to include them. I could have kept going further into the story, but I feared we would wander into repeat territory, so I chose to end Dillon's book just after Reeve's passing.

Every author's dream is to see their work on the big or small screen someday. If it was to happen for me, for any book or series, I would love it to be this one. Fingers crossed that someday that dream might come true.

Thank you for supporting me on this journey. Thank you for loving these characters and this world as much as I do. This was only meant to be a duet, but I wrote more in this world because you guys were as passionate as me. I hope you have enjoyed *Dillon* and that I've done him justice.

If you want to read more angsty emotional romance from me, please check out these titles: *Inseparable, When Forever Changes, The One I Want Duet, Always Meant to Be, Still Falling for You, Incognito, No Feelings Involved, Tell It to My Heart* or *Surviving Amber Springs*. Keep a look out for *Never Stopped Loving You* which is coming very soon! This is my next stand-alone angsty romance release with brand-new characters and a brand-new world.

***A childhood promise. An unbreakable bond. One tragic event
that shatters everything.***

It all started with the boys next door...

Devin and Ayden were my best friends. We were practically joined at the
hip since age two. When we were kids, we thought we were invincible,
inseparable, that nothing or no one could come between us.

But we were wrong.

Everything turned to crap our senior year of high school.

Devin was turning into a clone of his deadbeat lowlife father—fighting,
getting wasted, and screwing his way through every girl in town. I'd been
hiding a secret crush on him for years. Afraid to tell him how I felt in case I
ruined everything. So, I kept quiet and slowly watched him self-destruct with
a constant ache in my heart.

Where Devin was all brooding darkness, Ayden was the shining light. Our
star quarterback with the bright future whom everyone loved. But something
wasn't right. He was so guarded, and he wouldn't let me in.

When Devin publicly shamed me, Ayden took my side, and our awesome-threesome bond was severed. The split was devastating. The heartbreak inevitable.

Ayden and I moved on with our lives, but the pain never lessened, and Devin was never far from our thoughts.

Until it all came to a head in college, and one eventful night changed everything.

Now, I've lost the two people who matter more to me than life itself. Nothing will ever be the same again.

————

Available now in ebook, paperback, alternate paperback, hardcover and audio.

**CLAIM YOUR FREE EBOOK – ONLY AVAILABLE TO
NEWSLETTER SUBSCRIBERS!**

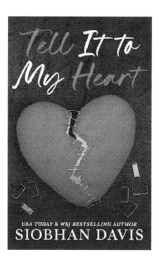

The boy who broke my heart is now the man who wants to mend it.

Jared was my everything until an ocean separated us and he abandoned me when I needed him most.

He forgot the promises he made.

Forgot the love he swore was eternal.

It was over before it began.

Now, he's a hot commodity, universally adored, and I'm the woman no one wants.

Pining for a boy who no longer exists is pathetic. Years pass, men come and go, but I cannot move on.

I didn't believe my fractured heart and broken soul could endure any more pain. Until Jared rocks up to the art gallery where I work, with his fiancée in tow, and I'm drowning again.

Seeing him brings everything to the surface, so I flee. Placing distance between us again, I'm determined to put him behind me once and for all.

Then he reappears at my door, begging me for another chance.

I know I should turn him away.

Try telling that to my heart.

This angsty, new adult romance is a FREE full-length ebook, exclusively available to newsletter subscribers.

Type this link into your browser to claim your free copy:

https://bit.ly/TITMHFBB

OR

Scan this code to claim your free copy:

About the Author

Siobhan Davis™ is a *USA Today, Wall Street Journal*, and Amazon Top 5 bestselling romance author. **Siobhan** writes emotionally intense stories with swoon-worthy romance, complex characters, and tons of unexpected plot twists and turns that will have you flipping the pages beyond bedtime! She has sold over 2 million books, and her titles are translated into several languages.

Prior to becoming a full-time writer, Siobhan forged a successful corporate career in human resource management.

Siobhan currently lives with her husband in Cyprus while their two grown-up sons reside at the family home in Ireland.

You can connect with Siobhan in the following ways:

Website: www.siobhandavis.com
Facebook: AuthorSiobhanDavis
Instagram: @siobhandavisauthor
Tiktok: @siobhandavisauthor
Email: siobhan@siobhandavis.com

Books By Siobhan Davis

NEW ADULT ROMANCE SERIES

The Kennedy Boys® Series
Rydeville Elite Series
All of Me Series
Forever Love Duet
The One I Want Duet

NEW ADULT ROMANCE STAND-ALONES

Inseparable
Incognito
Still Falling for You
Holding on to Forever
Always Meant to Be
Tell It to My Heart
Never Stopped Loving You*

REVERSE HAREM

Sainthood Series
Dirty Crazy Bad Duet
Surviving Amber Springs (stand-alone)
Alinthia Series

DARK MAFIA ROMANCE

Condemned to Love

Forbidden to Love

Scared to Love

Vengeance of a Mafia Queen

Cold King of New York (The Accardi Twins #1)

Cold King of New York (The Accardi Twins #2)

Taking What's Mine

*Protecting What's Mine**

YA SCI-FI & PARANORMAL ROMANCE

Saven Series

*Broken World Series^*

---

*Coming 2025

^Previously the *True Calling Series*

www.siobhandavis.com

Made in the USA
Monee, IL
29 December 2024